AN EX-SLAVE CATHCHER'S NARRATIVE
VOLUME 2

L. ALLEN FARMER

EMMI PUBLICATIONS

EMMI PUBLICATIONS
Edgewater, NJ 07020

Publisher's Note: This is a work of fiction. Names, characters, places, and incidents are a product of the author's imagination. Locales and public names are sometimes used for atmospheric purposes. Any resemblance to actual people, living or dead, or to businesses, companies, events, institutions, or locales is completely coincidental.

Copy Editor – Claudia Mason
Cover Art – Jay Durrah
Cover Design – Clayton Prawl

An Ex-Slave Catcher's Narrative Vol. 2/ L. Allen Farmer – 3rd ed.
ISBN 978-0692315941

Acknowledgements

Dedicated to Johnny Ray, Carlton, Sir Robert, Bob, Zana, Ericka, Valerie and Blake, Taylor, Eliazabeth, Avalyn, Robin, Tonya, Stacey, Monique, Anita, Joey, Andre, Grace, Janay, Sheldon, Dr. Juan, Theiron, Paul, Al, Clark, PC Jr, Yvette, BJ, Kenny-Rodgers, Mike and Shawn Bell, Troy, T-Rice, Chris, Jay, Eddie, Manotii, Aaron, Marion, Fatima, Effegia, Ivonne and the twins, Jason, Jitesh, Kendal, PW, Channing, Carla, Randy Mike-C, Nevin, Dr. Gary, Lori, Marcus, Brett, Keith, Max, Darius, Offley, Olivia, Danny, Jordan, Jonathan, Aggie, Carla, Katrina, Terri, Taylor, Lil Flower-RN, Tammi, Spoon- er, Philip, Kadidia, Sevil, Renae, Nicole, Mary, Nigel, Mona, Michelle, Kim, Nikki, Wally-Poobah, Lita, Carmelita, Ruthanne, Lisa, Julie, Violet- Lolita, Pam, Nellie, Amos, Kendell, Darlene-Carol, Dr. Shelly, Reggie, Bruce, Raquel, Snow White, Stephanie, Larry, Victor, Colette, Susan, Pablo, Irene, Icaro, Lucy, Simone, Shevon, Archie, Giselle, Ray-Ray, Sheila-Patrice, Tim, Teresa, Joy, Hazel, Tekachew, Jennifer, Alphonso Jr, Fletcher, the Furious 5 of 5, Aurther Joe Jr, Beatrice, Marta, KO, Theo, Mark, Delvin, Bubba, Terry, Sam, Mikey, Ada, Karen, Tani, Betty, Sherwood, Allison, Carmela, Deirde, Doree, Georgiana, Lady Emily, Vernita, Wesley, Vanessa, Natalie, Kevin, Amy, Katrice, Angela, Hazel, Shawn, and of course Kara.

EMMI PUBLICATIONS

PART FOUR

SERRA ME, SERVANT TE

SAVE ME, AND I SAVE YOU

QUOTE: OPTIMISM IS THE MADNESS OF

INSISTING THAT ALL IS WELL WHEN WE

ARE MISERABLE

A fter the freedom celebration was over, and we had begun the preparations to build a shelter, we sat down as a family to discuss our situation. We had decided to go into Ontario because Master Jack had both a lot of money and power, and in America an extremely long reach. So Canada provided the best and safest option for the entire family, and it would not be the last time that Canada would provide such an alternative. Abuelo, had been tasked to figure out a way to ensure the family's survival, and after he had thought both long and hard, he had come up with the codes for survival and freedom. In creating these codes he said he was influenced by *The Book of Noah* now called the *New Testament* because it was very valuable to the peoples of the days and times after which it was written and it was used by these people to govern themselves and to thereby live in a rightful manner. These codes were our family's version of the *Book of Noah*. These codes were enacted right after the main body of the family was delivered to that place called freedom. These codes were also the last greatest act of mi Abuelo, as he crafted a set of rules that were designed to ensure our survival, and each rule must be followed and adhered to at all times, and we must always try to stick together, because there is always strength in numbers.

So when he first gathered us together after our celebration to acknowledge our ascent up into freedom, he made everyone be still and quiet, and he then said in a kind of low voice 'so say we all' as he looked around at everyone, I am guessing, to gauge everyone's response. He said it again 'so say we all', only this time louder than the first time and with more force in his voice, 'so say we all,' and he did this in a manner—now that I am looking back—that reminded me of the way in which certain religious ministers use the call and response method with their flocks, for approval and clarity about a topic; 'so say we all.' So, I guess after four or five of these, 'so say we all's,' we all finally, as a group, began to realize that he wanted us to acknowledge what he was saying, by chanting altogether in one unified voice, 'so say we all.' Finally, when and only when we had gotten this hint, did he then begin to speak about our codes of survival and freedom, which he said that all of us must follow, 'so say we all. So say we all!' We must avoid contact with the Blancos at all times, and we must never trust anyone outside of the family, 'so say we all. So say we all!' We would never travel alone, with the exception being any warrior, and this must always be in pairs, so one would have the other's back. He called this the rule of two, 'so say we all. So say we all!' Everyone must adhere at all times to the rule of two, except the Prime. 'So say we all!' A young warrior caste must be established, which would be called the House of Calais-Vega, which would be our family's army, and this army therefore needed soldiers, of all ages to help protect our second most valuable commodity, which was called freedom, 'so say we all. So say we all!' Everyone in the family, of all ages and genders must be given basic warrior training on how to defend themselves, because anyone traveling outside of the family compound, must be armed at all times, because you never know when you may have to defend your freedom or that of a lovec one, 'so say we all. So say we all!' I am the one that he had selected as the leader or prime number of the House, and as we already know, what he says goes, at all times, 'so say we all. So say we al.!' He already knows how to develop the warrior caste, so he naturally will have final say so in all matters regarding our House's young warriors, 'so say we all. So say we all!'

Everyone will have a role in the House, and we will conserve all of our resources, and nothing will be wasted, 'so say we all'. "So say we all!" We will at all times respect everything of an in nature, and we will try hard to respect all people, at all times, until they show their true natures, so say we all. 'So say we all!' All young ones must be educated, because learning how to read and write has been critical to the advancement of the so- called modern man and es- pecially this family, 'so say we all!' 'So say we all!' So all children, including the young warriors must be made to get some sort of schooling, even if it is just on a basic level of reading and writing and mathematics, because look what schooling did for the Prime of the House, 'so say we all.' 'So say we all!' Even the adults must be educated, no matter the age, because we are going to be an edu- cated family of individuals, and not some mob of ruthless people, 'so say we all.' 'So say we all!' These are the first set of codes or rules that we must solemnly swear to follow and obey, at all times, and the Prime will have his own additions, as will the next Prime that follows him, and so on and so on, so say we all.' So say we all!' So let us have a solemn moment of silence, as we dedicate our new lives, towards seeking a new beginning, and following the codes. Because these codes have been put in place and devised to ensure that we ultimately stay free at all times, and that we remember what it (freedom) tastes like, and what it smells like and how it feels like upon your body and mind, because if one day you happen to lose it, this may very well motivate you to regain it, 'so say we all.' 'So say we all!'

When the moment of silence was over, my first act as Prime, was to make mi Abuelo, the Ultimate Prime, and to declare that he was to be involved and consulted on all House matters, as long as he had breath in his body. 'So say we all.' He would also lead the training of all young warriors, until he chose to no longer do so, and he was our family's greatest resource whom everyone was bound to both respect and honor. 'So say we all.' The commanders would naturally be the first three young warriors of The House and their training would begin tomorrow, as everyone enthusiastically agreed, by saying 'So say we all.' Men and women would have equal rank in The House, and one's gender had nothing to do with their position. 'So say we all.' We will get the children enrolled in school as soon as possible, and then sort out the rest for everyone else, because now was not the time to get lazy or shiftless. It was the time to get going and carve out a life from nothingness. We would survive together in these strange and savage lands, and no matter where we lived or moved to, we would be as one. The house in Xenia would be like a listening and observation post, in the United Snakes, where everyone would have a turn to be stationed, on a rotational basis, where we could all learn and observe what it was like to be Americans and we, as a family, would only go back to America, if the situation of slavery ever changed in the United Snakes, which did not seem very likely, or so I thought. 'So say we all.'

Many weeks later, after the foundation and the roof and walls of the family shelter had been completed, I sat down with Mamie and mi Abuelo, to have a heart to heart with them, because they could sense that something was going on inside of me that was nagging and pulling on my soul. I was going back, to the Strickland Plantation, and no I was not going to be talked out of it either. I felt that I owed them an explanation or reason why, even though they knew why, and that was because of mi Madre. For she was not going to be left behind in that strange land called America or be like a heroic casualty who symbolically dies to save everyone else. No matter how long it took, I was going to free her from bondage, or die trying. I really should have not left there without her, but she forbade me to change the plan, just because of her, and actually she was the real hero in the mess, because she is the one who sacrificed herself so that everyone else in her family could truly be free. She was totally right, as I looked back upon it over and over again in my mind, but she was now alone with no family to love and care for her, and I can only wonder how Master Jack would now be acting towards her, once the slave hunters returned empty handed, and all beat up and mangled. He would be furious and probably try to take it out on her, in any and all types of cruel manners. So we had unfinished business in America, and if I had to kill them all, every single one of those Blancos, I was going to free her no matter what it took.

Mamie and mi Abuelo sat there, and both said nothing for a long time, but I guess the look of determination within me was extremely strong. They both agreed with me, and actually said that they both had already figured out what I was up to because I had been unusually quiet since my return with the family. They could tell that I was going hunting and that my mind was calculating back and forth, so something was happening within me. They both hugged me, at the same time, and said that they were proud of me, because I always seemed determined to do the right thing. This was one of those right things, and we would keep this between the three of us, and on the down low, and really on a need-to-know basis with everyone else. Mamie would run the day-to-day family business, like she does anyway while Abuelo would run The House, like he does every day, in my absence. I was not to worry, because the family was now safe, and things were operating smoothly and efficiently. I would get a list of the things that I felt that I would need, and once everything was in order, I would take my leave and slip away in the night, to try to free mi Madre or die trying to change her life. This then is how my conductor days officially began, and even though I did not change her life, I did change many other lives in a truly worthwhile manner. But those days of being a conductor on the so-called Underground Railroad were mostly filled with a lot of personal unhappiness and a sickening feeling within the bottom of my stomach. I had entered into the job, as a means of liberating the soulless ones, because of my commitment to finding my mother. On the return trips back north, I would conduct or act as a guide, to those escapees that were looking for a better way and seeking a new beginning.

My days of being a conductor were challenging and very lonely. I was never home, and my life was really like that of a lone wolf, that continually runs the boundaries of its territory in solitude. I would make these trips about every three to five months, and to most of the townspeople, I was away surveying lands in the badlands, and the territories beyond our realm. These trips, that numbered somewhere between 20 and 30 all total for me, and my family were unsuccessful, because I could never track down Master Jack and mi Madre. They always seemed to be one step in front of me, or I always seemed to be one step behind them, but never at the same time in the same place. Master Jack knew that mi Madre, was his only insurance against me, and by moving her about he could be spared any mysterious fate. Because many slave owners were now scared, of a mysterious and ghostly figure that was like a ghost that walked. This ghost had some very unusual abilities and had dispatched many men and then appeared to line the bodies up like prey, and a lot of slave catchers had similar stories about this figure.

This ghost also had, some said, an extremely sharp sword or some kind of knife. So because of all of this and more, Master Jack was now not taking any chances, and thus, all of my trips were empty, and they only seemed to make my frustration grow and fester in my mind. But on the other hand, to the forgotter and lost souls, this journey when completed for them always produced unbridled joy and happiness. This did, on a certain level, give me a lot of satisfaction, for after Mamie had a meeting with some of the leaders of the Ontario Freemen settlements a need for this kind of service was identified. They together one day all sat down and devised a way to strategically advertise our services in the various local newspapers in and 'round the Province of Ontario, and in the Ohio and Michigan territories by taking out carefully worded advertisements that sounded religious in nature, to get the word out.

So once the word had gotten out with the right people, primarily the abolitionists and Quakers, that there was a certain someone, an angel or an angelos, who had come down from the heavens to earth who could be persuaded if the price or the timing or the logic of the conversation were right, to conduct certain lost individuals who were seeking a new beginning to become found, and thus born again, in the eyes of God. The conductor business really started to bloom and prosper, like flowers do in the springtime. Another cleverly worded advertisement stated, "For anyone that was seeking the services of a Seraphim for lost souls, as described in the Good Book, in the Books of Acts 12, and Daniel 6:22, please inquire in and around Xenia, Ohio, and ask for Mal'ak". Mamie would set everything up, and provide the location of the passengers, and everything was based upon her intuition or faith or really a little bit of both. She was the businessperson in the family so this was her or shall I say, our side job but she did all of the leg work for her project, and she secured the money and created the passenger's manifest. I would ride down to survey the scene and to set up the return trip, all the while being on the hunt for mi Madre.

If I had extra passengers, every once in a while, I would take the commanders with me out in the field to assist in the retrieval process. It was always funny because in the beginning they were all so little that they could all ride together on the same horse, all in a neat little row with the one in the back, at the end, always turned around backwards, guarding our tails. It was during this time that I, more importantly, learned on a deeper level just how this Underground Railroad really operated and was designed, and how songs and music played a big part in the total operation. For most slaves had been told from childhood to commit to memory certain songs that either told slaves about who was who, and what was what, and about staying strong in the face of an ever-changing uncertainty, which is how the life of any slave was from one day to the next. When one was actually escaping, the songs described the routes to freedom, like the song *Follow the Drinking Gourd*, where the drinking gourd was a secret code or instruction for the location of Polaris, which is the North or Pole star. The code or instructions used the stars in the Big Dipper's star formation, which is called an asterism, to point to the location or exact spot of the North Star, which they could always use to find their way by traveling north, which would lead them from the South up to the North, and past the Northern states to real freedom that was Canada.

The North or Pole Star was the key because it is always at the same fixed point in the nighttime sky, each and every night. The song was basically escape instructions, and a star map, from Mobile, Alabama up the Tombigbee River, over the great divide, which is Woodall Mountain, to the Tennessee River, and then down river to where the Tennessee and the mighty Ohio Rivers meet in and around the area of Paducah, Kentucky. It also spoke of dead trees showing the way, which were marked trees and other landmarks, all displaying the charcoal or in some cases mud outline of a human left foot and a round spot in place of the right foot. This was the mark of the conductor, a former sailor who was known as Peg Leg Joe. Some say that once he got you to the pickup point, which was on the River, he used his boat to sail the lost souls to freedom in Canada on the other side of the lake called Erie, and into a new beginning. He had left a series of clues and hints of the path to follow, that eventually led folks to freedom, and it was said that he had saved hundreds, if not thousands of lives in his lifetime.

Another song, 'The Song of the Free,' was about a man that was fleeing slavery in Tennessee, by using the Underground Railroad, to escape to Canada. Other songs like this were, Now Let Me Fly, which used the biblical story of Ezekiel's wheels, or 'Wade in the Water,' which recommended leaving the dry land and taking to the water to throw off the bloodhounds and trackers from off of one's trail, John 5:4. And let's not forget about the Gospel Train, or Swing Low, Sweet Chariot, or the impressive 'Steal Away,' or also known as Steal Away to Jesus, which encouraged slaves to run away on their own, or with the help of the Underground Railroad, and more importantly to always keep moving, and don't stay at one place or another too long on this stealing away journey or mission to Freedom, by cleverly implanting a code into the chorus line, which smartly said, I ain't got long to stay here. I also learned how music itself was a part of this whole sordid affair, because all of the songs eventually had music that accompanied them, and thus the music itself, became part of the lore surrounding these songs. All that you had to do was play the music and see how people responded to it.

I usually did not accept any money on these trips back North, and everything was on a pay up front basis, so that Mamie could handle the business of getting paid in full. But once the abolitionists put the coin into circulation, the coin became my most frequent method of payment when I picked up lost souls, or folks locking to immediately hire my services. This coin was minted by a group of northern men and women, who wanted to abolish slavery all over the Americas. These people were both dedicated and more importantly committed to ending this practice of inhumane treatment. So they created these coins, and then released them all throughout the Southern states, as a way to give slaves hope, and to have a currency that they could trade in for real United States currency, once they were free. The southern gentlemen were of course, naturally upset with this situation, and any slave even caught with one of these coins, was tortured and eventually put to death, quicker than they were, if they had been caught reading.

Now the actual conducting part for me, was really like a game of hide and find, that all slave children play in their youths, but this grown up game was extremely dangerous and ever changing from moment to moment. I have been shot at, chased down by men and dogs, and even one time stuck in a hiding place for two days in silence, as we out waited a group of determined slave catchers. I was ferrying a group of six, and we could not even light a fire on a very cold night, because we knew that the forces of evil and darkness were close by and lurking in the woods nearby our position. They finally moved on down the trail, thinking that they had just missed us, when we actually were just a breath away, and right beneath their feet the whole time. I therefore had decided to be like the great Haitian general, Toussaint L'Ouverture, who as history has stated, was always unpredictable. So our movements, when on conducting duty, were always changing so that we would be unpredictable and hard to trace or track. We used all of the tricks and one trick that I always used was to at first go south, or southwest, instead of north or northeast, because the forces of evil were expecting that these dumb slaves would always only know one route, and follow a northern route. But if I was following the 'Drinking Gourd' then I had to first get to Mobile Bay, Alabama, and then turn north, to follow the directions. So while the so-called intelligent slave catchers waited at the obvious places, I was guiding my passengers south, to the back door, and then up to freedom. I also liked to act as a guide or guardian angel, because it always worked better that way, because I could direct my passengers, but remain out of sight, and swoop down in the nick of time, to save the lost souls, from returning from their old hellish fates.

Once when I was on angel duty, a group of five tracers had gotten the bead on a group of runaways and had them trapped with their backs to a ravine. As the blood thirsty savages moved in for the kill, and most of the times it was kill, because dead or alive, always sadly meant dead; they seemed startled because when they turned, there I was, at their backs. I will always remember what one of these men, whose eyes were big and bugging out of his head said that he was "out of there, because the stories about a ghost are real." And with that, the cowards quickly, and I mean quckly, exited in the other direction. They had completely forgotten about the lost souls, and they really seemed to be terrified at the sight of me, or my appearance, and more so because of the gleam from our friend named Destiny. The cowards ran like scared animals, with their tails between their legs, and because for them, that night was not a good night to die. I have had a range of passengers that I have conducted, from slaves, to ex-slaves, with barely no clothing or possessions, to some well-dressed folks, and all in between, from a doctor, to a lawyer to even an old First American chief. But there were two of my passengers that really stick out in my mind, and whom I will never ever forget. One was a very beautiful colored lady, who was as beautiful as my wife, who could have passed for a Blanca, and when you saw her, you had to take a double take, because she was a real head turner, and she always made all men swallow hard whenever she floated by, into eye range.

Her name was Ms. Mona-Lisa and she was the mistress of a certain plantation owner, and this plantation owner, was eager to help her to get established, up north beyond the borders of this country, so that nothing would ever happen to her, involving slavery ever again, and really so that her beauty would be protected. He really, I think, was getting her away from all of the craziness of slavery so that he, and, only he only, would possess this beautiful creature like he was protecting his asset. So she came with a wagon and a bunch of bags, and she even had some kind of little dog that yapped a lot until she told it to be quiet. But for all of the hardships that revolved around this kept woman, or lady in waiting, the method of payment for her was in gold coin, which was extremely profitable, as Mamie had said in astonishment, 'REALLY' when she saw the coins, and I had quoted her the actual price, which was well over the agreed price, that WE were compensated for the trip. The trick was to figure out how to travel, but because she could easily pass, we used this to our advantage. I just dressed up like her butler and man servant, and we just rode the whole way to Nova Scotia, Canada in the open, in a fancy open topped, with soft pull up roof French-styled carriage. Not once did we get stopped or asked a single question, and the hardest part of the trip was the continual stopping that we did to attend to her constant requests and desires and wants and needs. She was actually like a headache, and she appeared to be one of the neediest people alive on the planet. But my most interesting passenger was without a doubt the strange and yet remarkable Mr. Anderson.

Yes, Osborne Perry Anderson, and I did not know his middle name until many, many years later, after I had heard that he was sick in the local newspaper and had died. He was an intriguing figure, who by chance became a passenger of mine. I was coming back from another trip to Nova Scotia, and I was doing a southern sweep, as I called it, to see if I could make some extra money by picking up a straggler or two, who were willing to pay for my services. Now many times I would just take any passenger whether they had the money or not, because as long as the desire to taste freedom was apparent, I took on all comers, be they rich or poor or indifferent. So in the state of Pennsylvania, about two hours past dusk, I came upon a well-dressed person, who happened to be an ex - slave, or so I thought. He was wearing a high-necked white collared shirt, with a dark cravat, a fancy vest, and a stylish jacket, with wide lapels and a fancy stickpin in one of them. His pants had a satin looking stripe down the outside of each leg. And, he was quite the sight hiding behind a big thicket bush, as a group of five angry looking Blancos rode extremely close nearby probably, as I look back on it, looking for him.

He looked as if he would jump right out of his clothes, when he finally realized that I was standing there behind him, and then his knees kind of buckled, as he slithered down to the ground. But once he understood that I was no ghost, and that I was an ex-slave myself, he seemed a bit relieved as he ever so slowly got up off the ground. I gave him the index finger over the lips, to signify for him to be quiet, because I could hear the riders coming back in the distance, and once they had passed by, we moved to a better defensive location, which was at the high point of a neighboring hill. He seemed extremely nervous and jittery and on edge, and he really seemed in fear of his life as he continually turned his head back and forth, left and right, as if he was being followed or stalked by some animal or something. He just had this look of despera-tion about himself, and finally once the danger had moved farther up the trail, he without notice, either sat down or really fell down backwards in exhaustion, as he crashed upon the ground with a loud thud. It took him a few minutes to gather himself as he began to whisper, all sad sounding, "I do not have any money, if money is what you are looking for or want. I am only trying to get back home, to a place called Chatham, which is in the Ontario Province in Canada. I am hungry, tired, and I fear that I am a wanted man, and even my very own father just a few days ago, threatened to have me arrested and turned me away from his door. I just need to rest a bit, and maybe once I have rested, I will be strong enough to get my bearings and find a way out of this wilderness of despair, called the United States of America, and get back home, to total freedom." With that, he kind of looked at me, kind of settled back, and went straight into sleep, as you do when you are totally exhausted and can go no further. So I covered him with a blanket and I let him sleep, while I played guard duty on his position, and I also rustled him up some grub for four, because the food would give him the energy that he would need on his long trek to Canada. I let him sleep for about half the night I think, and then woke him up because the birds would be chirping for the coming of the morning sunlight in about an hour or less— as I shoved a plate of food in his face to ensure that he would truly rise up. He seemed by his facial expression, that he was very thankful for both the blanket and the food, and he started gobbling down his food, so fast, I had to make him slow down, so he would not choke himself in his haste. After he had finished the first plate, I gave him another plate, and finally another plate, as he finally started to slow down, as his hunger subsided, to almost nothing. He moved towards the fire that I had constructed in a hole, that had rocks on top, as he scooped the last food on the plate in two quick chomps, and then handed me the metal plate back, and begin to warm himself up and stretch his legs, and rub his tired feet. He had this nervous way of talking, like he was really talking to himself, and I just happened to be there. He had this low but deep kind of voice, and he introduced himself as Osborne P. Anderson and said that he was originally born in nearby West Fallowfield Township in Chester County. This is close to Delaware and it is actually he said, "Two Townships, from the great city of Philadelphia." He then said with pride, that he was "a product of public schools in Chester County," and that he had briefly attended Oberlin College, in the Ohio territory, but he had a monetary problem and had to withdraw. He had immigrated to Canada, in 1851, one year after the passing of the Fugitive Slave Law, to the southwest corner of the Province of Ontario, Canada, to the town of Chatham, where over 2000 ex-slaves lived, worked, went to school, obeyed the laws, and lived in total freedom, which means peace and safety. He was just on his way back there, and he was fearful of the slave hunters and the patrols that routinely traveled between the north and the south on the Mason Dixon line of demarcation.

But strangely it was his actions that seemed out of place to me, because he was born a free man and he did have his papers, so why all of the jittery and acting scared type of actions did he constantly exhibit I wondered, as I told him that I was about to leave. I also wished him well and that I hoped that he would have a safe passage on his way back to Chatham, Canada. With that I turned around to leave, but he started running up to me, kind of like begging me, to hold on, and asked could he walk with me a ways, and what way was I going? I walked back to put out the fire, and he followed me like a newborn animal, does its mother. I told him that I had business that was of a hard nature, in the South, and that I was responsible for a lot of lost souls, who had lost their way, and who were only looking for the northern or pole star, that lied high in the nighttime sky, in the same place, each and every night. His mouth dropped open, in amazement, and he then closed his eyes, and dropped to his knees, and he bowed his head and acted as if he was silently praying, as if, I was a dream or a wish, or a prayer come true. He then jumped up, and asked me was I for hire. He actually had money. He was just separated from it, while on a business trip about cattle in Virginia, and if I agreed to conduct him at least as far as Lucas County, Ohio, I would be paid for my troubles, at double the going rate, whatever that may be, and I could even name the price, within reason that is.

Inasmuch that Mamie had been on me, about picking up stragglers who could not pay, and to 'at least charge the folks that could pay,' was her motto. I could only imagine her face when I told her that WE had gotten paid, and how she would probably say "RE-ALLY" in that funny and cute way that she had of saying that word when she was excited or happy, and of course she would be pleased with this outcome if it panned out that is. So because I was only thinking about making my wife happy, I said yes to this strange acting fellow, and I made him swear to a blood oath with me about his promise to pay "WE" when we reached Lucas County. He then swore the blood oath, and I then sliced his palm, to complete the deal, and away we both went, as he nervously looked around, and in his eyes I could see a bit of both sadness and determination. I decided that   we   could not risk the chance of riding double on my horse, because there were too many Blancos riding about searching for someone, so we had to walk the horse, until I deemed it safe enough to make a break for it. So we had to walk most of the early part of the journey and travel at night and hide out during the day. For most of the beginning part of the trip, he was silent, and as we moved further away, going par-allel to the Mason-Dixon line and as we began to travel further across Pennsylvania. Towards the western part, he seemed more relieved and thus ever so slowly more talkative.

By the middle of the first week or so, he started to ask me ques-tions, during the daytime rest period like who   was   I, did I know how scary I looked with that white macabre- looking face with bone looking drawings, and why was I carrying implements of war within my possession? And all I could do was just laugh, because of the way in which he asked me the questions, and all of this seemed to   only lead to more questions. After another round of the same questions, just asked in another way, which I did my best to answer but not answer, he then started to pick up on my language tones and inflections. And I guess he picked up on the fact that I had, had some kind of schooling in my past, and it was at that point I guess that he began to trust me, as if he now had only realized, that we were like on the same level or something.

Because this is when he began to share his numerous thoughts, and he had a plenty of them on a wide range of subjects; from the ills of slavery, then to what freedom was and is, then to education, and then the law, and then back on slavery and its ill effects on slave and slave master alike. By the end of the seventh day, he started to talk about an ill wind that was blowing and consuming all men, of all creeds and colors. I also started to notice how always around any mealtime is when he would always talk de talk, as if the food gave him the energy or passion to state his case, like any fine lawyer does before the judge or jury. But this time, he seemed extremely passionate, and sensing that he was amongst a true friend and fellow educated freeman; he began to tell his tale about his true mission to Virginia, and how he was really with a vanguard of raiders who were led by a white man named John Brown.

Now this John Brown was not an ordinary white man. He said, he was so very different, that he was at times simply spell binding. Mr. Anderson said that in the month of June, in the year 1856, he had went to work for a friend of his who was the editor of the newspaper named the 'Provincial Freeman,' first as a sub-scription salesperson, and then after some time had passed and he had paid his dues, he then became a printer. It was there at the newspaper, that he first became more acquainted with the exploits of Mr. Brown, who was a champion abolitionist in the Kansas Ter-ritories. Mr. Brown along with his family members, and fellow abolitionists, waged a protracted battle in Kansas against slavery and its evils. He had killed scores of slave owners and their families, burnt their property and killed their livestock, and set their slaves free, all in an attempt to rally everyone against the proslavery forces, and to really bring attention to their cause, which was to end slavery all together. This would also be a means of bringing the battle to the Southern states, and to make them feel what terror felt like, and more importantly to symbolically throw this issue up in their faces. Mr. Anderson said that it was an article that he himself had written, I believe he said, 'in the second week edition of the month of August, either the 7th or the 8th, in the year of 1857,' that had drawn attention to himself, as a new and great anti-slavery voice, as someone who seemed determined to talk the talk, and fight the fight.

Mr. Brown, who at this point was a wanted federal fugitive in certain, if not most all, Southern states, had since secretly moved to a farm in North Elba, New York, to live a quiet life and to really let things cool off for a while, but the federal officials had gotten wind of his hiding place, and so he had to quickly immigrate to Canada to avoid persecution. So this is why he was able to read the newspaper article that Mr. Anderson had written, and he was quite impressed, to say the very least. Mr. Brown then issued a mail call, for a quiet convention to be held in Chatham on or around May 8, 1858, to discuss the formation of a Negro state that would be in the southern region of the United States. In all total 46 people showed up, on that day in May, all men 12 white and 34 black that was convened by Martin R. Delany and John Brown, and their strategy would be that they would use a general slave rebellion, that they would organize and lead and this rebellion would be how they would create their State. This revolution would be known as Helter Skelter and it would be the tip of the spear. They even ratified a provisional constitution and ordinances, that everyone would adhere to, once this State was up and running. But their problem was that they would need to protect themselves and their State, so they would need loads of guns and rifles to furnish their large army that they would need to create, by using all of the scores of freedmen that they would liberate to become their soldiers. At that point, Mr. Anderson said that not only was he voted in as one of the two secretaries, but he was also elected as one of the founding members of the future

Congress of this colored State, all because of the article that he had written. At the end of the meeting, John Brown had personally sought him out, and had also spoken directly to him, by name and he commented on how he had especially liked the language or specifically the words that he had used in the article. These words were important because they rang out in both eloquence, and in the truth. He also had liked the quote by Sir Francis Bacon, "...against the winds, against the tide, now steady on with upright zeal,' because it gave a nice touch to the article at the end.

So with that, everyone in Chatham was smitten with the aura of John Brown, whose long white bread and hard chiseled looks cut quite the imposing figure. For John Brown was larger than life itself, Mr. Anderson said, and right there in their midst was a man, a white man who scared all white folks to death. But he seemed so opposite of what the stories had said, and he was gentle and thoughtful, and very wise, and not the Devil that the stories had all described. He treated all free men and women as equals, and he loved to go to the house of his editor friend, Mary Ann Shadd, and eat and talk, and tell powerful Bible versed stories about his battles in Kansas. Mr. Brown came and went a lot in the almost the next two years, but in late August of this year of 1859, word had been passed up to them, in the town of Chatham, that John Brown had moved down to the vicinity of Harpers Ferry, which was still in Virginia in those days which is about 60 miles from the Federal District of Columbia, to conduct an undercover intelligence gathering mission. He was using the name Isaac Smith, who was a cattle breeder, to survey the area and to look into the possibility of conducting a raid against the Second Federal Arsenal that was located in Harpers Ferry, to secure weapons that were needed to furnish their future army that would be used to protect their future state.

They say that he even first had asked Harriet Tubman and Fredrick Douglas, to join him, but she was sick, and Mr. Douglas told him that his plan would fail and they would get caught, and that it felt to him like a suicide mission to attack the Federal Government. Well of course, the whole town seemed mortified, and most felt that John Brown was acting on his own, and that he had not even properly discussed his plans with anyone before he boldly set out. His actions seemed both ill-advised and ill thought out—like no matter what, he was determined to strike the first national blow of freedom and force this issue into people's hearts and minds. Now everyone seemed unsure of the next course of action, but because of his alliance with the newspaper's owners, they felt obligated towards helping him, and so they decided to draw lots, so that they could send John Brown at least one recruit, from the town of Chatham. The very wind went out of me, said Mr. Anderson, once he realized that it was, he, who had drawn the smallest stick. And even though he protested he was pressured to make a "good showing of it and to have some courage." So he left Chatham on September 13th, 1859 and low and behold it was John Brown himself, in the flesh, who picked him up at the pickup point that was on the Mason Dixon Line between Pennsylvania and Maryland, in a wagon. In twelve days they arrived at a farm, which was owned by a family named Kennedy , which was on the Maryland side of the Potomac River, in Washington County, and this became their base of operations as everyone called him, to his surprise, "Chatham Anderson."

On the 12 day ride into the farm, John Brown, had steadied his resolve, and talked over and over to him about the evils of slavery and why their mission was so important, and after all of this, he was ready for war or so he thought, but it was the waiting part for additional recruits that never came which was the worst part for him and others. So finally when things started to become unraveled and everyone was starting to ask a lot of questions, and have and show doubts, Captain (John) Brown decided that it was time to go. So in a last minute parley, on October 16, 1859, he left three of his men behinc, his son Owen and two fellows named Coppoc and Meriam, to cover their rear flank and he took the rest of his raiding party to Harpers Ferry. They sounded like thunder, as they raced along on their horses about to fulfill their destinies and strike the blow, that would begin the long and hard process that would change things in the United States, or so they thought. But n a moment's notice things changed, as if by some cruel twist of fate, and John Brown or really Captain (John) Brown's true intentions came out of the darkness and into the light.

Because as they approached the rail station on the west side of the Federal Arsenal, they came upon a colored man who was wearing a uniform while minding his own business, and he was walking closely to the tracks. The man seemed a bit frightened by the riders, and because he did not heed their commands, they shot him down killing him right on the very spot just as he had started to look back again, for the second or really maybe third time. His life was gone in a heartbeat, and the only thing that he had really done was to be in the wrong place at the wrong time. Also why was killing him so important, and why coulc not he have been the first of many hostages, that they were about to take. So it was right then and there, that Mr. Anderson said that he felt, that Captain (John) Brown, would kill anyone who ever got into his way or his plans, be that white, ex-slaves, slaves, or whomever, and how ironic that an descendant of slaves was the first casualty of the raid. His true nature had been exposed right then and there for Mr. Anderson, and John Brown could sense that he had lost Mr. Anderson in the service of his cause forever more.

So the raiders took control of the town, and Captain (John) Brown, then sent Mr. Anderson and John Cook who was in command, and four others to The Beall-Air estate, which was the home of Col. Lewis W. Washington, the great grandnephew of the original President of the United States, to retrieve a few certain spoils of victory, which was a sword that Fredrick the Great, had given to George Washington, and two dueling pistols that had at one time belonged to the Marquis de Lafayette and to take him hostage. Captain (John) Brown was doing this, to send a message, that he wanted a descendent of Washington himself, to surrender these spoils to a colored man from Chatham, because of the symbolism that it would create in the minds of men in the south. It would be like a slap to their faces, and this was the real and only reason why he needed someone from Chatham, to accompany him on his vanguard mission, plain and simple.

It was as if he was using and leading the free men and woman of Chatham towards some unknown destination that only he, John Brown, knew, in his evil and twisted mind. So he really was just using everybody, to further his own plans or the desires, of his very own state, or nation where he would no doubt be in control or charge of, and more importantly, be the most powerful person in and this seemed like it was his real objective or end game, the whole time. He had this ability to pull you in with his words, and the way he could look sad or hurt or lost, and he seemed so civilized and God fearing. But this man was a master of deception, and he really was the beast that everyone had de- scribed, in the newspapers, without question. So Mr. Anderson and his party took Col. Washington hostage, freed his slaves, who all but one, seemed dumbstruck by suddenly being set free, and that one joined up with the raiders and their cause. They then took the weapons and returned via the Allstadt House, where they took more hostages, and freed those slaves, and there was one in that group, who also wanted to join up with the raiders.

When they got back to Harpers Ferry, they gave the weapons to Captain (John) Brown, who by then had taken over the whole town, and had set up the fire engine building as his base headquar- ters, because it was big enough to act as a temporary jail, for all of the hostages that they had captured. Once back, Captain (John) Brown could sense the change in Mr. Anderson's attitude, so he had pulled him aside outside of the engine house and tried to 'talk' him back into believing in the cause. But Mr. Anderson said that it was if that he had been self-awakened, and he could now see the true nature of the man, and past the disguise. So angrily, but in private, as to not affect the raiders' morale, Captain (John) Brown, in a low voice that was almost like a whisper, rebuked him in a kind of stinging to the ears type of manner. And then he sent him, and two others to guard the Federal Arsenal, and strangely he felt that Captain (John) Brown had sent one of these two others along one who was a fugitive slave named Green just to watch him he probably was told to kill him, if he tried to run. But Captain (John) Brown had unknowingly done him a favor, because if he had not made him move to guard the Arsenal, then he too would have suffered the similar fate of all of the others who became trapped in the fire engine house. But as fate would have it, the Federal troops and militia rushed right past the Arsenal in their haste to get at John Brown, who was a long time notorious and infamous nemesis of the Federal Government. Mr. Anderson said that they had stayed very quiet, when they heard the sounds of a large number of riders and men passing by, and a lot of shouting and general confusion. The Federal troops amassed their forces as they waited for a Colonel named Robert E. Lee to arrive and take command of the situation. Once he finally arrived, which was right during a break in a constant rainstorm, he asked John Brown to surrender. And, when he said no, he immediately had the fire engine house stormed with a detachment of U.S. Marines from Baltimore, Maryland, with an attack that was relentless and savagely stunning in its operation and methods. It was during this attack, that Mr. Anderson and a white man, whose name he said was Hazlett, were both sensing that they could no longer aid Captain (John)

Brown, were able to escape as fast as they could in the direction of the farm house which lay about four miles north in Washington County, Maryland. Green, on the other hand, decided that his fate was with Captain (John) Brown, so early on, while the militias were amassing, and before the federal troops with the Colonel had arrived, he choose to try to go back to the fire engine house, and it appears that somehow, he was able to sneak back past the militia troops, into the engine house and join back up with the remaining raiders.

Mr. Anderson said that they never looked back once, until they were out of the town. They hid on a hill that was outside of town for three or four hours, as they could hear the shooting die down and then eventually stop. There were sporadic shots, and a lot of dust and noise swirling all about in the air, which was being driven by the wind, which strangely almost seemed to have a cleansing effect upon Mr. Anderson. He said, it was as if, he was getting a symbolic release from both John Brown, and more importantly his ideas and notions about things, and that he could do more for the cause alive than dead. With that, Mr. Anderson seemed winded and tired, so he just looked at me, and then he slowly sat back, and passed out to sleep.

On the next day, at the next rest stop, Mr. Anderson began to continue his tale, right where he had left off and his next recollections, seemed a bit vague and as if he was walking around in a daze. They hid out, then returned to Harpers Ferry, followed the railroad tracks, stole a boat, then took a hostage, and then he changed his story to taking a hostage and then stealing a boat to cross the Potomac River, and then walking for hours it seemed. They finally got to the farmhouse, that showed signs of people leaving in a great haste, as if they suddenly had to leave and right then. Years later, he would find out that when Owen Brown heard the shooting, he left out to join the fight, and be at his father's side, while both Coppoc and Meriam, both had hightailed it due north as fast as they could, and because of their cowardice actions that day they both lived to fight in the great War amongst the States. He then talked about being very scared, and of it being dark, cold, wet, and very rainy, and of them trying hard to get to Chambersburg, which is in the Commonwealth of Pennsylvania, because there was an Underground Railroad stop there, that was run by a Henry Watson. Mr. Anderson said that he left Hazlett who had no more energy behind, before they reached the Chambersburg stop at Hazlett's suggestion, because he felt that he was only slowing them both down. Because, his legs were giving out on him, and by now a federal manhunt must be occurring nationwide. After bidding him goodbye, Mr. Anderson went to Chambersburg, and was with great haste whisked away and onward to York, Pennsylvania, to the next Underground Railroad stop. A colored man named William Goodridge, who owned a photography studio which secretly was the actual stop itself, was the conductor. Mr. Goodridge, after listening to his story, quickly put him aboard a train that was bound for Philadelphia, and the stop that William still ran, and where Mr. Goodridge thought that he would be safe. But everyone there in Philadelphia, and in Chester County, saw him as bad news, and that their actions at Harpers Ferry had now made it harder on all colored people, be they free or still in slavery in all of the United States. It was his very own father who commented that here he was, all caught up in this mess, and why didn't he think about what he was doing before getting in all of this mess?

He was a so-called educated colored free man, who had so-called higher reasoning, yet he had not thought about the effect of what their actions would have on the masses. The masses would all be judged, even if it were unfair by their actions, which were the actions of a few individuals and not the whole group. The white folks would not all think fairly and honestly, and in a Christian manner about the whole situation, and they would immediately group or lump everyone into the same boat. And thus, everyone would

be judged because of John Brown and his raiders' ill-timed
actions. So no matter how grand and noble his, John Brown's,
ideas were or had seemed at the time, anyone associating with
him, no matter how inspiring or uplifting the person or persons,
everyone will be judged and lumped into this unfortunate association. "So you will have to leave right now, my son, and do not
think, for a single minute that I do not love you, Osborne, because
I do, but you must go away from my door right now because
your actions have put us all in jeopardy," his father had said. And
with that, he gave me a bundle of some clothes and a little bit of
food, and then he shut the door right in my face Mr. Anderson
recounted.

Now to Mr. Anderson, he felt that everyone's actions
in Chester County were unfair, but life at times is not fair, and
this was a part of life, so he immediately left with hunters and
killers on his trail. "And, they were about to catch me, when I met
you," he said, "or really when you happened upon me. So once I
had figured out that you were not a ghost or some ghoulish
figure, but a real man, who was employed in a certain business ar-
rangement, I felt that my true safety lied with you. So only being
moments from capture or death or both, it was not a hard choice
to make. I just had to convince you to take me on as a passenger,
which ultimately has saved my life thus far," he'd said I just sat
there waiting to see if he had any more to say, but he was
strangely quiet in an odd sort of way. We continued on, now
riding some and walking some, and in a couple of days we were in
Cleveland and we went to visit someone that he knew, a Blanco
fellow named Charles Tidd, who seemed extremely happy to see
him, and who paid me double in gold coin, for my conducting
services. I found out later that this Tidd fellow had also been a
part of the ill-fated raid day those days in October, and that
he had three or four others that were assigned to move the stolen weapons, and right before the militia had captured and

cut off the bridge across the Potomac River, they barely escaped with their lives. He gave Mr. Anderson his own horse to ride, and we then left there and traveled first to Lucas County, so that he could see from friends, and where we could both rest up, eat, and wash up, and then proceeded the rest of the way to Canada. These folks also gave me payment for my services, so he must really be an important person I thought.

We crossed over at Sandusky by boat across Lake Erie, and when we finally got to Chatham, a lot of people were happy to see him, as if he was a ghost or something and he was greeted with a lot of shouts of joy and praise and plenty of hugs. Because, everyone assumed that he was dead, due to the letter that John Brown sent to his wife from prison telling her the situation. So with that, folks started to run up, as the word rapidly spread of his sudden appearance, and it was if the dead had arisen back to life. He then introduced me to Mrs. Mary Cary, who then introduced me to most of the inhabitants of the town, and yes this did feel like a very unique place, which seemed out of time and where total freedom reigned supreme. Now the big question is, did I believe his story? And was any of it true, or was it just all made up, by a fellow who was both scared and a little crazy—but a well-dressed person who smelled a bit ripe with both sweat and fear. Now whether he just lying or just making up his incredible story was the one and only question that just kept going in and out of my mind. Well looking back on it, history has or will continue to be his judge and jury. He did seem a bit talkative for my taste, and maybe it was just the continual cutting of his eyes, like he was about to lie and change his story, which made me suspicious, and all of the nervous talk about death or the specter of death hovering nearby, but he did appear to be who he said that he was.

History has been his judge, and he did participate in this tactical first strike mission with John Brown and his 16 or more, other unfortunate souls at Harpers Ferry, Virginia. He did take part in a memorial at John Brown's farm, in North Elba, New York, that occurred on July 4th, 1860. And, he was recognized by John Brown's daughter Annie, as Chatham Anderson because, she had met him at the Kennedy Farm in the summer of 1859, only days before the ill-fated raid. He did write a book that was entitled *A Voice from Harpers Ferry*, in 1861. Some folks in history dismiss him, and say that he was lying, because his version of this infamous event in United States history was wrong, and a full day earlier, than most know accounts. But looking back, it was not my job or task to judge him, because he was a fellow human being, who also lived during a very troubling and confusing point in time, as we all did, in this particular part of the world. He seemed rational and he did seem to possess all of his facilities and senses, even though he talked a lot. He did seem very believable, and he was highly aware of what he was saying. He also seemed afraid of what had happened, and this was perfectly natural considering everything that he claimed to have witnessed and therefore experienced on that fateful day in October of 1859. But he was also said to have taken issue over the actual facts that surrounded the raid, because in the official report that was made to the President of the United States, James Buchan- an, by the Col. Robert E Lee. In this report, Col. Lee indicated, that he felt that John Brown was insane and that the slaves belonging to Washington and Allstadt, both were forced to participate in the raid, and that they did not do so of their own free will. This issue always incensed Mr. Anderson, because he, even up to his death, stated that these slaves had joined the cause, because they felt that the cause was just, and righteous.

They were both honored to take up the first strike against southern slavery, and it was always funny he said how these slaves' involvement was suppressed, no less by a southern gentleman, Col Lee, so as to not give any other slaves in any of the southern states, a similar idea. So to some Mr. Anderson was considered a hero who went on to become a recruiter for the Great War amongst the States, and he became a great speaker, who could sway people with his insightful words of wisdom and spiritual conviction. I was saddened to hear that he had passed on to the next life, on December 11th, 1872, at the age of 42 years young, because no matter what, to me he probably was my most interesting passenger ever, that I had the honor of conducting on the rails of the Underground Railroad. Now my conducting days slowed really down and became very limited, because of the John Brown raid, which changed a lot of things in the United States. The southern states assumed that the northern states were in league with John Brown, and that they condoned his actions. So the southern states built up their state militias as a response to a new and growing threat, which was an invasion from the north. They also heavily patrolled their state borders, and where the northern states bordered the southern ones, on the Mason Dixon Line, these areas were like a military zone, and thus extremely tough to try to sneak people across.

John Brown's last prophecy on the day of his execution was "I, John Brown, am now certain that the crimes of this guilty land: will never be purged away, but with Blood. I had as I now think vainly flattered myself that without very much bloodshed, it might be done." So this changed the whole landscape, and made a tense situation even tenser, because everyone could sense that there was going to be no way out of this situation, but by armed conflict. Which all of which really made me think of Master Jack's words, concerning the way in which the southern states would be forced to act if they felt threatened or backed into a corner. Then in January of 1861, Abraham Lincoln, a Republican, who was a somewhat known opponent of slavery, was elected as the next President of America, and things really began to change. The state of South Carolina's State

Legislature not truly knowing what Lincoln's next moves would be, seceded from the Union, then followed by the secession of six more States. The leading freeman abolitionist of his time, the great Fredrick Douglas, was himself, even skeptical of Lincoln, and his freeing of the slaves, and he called him, the 'King Slave Catcher,' and it was known in many circles that Lincoln told darkie jokes, and freely used the word 'Nigger.'

Douglas was a powerful critic of Lincoln, because he refused to address the slavery issue, and because he appeared to be going too slow, and somewhat reluctant in moving in that direction, either in action, or speeches. He called him a proslavery wolf, in antislavery sheep's clothing, and voiced that, "Lincoln was no more fit for the place that he holds, than was James Buchanan, and the latter was no more the miserable tool of traitors, than the former, is allowing himself to be." Lincoln early on in his presidency stated that his goal was to preserve the Union, and not end slavery. He actually supported the Corwin Amendment, which would permanently allow slavery in the states where it was presently legal and also would have forbidden any attempt to amend the Constitution to abolish or interfere with the domestic institutions of the states, including persons   held to labor or service which meant slavery. Lincoln wanted the Southern states to accept it, but they refused, thinking that it was a trick to entrap them with, to   eventually   change their way of life, not realizing that all they had to do was to accept the Corwin Amendment, and not succeed, and then they would be able to keep slavery alive and well in its present shape or form. But to the South, they needed to be able to control their own destinies, and not have anyone dictate political terms to them, about what their way of life would, or more importantly should be.

The Civil War began in April of 1861, with the attack on Fort Sumter that is in South Carolina, by forces loyal to the newly established Confederacy. The actual ground campaign began in May of 1861 in western Virginia, which is now called West Virginia, in the hills and mountain regions, as President Lincoln commanded the Army of the Department of Ohio, which was under the command of General McClellan, to cross the Ohio River and secure western Virginia, which was loyal to the Union. For the Union. The only thing that slowed things down was a very terrible winter, and by the time 1862 came around; the war shifted to the southeast region of the divided nation. Lincoln suspended the Rite of Habeas Corpus, closed down newspapers, and jailed dozens of citizens in an attempt to control and already worsening situation. The thing that I wi.l always remember about that year, of 1862 was that in April, I was witness to the slaughter that was known as the Battle of Shiloh. I was cutting through and around the troops on either side of this crazy war, leading a group of runaways towards freedom that lie in the North. Because of the current situation, we had to move ever so slowly, in a western route, as we went from state to state, and we had just gotten around the area of Shiloh Tennessee, about to finally make that turn to the north, when on April 6th, the Confederate forces attacked the Union forces that were encamped along the Tennessee River, at the Pittsburg Landing area. We barely had a chance to get settled down, on a nearby hillside and seek cover when the battle began, and let me say that from our position, that had a commanding view of the battle field, we saw everything as it unfolded, for the next two days. Almost 24,000 men died, and it was like a blood bath, as the generals stood back and continually threw their men into the fray without a regard for human life or the consequences of such actions. On day one, which was April 6th, the Confederates looked as if they were about to route the Federal troops, and it looked many times during that day as if they were about to be defeated, yet they hung on until nighttime fell, which ended the main hostilities, except for the occasional gun shots from the snipers from both sides, who were picking off any easy and upright moving or plain ole obvious targets. As nighttime came, the Federal's reinforcements arrived on the other side of the River, and these troops were ferried across, and in the morning just as the daybreak was starting to wake up, the Federals viciously counterattacked, driving the Confederates off the field.

We were stuck in our location for about three days' time, because we had to wait until we were absolutely sure that both armies had gone, before we even moved an inch. The loss of life was enormous, and it is hard to explain what we were truly witness to, and once we got back under way, which was on April 8th, no one said anything for days, because the shock to our body systems was just too great, I always assumed, and all of that death is simply too hard for the mind to comprehend, and deal with. I really right then, saw the real deal about these Blancos locos, and how they are determined to kill or be killed just because of a reason that really did not make any sense to me at all. There were so many dead men around, with loads of weapons lying everywhere on the battlefield, that both of the armies only removed the casualties, but not the bodies of the fallen from the field, so we had to walk through scores and scores of the dead, and we saw firsthand what the horrors of war are really about. Dead men with holes all throughout their bodies, bodies burned up looking bodies with eyes shot out, noses missing, parts of men, arms and legs and even fingers and toes, and teeth were all spread about the entire length of the field of battle.

Nothing was spared, not even animals, and even the land area itself was torn up and worn looking in places. Some of the dead had arms or legs blown off, while some of the dead had these horrible twisted looks of death on their faces. I was determined because of this, right then to never again expose myself or my loved ones, to the crazy ways of the Blancos, or to die trying. Because the real truth about the Battle of Shiloh was that both sides appeared to have nothing to lose and sadly nothing to gain either. They killed each other like it was a game or better yet a competition that had no clear-cut rules, or order and it was like the ultimate game of survival. So the family would move westward, hopefully before the end of this conflict, when it was safe and try to stay as far away from the Blancos as possible, because depending upon who ultimately won this contest, between two bears, we, as in our race or creed could be worse off than ever before. The only good thing, if it could be called a good thing, about the battle of Shiloh, was that I was able to pick up my very first Henry model 1860 repeating rifle, from some unfortunate soul who had it in his clutches at the time of his demise.

PART FIVE

AUDACES FORTUNA LAVAT

FORTUNE FAVORS THE BOLD

QUOT E: STAND UPRIGHT, SPEAK THY

THOUGHTS, DECLARE THE TRUTH THOU

HAST , THAT ALL MAY SHARE; BE BOLD,

PRO-CLAIM IT EVERYWHERE.

THEY ONLY LIVE TO DARE

The so called Civil War lasted for about five long years and the loss of life on both sides was high, over 600 thousand people were killed some said, and the initial reason why the war had even started, seemed to become lost or misplaced, I shall say. The newspapers from all around the country, covered the war from all sides and angles, and the names of the different major battles: 'Bull Run, Monitoverses, Merrimac, Shiloh, Seven Pines, Seven Days, Stone Mountain, Antietam, Fredericksburg, Chancellorsville, Gettysburg, Chickamauga, Chattanooga, Spotsylvania, Cold Harbor, Petersburg,' that all of the newspapers covered, sounded strange and far off from our families' new world. This appears to be the first war of a new age, where technology had made the killing easier and more efficient, and where the newspapers each and every day brought every detail of this tragedy, to our minds, hearts and souls. On January 1st, 1863, Lincoln issued the Emancipation Proclamation, which stated that all slaves in the areas that were still in rebellion were in the eyes of the Federal government, now free.

But it did not free the slaves who were in pro-Union slave states or territories like Kansas, so in reality it was only directed at the slaves in the Confederate states. So all that meant is that, once again freedom ain't free. In 1864 Lincoln was re-elected, to a second term and then on April 9th, 1865 the South surrendered at the Appomattox Courthouse, with a General Robert E. Lee representing the South. This ironically was the same Robert

E. Lee, who in October of 1859, then as a Colonel, defeated John Brown and his raiders in Harpers Ferry, and it was always interesting to see where, because of his choices, that his life had taken him.

Then only five days later, on April 14th, 1865, on what they call Good Friday, Lincoln was shot in the head, and died the next morning, on April 15th, 1865, throwing everyone in the United Snakes into both chaos, and turmoil. Now our family had been getting ready the whole time, for the day that the war amongst the states would officially end. We had come up with an ambitious five-year plan that we had stuck to, and when the time came, we would be ready if anything changed. A lot of the freedmen and women, in the Ontario Province, had decided to go back to America, because we were all now, as a group, suddenly free. So the places where freedom itself had thrived in a real sense, suddenly became like ghost towns and almost vacant. Some folks went back, as early as 1863 to enlist and join up with Colored Outfits, to fight against the South, and it's now outlawed way of life that was known as slavery. An all Freedmen's infantry outfit, the 54th of Massachusetts was even created, and two of Fredrick Douglas' sons were a part of it, and this unit of men served with both honor and distinction.

Then also at the war's end, people started going back, in droves, to try to reunite with their loved ones, because we were all now supposedly free, and we would be treated much different now, than before, or so they thought. But this was sadly not the reality of the situation for freed people on a whole. Things seemed to get or be as worse, or worse than before the war, and just because the war was over and the reconstruction period had begun, we would not give our trust over so easily or blindly.

But we had been trained by Abuelo to not trust anyone, and to figure out a way out of no way, our mission was clear, 'so said we all.' Since 1862, as the states of the once United Snakes battled one another, I had scouted the western territories beyond Ohio, and I had really began to respect the First Americans, for their ability to survive and conquer all foes based upon a concept that was called the right of conquest. Some of them, like those that lived on the plains were warrior clans, while some of them were peaceful and non-threatening clans, and if we just took our time and really looked, things would work out. We would find a suitable place beyond the reaches of everyone, and stick together as a family, and then learn to respect everything in nature, be that man, and or beast, and even the weather. We used my initial intelligence gathering and scouting missions in- formation, to find a very suitable location that was in the land, which was just beyond the Land of the 10,000 Lakes, that was called, 'Mini Ota' or 'Much Water.' One of the groups of First Americans that resided there families to the surface of Maka or the Earth, by Inktomi, the spider. Because before this, the people lived below the surface of Maka Ina (Mother Earth), with no culture and no contact with Wakan Tanka, or The Great Mystery. They were a deeply spiritual people, who believed in one all-pervasive God, the 'Great Mystery' who controlled every aspect of their daily lives. They communed with the spirit world through music and dance. There were three divisions within the Ochethi Sakowin and within the divisions were bands, with the Santee Dakota having four bands, the Yankton Nakota having two bands which eventually became three, and the Teton Lakota having one band, that was then divided after the move to the plains, into seven sub bands, which they called the seven tents, which seems to be based upon the same concept as the original Seven Council Fires. Each of the seven divisions would select four leaders known as Wichasa Yatapika, and there was no greater honor amongst the Ochethi Sakowin, than to be voted in as one of these leaders. The Santee (Dwellers of the Knife Lake) Dakota were a peaceful sort of folk and they were accepting of outsiders who were honest, respectful and peaceful, so they had no problem with us.

Their distant cousins, the Teton (Prairie Dwellers) Lakota and Yanktonai (The Dwellers of the End Village) Nakotas that lived even farther west of them, on the lands of The Great Plains, around the area where the spiritual center of their nation was, in a place that was called Paha Sapa or the Black Hills, because within these hills contained the wind cave that Tokahe had first emerged from. I had even once met one of the Oglala Lakota clans, and they were to me, quite an impressive lot. From their style of dress, to their implements of war, and to the way in which they just rode their horses, they seemed like a very formidable and battle tested bunch. They had come as they did every year, to return to the original stomping groups and homelands of their ancient and original tribe for the yearly Sun Dance ritual. For this is where everything had begun, in the Land of the 10,000 Lakes, before this original tribe had split, into three parts, as two parts moved westward in search of new hunting grounds and a new beginning, and they settled in the Black Hills area because it was on the edge of the Great Trail that the Bison used in their yearly migration. So all Ochethi Sakowin warriors at some time or point in their lives, were required to make this journey to the ancient homeland, and honor their original forefathers by performing the Sun Dance, at the annual Seven Fires Council meeting, which was held each and every summer up until 1850.

After 1850, the Ochethi Sakowin Oyate met, although it was not because of the Seven Fires council meeting any longer, but it was less formal and it really was the warriors from the bands, who continued to follow the traditions and ways of the Oyate and to perform the Sun Dance because for them, it was like a pilgrimage which their way of life required them to do.

This 12 day summer ritual of self-sacrifice was a testimony to endurance and individual courage in serving the Great Spirit Wakan Takan. It was a shared experience among the men and was also used to instill a sense of tribal unity. The dancing and enduring the pain of self-inflicted wounds, was the way to reassert the identity of the warrior that lay within the man. So by the time that the Great War between the United Snakes was finally over, we had already built a homestead within Santee lands, and had set the plan, just in case we had to move. But what we all had not seen coming was that once the great war was over, and everything settled back down, the Blanco's went right back to their ways of nation building, and removal of the First Americans, to steal their lands, and to expand the Union of Snakes. Because they really had never ever stopped removing the First Ones, and even though it seemed like it did because of the newspapers' constant coverage of the Great Civil War was the only topic on everyone's mind, but the double talking Federal Government had just used volunteer troops, in place of the Federal ones that were being used in the Great War, to continue its secret extermination policies of Nation Building.

Around 1850, the United States Federal Government began an effort to exterminate the buffalo herds that roamed the plains, because it was believed that by killing the main food source, the buffalo, it would make it possible for the Federal Government to better control the Great Plains tribes of First Ones who were all expanding and who were always at war with one another. But what it really did was to make the competition more fierce between natural rivals, as the food source began to dwindle, and became nonexistent.

The Fort Laramie Treaties of 1851 was the Federal Governments' plan to convince The Plains Tribes to stop fighting one another, and it had also given safe passage to the settlers who were crossing the Great Plains, on the way to California because of the Gold Rush, in return for $50,000 per year annuity payments of supplies for 50 (later changed to 15) years for each tribe, of the First Ones and more importantly, it had created First One Territories that were not supposed to be trespassed against by anyone, in no way, shape or manner. There was also a provision in small print that also allowed or granted the Army the right to build Forts, if it so chose.

Then came the Homestead Act of 1862, which by law allowed the American settlers to apply for grants that entitled them to the lands of the First Ones. And because of this new Federal law, in August of 1862, under the leadership of Taoyateduta (Little Crow), the Dakota War took place between the Santee, with help from some of their Teton cousins, and the American settlements on the Minnesota River. When order was finally restored, over 600 settlers had been killed, and 303 Santee and Teton were found guilty of rape and murder of American Settlers, and President Lincoln commuted the death sentence for 284 warriors, but signed off on the execution notice that 38 Santee men were to hang, in Mankato, Mini Ota (Minnesota), in December of the same year. With that, many Santee fled either to the Plains area, or to Canada for safety, and this hanging became the largest mass hanging in United States history. So by 1865, at the end of the Great War, we had a decision to make, whether we would move back to Xenia in the Ohio territories, or move westward, to our new homestead that lay in the Santee Dakota lands beyond 'Mini Ota,' and once again seek a new beginning. Even though the Northern Yankees had won the Great War amongst the Snakes, we were as a group, not comfortable with the current situation of Reconstruction, in the United States, and so the all important family vote was taken to see what would be our fate. We also decided that if anyone felt compelled to stay in Ontario, they could, and we would leave route markers and clues to where we had moved onward to, if they ever decided to join up with us.

The vote came and three of our family voted to stay, and so that is how and why they remained behind in this new land of freedom, called Canada. Our first stop was in Xenia, as we decided to yet vote again to see who wanted to stay here or who wanted to push onwards into the west. This is where Mamie's parents wanted to stay, because they liked the makeup of the town, and also because they liked the house that we had built, while the rest of us, wanted to stick together as a group, and once again at least try to seek another new beginning. We then decided to have a planned approach towards the next move and not just move without knowing if things were still in place. We would go in search of our friends, the Woodland people who called themselves the Santee, who had let us live with them, and have a homestead. They seemed to like us, because they had given us our very own Teepee and had treated us like we mattered to them in their world. They had taught us their language and had shown us how to survive in their world, which is what you do with your family members.

But when we got to the old location, everything was desert- ed and they had all gone or left, and it was like a mystery as to where they had really gone. Our teepee, which meant dwelling, was also gone, and this only served to deepen the mystery for us, as we scoured the area for anything that could give us a hint of just where our friends were now.

The only clue was a set of carefully chosen, medium sized inyans or stones, that was fashioned to look like an arrow head, that was pointing due wiohpeya or West, as if it were a clue that was left for us, or for our benefit, to show us the way or direction that they had gone in.

Now I knew that the Santee were the last of the Ochethi Sakowin to acquire and use the horse, so I remembered wondering in my mind, just how far they could have truly gone, on foot. So we must now just go further into the wild to catch up to them, and maybe we will be blessed enough to reconnect with our friends, somewhere out there in the land of their fathers and mothers. So with that we did scouting missions that were getting to be further and further from the comfort of the Ohio territories, and deeper into the central and northern Great Plains area, as we searched high and low, but with no luck, for our friends. The last known location of our Santee Dakota friends, became our new forward base camp, as we built a sanctuary into the hillside, that was well protected and even had its own fence, that was great because the livestock were protected and not out in the open.

At the same time, the terrible or treacherous three were becoming quite the warriors in their own right, and the four of us, became quite the team, with our long-hooded robes that masked our identities and weapons. I always will remember how people in general, seemed quite afraid of us, whenever we would ride up on them, and most of the time, we had no trouble riding right by and not even stopping or appearing remotely interested in them whatsoever. Which was kind of funny, because when you rode up on the settlers in their covered wagons, some in wagon trains, or single wagons, out on the Plains, they seemed curious of us and for a lot of them, they were thinking of their own safety, so why did not these four riders not even want to speak or inquire of how they were doing. A lot of them would yell 'hello' or even wave, like we all knew one another but we would ignore them, as if they were ghosts or the walking dead, or really lepers that needed to be avoided at all cost.

One day, just a few hours before dusk, we came upon a group of church people, in four wagons and as we got closer to them, they became quite scared and some of them even had the gall to start to praying and lamenting all out loud, so we could hear them, and they seemed to think that we were going to do something to them. One man was so nervous that he picked up his trusty Good Book (Bible), and started reading out very loudly, so that we could hear him mind you, Revelation six, verse seven, "And when he had opened the fourth seal, I heard a voice of the fourth beast say, "Come and see," verse eight, "And I looked and behold a pale horse: and his name that sat on him was Death, and Hell followed with him. And power was given unto them over the fourth part of the earth to kill with sword, and with hunger and with death and with the beasts of the earth." He then looked up and they all just stared at us all hard like, as it got strangely quiet and everything stopped moving, and then as we passed, and as our backs were finally to them, he yelled, "Behold brothers and sisters, there go the four crown Prince's of hell, Satan, Lucifer, Leviathan, and Belial, yes my brothers and sisters, the real four horsemen of the apocalypse, and pray that we never cross their paths ever again, in this lifetime." It was right then, that we decided to look as menacing as ever, and ride mostly at night, so that we would be left alone, on our mission, and trek into this stunning beautiful and immense land, of the First Ones, the true first Americans.

Also about this time, is when the terrible three started going out on missions by themselves, and they proved time and time again that they could hold their own. They were not to be played with ever and they have been many things to many different people. For they were seen by some as cold-blooded killers, who killed on a look, for no reason, seemingly just to do it, which is why folks in the various towns that they would on occasion visit, always seem to scatter and run for cover whenever they showed up, as everything would close up and shut down, as if they knew something about the three, that was sinister in its design. They have also been seen as saviors or liberators by some folks, and that is why these folks displayed an enormous amount of family type of love for the three, whenever they showed up. They are also seen as highway men or robbers and although I personally never saw anything that proved or disproved this fact, their reports from the field, state field oper-ations for the House, which could mean a lot of different things.

But who really knows? They have always displayed a certain amount of pride in their tasks, and they always seemed very grown up, despite their young ages. They always exhibited an enormous amount of courage and teamwork through any adversity. They were drilled endlessly in Abuelo's five P's, which was a motto or saying that stood for 'proper preparation prevents poor perfor-mance.' So they were ready at all times for any situation when they were in the field, and because they received all seven levels of Abuelo's training, they were extremely formidable and efficient at dispatching any and all foes. They were warriors at all times, when-ever they were on any business in the field for the house, and they were afraid of nothing, and because of their dark sided beliefs, which they acquired from their initial experience when they were young children, during the great battle for the family's freedom, with me and El Diablo, and Freedom the horses. So they had no qualms about mixing it up, and as they got older and more skilled, they were really something else. Because they could shoot and cut or stab at the same time, and all at once, with a certain precision that was stunning to view. They had superior hunting and tracking skills, and they were quite accomplished with an array of talents and skills.

They were also trained, as I was, to hide or evade, in certain situations, and were able to move about like wanagis or ghosts, anytime the moon rose up, and appeared in the nighttime sky. They came up with their own face painting styles, and they seemed to resemble skulls with boney teeth showing, with Egyptian eyes, and they actually painted their whole bodies with the white powder, so that they had an eerie white skinned dead look, which scared people even more so, which seemed like this was their plan the whole time. Because they seemed the happiest, when they could scare any hostiles, and not have to go into battle mode, and they really seemed to be amused by all of this. And they would just laugh and laugh with delight, when they were able to scare folks into submission. The three were also different from one another in their individual battlefield skill sets, which was unique because they seemingly had this ability to become one unified machine, with ruthless efficiency. For although they all had different skill sets that they had mastered, they were all equally as skilled, and able to compete as a unit, in all areas of battlefield weapons. There were two stories that stood out in my mind, that ex- plain just how efficient they really were. One story was about how the three were holding the high ground, but boxed in by greater numbers, on one of the most pitch black nights ever, with no stars even showing up in the nighttime sky. They huddled together, which is their customary procedure, and when they broke their huddle, they set up in a sitting down triangle formation, and then let Gabriel take most of the shots, using his trusty bow and arrows, at every sound that crossed their ears' thresholds.

Hours later, when the morning had blown the darkness away, they counted 14 dead, and every single one of them had killed themselves by giving away their positions, to six trained ears. It was, they say, as if Gabriel could see in the dark, while using some kind of superior hearing, (six trained ears) and although they all took and made shots, Gabriel had taken 12 of them, and he had made every single one count.

Another story involved Aaron, who was the absolute master of long and short rifles, and this was his thing, what he was good at, and destined to be. He was extremely, extremely deadly and accurate from all ranges, but especially from long range. He rode with two long rifles that were attached to both sides of his saddle, with two short rifles attached to his waist for easy and anytime access. So once during a skirmish that began just as it started to become dusk, one of the combatants tried to get away, as he popped up on his horse, from the shadows in the tall grass, in sort of a coward's battle mode mentality. He, was the look out, and had seen the three coming, so he was sly like the fox, and he had made his horse lie down, and hide with him, and as the three passed by his position, to close the noose and mopped up the rest of his group. He remained perfectly quiet, and only made a break for it, when the three had turned their backs upon him, and were concentrating on the rest of his group. He almost got away with it, if Aaron was not present, for Aaron calmly trotted to his horse double quick time, and pulled out his two long barreled rifles, and wheeled about to make a visual sighting of his target.

He then never took his eyes off his prey once he made visual contact with it. He squared up his body and feet towards his prey, he squatted with one knee flat upon the ground, and then leaned the barrel of one of his long rifles, against the opposite leg that was positioned up in a 90 degree angle, with the foot flat against the ground, he took one deep yoguy's breath, and with smooth and stunning precision, he calculated the distance between time and the space between him and the rider, fired the first long, then dropped it, and in one continuous motion grabbed the second long that was resting upon his leg, and fired it, all in the time it took for him to exhale the yoguy's breath from his body.

The first shot hit the rider, in the back, taking him completely off his horse, which was still moving under full steam. The second shot hit the horse in the head, killing it instantly in its tracks, and without saying a word or displaying any emotion, he bounced up, and went to retrieve the prey, so they could line them all up together in the lineup, which was our way of giving a warning to beware of things that move about by the light of the moon.

Now while the three were growing daily with skill and experience mixed with determination, mi Abuelo was trying hard to figure out who in the commander's group would be the leader. All three had the attributes and leadership abilities so he was having a hard time, trying to figure how who and how to pick a leader? What could he use to solve this riddle, and so one day while he was talking to me, and Mamie, about his problem, which was a nice one to have, mind you because whoever got picked would be a nice choice, it was Mamie who gave him the solution that he was seeking. She said that if all three are similar in most respects, and all three had their strengths and things that they were naturally good at, then a test must be created, that was a combination of everything that they had learned up unto that point, to solve the issue. A series of challenges must be created, and the winner of the most of these should be considered the leader who would be given a title or name that was chosen by the House, 'so say we all.'

We also thought about making the name something in Latin, but in the end we decided, in honor of our Santee friends, we would give it a First One's name, and this is what we would all call the leader of the commanders. After many nights of healthy debate, we as a group decided on the formal name as Tatanka Sica Ohitike, which in English meant Brave Bad Buffalo, or Tatanka Sica which meant Bad Buffalo, for short. These tests should not only be physical in nature, but also be mental ones, because all good leaders must be able to think on their feet and use mental as well as physical solutions to accomplish goals. So Abuelo should also use schooling and mental exercises, in his challenges to create this leader of the three. With that we all, (Abuelo, Mamie and myself) developed a plan that contained a series of tests, that contained skill tests with all of the various weapons that we were trained with, along with school tests that combined math, and history and writing and Latin, and then the game of chess and then lastly, an in-the-field related exercise that involved a riddle that must be answered.

The question involved asking each commander what he or she should or would do in a mock battlefield scenario with a no win situation, where victory was not possible, and where the lives of all of the members of The House were at risk. Well to everyone's surprise, Kara was the eventual winner, because in the contest, everything was close and they were evenly matched, but she was the only one who passed the last test, and correctly deduced that retreat was also a possible solution, so that, you could live to fight another day in the war and ultimately save the lives of everyone in the House, so that the next generations would be possible.

So with that, Kara became Tatanka Sica Ohitike whenever she was in the field on House business, and the only one that she deferred to, was only to me. She then named the other two commanders Akicitas Chanzee or Shadow Warriors, and that is how the term Shadow Warriors of the House of Calais Vega came about, and has been used ever since. Once she became Tatanka Sica Ohitike, Kara was like an even more changed child, because she understood the great responsibility that was now placed upon her shoulders. She had this razor-sharp focus and attention to detail, and she was always asking questions, that once she got the answers for, she would never ever forget. She drilled the three even harder, and they moved like they were one machine. They trained as much as possible with Abuelo, and she even picked the next Akicitas Chanzee. She became a dedicated and highly disciplined student of her new trade, and she took her role as my number one, very seriously.

She dedicated herself to educating the young warriors in the ways of redrum, which is murder spelled backwards. She seemed to like it when it was just me and her, practicing in private, even though she really seemed to enjoy, it much more when the whole House trained as one, from the youngest to me and let Abuelo lead the session.

The terrible three began using an even wider range of weapons, and they became very good at using the metal stars from the land of mi Abeula, and all the various lengths of the bushido's, be that the smallest of blades to the longest ones. She developed more fully the hiding and evading techniques that all young shadow warriors of the House have been taught as a part of their basic training. She is the one that conceived of creating safe havens and weapon stores out on the field at various locations and points of interest to, and for the House. She drilled into everyone that while in the field at night never light a open fire for a meal, at your camp, so that you never ever give your camp's location away. She incorporated a lot of balance and stretching poses into the training, and she required that everything was to be done, as a group to help build morale and confidence in the younger warriors, and in the group as a whole. She used a joint training routine were everyone trained one another, as a way to ensure that the proper techniques were being used at all times, no matter what the situation or occurrence, be that the upkeep and cleaning of weapons, to shooting an arrow with a bow from any distance, or even how to ride a horse. She drilled into everyone, the concept of making each and every shot count, in any kind of action, that involved a knife, a gun, a rifle, a tomahawk, a bow and arrow, a spear, a five pointed metal star, and hitting the target was the key for her and accuracy at various distances, along with either fixed or moving targets was part of her routine, and thus her gun warfare was second to none. She also developed and maintained what history has called the road agent's spin, which was a gun fighting maneuver ruse that was used when forced to surrender a side arm to a hostile. This tactic was ingenious because when you normally surrendered a loaded pistol, you handed it over upside down, and gun butt first. She developed this way of holding the pistol upside down, by the trigger guard, using the index finger and then extend the pistol towards the hostile as a sign of giving up. When the hostile reached for the pistol, she used a quick and well practice twist of her wrist, that would flip the pistol forward and back into the basic firing position, which nine times out of ten would always catch the hostile off guard. Now this trick was also called at some point the 'Curley Bill' spin, after Curly Bill Brocius, but to be honest, he probably had seen or heard of her doing it first, because for all young warriors, this is a maneuver that is a part of basic young warrior training, starting with Group Three, so it's probably safe to say that she was the first to invent her version of this gun fighters' trick, that she then passed on to the House of Calais-Vega. She also drilled the classroom into all of the Warrior generations of the House, so that they would think smart at all times, and use that education that they were receiving, in a constructive manner, in situations that they may encounter while on or in the field.

We started going further wiohpeva (west) on sentinel missions in search of our old kolas (friends), and this was just about the time that the so-called Bozeman Trail War, really began to pick up. The Bozeman Trail War was from 1866 to 1868, in the Wyoming and Montana Territories for control of the Powder River country, in North central Wyoming, which lay adjacent to the Bozeman Trail, which was one of only two access routes to the Montana gold fields and the Oregon territories. The Powder River country was south of the Yellowstone River, and northeast of the Bighorn Mountains, and it is a beautiful piece of country. Now before, I continue, we first need to go back, some 15 years earlier, to the first treaty of

Fort Laramie in 1851, because this will set the table, so to speak, about why Mahpiya Luta (Scarlet (Red) Cloud), the great Teton Ogalala Chief was so determined to drive out the wacicu (white) invaders. When the Federal government was deciding on how to convince the Plains Tribes to stop fighting one another and attacking the settlers that were going West, they decided to invite them all, and see who would come.

The Kiowas and the mighty Comanches both would not come because they flatly stated that they had too many horses, and that the Great Father had invited too many notorious horse thieves, primarily the Crows and the Ochethi Sakowin, so thanks but no thanks. The Pawnees also refused to come, because they were afraid of the Ochethi Sakowin, and for any Sakowin any day was a great day to die, when facing one of your mortal enemies. But in the end over 10,000 First Ones showed up, which caused the Federal troops to move the gathering some 30 miles away from the Fort, for security and comfort reasons. They say that it was a grand sight to see, so many different tribes represented, and to conclude the treaty and make it all official and binding, the Federal troops insisted that each tribe head, name a head chief that would then sign for his people. But with most Plains tribes, there is no one single leader, and there are many chiefs, and holy men. So the Federal troops picked the Chiefs from each tribe, and a warrior chief named Mato Wayuhi (Conquering Bear) who was a Teton Brule Lakota, a known man of peace, was picked to represent the entire Teton Lakota band of tribes. Mainly, everyone thought, because his tribe lived close to the Fort and because they only wanted to live in peace and tolerate the first wacicu (white) invaders, and he was recognizable to the soldiers. But then in August of 1854, the fragile peace was broken due to cultural misunderstanding and hatred, due to what some say was a cow, but what was really an ox. The wayward animal had mistakenly wandered near Mato Wayuhi's camp, and a hungry Miniconjou warrior, that was visiting the camp with his family during the end of the spring summer season festival, shot it with an arrow, and they ate it. The animals' owners who were a family of religious people, passing through the area headed to the city that was called Salt Lake reported the animal had been stolen by, the First Ones. Mato Wayuhi went to the Fort, as he responded to the Federal Troops inquiry concerning the animal, and he even attempted to negotiate some form of compensation for the animal by offering up some of his own horses in an exchange. But the settlers refused, and the Fort's commanding officer demanded that he give up the offender, but Mato Wayuhi refused, and finally went home. Then a few days later, Lieutenant Grattan was ordered to take 25 men, but it really ended up as 30, to the camp to arrest the Miniconjou offender. Lt. Grattan, when he arrived at the camp, that was filled with family visitors from other tribes, trained his guns and two cannons on the teepees and demanded that the warrior surrender or be given up. Mato Wayuhi once again apologized for the act of killing the animal, but politely refused, and even attempted to pay more than what the animal was worth, and the two sides argued for almost an hour.

Finally, after seeing that the Federal troops would not listen to reason or sense, he refused one last time, and turned and began to walk away, as the officer, Lt. Grattan feeling as if Mato Wayuhi was disrespecting his authority as an officer in the US. Army ordered his men to open fire. Only one man, who history claims was still in a drunken state from the night before, followed through with his order, and as a shot rang out, Mato Wayuhi lay on the ground, shot in the back, mortally wounded and dying. So angered by the senseless shooting of a highly respected man of peace, the Ochethi Sakowin, who were led by the mighty Sinte Gleska (Spotted Tail) and others, rose up, and surrounded and then killed the entire group, except for one mortally wounded soldier, who was allowed to crawl back, so he could tell the story of what had happened to his superiors, but he eventually died too. But to the Ochethi

Sakowin, none of this made any sense, because Mato Wayuhi was supposed to be the person who could settle this in the appropriate manner, and they killed the agent of their own relationship. They killed Mato Wayuhi their handpicked leader who had always promoted peace and tolerance towards the wacicu invaders, over what had been a minor dispute over an animal, which became an obvious sign to the Ochethi Sakowin of, blatant untrustworthiness, and the question then for everyone became so how could anyone ever trust these people!

This killing sent shock waves through the Ochethi Sakowin, and each one who had witnessed it, told the story over and over again to every and anyone, who would listen, including every detail. The murder made a distinct impression upon all of the viewers there that day, one of who was a curly haired boy of 12 who was visiting his mother's family, and who would later be known to the world as, Tashunca Uitco (Crazy Horse). Then after a series of continued offenses each and every year, including the Santee Dakota War of 1862, in 1863 gold was discovered in the area of Bannack, which is in western Montana, which created another violation of the treaty of 1851, as the wacicu settlers sought a quicker way to the gold fields, which is where the Bozeman Trail came into the picture. This trail was the incentive to get to the gold fields quicker, and so it needed to be protected, even though this protection violated The Fort Laramie Treaty of 1851.

Then in 1865, only two months after the end of the Great War between the States, The Powder River expedition, was ordered by the Federal Government against the Ochethi Sakowin, the Northern Cheyenne, and the Arapaho, and it culminated in the Battle of the Tongue River, which ruined the ability of the Arapaho to wage any more war on the Bozeman Trail. A council was called between the Northern Cheyenne, and the Ochethi Sakowin, and the U.S. Government at Fort Laramie, in the spring of 1866. Mahpiya Luta (Scarlet (Red) Cloud) was present at this meeting and he was outraged that the Federal Army, was bringing in troops before the Ochethi Sakowin, and had even agreed to a military road through the area, to protect the Bozeman Trails at key military locations. Eventually Mahpiya Luta and his followers left the meeting upset but determined, and promising resistance to any wacicu invader who sought to use the trail or occupy the Powder River country. His words as he walked out were, "You are the white eagle who has come to steal the road. The great father sends us presents and wants us to sell him the road, but the White Chief comes with the soldiers to steal it before the Indian says, 'yes or no'. I will talk with you no more. I will go now and fight you. As long as I live, I will fight you for the last hunting grounds of my people." Because, as Mahpiya Luta had said, this area was supposed to be off limits to any and all wacicu invaders, since the Fort Laramie treaty of 1851, and why now because of the zi (yellow) shiny metal, which was not even on their land, did they seem so intent upon going back on their words. We had trusted them, yet they killed Mato Wayuhi, by shooting him in his back, over something minor, in less than three years after he had signed their so called treaty for them. Now 12 years later, they were up to their usual lying and double-dealing ways, and once again they with their big words, were to be trusted? So what were the soldiers and the Forts really going to be used for, and why did the words of the wacicu invader never ever have any meaning?

So Mahpiya Luta, took the fight to the invaders, and he was determined to have the Forts abandoned or burnt down or a combination of both. He created storehouses of weapons and food supplies for his warriors at strategic points that could be easily accessed, and he coordinated his attacks, based upon his observations of the soldiers' behavior. He invited all warriors from far and wide to speak to him, so that he could gain a total understanding of what they were up against. He then took all of this information and brilliantly used it to create havoc and chaos amongst all wacicu invaders, and used their arrogance against them, in a way never seen or even thought of before. Because most of the soldiers' officers, had participated in the great Civil War, and they seemed to respect no one, so why not use this against them, and they seemed intent upon blindly following decoy parties. So outside of Fort Kearny, he waited to spring the trap, and by killing an officer, he felt that he could accomplish his goal of entrapping some soldiers. Finally in December of 1866, a junior officer who was being sent out with a patrol to guard the weekly wood train was killed during a skirmish right outside of the Fort, and the officer who was second in command, a Lt. Colonel Fetter- man felt out- raged by this murder, as he called it.

So 15 days later after mulling the so called ineffectiveness of his commanding officer, he left the security of the Fort with 80 men to aid the weekly wood train, disobeying his orders to not engage in any manner or follow any braves, no matter how they should try to tempt him. But once he got to the Lodge Trail Ridge, the bait from the decoy party, which contained Tashunka Witco (Crazy Horse) was too strong, and the soldiers rode all hell bent, up and over the ridge, into a well-designed trap, that had no escape. All 81 men were killed, and all of the bodies were mutilated, except for one, the young bugler, who had killed several warriors with his bugle. For this, his body was left untouched as a sign of respect, and it was covered in a buffalo robe, as a tribute to his bravery. The Fet- terman massacre, as it became to be known in history, was the worst army defeat on the Great Plains, and with that the Federal Government took notice and started to pull back its forces.

Then in 1867 came a series of battles, and finally in the spring of 1868, Peace Commissioners were sent from Fort Laramie, to negotiate a peace treaty with Mahpiya Luta, who refused to meet with these people, until the Powder River Forts of Phil Kearny and C. F. Smith were abandoned. In August of 1868, the Federal soldiers finally abandoned the Forts, and in November Mahpiya Luta signed the Treaty of Fort Laramie of 1868, which created what the wacicu called the Great Sioux Reservation, which included the Papa Sans, and created unceded territory as a reserve for any Lakota who did not want to live on the new reservation, and really it was a hunting reserve. Mahpiya Luta, history will state, was the one and only First One, to ever win a major war against the United Snakes, and it was known historically as (Scarlet) Red Cloud's war, that occurred from 1866 to 1868.

We traveled all over the Great Plains, in search of our lost Santee friends, and the life was becoming very lonely for me, because I was missing out on watching our family grow up and my woman's touch and smell. I was also experiencing headaches, which seemed like it was linked to the fact that I was using the mushroom chew strips too much, and only when I chewed a strip did, I feel somewhat normal again. I also was becoming very disturbed by how it had started to affect my mind in an evil and sinister manner, and I was losing control of my ability to use my rational thought in regards to killing just for the sake of killing, and I had started to display a kill first mentality. That to me then meant that I needed to stop, because I originally used the mushroom chew strips to give myself an edge in the Great Battle of our Family's freedom, and then during my Conductor days. Abuelo had always warned me to never ever swallow the chews, because everybody's bodies were different, and so the chews affected everyone differently, and this effect, if ever swallowed, would last for a while. For me, the chews right off the bat, killed my appetite and kept me awake for long periods of time, and on edge with a huge amount of anxiety, and in a heightened sense of battlefield awareness. Thus, the more that I used it, the more heightened were my sense of sight, smell, hearing, imagination, along with an increased ability to run, and use any form of weaponry, and everyone seemed to slow down, as I sped up.

But now after continual use, and because of the long hours that being out on the Great Plains requires, it became like using it was likened unto drinking a lot of the drink that is called cafe, and too much cafe can make you feel so crazy and hyped up, which could not be good for your body. I felt as if I was a prisoner to the effects of the mushroom chews, and I needed to break the hold that it had on both my body and mind. So I decided after consulting with my beloved Mamie, that I needed to stop using this battlefield edge, and try hard to step away from the effects of this addiction. But as in any addiction, it had many twists and turns, until one could finally beat the habit. I would do good and go for days without using the mushroom chew strips, and then something would occur that would cause me to seek the advantage that the mushroom chew strips offered, and I would slip back into that world of my habit, and convince even my own mind, that I was doing the right thing by using this advantage. So Mamie started removing the mushroom chew strip bag from my saddlebag, as I sought to hide the fact from her that I was still using the advantage even when I was not on the field of battle. Tatanka Sica, had sensed that something was wrong with me, and had gone to both Mamie, and mi Abuelo to find out what was wrong with me.

We all sat down, and I was told to not go into the field, and just get some plain ole rest, for the next few weeks, because I was extremely worn down, and had not gotten a proper night's sleep in years and years, since before my slave catching days. I protested, because these were difficult and draining times that our family was now experiencing, as we began our quest to continue moving wiohpeva and away from the Blancos. This required constant vigilance and dedication to our cause. Everyone was being stretched thin, because of this whole thing, and now was the time for leadership to step up, and lead in a strong and determined manner. All of the new and young Akicitas Chanzee, were learning their lessons and it was encouraging, but I still felt that the House remained vulnerable because they were still young, and still learning. They had not gotten the experiences that time provides, and so how they will act in any battle or in any matters of the House is still not really known. So we must be extremely careful with them, and bring them along as slowly as we can and develop them. So, I had to stop my habit and man up and do the right thing. But sadly I was only fooling myself, because I had a problem, that became out of control, because the mushroom chew strips kept me awake, and to pull the long hours that our family's kind of business required, the mushroom chew strips became my upper, and then slowly over time, I continued to increase the amount of gum chews that I used.

I was not resting properly, and I never allowed my body the chance to rid it of the lack of sleep and sped up effects that the mushrooms produced within me. I was taking chances and always living on the razor's edge, highly anxious and ready to kill for no reason until as fate would have it, I got caught out there, and almost did not make it back from the field. I finally, because of my lying and sneaking ways about my habit, was forbidden to go into the field, until my family felt that I was doing better, and cleaning up my act, and thus I had plenty of time on my hands. I could assist in the training exercises, but I could not conduct any in the field business for the House, and I was just plain old bored. Mamie told me that I could not stay in the homestead, and to go outside. So I devised a plan to get me back into the saddle and get me somewhat away for at least a few hours, as I took on the leadership of the young Akicitas Chanzee. We drilled and drilled, and then finally one night while out on a nighttime riding mission, we saw a meteor shower in the nighttime sky, and we could see in what direction the rocks had fallen to earth. It was a chance of the lifetime, I explained to the young Akicitas Chanzee, because this is how our friend named Destiny came into existence.

So maybe we could create another one on some kind of level, and so the retrieval of the rocks was our top priority. Also with the change in the seasons coming, the rocks may be lost forever once the snow came and covered all trails, and so this was the only chance that we may ever have. We were supposed to go back and check in. So sticking to the codes, we rode in and explained to everyone, that we were the only ones around who could do this, because the three were away on Family business, it would be easy, and we would be back in time for breakfast. We took minimum weapons, not much ammunition, and food stores for three day and off we set out, making great time actually. There were the two Akicitas Chanzee from The Third Warrior generation and the four from The Fourth Warrior generation. One of my own daughters was in The Fourth Warrior generation, so I was happy, but terrified of something happening to her that was beyond my control which as I look back on it, was just another effect of the mushroom chews.

The seven of us rode like the wind, and in two days we began to find the evidence of what we were seeking. We finally found the main area that the meteors impacted the earth, and we took our time to collect as many of them as we could, because the young warriors could add this metal from the heavens into the making of their new bushido's that all warriors were required to complete, as one of their tests of becoming a warrior for the House of Calais-Vega. But the biggest rocks were still hot, and they needed more time to cool down, so I decided to take it slow. Because the young warriors were tired from our hard ride, I decided to not push back towards home right then, and just rest up some. I did not bring any chew strips, because I needed to beat this habit, no matter what. I took the watch, as the young ones bedded down for the night. I was feeling out of sorts, and very unsure about my body and mind. After about a hour or so I decided to close my eyes just for a minute, and much later in the wee hours of the morning, just as the dark was about to change over to the light of morning I was awakened by the sounds of movement against our position.

I was shocked and upset at myself, because I was supposed to be on guard duty and yet I had slipped and committed the cardinal sin and had gone to sleep during my shift.

And now, an unknown number of opponents were moving upon us, from different directions with us trapped, like in the middle of a blacksmith's vise. I had lost my edge, and instead of being the razor's edge, I had lost my edge, and had fallen asleep on guard duty and gotten us into a sticky situation. So I made the young ones hurriedly wake up, then explained our situation and assumed a defensive position. We would fight our way out of the trap or go down trying. As they got closer, I spotted Crows, which is one of the First Americans tribes that we always have had trouble with, along with the Pawnees, and it was a raiding party of maybe 15 braves. They were going for our horses, and the fire had brought them to our position. We assumed a V formation with the horses in the middle, and just boldly waited until we could see them, because we were low on ammunition, but certainly not courage. Then suddenly out from nowhere El Diablo joins the fray, and as I found out much later, that Mamie had instructed him to follow us, and to keep his eyes on us. His first act was to run head long into the path of the hard charging Crow braves, which disrupted their advance, because he spooked their horses.

This gave him the advantage that he needed, and he then began to attack the riders on the horses, with his usual throat biting habit. Well, he started his murderous run, moving steadily towards our position, which threw the Crow braves into turmoil and a panic, which gave us the advantage that we needed. I ordered the Young Warriors to begin firing and to mount their horses, and then signaled that we were going to make a break for it and use the advantage that El Diablo gave to us. We kept firing, and I then ordered the Young Ones to stop firing and to throw all caution to the wind, and ride towards El Diablo, to not stop riding until they had made it home, and to not look back or come back no matter what sounds they heard. Meanwhile, I would provide covering fire for their retreat. The two young warriors, the two Hell Raisers from the Third Warrior generation, Stacey and Alphonso it is noted, vigorously protested and demanded that they be allowed to stay with El Diablo and myself to properly cover our retreat, but I repeated my orders, and made them commanders of the entire two groups. I turned and began to carefully take out targets, preferring to take out the horses and not kill the riders. But they kept coming, and I had to hold my position until the young warriors were in the clear. I fired all my bullets, and I had completely forgotten to tell the young warriors to leave me their remaining ammunition which was another mistake that I committed, so I then pulled out my personal bushido. And, I began wielding it and suddenly Abuelo's training kicked in, and I was mopping them up to my surprise, despite not using the mushroom chews. The first two riders had no chance, as I cut the legs of both of their horses, which caused the both of them to be forcefully dismounted, in a throwing type of manner. I dispatched both riders, grabbing one's rifle and then in the nick of time, I was able to see another fast moving rider coming in rapidly, leaning over his horse, while readying his hatchet as I wielded my bushido in a circular motion, that halfway sliced though his hand that was holding the hatchet. I threw a star at the next rider, and then I emptied the rifle at the remaining braves, who seemed stunned by my battlefield prowess. I took them all on, and they were not my equal and as soon as you knew it, the battle was over, as the remaining Crows took their leave, and El Diablo and myself, were the only two left standing. It strangely was very easy work, and I was about to take my leave, when I decided not to forget our prize, and I went and secured the remaining meteor rocks, because the biggest three pieces had finally cooled down, enough to handle. I picked up the rocks, and placed them within my saddlebag, then turned to look at El Diablo, who was now at my side and growling at something, just as a shot rang out, and El Diablo yelped out in pain, and immediately went down in a thud. I turned to see another completely new raiding party fast approaching, and this certainly did not bode well for us. I picked him up, and he was a bloody mess, yet he still was alive, but just barely, I recognized. I put him over the saddle as I lashed him down, and I then slapped Freedom the horse on his rear, as I looked directly into his big eyes and said 'home' to him as he suddenly dashed off like he was in a championship horserace. I turned to face the oncoming onslaught, just as another shot rang out, and something crashed into my throat area, and knocking me off my feet. I struggled up, as my lifeblood furiously squirted out all upon me and onto the ground, which was making me dizzy and weak. But before the lead rider could fire again, I dispatched him, taking him right off his horse. Another shot rang out, and I felt something burning, in my right thigh area, and I went down again.

As I struggled to lift myself up, something was painfully sticking me in my left shoulder, and then something, that felt like a rope, went over my head and shoulders, which immobilized my arms and hands and then something clubbed me in the back of my head, as I nearly passed out from the pain. I then, can remember only bits and pieces of what happened next. I think punches and kicks all over my body, and then of being dragged for miles, and miles upon the ground by both feet, bumping and crashing into objects, and things like bushes that were in my path on the ground. Finally I was strung up and being pelted with rocks and sticks for what seemed like days until I was finally thrown into some kind of enclosure, and then the curious feeling of small hands all over my body. The pain was excruciating, and my mind faded to black, and then hovered in a strange place, where I was not dead, but not alive either. It took a long time for me even to be able to focus on trying to wake myself up, because along with the pain of my injuries, my body was crying out for the mushroom chews, and it made me physically sicker, as if my body was going through some kind of withdrawal, because I had not taken my daily dose of the mushroom chews.

I also felt a lot of pain and passing out into the darkness helped, because being conscious was painful, and early on just learning to cope with the pain, was the hardest thing to accomplish. So, my body had to first heal and then my mind. I actually felt as if I was going to pass onwards from the physical phase, to the next phase of the human existence. I passed back and forth between the darkness and the light, and mostly I stayed within the dark region. I could hear water that was constantly running somewhere nearby, and I can remember thinking or wondering what had happened to El Diablo and whether the Young Warriors made it back home. This all was my fault I thought, and if El Diablo died, it would all be my fault. He is or was something that could not just be easily replaced. He was my protector and confidant, and I had gotten him killed, because he appeared to me, to be bleeding out as I threw him up upon Freedom's back. I then wondered when this bad dream would be ending, but this was no dream, and I was being held somewhere. Only after weeks, did I finally start to revive myself, and it was then that I realized that I was being held as a prisoner or really a hostage, but why was I being kept alive?

I also realized that the snow had fallen, and it appeared to be deep from what I could see from my cage. I was also not alone in my cage, and I was being kept alive by some of my fellow prisoners. I guess I was babbling in Ochethi Sakowin, when they threw me into the cage area, and a few of the women folk, who were Teton Lakota recognized the language and started taking care of this stranger who could speak bits and pieces of their original language. They openly did not want to be seen helping me, so they only helped me after dark when everyone else was asleep. I was being fed very little, and was constantly tied up very tightly, by the wrists and feet. They beat me daily and they used this big rock to smash my toes and fingers with, as a method of punishment, but whenever they untied my feet, they constantly had three or more braves watching me, as I crawled about the ground. My throat had a bullet hole in it, and the original sound of my voice was gone, and now replaced with a barely audible and extremely low and squeaky sounding version, that seemed both alien and foreign sounding. It hurt when I tried to speak, so I guessed that my voice was now gone, and I would never be able to speak out loud ever again. My left shoulder had a arrow wound, and my right leg had a bullet hole in it. While the other leg, my left appeared to be broken, which meant that my entire left side did not work properly. My eyelids had been severely scraped, as I was being pulled along the ground, so my vision was obscured until my eyelids became healed and the swelling had gone down. My entire body had little holes all over it, where it appears that I may have had been pulled through a sticker bush of some kind. I had no feelings in either of my wrists, and neither in both ankles, and part of the arrows' shaft was still within the wound, which caused it to become infected, and to be always sore. I was a mess but, alive and once my vision came back, I could finally really blurry like, see who my captors were. And to my horror, they were Pawnees. So even though I was really banged up, they were not taking any chances with me because I had choked out one of my captors when I had first arrived. Besides, they wanted to know of my magic, and how they could gain some of it. For they had watched us for some time and actually had been following us, as we tracked down the meteor rocks, some of which glowed a reddish color. Meanwhile, they wondered just what we were doing and what we had wanted, with these rocks that fell down from the nighttime sky. They then had remained silent, as their allies, the Crows attacked us for our horses. And, they'd seen with their own eyes how I had used powerful magic, with a shiny sword to dispatch these brave Crow warriors. Only when my back was turned, and I'd had gone back to get the rocks, did they show themselves, and they had more rifles than their allies the Crows did. And, they were not about to take a chance and fight up close, and within close quarters. Besides, to them, this man and his wolf were a formidable pair, and they would make the man reveal his magic, and keep him a hostage until he did, or he died, whatever came first.

A lot of braves were always punching me, or taunting me to fight, because I had killed their second in command and great warrior, so why was I being kept alive? They all wanted the honor of killing me, so that they could have their revenge for my killing of their tribe's Pipe Holder. Days turned into weeks, and then weeks into months. Then spring came and went, and then summer started to slowly show itself upon the land. I had been captured in the beginning of the Fall Season. So, three Seasons had come and gone, which meant that I was at least into eight to nine months of having been their prisoner.

I was getting stronger by the minute, and my fellow prisoners, had taken a liking to me because I had displayed an enormous amount of strength and courage. Not once during my daily and routine beatings did, I ever cry out or scream in pain. So they respected me, and they watched and listened to me with their eyes and gave me the support that I needed to survive. They cleaned my wounds, and when I was sick with the shakes, which are part of the effects from not using the mushrooms, they used their own bodies to keep me warm, and took turns holding me. So they are the ones in the end, who kept me alive until my help arrived. My fellow captives, who were all females, seemed aware that I was starting to move about better, and that my vision and strength were both coming back. Once the blurriness totally left me, I could see that some of them appeared to be from the same tribe, which was Teton Lakota. There were also two Cheyenne women who smiled at me and who sometimes even gave to me their food, because I had to gain back my strength if I was to survive this ordeal. They had been intrigued by the fact that here I was, this strange fellow who could speak

Dakota, and who was determined to fight against our common oppressors.

So they had taken me under their wing, and treated me with
kindness and decency, even though they did not know me from
Adam and they helped to make me somewhat whole again. It was
their tiny and smooth hands that I had felt when I first arrived at
my prison. So whether it was secretly taking turns feeding me, or
taking turns giving to me their rations for the day or setting my
broken leg and tending to my injuries and wounds, they were right
there for me.

And if I could ever get out of here, I would be taking them all
with me or certainly die trying. One of the women, who seemed to
be in charge, whose name was Takchawee Weeko (Pretty Doe),
really did a good job in looking out for me in a real way, over time.
She seemed to understand that I was getting better, but she made
me take it easy and pretend to still be hurt, so that I could get
stronger without their knowledge.

I even began to be able to withstand the daily beatings, and still
get stronger, and more importantly I had to learn to mask my anger
and hatred for my oppressors and seem weak and have a broken
spirit. This gave me plenty of time to think about everything, and
how swallowing of the mushroom chew had caused all of this to
unfold and cause the death of my friend El Diablo.

I then thought of my beloved Mamie, and my family and children.
I then thought about mi Abuelo, and of my apprentice Tatanka Sica,
of the Terrible Three and of the young Akicitas Chanzee. I then
strangely thought of mi Madre, and of Master Jack, and the Blancos
that we had escaped from. And, I really wondered how all of this
would really turn out.

But to be honest, not once was I ever scared, nor did I ever give
up any of my self-determination. Because, my beloved Abuelo had
instilled within me a belief in Amen-Ra, the Great Mystery, that determination was steadfast and hard as a rock. I would hold on and

survive, and the word 'Agon' kept popping up inside of my head and mind, which meant 'the pain to overcome.' And now, I see why he had drilled it so hard within my being and state of mind.

This was my real and true test of fire. And, if I was the true and rightful heir, the so called 'chosen one' of our family's destiny then I must survive at all costs and wait for my chance to escape. Finally, I got a chance to briefly see the main Chief and low and behold, he was holding my very own bushido tightly in his grip. And he went everywhere with it, I had on many occasions noticed, as if it was now a part of him even though he did not help to create the blade.

This was like a great prize or object of affection to him. And he held this like it was his, and his alone, which really only made me madder and more determined to wield my personal bushido once again. And once I got back my sword, I would avenge the death of our family's beloved El Diablo or die trying. But unknown to myself, El Diablo did not die that day because of the battle. He was gravely injured and about to pass on.

But Freedom the horse had saved his life, at the cost of his own. For once I had slapped his backsides and had uttered the phrase 'go home,' he set off with Pawnees in pursuit because, they had seen me place the rocks into the saddle bag which was a part of the saddle. They shot at him and chased him for miles, but he was determined to make it back home. He was wounded, but yet he kept running, for almost two days straight carrying El Diablo the whole way still lashed to his saddle.

And finally, after getting safely and far away from his pur-suers, he ran himself to death as his blood ran all out. He crashed to the earth, and his last movement was to try and cover El Diablo, because the first snowfall had just began to occur. Freedom's body heat had kept El Diablo alive long enough, so that he did not totally freeze under the weight of the first snowfall of the year.

In about a day, the Terrible Three found Freedom's dead body, with a still alive but badly shot up El Diablo partly underneath it.

The Three buried Freedom, recovered the rocks that were within the saddlebag and then took El Diablo back to the base camp, where Mamie immediately took care of his wounds. But because he had lost quite a bit of blood, and the bullet had to be removed and his condition was grim, and everyone in the family feared that he was going to die.

The young Akicitas Chanzee then took off to begin looking for me again, and they were able to find the battle site that was littered with snow covered dead bodies. And there was no hair or hide of me. Because of the snow, they could neither track my route or me because all of the clues had been covered up. Only when it started to snow heavier and deeper again, did they give up and return home. And, it was gloomy and very sad they said, because everyone except Mamie and mi Abuelo, feared that I had been lost in the field and was dead.

But Mamie and mi Abuelo, both never gave up hope on me. They both continued on as if I was out of town, and still alive. Mamie would confess to me later, that she knew that I was alive the whole time because her connection to me was never broken, and so she knew instinctively that I was still alive out there somewhere in the field. She also knew that keeping El Diablo alive was the key to finding out what had happened to me.

And if he died, then all could be lost as regards to me and my whereabouts because if anyone could find me, it would be El Diablo. Everything appeared rough, because after two months Diablo was barely holding on, and an infection had set in his wound, and he appeared many times to be a goner, but after another two months of constant and 'round the clock love and affection and care, he began to come around.

And truly it was Mamie's love that saved his life because she used a baby bottle to feed him, when he was at his lowest of lows, and about to go yonder, into the next life. She forced into his weakened body a concoction of milk and mashed up cooked potatoes, with a little gravy which was one of his favorite foods from since he had come to us as a mere pup. And she acted as if it was a beloved family member of hers, whose life she was desperately trying to save.

At seven months he started to try to open up his eyes, and to weakly sit up and look about. And that sleeping all of the time behavior started to slowly be replaced with barely opened eyes and low-pitched growling noises as if he was talking to himself and willing himself to get better. Then at eight to nine months he actually started to try to stand up, as he kept wobbly falling down, and then repeating the process. At 9 and a half months, to everyone's total amazement, his total strength came back and suddenly one day, he was his old self up and barking and growling and ready to go.

When he was ready, they say that he went to Mamie and used his nose to nuzzle her hands, letting her know that he was ready to find me, or my body. So after all of this time, he finally felt healed enough and he gently took her hand with his mouth and guided her to Tatanka Sica. So Tatanka Sica right then and there organized a raiding or really a recovery party, which included the Terrible Three along with the Two Hell Raisers from Group Three, while leaving Group Four behind to guard the base camp.

Before she left out, Mamie pulled Tatanka Sica off to the side and requested an audience. And she gave to her, Our Friend named Destiny, and all three of the remaining bottles of the awakening liquid, along with instructions on how to secretly awaken the spirit of the blade. She also gave to her the bag of mushroom chew sticks and instructed her on how to use them, which was right before any battle, but at no time must she ever swallow the chew stick, because the sticks once swallowed could make you a prisoner to its effects.

She also told her to bring my body back, be that alive or dead but bring the body back so that the family could have some kind of closure, if I was sadly indeed dead. "Retrieve the body," she firmly stated once again for effect "bring him home, because no one ever gets left behind in or on the field of battle." With that, the five Akicitas Chanzee's along with El Diablo at the point all lit out together like some wild animals with a wagon and six horses tied to the back of it. And it was of course El Diablo who found my scent, in about a week or so, and led everyone to my prison which was the Pawnee's camp. El Diablo wanted to immediately charge into the Camp, they all said. But they had to restrain him and drag him back, because they had to observe what was going on inside of the Camp to determine if I was even still alive. And more importantly, they did not want to lose their element of surprise. But El Diablo's actions meant that my body was there, and they needed to use caution and to remain in the shadows until they could scout the camp.

About the same time, I had started to notice that my strength was indeed coming back or was really back. And, my captors were getting lazy in guarding me, and they were not even tying up my feet any longer at night, because they still falsely assumed that my left side was still not properly working yet. They also stopped using many eyes upon me at night, and now only left one guard to watch over me, which seemed kind of downright disrespectful to me, even if I was still banged up pretty bad.

I then noticed a pattern in the guard's behavior, and when the majority of the braves were gone on the hunt, the remaining guards would leave us unattended, and go to get some sleep in their dwellings. I had used my time to construct a weapon, from a buffalo bone, by giving it to Takchawee Weeko (Pretty Doe) to be sharpened. She really did a good job at making the point very sharp, and when she eventually handed it back to me, she said tawaiciya (freedom) and smiled. She then seemed a bit startled when I tried to mouth the word pilamaya (thank you) in a low and squeaky sound, even though it hurt whenever I tried to vocalize, and so I just smiled back at her, and nodded which she seemed to understand.

I started to formulate an action plan and to me, I had figured that we would only have one, and only one chance as a group, to escape and to once again experience freedom. So the timing of our escape was the thing that had to be figured out. And maybe, I should just try, when the moment seemed right.

So I showed Takchawee Weeko what our tiospaye (extended family) hand signal was my index finger below my eye socket. And I decided to strike when the first chance came, and to not wait for a better day. In about four days' time, just after dusk when the camp's main nighttime fire had just been lit, it appeared that something had spooked the warriors, and there was a lot of commotion about the entire camp, and we realized that something big was happening.

Then, after a quickly put together meeting at the biggest dwelling, suddenly, most of the warriors mounted their horses and raced out of the camp crossed the river and bolted up and over a hill, and out of view. That left only the Main Council of the tribe who were still in the main dwelling, the women, children and old ones, along with only a few guards, and a few dogs. And there was only one sleepy looking guard watching us, or really a still half asleep one, with his eyes closed, who sat upon a nearby rock.

Then up over the hill, in the direction of where the braves had ridden off into, there were the sounds of rifle and gunfire. A lot of dirt swirled and billowed about through the air from that direction, as if a great battle was occurring. Now was then the time, I said to myself. And we may not have another chance like this, so I signaled Takchawee Weeko, and everyone got ready.

I lured the single guard close to the fence, by spitting upon him through the fence, and turned my back to him as he opened the gate and rushed into the enclosure to deliver my punishment. The look on his face was one of total astonishment, as I wheeled about and thrust the buffalo bone directly into his left eye, and snap-turned my wrist to the right, to make it dig deeper into his eye socket. I pulled the bone back, from the wound, as he crumpled to the ground.

Then I hobbled to the gate and began waving to signal my ti-ospaye (extended family) to get moving that we were to leave then. I heard feet running directly towards us and as I looked up, I saw a brave coming up quickly with his knife drawn, ready to strike. I blocked his initial thrust with my left forearm, and used the buffalo bone, that was in my right hand, in a sweeping hook type of motion that smashed just below the jaw line and into his face, as he yelped out in agony, and semi-staggered away in pain. I was then immediately knocked down from behind, and then I was on the ground clawing and fighting my next oppressor.

I could feel something slicing into my right side, as pain shot up and down the whole right side of my body. But I had gotten my hands around his neck, and I was choking the life from him, so no matter what the pain felt like, I was just going to hang on until he stopped moving. When I had finished dispatching him, I was breathing hard, as I rolled over onto my back while placing my hand over my wound, which was bleeding quite hard.

And, upside down I could see braves coming out of the main dwelling to see what was going on. I could then see the braves reading themselves, but for some reason they were strangely not approaching my position. I then heard something approaching me, and as I braced myself and lift- ed my head and looked down at my feet to see what was now coming, what I saw was the angel of death herself, Tatanka Sica, in the flesh, and she had this dark sided sinister look on her face, like she was not in any mood to play.

She had her face paint on, but it was streaked, and she seemed to be wet all over, from head to toes. When our eyes locked, she had tears in her eyes and her teeth were clenched. Her eyes flashed as she went into a mental rage of sorts that pushed her over the edge, and into the zone of the dark side of her personality. And that is when I noticed that 'Our Friend named Destiny' was in her hand,

and she was holding it by the handle with the blade facing downwards, and Destiny was awake and glowing. And she had this pot that was smoking, that she was holding by some strings of rope in the other hand.

She swooped down and hugged me tightly, gave me her bushido and then she yelled out a birdcall. And from out of nowhere, came El Diablo, who lay down upon my body as he snarled with his teeth flashing. And he would not let me get up, and anything that came near us, he dispatched with an ease that seemed not quite fair.

I, lying down flat on my back and upside down, could see Tatanka Sica moving swiftly and gracefully towards the main dwelling with her robe on. And, Our Friend named Destiny, who was glowing and awake, was kind of like cocked behind her back. The pointed end pointed skyward with the hand that was holding the pot, which was now smoking more heavily, clinched into a fist outstretched and pointed towards the braves.

Now maybe it was my mind playing tricks on me, because of all the stress and punishment that I had taken for all of those months. But she honestly seemed to hover above the ground, as she moved, and she ruthlessly dispatched the two braves that were guarding the entrance to the main dwelling before they even knew what was happening. All the while she swung the smoking pot in a small semi-circle by her head, and then threw it into the entrance. And as she then pulled the hood down over her head with only the lower half of her face showing, she smoothly walked into the entrance, and once inside all hell sounded like it had broken loose.

I could hear yells and gun shots and shouts and screams, and then a head came rolling outside through the entrance and came to a stop a few feet from the entrance opening.

This all happened in less than five minutes, and then every- thing became eerily quiet as smoke came from inside the dwelling and drifted into the outside air. And, out from within the smoke itself came Tatanka Sica, who savagely kicked the lifeless head with her foot.

And she was also holding in her hand, my bushido, which she tossed to me when she got closer to me. Then she dispatched any and all things that even moved towards us, be that old people, women or dogs or even children as Destiny hummed its song of death as she swung it from side to side. Nothing survived her on-slaught, and the yells of her victims pierced the nighttime air. And when everything was finally over, she whistled and her horse, with another horse that was tied to its saddle, both came a running at her command.

She tried to make me get up onto the extra horse, but I was not about to leave without my tiospaye, who were hiding behind a nearby dwelling. My voice did not work, but Tatanka Sica could un-derstand my hand signals, and see that those females were with us and so with that, we all were off. We crossed the river together, with the Lakota females on foot but moving quickly and silently, and we followed down a path that was adjacent to the river. Ta-tanka Sica told El Diablo to stay with us, as she rode over the hill to the sounds of guns and the great battle.

After the shooting had finally died down, we were joined by first a wagon that was being driven by the Two Hell raisers Akicitas Chanzee. And we, including El Diablo and our new tiwahe (immedi-ate family) members, all got up into the wagon and quickly rode off without even looking back. Takchawee Weeko attended to my side wound, and after a few minutes of applying pressure to the wound, it stopped bleeding so hard.

After an hour or so 'the Terrible Three' joined us all and, all of the Akicitas Chanzee seemed extremely pleased and tickled to death. All five of them seemed relieved, but serious and determined to get us all home. Tatanka Sica came right over, jumped down off of her horse then quickly tied its harness straps to the back of the wagon, and climbed up into the wagon. She then lovingly put her hand on my face, and then hugged me for a long time as tears streamed down her face. And it was then, that I noticed the marks within the palm of her hand that matched the skull carvings on Destiny's handle.

But her marks were upside down from mine and mi Abuelo's because of the way in which she had held the jade handle. So Tatanka Sica had now been joined with the Spirit of Destiny's bushido, when she had awakened its spirit and wielded 'Our Friend named Destiny', and there is no mistaking that she had felt its enormous power in her grip, as the marks on the palm of her hand would attest to.

She stayed seated next to me the whole time, for the rest of our return trip home and she also hugged each and every one of our new tiospaye and smiled and then shared our food with them. She became especially close to Takchawee Weeko, and despite at first, they not knowing each other's tongue or language they became immediate lifelong friends on the ride back home. I guess she was intrigued by Tatanka's age and that she was a woman warrior, who despite her age and beautiful looks was a coldblooded killer, and more importantly she was in command, a woman Pipe Holder!

For she had watched her dispatch some people and some animals, and she had done this with such an ease and grace, that she had been both in awe and impressed all at the same time. She had also seen her wield 'Our Friend named Destiny', and what kind of magic was it that this person was holding in her hand? Because it cut through everything, and when she cut you it was as if you did not even know that you were cut either, until the cut piece fell to the ground. We stopped a few times for meals and rest stops, but in less than a week we were back at our forward base camp.

They had sent word ahead, so everyone was waiting for us when we finally pulled into the enclosure. Mamie was standing there with tears streaming down her pretty face, and the kids were all right there around her, in a semi- circle, and they were crying too, as they opened up the back of the wagon. And, El Diablo who had gone to sleep over my lower legs finally lifted his head yawning got up and then hopped down off the back. Everyone, all together at one time, very gingerly lifted my battered body up, and placed me upon the ground.

Mamie bent down and hugged me like she did on our wedding day, not letting go forever, as everyone laughed and chuckled at our display of our love for one another. I remember that she at one point had hugged me so tightly that the stab wound on my side was affected by the pressure her arms had put on my neck, and on the sides of my body. This hurt a bit and made me wince, but I would take her hugs anytime, and so I did not even complain. Finally, the rest of the clan was allowed to get their hugs in, and it was if they had mobbed me up, with mi Abuelo being the last but not least.

Finally, they took me inside to one of the beds so that they could take a look at my injuries and feed us all. Before they took me inside though, I introduced our tiwahe (immediate family) members to the rest of the House of Calais -Vega.

And it was a beautiful thing to behold, seeing my clan accepting complete strangers in the loving manner in which they did, because they let them fill their plates first, as if they were our honored guests.

My body was a total mess and Mamie decided that I needed an extended break, to sleep in a real bed and to see a real doctor, so that I could get a total examination. So, the House sent us back to the Family's house in Xenia, guarded by 'the Two Hell Raisers,' Akicitas Chanzee, so that I could get some rest and rehabilitate my broken body. Mamie actually loved the chance for us to get away from it all, because we had never had an extended break or real honeymoon, so this break became like a late honeymoon.

I was taken to see our very trustworthy family doctor who placed my leg in a splint and gave me some sticks called crutches and who cleaned and dressed all of my wounds. My throat wound had finally started to heal, but there was no telling about my voice and, or my ability to ever talk or speak again. My shoulder was healing as well as my side, as well as the fingers on my hands. And the doctor also had determined that I had some busted ribs, and some broken toes on my feet, and a thigh wound, but all in all just being alive was nothing short of a miracle.

Mamie did not let me get out of the bed except for an out-house break, for almost a solid two weeks, and she doted on me like I was her newborn child. She just seemed so happy, and even though I could not talk, she could tell by my eyes that I was happy to just be around her, and the air that she breathed in. She was even more beautiful than when we had gotten married it seemed, because now she was a mother and a lady, and her beauty ran well below her skin. She had this way that her smile just radiated through, and it was so bright when she was happy, that at times it seemed as if it could blot the sun from out of the sky.

She pampered me and washed my body and massaged on me with her hands and touched my broken body. She fed me constantly 3 to 4 square meals each and every day, because she was making up for all of those meals that I had missed during my captivity. Six weeks came and left quickly, so we decided that it was time to get back to our real lives. And so, we headed back to our forward base camp, but we did take our time and just enjoyed being alive, and the beauty of nature that surrounded us.

When we finally got back and settled in, I was totally amazed by the way that Tatanka Sica and Takchawee Weeko had begun to speak one another's language. Takchawee Weeko was learning all of the basics of the language that is known as English, and it was good to see her at least trying and laughing (amapsa) with Tatanka Sica. Tatanka Sica on the other hand, had learned and mastered all of the basic colors—sapa (black), zi (yellow), tohca (blue), gi (brown) luta (red), ska (white), ziyato (green), and hota (grey). She also had learned and mastered directions, waziya (north), wiohiyanpa (east), wiohpeva (west), itokaga (south). She was now learning the various animal names, and learning how to say the numbers, and family terms. She seemed determined to learn as fast as she could, to communicate with her new best friend and the rest of our guests.

She said that in the language of the Ochethi Sakowin, that it was mandatory to understand the pronunciation of things, so that one may more fully express emotions, and thereby make a statement with feeling and meaning, because feelings are important in the language. This understanding of language also helped to understand their feelings and emotions and also reflects the environment, expresses philosophy, and more importantly it also affirmed spirituality. So in essence, their language is the life force of their entire culture. So Tatanka Sica was determined by any and all means necessary to bridge the language gap and be able to communicate with our guests with the correct meaning and feeling as rapidly as possible.

But what was also amazing was that the young warriors of the House had also taken it upon themselves to at least try to learn because of Tatanka Sica. Because she was now the role model of all young warriors of the House, because of her exploits while saving me. I was finally allowed to sit down, and this was when I was told of everything since my capture and of Tatanka Sica's rescue plan for me. Once El Diablo had alerted the rescue party that I was there, or that my body was, Tatanka Sica had decided that they would scout and observe the camp, to determine the strengths and weaknesses of the First Ones

They watched for days the comings and goings, and even had covertly sneaked into their camp, to study the layout. It was during this initial sneaking mission, when they realized that yes, I was alive, but badly damaged. And so, they would have to come and get me, and remove me from my captors. They also determined that there were at least 30 possible warriors and of this 30, the leader had 3 braves that stayed with him at all times. So there were 26 braves that needed to be accounted for at all times. And, to get the number of braves down to a manageable number, that they could control and then rescue me, they needed to create a diversion that would then hopefully lead the majority of these braves, into a well-designed trap.

Tatanka Sica would use four warriors for this part, and that left only one warrior, and El Diablo to conduct the actual grab and snatch portion of the mission. Instead of using triangular fire, this time they would use a square or box-like configuration, with four fixed points or four moving points on horseback that would cover each other's positions. They had to figure out a suitable diversion, and she had used Aaron's suggestion of using fire, dust and smoke to lure the braves out of their encampment at just before dusk.

And then, once they were away from the village, prevent them by any and all means necessary, from returning for as long as it took. They would cut some foliage and tie it up with some rope, that each of the four Akicitas Chanzee would light on fire and then drag behind their horses, upon the plateau area of the ridge, to kick up as much dirt and smoke needed to divert their attention.

The one warrior who would be doing the actual dirty work, would use the river as a cover, while using a reed that had a hole in its center to breathe through. This warrior would stay submerged under the water, until it was time to perform that part of the mission. A set of foliage would be cut, and a watertight bassinet would be formed, which would contain that warrior's weapons, but more importantly keep everything dry and ready for action. El Diablo would guard the flank and provide back up support, and once I was located, he would stay with me the whole time. This warrior would also use a pot that was filled with the leaves that once lit, created quite a bit of smoke to further confuse my captors.

Everything must work in concert and be performed with clockwork precision. There would be no excuses for any lapses of concentration. They had a job to do, and they all had owed me their lives so this was just how they repaid me for everything that I had done for them and for the family in general. They used El Diablo to lure the guards, who seemed at first taken aback by a wolf that seemed not to be scared or frightened of them. And then, as he ran off and went over the ridge, there appeared to be a big calamity in the air.

And something was kicking up a lot of dust and smoke into the air. The leader quickly dispatched a couple of scouts to see what was going on. The two were quickly killed and their rider less horses were sent back into the camp. This really appeared to spook the leader, who quickly organized a meeting, as he sent most of his remaining braves along with the new Pipe Holder to investigate. Meanwhile, he and his council, and his personal guard stayed behind, to await the findings and to ready the camp for a possible move just in case this was a prairie fire or weather event.

When the party of braves went up and over the ridge onto the plateau, Tatanka Sica had slipped down to the River with a rope that was tied around her waist, which was connected to the basket that held her dry weapons, as she went underneath the water slowly moving in the direction of the other side, using a hollow reed to breathe through, and to stay totally submerged until she felt that it was safe. The basket stayed on top of the surface, high and dry so, when she got to the camp side of the river, she eluded the people, as she took her weapons from the basket and quickly dressed herself for battle.

Then she quickly worked her way toward the main campfire. She flipped 'Our Friend named Destiny', into the fire, so that its point was sticking into the ground with the handle up. As she put a mushroom chew into her mouth, and violently threw the two bottles one at a time, into the fire they were breaking with force as the flames reacted to the concoction inside of the bottles. They then shot up higher and more intensely and seemed to crackle and hiss all around Destiny. She then grabbed the handle, like she was opening her hand and then closing it into a fist. And as the heat from the blade sheared her hand, and the pain shot through her entire body, forever connecting her essence to the spirit of the blade suddenly, she felt nothing. She spun around to meet the oncoming sound of feet that were running toward her position she immediately noticed just how light as a feather that Destiny had felt in her hand.

And she did a half circle flick of her wrist, and the running sound was no more. The brave had been cut through and through on an odd angle, and his body had separated itself into two pieces, to her amazement. She then quickly moved toward my position and once she saw me, and how badly damaged I was, she could not contain her anger, and this anger fueled her lust for revenge, and revenge is a dish that is best served cold they say. This lust pushed her over the edge, and her dark sided rage completely took over her personality.

Then coupled with the death that Destiny had caused, or seen, Tatanka Sica became seduced by the power that Destiny wielded, and she was never ever the same. She said that right then and there, her goal was to 'redrum' or to kill them all or as many as she could, for what they had done to me. She was going to use the smoking pot as a diversion, but she quickly changed her battle plan from a defensive recovery mission, to then strike out on her own, on the offensive and even the score for the House of Calais - Vega. She called El Diablo out from his hiding place, and made him guard me, pulled the hood of her cloak down over her head with only the lower half of her face below her nose showing while she went to chop the head off of the snake. She popped another mushroom chew into her mouth and began to quickly chew, and that is when she said that things all around her began to slow down, as she began to speed up.

She said that she felt as if she was floating as she approached the two men who were standing as guards on the outside of the lodge-type structure, and she was shocked just how light that 'Our

Friend named Destiny' felt in her hand. It felt like some kind of white bluish and greenish red-streaked glowing wand, that kind of like hummed when she waved it at first one, and then another, and they both dropped like rocks onto the ground. She swung the smoking pot around in a circle near to her head and tossed it into the opening as she pulled down the hood over her head.

She braced herself, and flowed inside, and was met by a brave, halfway through the opening in the middle of the drifting smoke. He seemed stunned when she waved at his waist in a half arc hooking motion, which caused him to fall into two separate pieces, as a gasp went around the enclosure. She threw off her cloak as she unveiled herself in all of her glory, and that is when the battle really began. She looked around the room, scanning and looking for her prey, and there he was standing at the back of the room with eleven people standing between them. She went to work, and she leapt into action before anyone could react. With a flick of her wrist, throwing three metal stars in rapid fire succession, with all three finding their mark, one impaled a victim in the eye, one victim was left grasping at his throat and the last one landed on the side of that victim's nose. She could feel something closing in on her from her right side, as she pulled her pistol with her left hand, and fired it from underneath her right elbow and directly into the face of her attacker and then re-holstered it. All in one smooth motion, she simultaneously swung 'Our Friend named Destiny' within a semi-circled arch with her right hand, while she pivoted her body within a circle and sliced off the next attacker's arm, at the shoulder blade. She then continued her murderous assault, spinning and turning, both shooting and stabbing with both hands all in one motion, continuously moving forward, as Destiny hummed its song of death and she became the real merchant of death, as she dispatched everything that got in her way. Her victims' blood splattered about all in the air, as she cut and shot a path through them. Just when she had finished off the last defender by waving at his stomach area as his guts tumbled out and spilled upon the ground, he groaned out in a painful anguish. And as her back was facing him, the gutless leader who wanted no parts of battle, tried to run past her. And, she just simply pivoted in a circle, and with two hands swung in an upward chopping motion, and off came his head as it flew through the opening, and onto the ground outside. She walked up to the headless body, spit upon it and then savagely snatched my bushido that was still being held tightly by the dead man's hand. She then looked around the room to ensure that there was nothing still alive, and then put back on her cloak, and pulled the hood down over her head. And then she walked through the doorway opening and savagely kicked out of her way, the head that lay upon the ground a few feet from the opening as a loud gasp could be heard from some onlookers. She scanned the area outside of the lodge and found that her lust for revenge was not yet satisfied, so she then took her murderous ways to the rest of the village. And if she were an artist, she would have then just painted her ultimate masterpiece called redrum. She killed to kill, not to eat, not to satisfy a hunger need, but just because of revenge for what was done to me. She worked her way around to our position, using just 'Our Friend named Destiny' to dispatch everything that came into her field of vision, and when she came upon the Ochethi Sakowin, who were hiding behind a group of tents, she looked them all in the eyes, and kind of half smiled and then she acted as if they were not even there, and went around them and simply continued her murderous ways. When she was finally finished, and her lust had been satisfied, she called for our ride, and we were out. She left to join the battle upon the plateau, but it really was already done, and they were actually mopping things up. The Akicitas Chanzee had handled their business, and the braves who had ridden into the trap, had never had a chance. They were trapped into a rectangular configuration, by walls of fire on four sides, and it was like a turkey shoot because they had no cover. So they never had a chance and the Akicitas

Chanzee were all crack shots. Thus, it became a slaughter, as they completed their part of my retrieval mission, which was to chop off the head of the snake and create confusion by holding them there in that place. The four of them killed everything, the men as well as the horses that they rode on. They centered their initial attentions on the Pipe Holder, or the leader of the warriors in battle and he was the first to go, which was by design. Because his death created confusion and turmoil within the ranks of the braves, which is what the Akicitas Chanzee wanted to really accomplish in the very first place, because this would keep their attention away from the Village. So the plan was pulled off and everyone was alive and well. They stacked up the bodies of their prey, as is our way, and then sent 'the Two Hell Raisers' on ahead to join us, while they guarded our escape. I was impressed by the whole operation, by the cutlay of the plan itself, and by the skill at which it was executed. Everyone had individual responsibilities that they carried out, and everyone did their jobs, which made them operate as a unified whole. But in everything good, there is bad, and in this case the dark side had once again surfaced, and Tatanka Sica was now finally in its grip. She oddly seemed normal enough, and she had not swallowed the mushroom chews, and had spit them out once they had put some distance between the Village and us. But there was just something different about her now, as if she now had a razor's edge about herself that was sinister in both design and nature. She was a dangerous tool because she had joined with the spirit of the Blade, and all of the death that it had experienced. And we all agreed that she now would need to be watched, because she had wielded Our Friend named Destiny and had tasted its awesome power for herself. All of which could be a very intoxicating experience to the human mind. In about two weeks' time Tatanka Sica asked for permission to take our new tiospaye, back home to their tribes, and of course we happily said yes. We all sat down together with Tatanka Sica acting as the interpreter and devised a plan that was based upon where the women thought that their tribes would be located in their yearly migration paths. We would roll out in battle mode, and so we had to provide our guests with horses, and ensure that they could ride them and then, and only then, would we be able to travel in a more comfortable manner. So the Akicitas Chanzee got horses for us all, and we broke them in and got ready for the trip

My horse, which I myself choose was extremely fast so I named him Pegasus, after the winged horse from Greek Mythology, because for me there would never ever be another horse named Freedom. Because his actions, had saved El Diablo, and El Diablo had saved me, so out of much respect and honor, Freedom became a treasured name in our family, which would never ever be forgotten. I took my time and trained Pegasus just like I had trained Freedom, and he seemed to also be a quick learner. Once the horses were fully broken in, and trained to our tastes, and our new family had all learned to properly ride their mounts, we had our big going away powwow. So, we all broke bread with one another one last time, got in our goodbyes, and made sure that our guests knew just how much that we truly appreciated them, for caring for me and ultimately saving my life. It was really kind of neat, because the guests got into a circle that surrounded the fire. And the family encircled them with our guests on inside close to the fire, and then everyone sat down upon the ground, and as we went around the circle of life. Everyone except me that is from Abuelo to the very young, all got a chance to say their piece, or simply what was on their minds. Tatanka Sica provided the translation for those new friends or really tiospaye (family) of ours, who had trouble with their limited English or who were shy, but everyone was able to say thanks in one way or another. Abuelo was the first to speak, and he said thank you in his usual humble manner, with his hands clasped in front him, and he actually had the nerve to be smiling. Then Takchawee Weeko got up, and to everyone's amazement her English was pretty good. She was just so happy to have met us,

and she always knew that I was something special, and that something about me was very familiar or comfortable to her. Then upon
meeting my family, she had never ever met invaders who displayed
the sense of family that we do, besides her own tribe that is. And
with that, she then began to cry tears of real joy, and she started
to sway as she began to sing a song that was in her native Ochethi
Sakowin. When she was finished, she told me thank you (pilamaya)
in English, for saving her as well as the rest of the captives', and
that stories will be told for generations to come, of our generosity
and kindness. She said that we will always be in her family, and in
her family's family. With that, Tatanka Sica jumped up and went
over to her, and gave her a big old long and deep hug, and they were
both crying tears of joy at that point. Then Ominotago (Beautiful
Voice) got, up and began to sing a song in her native tongue. and
this sweet natured Cheyenne sister of ours, simply shocked and
amazed everyone with the clarity and sweetness of her mature
sounding voice. Her voice just rocked your world, and it was the
most beautiful sounding voice that we all had ever heard is what
everyone kept saying over and over again. Tatanka Sica then got
up and said her part and told of how in a strange sort of way, she
was so indebted to me. For because of my situation, she now has
a true and dear best friend for life, in Tanchawee Weeko, and she
really had hoped that she felt the same way about her. She said
that although they had not met under the best of times, there was
something in her eyes, or about her eyes that spoke to both her
soul and heart. It was funny, because they seem as if they had been
close friends all of their lives, and she really now felt like a sister to
her. With that she started crying again as everyone started laughing at the two of them, because it was kind of sweet, the way that
they had connected. Mamie then got up and said pilamaya (thank
you) to our new tiospaye, because they had kept me alive until a
retrieval mission could be performed. She then hugged each and
every one of them one at a time, and when she got to Tanchawee

Weeko, she was also crying and she said that by their saving of me, they had also saved her from a lonely existence or life without her mate, her husband and very best friend. Tanchawee Weeko was one of the six new heroes in our Family, and her name as well as the other five, would always have a place of honor and respect within our Family. Next was El Diablo's turn. And, he rushed through the circle and started barking, growling and hopping about, as everyone laughed. Because, even he had something to say, and everyone said that it was as if he had sensed that it was finally now his turn to say something, and he wanted to get it in, and to be heard. So finally it was my turn, and although I could not talk, my eyes and hands told my story, and said what I needed to say. Because Tanchawee Weeko had truly saved my life, and I was determined to one day personally tell her pilamaya, but for right then, all that I had to use, was a nonverbal method. I stood up, and it suddenly got very quiet, and I extended my right arm out in front of me, pointing at everyone with my index finger, and then I started turning in a slow circle, so that I made eye contact with everyone in the circle of life. I proceeded to our new tiospaye and made them stand up. I then stared at them for a few long minutes, and then I slowly began to clap, and soon everyone was clapping and cheering. With that we all broke bread with one another, and after that we just enjoyed one another's company, as some of the kids were playing some kind of game and laughing with our new tiospaye. Abuelo was playing his funny shaped fiddle, which he had acquired in the land of mi Abuela. And he was belting out an extremely beautiful and haunting tune, as a small crowd huddled around him in appreciation and amazement. The nighttime sky was very pretty because it was filled full of stars, and there was a soft and cool breeze that cascaded down upon us, and there was this harmony that flowed over the whole group. Mamie was sitting in my lap, and she looked at the scene of happiness before us and leaned back, settling comfortably within my arms and whispered in a way that only the two of us could hear, "My darling Balaam do you know of any way possible to make this moment last," as she closed her eyes, and started to hum the tune that Abuelo was so eloquently playing. And, I held her firmly and tightly. The next day early in the morning, when we were all saddled up and about to push out into the field, Mamie told me right at the very last minute that she felt as if I should not go. Because I was, after all still healing, so her concerns are what stopped my participation in the bringing of our tiospaye home. I just gave each and every one a hug, and when I got to Tanchwee Weeko, she smiled and placed her hands upon my shoulders and said to my surprise, "Do not worry Balaam, when you get better, we will see then, okay? Because we are now family and we are forevermore a part of one another's lives, in a real way, so I will be seeing you soon." I smiled and just hugged her tightly, and she then jumped up onto her horse, and everyone waved goodbye. And some folks were weeping, as if someone had died or something and they rode out. Tatanka Sica chose 'the Terrible Three' as well as 'the Two Hell Raisers,' Stacey and Alphonso, to accompany them on the trip. We all watched them until they rode out of sight, and then the Akicitas Chanzees from the Fourth Warrior group assumed sentry duty, and the daily routine of The House kicked back in.

Then, in about thirty-seven days, the Sentries alerted the compound or base camp that riders were approaching fast. And n less than five minutes, the Akicitas Chanzee, were rolling back up into camp, each one with an extra pony that was laden down with many different and interesting things. They all seemed different in their dress and demeanor, as if they had experienced something that had seemingly changed them on a fundamental level. They were the same, yet something was now different about them. Seemingly, something was added to who they were. It was as if they had gained some kind of seasoning that had made them grow positively. And, it really was noticeable with 'the Two Hell Raisers,' Stacey and Alphonso because they seemed now older than what they actually were. They both seemed quieter now and much more focused and poised. And really, they seemed like they now had somehow acquired some of Tatanka Sica's poise and precision. Their under garb for battle was now different, lighter and flowing, and their face paint was different. Also, they used the in- the-field-of-battle black and white colors in a totally different paint scheme, which looked kind of slick. After they had all bathed and had something to eat, and were rested, Tatanka Sica explained during her mission debriefing, that our new tiospaye were not just some simple people. And, that they all were connected to some well known and respected leaders of their tribes. Our Sahiyela nupa (two Cheyenne) sisters, Ayashe Ayasha (Little one) and Ominotago (Beautiful Voice) whose nickname was Meoquanee (Wears Red), were family members of the mighty and respected warrior Chief Woqini (Roman Nose or Hook Nose), and distant cousins of Ishi'eyo Nissi (Two Moons). Upon riding into the encampment, they had been surrounded by many warriors, both young and old all of whom seemed ready to attack. But, the Akicitas Chanzee held their ground, with weapons drawn as Meoquanee (Wears Red), ushered the Sahiyela (Cheyenne) warriors back while she then told her story. They had been taken captive when they were out foraging for fruits and nuts, and everyone thought that they were either dead, or forever lost. And as the village gathered around in amazement, they repeated their stories about their capture. They spoke about me, our escape and about the Family's kindness to them with the elders and the council members. And everyone was very happy and excited, and smiling from ear to ear. The word started to spread quickly of the children warriors, and of their mighty medicine that they used in battle. So, people were just rolling up to get a look at these strange looking visitors. One brave rode up, and quickly jumped down off his mount and ran to Kimimela Magaskawee (Graceful Butterfly) who was related to his wife. He immediately started hugging her tightly, because they all had given her up as lost. She was a Teton

Hunkpapa Lakota, and the Lakota and the Sahiyela regularly inter-married within the two tribes, so it was common for the two tribes to be related by marriage to one another. Kimimela Magaskawee (Graceful Butterfly) saw a woman quickly approaching and she just squealed in approval, as they ran to one another and tightly embraced, because this lady, as it turned out was her tunwicu (aunt), her ina's (mother's) tanka (younger sister). A rider was sent out to send word ahead to the Lakota encampments that the four of them were still alive. And, that they would be on the way home with strange visitors. The next day the Akicitas Chanzee were given certain items of appreciation by the Sahiyela (Cheyenne) Village. They then headed out to take Tanchawee Weeko and the other three Lakota sisters of ours to their Village. They rode for over a day and a half, and on the way to where they were going, they saw some of the most beautiful scenery that they had ever witnessed, and it was humbling and awe inspiring all at the same time. The landscape was beautiful, and it seemed like it was right out of a picture, and everything seemed so free, open and beautiful. They finally arrived to where they were going, and the whole tribe was abuzz when they rode in. Escorted by many happy and curious Lakota warriors into camp, they were taken straight to the chief, who happened to be none other than the mighty Hunkpapa warrior Pizi (Gail) himself, in the flesh. Pizi (Gail) was extremely thankful and impressed, once he had heard Tanchawee Weeko's reciting of her story, and once she was finished, the whole village broke out in cheers and songs. It was as if a party had just broken out, because everyone was happy about them being alive and safe. There were songs sung and plenty of food, and dancing or really hopping around the main fire of the village. And, all of the warriors just gathered around the Akicitas Chanzee observing our weapons and mode of dress for battle. Pizi seemed very intent upon gaining as much knowledge about us as possible. He asked endless questions, that Tatanka Sica answered back in prefect Lakota, which was even more amazing and mind-boggling to him. He was more impressed with Tanchawee Weeko's and Tatanka Sica's closeness. To him it appeared as if the two of them could pass for actual blood sisters and had came from the same ate (father), and through the same Ina (mother). A lone rider raced into the camp all excited and out of breath, and when he finally could catch his breath to speak, he kept saying Tatanka, Tatanka, Tatanka. Pizi then asked or really requested that the Akicitas Chanzee accompany them on the hunt. We did, and everyone seemed excited, as the village was quickly and quietly dismantled, and everyone started moving in the general location of the Tatanka.

The braves donned their war paint and pulled out their finest weapons. The overall excitement was so much that it was as if they hardly could contain themselves. We then mounted up and rode until we got to where a group of braves were excitedly and quietly waiting for us at the base of a medium sized ridge. And there was one brave or lookout, already on the top peering down, and pointing at something. And then we all crept up the hill on all fours, and when we looked over the crest, there were buffalo for what seemed like miles. Their black brown silhouettes stood out against the green grass filled plain, as far as one could see to the horizon. We quietly went back smiling all of the way to our horses and mounted up. Then we rode around a series of small hills, as our pace increased until we came to a break between them. And when we turned right through the break, towards the buffaloes' direction, we were already up to nearly full speed on our horses. We rode with reckless abandonment, as we charged into the herd. And as the buffalo sensed our presence, they broke out into a dead run, and this only increased the excitement. To us it was like target practice, but what we noticed was that anyone could kill a tatanka with a gun. But the real skill was to use bows and arrows or specially designed spears to dispatch the tatanka with, which was really an art form and something to behold. All of this was extremely exciting as we raced along, the wind blowing in our hair, as we raced with and chased down our fast moving prey. We took what we wanted of what we killed, and we then gave the rest to Tanchawee Weeko, and to the village. Pizi was really impressed with our hunting skills and prowess. Because as first timers we displayed a certain style that comes through experience. And for our generosity, we were all given tashina pte (buffalo robes) as a sign of both respect and honor. Pizi was extremely intrigued with us because of all of this, and he then wanted to know when he would meet the one who is known as 'Balaam, The Liberator.' He looked deeply into my eyes and told me to my face, to tell The Liberator of his people, from the hohe (enemy), that he was always welcome. And once he had gotten better, to please come back, so that they could meet, be-cause, the hohe (enemy) of his hohe (enemy) was his kola (friend). Our tribe, The House of Calais -Vega would always be welcome to his village, and that's because of our generosity and kindness to his family members. We would always be considered as family to them, and, if we ever needed anything, for us to simply ask, and they would try to help us out. So we must all come back, once I was ready to ride so that we all could meet one another. We then sat back and ate buffalo meat, until we had stuffed ourselves and could not eat any more.

Five weeks' time from then, at our usual Good Days fest, every-one almost fell out and died, when I said, 'thank you,' to my Beloved for her giving my meal plate to me. Mamie stared in both shock and amazement. And, even though it was barely heard and sounded weak and windy-like, all began to celebrate and rejoice. Because, I'd been told that I might not ever speak again, and besides up until then it actually hurt to speak, since the bullet had severely damaged my vocal chords. So my new voice was now very low and raspy, and it was feint like the wind, and sounded very foreign to me. It was a struggle to adjust to because all of my life, I had known and under-stood the sound of my voice. And, now I had to adjust to a whole new sound. But hey it was better than nothing, so I was not complaining, just observing. Two weeks later, my Beloved thought and really felt that I was finally ready to ride again and could withstand the rigors associated with hard riding. She gave me her consent, and off we went. 'The Two Hell Raisers,' Stacey and Alphonso who of course also wanted to come, were left in command. 'The Terrible Three' and I all rode off, laden with gifts from Mamie, so that I could get my audience with Pizi. We hunted and fished along the way, so that we would have something to give and share with our tiospaye, once we reached the village's location. The Village was camped along Chaka dee Wakpa (The Powder River). It seemed as if everyone knew that we were coming, long before we had even gotten close to the Village. The whole tribe was standing there waiting for us when we rode in. Our four new family members started running to us, with their family members, as soon as we came into their eyesight. We could barely make it down off our mounts, before they hugged us up. Tanchawee Weeko and Tatanka Sica, both started crying as soon as they hugged one another. Then, they acted as if they had not seen one another in many, many years which caused everyone to laugh in amazement. Tanchawee Weeko's Ina (mother) then joined the hug, and she too started to cry, because her long-lost daughter had finally made it back home. Because of this, she knew that she would have a good meal tonight, because she had come back home bearing gifts. Tanchawee Weeko, acting somewhat both shocked and embarrassed by her Ina's words shooed her with her hand and asked her to stop. Everyone in the group really got a deep laugh, as Tatanka Sica playfully said 'Ina,' and tightly hugged her, as she handed her a line of six freshly caught fish. And finally, after all of the hugs and kisses upon the cheeks, and touches and pats on the head were all done, we as a unified group, together went to meet Pizi and the rest of the assembled tribe that was standing a ways away, looking at our commotion. Kimimela Magaskawee (Graceful Butterfly), would not let go of my hand, and her Taksi (little sister), Tanagila Hopa (Beautiful Hummingbird) held fast to the other one. As we got close to the tribe, I had to struggle to even lower my hood over my head and face, and then quickly bow my head, as I walked straight up to Pizi. When I got within two paces of him, everyone else had dropped back, as a sign of respect and honor. I dropped down to one knee, with one arm extended outwards with the palm of my hand facing up and bowed my head. Pizi could only see the lower part of my face, and he studied me for a couple of long moments, as everything became deftly quiet, as if time itself was standing still. Pizi 's arm came down to meet mine, and my hand touched his outer elbow as his hand touched my inner elbow at the bend part. And, as we strongly and firmly gripped one another in this manner, he pulled me forward and up onto both feet. Meanwhile, I used my free hand to pull back my hood to display my face, which caused him to smile and say loudly, 'Kizzen/hohahe (Welcome). All of which caused time to start again, as the entire tribe burst out in expressions of approval and happiness. "Ya ta say" (Greetings), "Mieyebo" (I am) "Pizi, miyelo ca kola" (I am friend). You are home, he then loudly stated, and he patted me on the back and hugged me as if I were a brother, or other family member to him. "At last," he stated, "at last, we get to meet the liberator of our family from the clutches of the murderous and cowardly hohe (enemy)." He smiled and the entire tribe just roared with its approval. And as he led me to his teepee, he seemed amazed, when I stopped and whistled, and Pegasus came trotting up to me. I then retrieved the gift package of nuts, dried fruit, and dried meats that Mamie had given me, to give to him and his family. He was even more taken aback, when I whistled again, and Pegasus trotted back to regain his place with the rest of the horses. We walked into his teepee, and sat down upon buffalo rugs, and everyone crowded into the dwelling, until it was packed, with no place to move. Tatanka Sica sat between him and me, so that she could translate to me what he wanted to say and say to him what I wanted to say back. I looked around the room and said, "My friend (le mita cola), I am (waun/mieyebo) Balaam, and thank you (ashoge) for inviting (kico) me (miye) to your village (wicoti). We (unkis) are blessed (yuwakape) by your generous (tawaci waste) offer to (ki-yuga), visit you (niye) and it (iye) is important to (wakal u) me (miye) that we (unkis) learn (ospewakiye) as much about (wa hecel) one (wanji) another (tokeca) as possible (pica). Because if we (unkis) are to truly (awecakeya) trust one (wanji) another (tokeca), then we must know who we (unkis) each are and learn to move past the words (wico iye) and rely upon our innermost feelings." For as the elders say, 'we (unkis) can say a thousand (kiktopawige) words (wico iye) and not mean a single (isnala) one (wanji) of them.' "So (Ca) Pizi who are you (nituwe he)?" Pizi looked around into the faces of eve-ryone whom had crowded into the room, and slowly he began telling his story. I am Pizi, a Teton Hunkapapa Lakota, of the Sihasapa (Blackfoot) clan. My clan were the bear hunters of the Nation. And, I come from Mato Kute (Shoot the Bear) and Hi Waste (Good Fur). My name in my youth was 'Matohinshda (Bear shedding his hair),' and there are many stories of me during this wonderful time that may help you to understand just who I really am. One is of me, at three years old, riding in a travois, which is a basket, placed upon the back of our trusty family dog. I had one hand on one of the basket's poles and the other one, my left, was holding the dog's tail as it chased down and finally caught a jackrabbit. The ride itself was a bit crazy and confusing, but instead of being scared, I had enjoyed the whole thing. And, I really was amazed at how brave my dog was. I also remember that day, how my Grandmother poured water into a drinking basin, so that our dog could have a drink. Or the story that happened during one winter of a great snowball fight amongst all of the boys and at the end, my being the only one left on my side, against 11 boys of the other side. I remember how I ducked down, to evade the onslaught, and as I turned out came a slumber-ing huge grey wolf from its den. And it just ran by me and took my exact former place. My opponents, seeing the wolf, superstitiously took off running in all directions, thinking that somehow, I had been transformed into the animal. Really, I had just ducked down, and crawled a bit. Then I just came out on the other far side, of the washout and had just crossed the line to become the winner. This had caught everyone by complete surprise. Another story that stands out is of my Che-hoo-hoo match with the mighty Sahiyela (Cheyenne) boy Woqini (Roman Nose). During the time of the annual gathering amongst the tribes I was placed opposite him. And in the end, it was just he and I battling back and forth—some say like two forces of nature. I do not really remember how I did it, but I was finally able to hoist and then throw Woqini (Roman Nose) to the ground. And hold him fast for over a minute, all of which left me tired, but the winner. I remember the shouts that went up, and how Woqini's mother came forward and presented me with a fine buffalo robe. Meanwhile, my mother then returned the compliment by presenting Woqini with a blanket. And to this day, people still talk about that epic battle between us. I also remember how everyone was so excited and happy, and how both tribes seemed pleased by the whole thing. The Che-hoo-hoo game is really meant to establish both the physical and mental abilities of the boys in the tribe. So, this battle showed everyone that both tribes had strong and future leaders amongst the boys, and that I was truly on my way towards leadership.

As a man, I am peaceful and good spirited, but I do not accept any injustices toward my people or towards our way of life. My strengths, I have been told many times, lie in quick thinking and organizing. And, I will never ever hesitate when courage, or endurance are needed. I like to ask a lot of questions, and I learn from other people's experiences and lessons. I have not done everything right, nor have I done everything wrong, but I have learned from everything that I have experienced. I also like to advise the youth, and sit around and listen to the elders, because in life hopefully you will be both. And, we do really learn from one another despite the age differences between us. So, this is why I just had to meet you, because both your courage and determination already have stories and songs told and sung about them. You survived constant pain and suffering from our enemy, and when you were able to escape, you could have done this alone, but yet you took our Family members with you. And, then once free you treated them like they were your own Family members. What kind of person displays these abilities? What kind of person displays this kind of honor? "I have to ask myself, Balaam, if I were in your situation, would I or could I have done the same thing? You intrigue me, Balaam, and I hope that you give me an opportunity to learn from you, and hopefully become your friend. Because Tatanka Sica is a wonderful warrior, but she said that you are the best, and that she has learned a lot from you, so I just had to meet you," he exclaimed. I then began to tell my tale and all during this, Pizi's eyes just twinkled and shone, as he heard my story. When I was finally finished, he smiled and then said that my story was interesting and that he wanted to learn even more, because I had many experiences that he could study and learn from. He wanted to know if I could spend time with his village and if I could teach him the ways of the wacicu invader. Because the wacicu always spoke with a forked tongue, and he most certainly could not never ever be trusted.

I said yes, and it would be an honor if I could help him in any way to understand this invader. Because this invader respected no one, not even his own kind, and even though this land was so called discovered by him and his kind, the First Ones had inhabited it for many countless ages. And, the First Ones' only fault was that they did not recognize 'individual ownership' of the land. So because the First Ones did not covet the ownership of land, they were mandated to relinquish its occupancy, so that the wacicu's ideas of nation building could go forward. But how can one claim to discover something, which was never lost in the first place? Pizi then got up and asked if I would walk with him, and we left the teepee as a group followed us at a distance, matching our every movement stride for stride.

As we walked, it was then that I started to see the true natural beauty of the land. This was truly a remarkable place that was filled with a remarkable people, and at that moment, I felt determined to assist them in any way possible. Because, this Warrior Plains culture was worth helping and saving, and it was the first time that I felt at home, among people with whom I felt a natural connection too and possessed an affinity for.

This reminded me of the words of the great Irish statesman, author, orator, political theorist and author, Edmund Burke who stated that, "The only way for evil to triumph is for good men or women to do nothing," which was just another way of saying that "evil prevails, when good men and women fail to act!" With that, Pizi and I became lasting and seemingly lifelong friends. And, we spent a lot of time with one another as we developed our friendship through time and understanding.

We became so close, that even our wives became good friends. Our families became intertwined with one another, and it felt both right and good. We then started to travel around, so that I could see the entire area, and I was amazed by what I experienced. As I look back on those times, everything seemed truly wonderful because, for the first time in my life I felt free, totally free, and also because the landscape was so beautiful and never ending. The Plains were like an endless sea of short grass and was called awanka toyala (greenness of the world), and this seemingly endless heartland, was only interrupted by rivers and mountains.

This awanka toyala (greenness of the world) was presently a much smaller area, Pizi had stated, because of the wacicu invaders, in their quest to consume and own everything. There used to be many places that contained everything that his people needed to live on. But now, everything was slowly shrinking, and change was everywhere. No more were the places that contained the currants, plums, different types of berries, and the chokecherries that were once in abundance and used for food by the people.

The many places where they used to look for the violet-colored blossoms on the exposed green roots that showed where the sweet tinpsila (prairie turnips) were, also were sadly going away. And, even the tall grasses called oblayela (wideness of the world), were no longer a part of their hunting grounds. So this change was happening very fast, within his generation and it was obvious and heartbreaking for all to see.

He stated that his way of life was threatened and was slowly going away. And, that this is what he and others were so determined to preserve for the children of the future generations. Pizi took me to see the MaTo Tipila Papa (Devils Tower), which is also known as Mato (Bear) Lodge, that lies some sixty miles in present day Wyoming, from the Papa Sapa, but is still considered by the elders to be a part of the Chan Gleshka Wakan (Sacred Racetrack).

He then took me to the Papa Sapa (Black Hills), which are the 'sacred heart' to many tribes of The Great Plains First Ones because in their oral traditions, this is the place of their creation where they first appeared on the maka (land), their Garden of Eden so to speak. The Ochethi Sakowin call this area Wamaka Ognaka Icante (the heart of everything that is), which means to them that this area is the actual center of their universe, and they have lived in this area since the beginning of time itself.

He said that the Papa Sapa also contains the Wind Cave that Tokahe the First One and the Other Six and their families first emerged from, to become surface dwellers. He then took me to Hinhan Kaga Paha (Harney Peak), which was known by the First Ones as 'the center of the world,' and a place where one could meet the great powers of the world and receive special abilities from them.

It was also a place where the wakan was powerful, and extremely strong, and Pizi explained that every object in the known world has a spirit, and that spirit is Wakan. Wakan comes from Wakan beings, and Wakan beings are greater than mankind, in the same manner that mankind is greater than animals, and thus they can do many things that mankind cannot. Mankind then must never ever forget its place, he said, and it must continue to pray to these Wakan beings for help and guidance, he believed.

So the Papa Sapa is the place on Maka Ina (Mother Earth) that these Wakan beings connect with mankind, and their energy can be felt all over this mystical place. That is why the Papa Sapa was so scared and revered, and unlike any other place in the known world to his people. We next visited the saglohan (eight) sacred places of historical importance, located around and within the oval valley that encircles the Papa Sapa.

They are the Pe Sla (Old Baldy); Wakinyan Paha (Thunder Butte); Hinhan Kaga Papa (Ghost Owl Butte); Pte Tali Yapa (Buffalo Gap); Papa Zipela (Slim Buttes); Mnikata (Hot Springs); Mato Papa (Bear Butte); and, then finally to Chan Gleshka Wakan (Sacred Hoop), which is also known as Ki Inyanka Ocanku (The Red Race Track).

He also took me to a place that had a dry grassless and rough landscape about it, which he called Mako Sica (strange lands of the world or bad earth or bad lands)—that the wacicu invaders were downright scared of and steered clear of at all times. This place was also amazing in its own right, because everything seemed so vastly different from everywhere else that we had visited. It was as if this area was its own foreign and rough place, and nothing seemed to flourish and survive within the entire region. So as I now look back upon it, Pizi was showing his culture and heritage to me in a very unique and hands-on type of manner, so that I could truly grasp why his people were so determined to maintain and control these sacred areas by any and all means necessary, or to die trying. He told me some of the ancient stories surrounding Wicahpi Hihpa Ya (Fallen Star), and of his many exploits, like his creation of the MaTo Tipila Papa (Devils Tower) to help a brother and sister avoid a pursuing mato (bear). And of his epic sky battle to defeat a wanbli (eagle), so the wincincala sakowin (seven girls) could be returned to earth, while he left their spirits in the sky. Another thing to me, that was simply awe inspiring about this place, was the nighttime sky. It had so many huge looking stars that it seemed unreal, and at times reminded me of a painted picture. This certainly was 'big sky country,' and it was a breathtaking and a wonderful sight to behold. I remember just sitting for hours looking up, and marveling at the peacefulness of the nighttime sky. For some stars were so big that it was as if one could just reach right up into the nighttime sky, and pluck them down, just as if they were fruit that is on a tree. I can remember being totally amazed by all of this and I distinctly remember that I never, ever wanted this great time of peace and happiness, for me and my family to never, ever end. But the time flew by, and before we knew it, change once again was rearing its head. And just like before, the words of the waccicu invader meant nothing. The Fort Laramie treaty of 1868 had designated the Powder River (Chaka dee Wakpa) country of Montana and Wyoming plus all of what is present day South Dakota, west of the Missouri River as the Great Sioux Reservation. And within these lands, lie the Papa Sapa, which were held sacred by many tribes, including the Lakota, Cheyenne, Kiowa, and Crow. But in July of 1874, the Great Civil War, General Sherman dispatched an illegal survey expedition into these lands. This expedition was guarded by a military escort, which was headed by Brevet Major General George Armstrong Custer, to finally put to rest the rumors that had been spread for years by various mountain men and priests, that there was gold in the Black Hills. The survey did indeed find plenty of gold in the Papa Sapa. After the word was publicly announced by Custer himself to the Eastern newspapers, the mining increased by twenty-fold, and people flocked to the area. When gold strikes were made in the towns of Deadwood, Central City, and Lead in late 1875 and early 1876, thousands more of wacicu invaders flooded into the area. The track that was cut by Custer's supply train was called 'the Freedom Trail' by the wacicu invaders, but to the First Americans it was known as "the 'Thieves' Road,' and it be-came the main path that the wagon trains of the wacicu invaders used, as they illegally entered into Teton Lakota territory. Then once they arrived and started setting down roots, other businesses popped up, to accommodate the rush of people like lumber companies, saloons, trading stores, whore-houses and churches. And of course the military, which was sent there to guard the settlers, miners and the whores. The Lakota felt enraged because their sanctuary had been invaded in an obvious violation of the 1868 Treaty.

This became the very last slap to the face, for the Teton Lakota of the Ochethi Sakowin, by the wacicu invaders. For to them starting in early 1875, this now was about the survival of their way of life, and the loss of their ancestral and sacred homelands. So the calls went out for all warriors to gather at the next coming full moon in the nighttime sky, at the camp of Tatanka Iyotake (Sitting Bull), so that everyone would get a chance to have their say.

Pizi asked me if I would honor him by attending. He always knew that I was special, when he first had heard the stories of a great warrior clan, that were trying to do the very same thing that the Teton Lakota were, which was stay alive and free, or die trying, by any and all means necessary. I felt honored by the invite, but I would only go if my apprentice could also attend. He said yes that it was okay for her to attend, and he wanted one more thing from me; and that was to go with him, to meet Mahpiya Luta, before we went to the big powwow of the meeting of the minds. I said yes, and I knew that my apprentice would be simply thrilled to be out in the field with just her and me alone, experiencing the master and apprentice roles together. She also would be getting a chance to take the Winchester Model 1873's out into the field for the first time. We up until then had a few well-used Henry's 1860, and three Model 1866 which were called 'Yellow Boys' because of their shiny brass frame.

Our order from the Winchester and Henry Company, now called the Win-chester Repeating Arms Company, located in New Haven, Connecticut, had finally arrived. The order was shipped to and arrived in Xenia, at the General Store. And once the word had filtered out to us that it had arrived, the Akici-tas Chanzee all hurriedly put together a retrieval mission and off they scampered, leaving only the Fourth Warrior group in charge of the base camp.

They had ordered an original order of eight, and six had come with the other two being shipped under another name for security purposes. And, this part of the order was due in about another week. So as chance would have it, they had just gotten back with all eight when I was summoned to meet Pizi. The Model 1873 had a side-loading gate in a frame and was easier to load because of the center fire cartridge, and it continued to use the .44 rim fire cartridge. It was trim, easy to carry and very popular with a lot of people. The Model 1873 was stronger and simpler, and lighter in weight than the Model 1866. The Model 1866's only drawbacks were its lack of impact and range, but these two issues were addressed with the Model 1873.

So we left out and met up with Pizi, and he took us straight to Mahpiya Luta's encampment. I distinctly remember being a bit in awe at the prospect of meeting him because he was a living legend in his own time. As we approached, Pizi was greeted with warmth and much love, so that made me and my apprentice both comfortable and at ease. The nervousness seemed to just go away and as we jumped down off of our mounts, and walked into his teepee; a sitting figure quickly rose up from the shadows and greeted us in the familiar way that one does with family members.

He had these strong piercing eyes, firm, strong hands and his smile was easy and genuine. He hugged all three of us, and then offered us a place to sit by him. And he gave us a gourd to drink cool water from, as he made sure that all of our needs were taken care of first and foremost. He then began to listen to Pizi, who talked to him in revered manner, just as one does to royalty or to any other dignitary. Pizi stated that we were the strangers from the East, who were only seeking a new beginning and who were escaping 'the long knives,' and all wacicu invaders. Mahpiya Luta seemed uneasy at times, as if he was holding back something; and only after Pizi had finally finished did he begin to talk.

He stated that he had a problem, because of the vision in his dream quest and that he could not talk about it with anyone of the Teton Lakota or any other Nation. With that, Pizi just got up and left like it was a prearranged deal leaving just Mahpiya Luta, my apprentice and myself in the teepee. Mahpiya Luta got up and went to see if anyone was at the opening to the teepee and seeing no one, he came back and then sat down really close to us, so that he could lower his voice but still be heard by us in the room.

He had a very troubling problem because of his dream quest, and it scared him. He stated that for a while, he had been troubled by the changing times, so he spoke to the medicine man who told him that he should embark on a dream quest to clear his mind of the many things that troubled it. In his dream quest he would be given the answers to many of his troubling questions and concerns, and that he must submit to the forceful power of wakan, so that he could truly see what needs to be seen.

He went to the Papa Sapa, to the sacred wind cave, and in the hills above it he set up his smoke shack, and stripped down to his naked body, crawled inside and began his journey. In about two days, his mind began to cross over the great divide to a place where he was not alive, but not yet dead either. He went into a trance-like state, where everything seemed beautiful and flowing. The mako all around him was beautiful, and extremely enticing, and there was a slight but cool breeze that was blew onto the front of his body.

Everything seemed nice and relaxing; it was as if all of his worries had gone away, and he was in a place where he felt at home. He was somewhere in the Papa Sapa he had recognized and he was standing in a clearing that had many trees all around it. He started to run, and it was as if the harder he ran, the further away everything seemed to be from him. And, only when he stood still, did everything around him start to move normally all around him again. He could hear this sound, like a bell or chime, distinctly in the distance, close, but far. He then noticed a Mato (bear) who walked through some wagichun wagi (cottonwood) trees, right up to him and when it got right in front of him, it stood up on its hind legs. And, as the Mato began to speak, the area around them suddenly became smoky or foggy as the sun covered itself up which changed the sky from daytime light into nighttime light. The bell chime sound changed to that of Wakiya Tuwapi (thunder), as the Wakinyan Towa Pi (lightning) struck angrily, momentarily bringing flashes of daylight to the darkness of the sky. The Mato began by saying that Mahpiya Luta was a great warrior; his accomplishments on the battlefield were the stuff of legends, but that had to change because it was now a new season. Now he had a new role for his Nation, which was to be the Iyeye Ocaku (pathfinder) for a new way of life. And, no matter what he thought or felt about this new role; this change must and would happen. That he, Mahpiya Luta, must never going forward ever again participate in any kind of battles or military related campaigns. So he must be careful to in no way take part in the upcoming battle between the Oyates Yamni (Three Nations) and the Mighty Zuzeca Ska (white snake). This battle will occur on a Great Plain, and the wacicu invaders would be driven back and many of them would die that day, but sadly because of this great and mighty battle, this would eventually lead to the destruction of the entire Teton Lakota people. Yes, they would win the greatest battle of present-day times, but they would sadly lose the war and doom the people to a life of cruel punishment for 15 generations to come.

This is why the Mato had come into his dream quest to speak to him. Because, yes, he was a great and mighty warrior but now he had to be an even greater man of peace. No matter what the wacicu had previously done, or were doing, because the survival of the entire Lakota Nation of Tribes depended upon his non-involvement in the upcoming battle. "So lay down your weapons brother," said the wise and knowledgeable Mato, but sadly you must never ever tell anyone from any of the Nations this story, because if you do you are dooming to death, the one thing that you love and care for the most. So this therefore becomes your greatest struggle, to save the lives of one or to save the many, or to keep quiet and work within this struggle and become part of a meaningful solution.

Mahpiya Luta said he seemed dumbfounded, trying to figure out the riddle that the Mato had just spoken to him. With that, the fog seemed to lift away, the sun uncovered itself and the sky turned back to its usual daytime look, as the sound changed back over to the bell or chime in the distance. And the Mato dropped down back onto all fours and moved onward and eventually out of sight through the woods. As he stood there, trying to make sense out of what the Mato had said, down from the sky came two birds, one a Kagi Taka (raven) and the other a Wakinyan (thunderbird). The Kagi Taka (raven) said, 'Look for the mysterious stranger from the East, that carries a light in his hand, and with this Mani Wana Gi (ghost that walks) you should seek refuge and council.

The wakinyan (thunderbird) then said, "This Mani Wana Gi (ghost that walks), whose voice sounds like the wind, can always be trusted because he knows the ways of the wacicu better than the wacicu know themselves." He is the one that can answer the riddle for you and assist you on this part of your journey through this life. So remember Mahpiya Luta, to never trust anyone but the mysterious stranger, and also remember what the Mato told you about not telling anyone of what he had told you 'Because if you tell anyone, this will bring about the death of the thing that you love the most.' They then looked at one another and screeched some kind of bird sound or call, and then took off together at the same time and up they went, straight up and out of sight, back into the clouds that hung in the daytime sky.

With that, he was awakened out of his vision, back to the real world that we live in, startled and extremely concerned about what he had just witnessed. He was extremely shaken and devastated, and it took him days to get himself together and move beyond just continually pondering upon his ill-fated plight. He was really worried until news had reached his encampment of a mysterious group of strangers, of one the hero who saved the day, and brought back our family members to us, as well as to our Sahiyela (Cheyenne) brothers and sisters. This person had strong magic, and had battled all alone and by himself against both Crows and Pawnees, and had come out on top. He was a part of some mysterious warrior clan that had a female child leading its warriors, who all appear to be nothing more than children. And, the hero was searching for what we all had wanted, which was to live free and far away from the wacicu, and their troubling ways. He had in a very short time become extremely close to Pizi, almost like a brother they all say, and he had without hesitation accepted my offer of meeting before the pow-wow at Ta-tanka Iyotake's (Sitting Bull's) encampment. Were the Wakinyan and the Kagi Taka both right? He wondered, but upon meeting me he had decided that I was truly The Mysterious One, and that he could trust me with his secret.

Mahpiya Luta then told us of his troubles, and he wondered how I could really help him. My apprentice said, "So you must not participate in any way or the thing that you love the most will die? So if I may respectfully be permitted to ask you Mahpiya Luta, one question? What is the thing that you love the most?" Mahpiya Luta swallowed hard and said, that the thing that he loved most, was' his people themselves, and then their way of life'. So how could he guard his people and keep them safe, when if he tells anyone of his dream, then what the Mato said would come true. "Let him accompany you to the powwow and once there, you keep quiet, and let him speak in your place. Now this will ensure that you are there but being silent will not break your oath to the Mato. Let Balaam devise the battle plan and give it to the warriors all assembled," she spoke.

I said through Tatanka Sica to Mahpiya Luta, "You should try to meet the wacicu invaders and see if they will honor their Treaty. and, make the invaders leave the Papa Sapa, and the surrounding areas. Send your most trusted men either two or three east to the wacicu's main meeting place, and big lodge of the Great Father that lies within it, to see if they can meet either the Great Father, or meet someone under him who can stop this before it gets uglier because the rights of the Teton Lakota must be upheld at all times.

This will catch the wacicu off guard because he will not be expecting you to come to him because he always talks the good talk with big words but trust me when I say that the Great Father, will never come to you. This will give your Nation time, and this will give us additional time to create the correct battle plan.

Also, instruct your men to ask for a price for the land, and when they ask the price, make it be a price that he will not be willing to pay. He will then have to confer with his higher ups, but really, he will be stalling and beating the drum, and sending out signals to his turncoats within the Nation to start causing confusion and doubt. Also, remember that whatever you see is false as in fake, not real and whatever he tells you; it is a lie and cannot be trusted. Because, his words have always been empty and have no meaning, so trust no one, not even yourself.

And maybe you should even think about going along to, just for the effect because the wacicu is afraid of you, and your military genius, and upon seeing you; it will cause him to freeze like a river in the winter and seek to regroup. Mahpiya Luta, sat there for a while pondering what I had told him through Tatanka Sica, and after a while he stated that he agreed with me, and that he would follow my instructions. He would go to the place where the Great Father's Lodge was located, and he would ask Sinte Gleska (Spotted Tail) and Heh won ge chat (Lone Horn) to accompany him, on this trip.

He also would have no intention of taking any money from the wacicu, but he was trying to learn their funny ways. So he would in private, and only to certain people, give a price for the land and then see how the wacicu would react. But all of the while, he would remain in contact with me, through Pizi, and he would let me take his place at the powwow and speak for him, at the gathering of the warriors.

What incredible price for the Papa Sapa, should he ask for, he asked me? How about sixty million, or a million for each acre, I answered through Tatanka Sica. Mahpiya Luta looked at me, and then at Tatanka Sica, as we then all broke out into laughter, because we all knew that the wacicu would be shocked and hurt by our attempt to be businessmen like themselves. A sixty million dollar asking price would make them all swallow very hard and pull back in horror, as if we had asked them to give us their wives or their way of life or something as honorable as that.

Then Tatanka Sica said, "You know sixty million is way too low, and to me, it is worth triple of that, if we are thinking serious about this whole thing." We all looked at one another, and right then and there I said, "Mahpiya Luta, let's make a pact right here and now, with one another to use our heads and become one mind so that we can save as many of your beautiful and vibrant people as we possibly can." Mahpiya Luta looked me in the eye and said," You are a blessing and you are the mysterious stranger that the Mato anc the Zitkalas (birds) were all talking about".

"But may I ask one question he asked?" I said, Sure. And with that, he looked me directly into my eyes and asked me, "Who are you really and why are you called the Mani Wana Gi? And Tatanka Sica looked at me, and asked, "How does he know about 'the ghost that walks' you reckon?" I just smiled back at him, and then through Tatanka Sica, I began to explain my own story to him, and also how I was only a man of peace from slavery, and that we were only truly seeking a new beginning away from the wacicu. I also explained how and why I became this 'Wana Gi' (Ghost), so that ultimately, I could strike fear into both the hearts and minds of the wacicu during the family's escape to total and true freedom.

It is just a costume or a trick to confuse the wacicu into seeing what they believed that they were seeing, which was some kind of scary figure that appeared in the night and so far it has worked as intended. So yes, I am this strange land's version of the 'Mani Wana Gi ', and as this Wana Gi (Ghost). I have pledged an oath, to protect his people, because it is the right thing to do, so that evil will not again triumph. Mahpiya Luta smiled and reached over to extend me his forearm, as we gripped one another's forearms with our hands at the outside of the elbow area. So with that, we made an oath with one another to become one mind. And I would help him, in any and all ways to overcome this deadly trap that had ensnared his people.

Because, when I had a chance to see a copy of the 1868 Second Fort Laramie Treaty, the whole situation smelled like a pigpen. There were many grey areas in its wording because, it was a treaty that ceded territory admittedly unceded, that confined the First Americans to a reservation while allowing them to roam freely elsewhere. It also guaranteed against trespass, unless a trespasser appeared.

The First Americans were given to understand that they retained their full rights to live in the old way, in a vast unceded territory (60 million acres), without trespass in any manner by the wacicu. The treaty did say exactly this, but the fact that it also denies it, was no fault to the First Americans. It was the wacicu's so called Commission of Indian Affairs that wrote the contradictions, into the treaty itself.

Which therefore only means, that they wrote one set of provisions to trick or beguile, and another set of provisions to be enforced by military force when they deemed it had become necessary to do so. Therefore, this was their endgame, to steal and or kill, if necessary, for what they wanted. And, to legislate in a manner that enabled deceitful ways by law that benefited them because after all, nation building was a part of their manifest destiny.

In Canwapeto Wi (Moon of Green Leaves) or May of 1875, Mahpiya Luta, Heh won ge Chat, and Sinte Gleska, all made the trip by railroad, to the Federal District of Washington. And, they actually were allowed to meet President Grant, the scandalous William W. Belknap, who was the Secretary of War, Columbus Delano who was the Secretary of the Interior, and Edwin Smith who was the Commissioner of Indian Affairs.

Everything worked out just like I had stated that it would, and the look of surprise was obvious when they had shown up, asking for an audience with these key men of the current political administration. Although it was rumored that they had been invited to visit the Federal District of Washington, by the Grant Administration, no one in the Administration had even thought that they would have really shown up.

In private, Mahpiya Luta had even spoke of the $60 million dollars figure, and he was amazed at how ruffled they had all become as they absorbed his words into their minds. He then started to have a lot of different people seeking to have a private word or audience with him, and just like I had said, they all seemed intent upon making him bend to their will and agree to sell the land but at a very reduced price from the original suggestion of the $60 million asking price.

Then something started happening and for the next few days, the three of them were all conveniently separated from one another. For this reason or for that reason, it was stated, and it seemed as if the wacicu were having meetings and dinners only with Sinte Gleska, as something certainly seemed to be happening behind the scenes and in the shadows.

Heh won ge Chat seemed to also notice that something was happening, and he stated that he felt as if he was being closely followed and watched at all times. And, he was certain that each and every night when he went to rest or sleep, that he was being held captive in his room for safekeeping. Because one night, after he had turned down his light, he opened the window for some fresh air, and he thought that he heard a set of familiar sounding voices. And when he looked out of the window, to his amazement he could see Sinte Gleska walking and talking with the one named Edwin Smith and three other men one of whom was carrying what the wacicu called a lantern. As he hid by the window and watched them eventually disappear into the darkness, he could hear the one named Edwin Smith laughing.

He became startled by this soft clicking sound at the door to his room, and when he went to check what that sound was, he noticed that the door seemed stuck in place and would not open. Mahpiya Luta said that he too had heard the strange clicking sound at his door, and more importantly that they must stay united with one another no matter what, because the wacicu was like the wily fox and, the wacicu were never ever to be trusted.

Because they were just trying to make Sinte Gleska become their inside man their agent of deception, and a true traitor to his people. But, Mahpiya Luta had remembered my words, and he did not try to judge Sinte Gleska, but just observed his actions and behavior. As a result, he trusted nothing that he saw or heard. He hoped that Heh won ge Chat, would also do the same and that he would more importantly always keep an open mind about this whole thing.

The U.S. leaders came back to them after a lengthy meeting and said that the Congress of the United States wanted to pay the tribes $25,000 for the land and have them relocate to Indian Territory that is located in present day Oklahoma. The Lakota delegation refused to sign a new treaty with these new stipulations. Sinte Gleska's reply to them, which appeared to catch them off guard was, "My Father, I have considered all that the Great Father has told me and have come here to give you an answer. When I was here before, the President gave me my Country, and I put my stake down in a good place, and there I wanted to stay. I respect the Treaty, but the white men who come into our Country do not. You speak of another Country, but it is not my Country, and it does not concern me, and I want nothing to do with it. I was not born there, and, if it is such a good Country, you ought to send the white men now in our Country, there—and let us alone."

So with that, they all came back from Washington to their lands. Within a few months later, a U.S. Commission that consisted of politicians, traders, missionaries, and the military, were sent to the Great Sioux reservation to gain the people's approval and to bring pressure, thereby personally upon the

leaders of the Teton tribes, to sign a new Treaty which was intended to negotiate the purchase of the Paha Sapa.

Four meetings were held, and nothing became of them, except that all of
the chiefs professed an undying friendship for the white man. But should anything be sold, that would only be the part of the Papa Sapa that contained
the shiny metal, and nothing else. They would only accept a figure of $70
million, along with tribal support, for seven generations. The younger chiefs
refused to sell at any price, and Mahpiya Luta got tired and stopped even
attending such foolishness, so he sent me in his place to observe what was
going on. The meetings were eventually adjourned because the Commission
lacked any real authority to comply with the First American's idea of value
and compensation.

The one thing that I did notice was that Sinte Gleska, had somehow been
picked to be the only chief that the wacicu dealt with as if he was now in
their pocket. Many other members, of the Teton Lakota Nation, also noticed
this fact. And, it created a lot of rumbling and grumbling within the Nation,
as folks sought to make sense out of all of this confusion and deception.

A few weeks later, in Mahpiya Luta's last great speech to the Teton Nation that had gathered upon the Little Rosebud River to discuss everything
in an open forum, he said, "We are told that Sinte Gleska has consented to
be the Beggars Chief. Those ones who go over to the wacicu can be nothing
but beggars for he respects only riches, and how can any one of the Teton
Lakota Nation be a rich man? He cannot, without ceasing to be what the
wacicu call an Indian. As for me, I have listened patiently to the promises of
the Great Father, but his memory is short. I am now done with him. This is all
that I have to say."

Now while all of this was going on, I was secretly meeting with Pizi and
Mahpiya Luta, constructing a sound battle plan. Because I knew that once
the wacicu could not secure a Treaty, he would be then figuring out a way to
take what he wanted, but then make it look like it was the fault of the Teton
Lakota. So he would quietly amass his soldiers, at the borders of the Great
Sioux reservation under the pretense of trying to enforce the treaty against
the miners and settlers. Even though the soldiers would let them freely pass

by through their ranks, when the time was right and at his own choosing, he would use these very same Federal soldiers to attack and destroy the Teton Lakota Nation.

The Great Father would telegraph to his Generals the so-called secret and sinister executive order and immediately the Federal soldiers, like the coldblooded killers that they really were, would turn on the very ones that they were there to protect. I studied the various battle movements of our prey, the wacicu soldiers, and especially those of the one that was known as Yellow or Long Hair. I tried to learn as much about him as possible, because when the time was right, he would be one of the ones who would be coming to destroy the Teton Lakota Oyate (Nation).

He was one of the Great Father's greatest warriors, in the so-called Civil War. And, this son of the Morning Star, was determined to quickly make a name for himself, as an Indian killer, so that one day he could legitimately get at least one star on the shoulders of his blue military field jacket. He would then use the newspapers to help him run for public office. And then, by the use of kickbacks and or bribery, which sadly go hand in hand with all Federal public offices, to become quite a wealthy man.

He would then live out his old age, in a northeastern city, like New York or Boston, as a refined English acting man of leisure. Yellow or Long Hair seemed to enjoy the thrill of battle and he was always it appeared, leading the charge into battle. This was unlike most officers of the wacicu's army, who tended to stay in the back behind the lines and from there, lead the action in field. He had been called a coldblooded, untruthful man with no prin-ciples, who was universally despised by most of the officers and men of his regiment.

He was always right, and never wrong, but yet he changed his mind far too often. And he seemed to rely a lot upon his impulses, which made no sense because he appeared to never have a set plan of battle or attack. He never conferred with any of his officers, except the ones who were his broth-ers, as if their opinions were the only ones in his life that had ever mattered.

This haphazard way of doing business in the field of battle could be fatal, for he liked to improvise a lot with hairbrained notions and schemes. He had been one of the ones, who had been leading a secret Federal war against our Sahiyela (Cheyenne) brothers and sisters. And in 1868, at the Battle of Washita, he used a tactic that I made a mental note to myself to always remember.

Because, as mi Abuelo would always say, 'history always has a way of repeating itself. 'He was a Calvary officer, a Lieutenant Colonel, a horse guy who relied upon speed to attack. And, who liked to split his command into at least two or three columns or pieces, and then use a single column that he would always lead, to attack at the heart of any tribe which were the nnocents ones, the women and the children and old ones, right as the morning sun was rising.

This attack would also be from out of the sun if at all possible. It always was to the flank, or exposed area in any defense. He did this because he knew that the warriors would not want to attack him because of his position in the camp, that of being surrounded by the innocents who would not be expecting their teepees to be in the center of a battle.

He used the innocents as a shield to protect his backsides. And he was quick to use this tactic over and over again, as if everyone was not smart enough to realize what he was repeatedly doing. So his column would charge through the center of the encampments guns blazing, taking no prisoners or hostages until after the shooting had ended. He would create panic and turmoil within the heart of the encampment, and this tactic seemed to always make the warriors of the First Americans wilt and lose their appetite for battle.

So, this tactic of his own device would be used against him and we would exploit his greed for fame, and cutthroat ways. We would use his own aggressive actions against him, to trap him into our snare and then steer him and his men to where we wanted them to go. And, hopefully, he and his men would never even see it coming, until it was too late. We would kill them all, and more importantly we would instruct all of the warriors to resist initially counting coups, and to go in straight for the kill. Because, all of the Plains First Americans' cultures were based upon the warrior ethos, and, within this ethos was contained an honor bound principle of counting coups.

Counting coups was a French word, that meant 'to strike,' and it could signify any sort of damage or humiliation inflicted upon an enemy in war. So striking an enemy with a gun, bow or lance was considered a higher achievement at times, than actually killing him. These coups were the means by which a warrior gained status in his or her tribe, but this would not be that kind of mission. Our mission was to prove a point to the Great Father, and really to grab his and his minions' attention. We would kill them all, and this would make them freeze like a river does in winter.

And secretly, this would give us the precious time that we would need to move the innocents and also those who wished to continue to live in the old ways to the Province of Saskatchewan, Canada. We should also instruct the innocents not to mutilate his body, after the battle was over. This mutilation was done so that the enemy warrior would be left to eternally wander around in the spirit realm, and thus be unable to enter heaven. And also, because we would want the Great Father to see that we too had an ability to wage war on his level, and to take out from this life or journey his greatest warrior right before his very eyes.

We would even leave a note that will be addressed to him, in his own language, on the body of Yellow or Long Hair. Then once the battle was over, we would all scatter like wolves do in the woods when their dinner is over. And, all of this will make him fear you and stop and think. He will fear you, because in his mind, he was the only of your opponents who had access to the precise and focused West Point military expertise and battlefield genius, not the bunch of homemade savages.

So next we would need to choose a suitable place to conduct our attack, and it had to be where they would least expect it. It had to be somewhere that was common and familiar to us all. So why would it not be at a place where all paths converge or meet in the up country? This area had the greatest number of crossing paths and it was also the place of the Many Rivers, where the wakan was strong, so strong it attracted to it both the animals of nature and man.

It was also where a lot of rivers were very close to one another, and this made our choice easy. We decided on either the Rosebud Creek or the Greasy

Grass (Little Bighorn) areas, because of the way in which the bluffs rose up from the wood filled riverbeds towards high ground plateaus. These areas would give us protection on all sides, because of the many ravines that came up to meet the bluffs and plateaus and ridges. So that any enemy could not just flat out ride up onto the village or encampment.

The rivers would also provide additional protection because any enemy would have to cross the rivers to attack the encampments, and all of this crossing action would be detectable, at all times. We would then use teepees to lure him in which is designed to let him see what he wants to see, and once he rides for higher ground to escape; we will already be waiting for him with warriors already stationed on two or three sides.

The last and fourth side would close slowly and once it closed, we would have them. So we would anticipate his every move, so that we could trap him in what would be a four-sided or square box. His tactics will be easy to decipher, and as usual he will break into at least three pieces. Then have one piece that would attack from the north as another simultaneously attacks from the south. He will wait until the shooting had begun, and then use the third piece to smash either through the middle or through at an angle on the flank, to conduct what West Point teaches, the classic 'hammer and anvil on horseback maneuver.'

He will expect that all of the braves would start riding or running towards the sounds of the gunfire. But the key is, for the warriors in the middle to remain where they are, to hold, and resist the notion or impulse to go towards the sounds of battle. They will then meet the enemy head on, which should cause the wacicu soldiers to retreat. And as they are pushed back from whence they came, the two sides would already be waiting.

We will then use Tashunka Witco (Crazy Horse) as our Calvary, and he and his men will first rush to meet the first attacking piece, either to the south or to the north. But after pushing them back, which will hold them in place and leave them unable to provide support for Yellow or Long Hair, he and his men will thus become the fourth side of our square sided trap.

Our Calvary will then double back in an arc maneuver, and appear seemingly out of nowhere, and break through the skirmish line. With that, all chaos would break out because they would be surrounded on all sides in a carefully designed trap that was meant for only them. There would be no escape or chance of surviving, and they will not know what was happening, until almost when the end was near and death was lurking closely by.

The key therefore, is that whatever area experiences the first wave of attackers in the south or the north, those braves in that area must remain in place and keep the wacicu invaders' army engaged and constantly busy, and not try to rush off and join the main battle. Everyone has a part to perform, and holding the wacicu invaders in place is how the battle will be really won. For he expects us to run and try to escape from the soldiers, and never ever stand up to him and fight with cunning and guile. So, standing up to him will catch him off guard and helpless.

If this works, all three pieces of the invader's army will be cut off from one another, and we will destroy them where they stand, as easy as one, two, three. But, also always remember that from whatever location we choose to conduct the attack upon the soldiers, we must control the high ground at all times. Pizi, Mahpiya Luta , and Tatanka Sica all nodded in approval. And Pizi was amazed as to the level of the attack, and he stated that it was as if I had an ability to be inside of the wacicu's own mind and thoughts.

This plan had been thought out in every detail and it was sound, they all stated, so we were now ready to put it into action. Mahpiya Luta told Pizi that he wanted him to be the shirt wearer for this upcoming battle, and that Tatanka Iyotake had already agreed that this was sound judgement. Pizi looked a bit surprised, but he realized that Mahpiya Luta trusted him, and was entrusting him with a great honor. So, he agreed and said that he was honored, to be given this responsibility and that he would do the right thing and bring honor to the Teton Lakota Nation.

Pizi , Tatanka Sica and myself then said our goodbyes to Mahpiya Luta and then we rode off, with the wind at our backs at a fast pace towards Tatanka Iyotake (Sitting Bull)'s encampment. When we were about five or more hours into the ride, we came across a curious sight, a black man who seemed right at home, who was trapping on a nice medium sized lake that for some reason or another contained a lot of beavers. He seemed quite startled when he saw us, as he kind of quickly sprang to get his rifle.

But when he saw Tatanka Sica, who was flashing her brand new Winchester Model 1873 in plain sight and then me he seemed to ease himself, and he actually started smiling. He was a big and burly man with big and strong looking hands. Pizi recognized him right away, and said that his name is Azinpi, which meant Buffalo Teat, and he was called this because of his black skin and curly hair, that reminded everyone in the Teton Lakota Nation of a Tatanka. We rode right up to him, and as we looked down upon him from our mounts. Pizi then greeted him, in the customary fashion, and both men smiled at one another because over time they had become acquainted with one another, and it seemed as if they were on friendly terms with each another. He raised his hand up, and then wiped it off on his pants, and then raised it up again. Tatanka Sica and then I, both shook his hand and he had a very strong and firm grip that felt like a vise.

He tried to explain to Pizi, that he was there to only hunt and trap, and that when he was finished that he would be on his way. Because this spot on the lake had always been lucky for him, and the beavers were plentiful and he had always been blessed by making a lot of money in his lucky spot. He then turned to Tatanka Sica and myself, and said, "Howdy, my name is Isaiah Dorman, and I escaped from my slave owners, the D'Ormans, from down in Lousiana."

He had been in these parts for well over 23 years, and he said that he was a guide, interpreter, miner, cook, trapper and trader. And he was also at one time the one who carried the mail, between the forts for one hundred dollars a month, which was good money, for any man. He said that he was given that amount, because the job was considered extremely dangerous.

But, because he had married a woman of the Inkpaduta tribe of the Santee nation, he was able to move about without any resistance or trouble. He now was working part time, for the Northern Pacific railroad as a scout and guide, because he knew the area so well. And, on his last job, he had been hired by none other than the great Lt Colonel Custer, himself, to accompany the soldiers and surveyors in 1874, on the initial survey to determine if the stories were true of gold in the Black Hills.

He now did mostly odd jobs, and whoever wanted to pay him could gain his services. If a former slave could be paid a handsome price for his labor, then he was glad that the South had lost the Great War, because it had changed his life in so many ways. He was making plenty of money, and as a slave all of the money that he had made thus far, would have gone to his owners. So he was glad to be where he was, and one day he was gonna be a very rich ex-slave.

He then offered us some of his food and coffee that he had rustled up and said that he was just about to begin to eat and drink, when he first decided to check his traps. Leaving his rifle behind, when up from nowhere, here we'd ridden in. We had startled him a bit, but once he saw Negro folks like himself, it immediately eased his soul and mind. Because these times were now a bit unsettling and worrisome, and it does a body good to always stay alert and ready for anything.

We declined his offer with a kind of mean sounding, 'No Thanks' and said that we had to be on our way. And, that it was good meeting him, and that we would always remember his hospitality and kindness. As we rode away, still not ever having formally introduced ourselves to him, I looked at Tatanka Sica, who looked back at him.

And then, she spit in disgust in his general direction, as he wildly waved goodbye to us as if we were some of his lifelong friends. She then just shook her head side to side, kind of in disbelief, because no matter who or what he had claimed to b; there was one fact that stood out to the both of us and that was the coat that he had on.

It was a blue Federal Army issued coat that he seemed to wear with either a false pride or simple stupidity. And no matter how long he had lived in the Territories, that bluecoat made him stick out like a sore thumb. He had also told on himself, with all of his big talk, which was his way of trying to impress us folks that he had just met in a chance encounter on the road of life, and trying kind of hard, in an offbeat sort of way to gain our confidence.

But he was in the end a traitor, who had aligned himself with the Blue-coats against the Teton Lakota oyate of people, the same nation of people who had taken him in when he had nowhere to go, when he was desperately seeking a new beginning from his old existence of forced servitude. This oyate of people had even treated him like he was a part of their family for no reason other than that; it was the right thing to do.

This modern-day Judas, one day, would get what all traitors get. And let's hope that he had sense enough to turn away from the mighty Caesar's gold, and to do the right thing, which was, to stay clear of, and as far away from the upcoming storm as possible. Because a storm truly was coming, you could feel it in the winds. And, it was going to be ugly for anyone who was caught outside in it.

But only time would tell for this lost soul, who had thought that he had somehow now found his way to redemption with the wacicu who were related to some of the very same ones that had once had owned him. I looked at Pizi, who seemed inquisitive as to what we were saying in English to one another, and I said, "Gnaye (fool)," which made him laugh loudly, and then chuckle for a long time.

The ride itself took about two full days. And it was as if everyone was waiting for us to show up, because as soon as we got there, the call to assemble went out camp wide. The last three to arrive to the meeting of the minds, were first Tatanka Iyotake (Sitting Bull), and then finally last but not least Tashunka Witco and Wicasa Tanka Sikala (Little Big Man).

Everyone gathered around the main fire, and Tatanka Iyotake (Sitting Bull) first welcomed everyone for coming to this important gathering, and then he asked everyone to please be seated. Still standing, he stated that this was a chance for all to have their say. And, to honestly speak their minds and that this meeting would last until everyone and he meant everyone, from the youngest to the oldest and all in between, had a chance to say what was really on their minds.

As he then sat down, different individuals stood up one by one and had their say. There was quite a collection of individuals assembled, and together they were quite an impressive lot, as I look back on it. There were some very

interesting things that were said, which created a lot of mumbling and grumbling from throughout the crowd of onlookers and everything that was said
by everyone seemed to point to the fact that the wacicu invaders were doing
a lot of underhanded things to the Teton Lakota Nation.

After many hours, Pizi stood up and he first introduced himself, that he
was Pizi, son of Iciskhan (Making many Sister/Running Horses) and
Cajeotawin (Walks with Many Names) ancestor of Hanhepi Wi Sapa (Black
Moon), married to Coka El Naji(Stand in Center) and Martina Makoce To (
Blue Earth). He then in a very humble manner, introduced the mighty child
warrior by her formal name Tatanka Sica Ohitike, and then finally he intro-
duced me, the Mani Wana Gi (Ghost that Walks) to everyone present as
Mahpiya Luta's personal handpicked representative or envoy.

He then spoke his mind. And he also stated that in his heart and mind
specifically, he felt as if their survival was truly at stake. That if they sat
around and did nothing, it could spell doom for the Teton Lakota nation. The
wacicu were plotting against them, and that no matter what, the old ways
were being threatened. He then sat down.

And, Wicasa Tanka Sikala (Little Big Man) jumped to his feet. His eyes
were blazing and bugging out of his head, as he held one hand on one of his
two pistols that were hanging from his hip. As the other hand clutched his
knife, he then yelled, that he would kill anyone, and he meant anyone even a
chief or medicine man, who tried to sell the land, and that this was not a
threat but a promise. He then swirled around and looked everyone in his or
her eyes, as he then abruptly sat back down, as the crowd again mumbled
and grumbled.

Next was Tashunka Witco's turn, and as he slowly rose, he at first said
nothing. He just looked into everyone's eyes, with his piercing black eyes, and
made sure that he had everyone's attention before he even uttered a word.
He was a medium sized man, with a slight build, with a long straight nose, and
flowing curly brown hair that went past his shoulders, and he had a yellow
lightning bolt that went down the left side of his face. He also had three finger
marks of a white powder, that when dried, were used to resemble hailstones
that were on all over his body.

Unlike a lot of other warriors, he had no face paint make up on his fore-head, and he wore no war bonnet. He had a very noticeable scar on the right side of his face, and he had slight or faint gun- powder marks on the left side of his face. He was an Oglala who

was originally given the title of an Ogle Tanka Un (Shirt Wearer or War Leader) because of his fighting ability in 1865.

And even though he was officially stripped of this title, around 1874, he still was to most tribes an unofficial Ogle Tanka Un. He had been in many battles between the Lakota and their natural enemies like the Crow, Sho-Shone, Arikara, Blackfeet and Pawnee. And, he was one of Mahpiya Luta's decoys in The Fetterman Massacre.

He was at the battles of Red Buttes, and the Platte River Bridge Station, and he was very respected by the whole Teton Lakota nation. He finally started to speak, and first off, he said that for those who did not know him, he was Tashunka Witco, son of Waglula (Worm) and Wiya Sina Wagma Ha (Rattling Blanket Woman), and the nephew of Sine Gleska, and the grandson of Tatanka Sapa (Black Buffalo) and Pte Ska (White Cow). He then said that these times were extremely difficult for everyone, because he believed that the wacicu invaders plan was to end the traditions and values of the Teton Lakota way of life.

He was there as a youth, when the mighty Mato Wayuhi was killed for no reason by the wacicu soldiers, and their behaviors had never changed one bit, because they have always seemed to not respect any of the Plains Nations, and that they were only doing the evil-bidding of the Great Father himself. They actually, he felt, were conducting a secret war against their Sahiyela brothers and sisters, because the Sahiyela were the first of the Great Plains tribes to wage tribe warfare because of their centralized tribal unity.

They also were the first of the Plains tribes to use the horse, and they actually were the ones who first introduced the horse culture to the many, and some say to all, of the many Plains Tribes including the Teton Lakotas, and because of all of this, since around 1860, the Sahiyela were a major force on the Great Grass Sea. So the wacicu's goal it appeared was to go after the most organized of the Plains tribes. And the Sahiyela culture being a leader in this capacity was the initial but not the only target of this plan. He then stated that the wacicu soldiers had destroyed seven Sahiyela encampments, before the present year (1875) and, if this continued our Sahiyela brothers and sister's way of life, would be at great risk. Also, since the Sahiyela and Lakota were treaty bound allies, for what seemed like many, moons then if the wacicu attacked the Sahiyela, then they were also attacking them.

As the crowd mumbled their agreement in unity, he then stated that after the wacicu invaders were through with the Sahiyela that they, the Teton Lakota oyate would be next because they had already many, many times blatantly violated the treaty that was of their own making and design, with the Teton Lakota Nation. So he was not in favor of dealing with the wacicu on any level, because it was crazy to think that anyone could own or sell the land.

The land was a gift from the ancestors for the children, and it simply could not be owned. So, he would kill any wacicu invaders that crossed into their territory first, and then talk later. He also had solid evidence that the surveyors of the Great Iron Horse (The Northern Pacific Railroad) were secretly also in their territory and were trying to build right under their very noses, this 'iron horse' right through their sacred lands.

So since 1870 he and Tatanka Iyotake, were waging their own secret attack and disappear war against any and all wacicus. And, more importantly, he wanted nothing to do with any wacicu, and he definitely was against selling them anything. He then looked everyone that was gathered around the fire in their eyes for a long time, and there was absolute silence from everyone in attendance, as if everyone was pondering his words of wisdom.

And with that, he then slowly sat down and the last person's turn to speak was finally Tatanka Iyotake himself. Tatanka Iyotake was a Hunkpapa wichasha wakan (holy man) since his early twenties, and he was a member of both the Tatanka (Buffalo) and Heyokh (Thunderbird) Societies and he had been fighting with the Dakota's who were expelled from Minn ola (Minnesota) since 1863. He had participated in numerous battles in 1863 and 1864 against the Federal Bluecoat soldiers.

And, all of these many battles it was said was what had hardened his views about the wacicu invaders. This is why he had assumed a sense of uncompromising militancy towards all wacicus. From 1865 to 1868 he had led numerous war parties against the Bluecoat Forts, and it was his attack and disappear actions along with Mahpiya Luta's warfare which caused the wacicu's to sign the Second Fort Laramie Treaty of 1868. But Tatanka Iyotake refused to sign the treaty, and he continued his attack and disappear tactics from 1868 through the early 1870's.

He had continued to make attacks on any and all wacicu invaders, and against the Forts. And it was he and Tashunka Witco, who had discovered in early 1871 that the wacicu's were secretly sending in survey parties for the Iron Horse (The Northern Pacific Railway), which was yet another clear violation of the 1868 Second Fort Laramie treaty. Tatanka Iyotake and Tashunka Witco were those among the tribes that had refused to move onto the reservation or sign any treaties.

And, they were determined to strike fear into the hearts and minds of all wacicu's that dared to enter into their territory. He seemed to be a man of few words, and yet he always commanded the ultimate of respect. And some say that he was installed as the symbolic Chief of all Chiefs around 1867 or 1868, because of his defiant view and attitude of living a free life in the old ways or to die trying.

So he was extremely respected, and some say he was of the same caliber as the highly respected and mighty warrior, the great Conquering Bear himself. He looked around at everyone in attendance with those piercing yet sleepy eyes of his, and then he began by saying that he was Tatanka Iyotake, son of Ptebloka Psice(Jumping Bull) and Tiyopa Waka Iye (Her Holy Door), brother of Wiyaka Waste (Good Feather), and half-brother to Si Tanka (Big Foot). He said that although he never liked to go to war, he had no problem with it, because war at times was a necessary part of life.

He said that he was never the aggressor against the wacicu, and that he had only fought to protect the children. He wanted everyone to realize, that yes they were at war with the wacicu and their Bluecoat soldiers. It was war and despite the so-called treaty, there was never ever a time of true and lasting peace. The wacicu always talked peace, yet their actions were not peaceful in any manner. And so, his actions would match theirs, and he would remain a thorn in their sides until he had no more breath in his body.

Because the wacicu had signed a so-called treaty, yet they really had never, ever stopped attacking the various Nations of the Great Grass Sea. And Tashunka Witco was right when he had said that the Great Father's Bluecoat soldiers were secretly trying to exterminate the Sahiyela Nation. He then said as he had sat there listening to what everyone was saying, that if he took everything that everyone had said and put it all together, then the only conclusion that he could make, was that the wacicu were trying to steal their sacred lands and exterminate their way of life.

These wacicu invaders and the Bluecoat soldiers of the Great Father must be stopped at all costs. So they must unite and become one, like they used to always do during the summer ritual of the Sun Dance, at the Seven Council fires. They would let the old ways unite them against a common foe and if anyone was seeking a return to the old ways, then they should listen for the call to gather. A call that, he, Tatanka Iyotake would be sending out as soon as the next spring was approaching. And that call, would be the call to meet, and return to their old ways.

They should also not seek to judge anyone who did not heed the call. Because everyone had an individual choice to make on this matter, and more importantly, it was not anyone's place to judge another. It was indeed a personal choice that each and every one had to make in their hearts and minds, on this matter. And, if they decided to believe in the old ways, and to let the Sun Dance bring us all together, then they would see that their choice proved right for them.

Also, it was important for all warriors to avoid contact with the wacicu when any of the innocents were around, because they were always the first targets of all wacicu's vengeance. So to keep as many of them as safe as possible, all warriors would have to now going forward pick their battles. And, we must remember to always use the virtue of wisdom, he continued, which is one of the four main virtues— generosity, fortitude, bravery and wisdom— of the Teton Lakota Nation. These virtues embody who we truly are, who we seek to be, and are those which we all have used to become productive members of our Tribes and Nation.

So seek wisdom, and do not let your actions betray any of us, because the wacicu is looking for any reason, be it big or small, to attack us before we are ready to show him our spirits and hearts. So scaring the wac cu is okay, he said, as many in the crowd laughed. But, please refrain from killing just to kill, he continued, until we are ready to make our stand for what is right and just. 'Do I make sense and is this clear for all in attendance?' he implored.

'And yes, for those in the crowd, who know that I am now talking to you that this request from me was directed at you, please heed my words. And, follow my instructions at all times, no matter what,' he said. He then gazed hard into Wicasa Tanka Sikala's eyes, and down into his soul. Wicasa Tanka Sikala's head slowly lowered toward the ground, as his eyes closed, as a lone snicker sound came from out of the crowd.

He then thanked everyone for coming and said that it was good to see so many known faces in the crowd that he had not seen in quite a while. He also expected everyone to stay and join the meal, and to relax from the long day and night.

Now if anyone wanted to or just had to leave for whatever reason, he would understand, he said, but there was plenty of prepared food, and rest does do a body good.

The nighttime sky was beautiful tonight. And it would be wonderful if they could all together as a united group experience the nighttime sky turn into morning, and then go through the process of being reborn all over again, he said. With that he waved his arms, and it was as if from out of nowhere, many women came up carrying food and cool water drinking gourds. Then to everyone's delight the children started coming out, playing and running and sounding happy.

With that, the whole scene turned into a big and happy holiday like event, which made me think and ask the obvious question that burned deep within my mind, as I soaked in all of this. Now who are supposed to be the so-called savages, again? As the crowd began to disperse about the encampments' main fire, a lot of warriors seemed to come up to get a better look at my apprentice and myself.

I guess trying to see just who this "Ghost That Walks" and his apprentice really were, and just what was so special about them anyways. For the Oceti Sakowin were an oral culture, and so the word had already started to spread like blood does in water, about these extremely friendly strangers who were new in these territories, yet they processed some very old familiar-like ways of friendship and trust building.

 Because trust is never given, it is earned. And yet amazingly, these new strangers had already become trusted within all levels of the Okawin Sakowin Nation. So, as everyone gathered around us in a semi-circle to either simply look at us, or to look at our weapons—especially Tatanka Sica's shiny new looking Model 1873, or to touch our clothing, Pizi started laughing. And, he just stood there and shook his head from side to side, in amazement.

"People seem taken with the both of you, and even Tatanka Iyotake himself, seems in awe of just being in your presence," he said." He has already asked me if the three of us would join him in his teepee to eat our meals, so that he may gain more insight, and therefore wisdom about the wacicu. He says that there is something intriguing and interesting about the two of you, and he seeks to be in the very air that you both breathe, to get a glimpse of who you both really are.

We of course, accepted his generous offer. And when we went to his teepee, it was funny, because it was extremely crowded with many people who were also seeking the answers to their questions about us. They actually had to make four of the young ones leave and go outside to play or eat. And, the young ones seemed a bit upset that they had to give up their places at all in the first place.

As they were leaving, they mumbled something that made Tatanka Sica just burst out in laughter. And she just laughed and laughed, and it seemed to tickle her to no end. Finally, when she had gotten it together, she told me what had made her laugh so. And, it was about what the littlest one of the four had said.

She said, it was he that looked like he was every bit of four or five years old, who had said so eloquently, and with much sense, "So why must we be made to go outside when, for half of these people assembled here, it is already way past their going to sleep time. And they would probably be sleep or dozing to sleep, way before we had even finished our meal together? So, make the sleepy and the tired ones leave, because they really are only here to say that they were here, to meet, and to eat with the new strangers, and nothing else."

It tickled me also. And I really started laughing, when I had noticed that the four of them who had just been thrown out, had already sneaked ɔack around to the back of the teepee. They had come from underneath the covering on the ground, close to where it is tied to the skinny poles that held the teepee upright and could now be seen with just the top halves of their little bodies showing. We ate and then sat back and listened to the various chatter around the room.

The talk was of a lighthearted nature. It was centered, around folk's tales and people of myth and legend. After a few hours or so, I was asked to tell any story. Or really told by some old heads, that it was now my turn to tell a story. And they all seemed taken aback in amazement, because I choose to speak of the many exploits of Wicahpi Hihpa Ya (Fallen Star), which made Pizi just beam and glow with admiration.

Because, not only did I listen to what he had told me about Wicahpi Hihpa Ya, I had also more importantly remembered the stories in all their exact details, which was even more of an impressive feat. Because, many adults did not even know all of the stories, let alone get all of the factual details correct. And, all that Tatanka Iyotake could do was to sit there and smile. Meanwhile, a small crowd that contained not only the innocents, but some warriors too, gathered around me, and Tatanka Sica. Each and everyone listened intently to me talking, through Tatanka Sica, about the exploits of the mighty Wicahpi Hihpa Ya, just like it was yesterday.

We left in about two days or so. And after everything that happened while we were at Tatanka Iyotake's encampment, there were two things for sure that stuck out in my mind. One, that Tatanka Sica definitely was one tough customer. Because, my Apprentice took every braves' best shot, and she always came out on top.

All of the aspiring warriors seemed as if they were out to test her, and she had no troubles holding her own. She had many braves that simply were just out to take her Model 1873, from her. And her grip on her Model 1873 was amazing. Because, as they tried to take or snatch her Model 1873 from her, she would never ever let go no matter what and she always was in control of her weapon.

A lot of braves were curious about the weapon, so they wanted to touch or inspect or really hold the weapon in their hands, up close and personal like. But a lot of them were not in the habit of asking to see, and they were used to taking what they wanted, as a clear-cut sign of their strength, for everyone to see. But Tatanka Sica was not about to take the loss of her weapon nor was she one to really show any sign of weakness, because mi Abuelo had trained her to never ever do so no matter what.

So, she went through a series of running skirmishes, which she felt were tests designed to her apprentice skill set. She was either slapping hands or pulling out one of her revolvers, especially her cute little two shot Derringer— that I did not even know that she had, or her trusty bushido. It all was meant to make the point of her being in control of the situation at all times.

She even once was pushed backwards and down toward the ground. Yet, she reacted with cat-like reflexes, so quickly at her attacker by using the rifle butt to brace her fall. And, in one graceful and stunning smooth motion, she then sprang back into the face of her attacker.

And then, she used the weapon as a wedge upon her attacker's neck, such that it caused all of the onlookers to gasp out in amazement and awe. And, some even laughed out loud. The Model 1873 seemed as if it was just an extension of her arm, and whatever she did the Model 1873 did it with her.

As we were riding away from Tatanka Iyotake's encampment, I told her that she and her boyfriend had both done well. And, that they both seemed to have impressed quite a lot of people, with how they acted as a couple. She looked at me all sheepishly, and started smiling and then said, "What boyfriend Balaam are you talking about, if I may be permitted to ask?" as she then started laughing.

I said, "You know your boyfriend." Kara looked all happy. And then I pointed at her Model 1873, which made her laugh so hard that she started crying with happiness. Because as I told her, she had held him tighter than Mamie at times had held me. And, the way that she held her boyfriend, it seemed kind of like true love-like the kind between a man and his woman, or in her case—between a woman and her man.

So, she had protected him, and she had let nothing get in between them. And her grip on her man was firm, and yet sure at all times. And she never once, did not think of his needs first and foremost. She had treated him all special, and her commitment to him was extremely noticeable and heart-warming. I then slyly said, "My Apprentice, since I see how this boyfriend thing is affecting you, we shall never ever bring it up again, and this will remain strictly between you and me." She then really started laughing, and I did right then, believe that this mission was extremely successful. Because, it did make Kara and me much closer, just like it was intended to do.

The second thing that I will always remember about this mission is that Pizi and Tatanka Iyotake had a long talk, just between the two of them. And then the two of them, along with Tashunka Witco, had their conversation with one another, and to see the Three Great Leaders of the Teton Lakota Nation all at the same time was a very impressive sight to behold. As we were riding back, Pizi said that all of our proper planning had been very successful. And, that my battle plans had been seen by both Tatanka Iyotake, and Tashunka Witco, as having been sound, and very thoroughly thought out.

They would also be coordinating their efforts, to assist our Sahiyela brothers and sisters, and provide strike groups that would provide defensive support and aid. For we all now knew that the Bluecoats were stalking the Sahiyela camps to kill off the innocents. This was their main tactic, and we therefore had to be able to ride like lightning, at a moment's notice in any direction, to assist our Sahiyela brothers and sisters

We would also be sending out Scouts daily from each village, which would ride out further and further into our territory, on each trip. Because, we needed to be able to see them before they saw us. We were to set up a network of riders that we would coordinate and use, to pass messages between one another, and to also sound the alarm if necessary. We were to use the innocents to set up a network of eyes that would aid us in our protection. They were to see and watch our backs at all times.

We also were to assume that the Great Father was now preparing for all-out war, so we had to be able to protect ourselves. What we needed was somehow for all of us, who were determined to live free in the way of our ancestors, to in some way come together. Maybe we could use the Sun Dance ritual to accomplish this goal, because it would bring out a lot of curious people, and strength is always in numbers.

So all in all, they were quite impressed with both me, and my Apprentice. And they had never ever met strangers who despite not knowing them had treated them like they were their family. We always would be welcome by all of the Oceti Sakowin Nation (oyate), and they wanted us to please come back with the entire tribe of the Calais Vega Nation.

I smiled and told Pizi thank you for good news, and that I was thankful for his friendship and guidance. Because, if it was not for his teaching me about his lovely people, and also taking me to the places that were special to them, I could not have recited the stories and legends that his people could relate to on a personal level. So he enabled me to be a guide to the past for his people, and I would never forget the look on their faces, which was priceless and awe inspiring to me on a personal level.

We then, did not have much time, so we must be ready at any time, for the Bluecoats to strike, because they would probably seek to attack in the winter, when travel for all Nations of the Great Grass Sea was hard to do. And if not then, surely in the springtime, which would even make more sense from a military standpoint, because they could bulk up their troops during the winter and get more sheer numbers onto the field of battle.

We both agreed to always be ready, and we then turned our attention to driving our horses pretty hard to make time, as we returned back to Mahpiya Luta's camp to discuss with him all that had transpired at Tatanka Iyotake's camp. Now while all of this was going on, in November of that same year,

1875, the Grant Administration began to consider what the next phase would be, now that the selling of the land was all but a moot point.

President Grant and key members of his cabinet, including his brother Orvil, decided to recall Generals Sheridan and Crook to Washington, to discuss the final solution to the Indian problem. They had crafted a plan, that they called The Final Solution: The Eradication of the Indian Infestation, or just The Final Solution for short. It was designed to exterminate their enemy and secure the Indians on the reservations.

And it had many different components, that all had to be carried out in unison for maximum success. They would all carry out their orders as soon as they got the command from headquarters. They would drill and train the soldiers every day, so that they would all know what their jobs would be, on zero hour.

So days later, after everyone had seen the Plan, they gathered again along with a few select individuals and had gone over it again to ensure that it was sound and logical. They all agreed that the army should also drop the pretense about stopping and evicting the trespassers. And more importantly, that they should begin to consider what a final military campaign or action would really look like, against the 'non-treaty signers' of the Second Fort Laramie Treaty of 1868—who had refused to turn themselves in to the Indian Agencies.

These Northern Cheyenne and Lakota bands would be considered hostiles. And they were in the way of the wacicu's goal, which was publicly one of manifest destiny and nation building by the right of conquest. But, in secret, it was to get the Northern Pacific Railroad that would be going straight through the Sioux Nation built at all costs. Because many of them, in the Cabinet had already received their kickback money, from the owners of the Railroad in order to make this happen.

So, they needed a way to make it look in the newspapers, like they were not launching a war against the Lakota and the Cheyenne without provocation. So they would send out an ultimatum through the Indian Agents in the region, but they would call it a notification. These Agents were to immediately begin notifying the bands of the non-treaty signers in their areas, to return to the Reservations by January 31, 1876, or face military action.

One General namely, General Sheridan thought that the plan was sound, but that the notification process was simply a waste of time. One Indian Inspector, named Edwin Watkins also agreed with the soundness of the plan, but he supported the notion, "...that the true policy should be, and is to send the troops against them in the winter—the sooner the better, and whip them into subjection." So, with everyone more or less in agreement, President Grant then gave his final instructions.

He wanted his Generals to be ready to move once he had telegraphed the code EO 66 for his Executive Order 66. This order would contain the blueprint plan for their domination over their enemy. And thus, every step had to be followed simultaneously at all costs and with no exceptions. This Final Solution was their end game, to the pursuit of their Manifest Destiny, and to their true desire of Nation building.

They also really wanted all of this to go away. Because, 1876 was the Centennial year of American Independence; this was to be celebrated with the First Official World's Fair, in the city of the framers of the Declaration of Independence Philadelphia, Pennsylvania. It was actually called, 'The International Exhibition of Arts, Manufactures and Products of the Soil and Mine.

This was to celebrate the 100th Anniversary of the signing of the Declaration of Independence. It was to run for six months from May 10th thru November 10th and was to be the focal event for activities of the Grant Administration in celebration of the building of the Nation. And, this was where the Grant Administration had wanted everyone's attentions, in the young and growing Nation to be focused on --with the help of the newspapers. And, really if the truth could be told, the Administration wanted them to be focused on no place else.

Because, if everyone's attention was focused upon the first ever World's Fair, then the Grant Administration could indeed conduct their sinister and evil business of the Final Solution out of the public eye. Now, all of this Centennial business was far, far away from all of the troubles that were happening out west. So if they could make this all go away, then it would be great for them.

The Council Lodges of the Non-Treaty's signers seriously discussed the "Notification" slash "Ultimatum." But it was too late in the season to travel into the Reservations because of the deepness of the winter snows of 1875. So they would first hunt the Tatanka, and then turn themselves in during the season of spring, of 1876.

When the deadline of Wiotehika Wi (Moon of Hard Winter) or January 31, 1876, had passed the newly appointed Commissioner of Indian Affairs, John Smith, wrote to his boss the Secretary of the Interior, Zachariah Chandler. He said that he "saw no reason why, in the discretion of the Honorable Secretary of War, that military action against the hostile bands especially one such as Sitting Bull, should begin at once."

Chandler agreed, and so he then turned these bands over to the War Department for such actions on the part of the Army, as they deemed proper under the circumstances. President Grant and his cabinet were then notified, and finally on or around Cannapopa Wi (Moon of Popping Trees) or February 7th, Grant telegraphed his secret four-character code: EO 66 (Executive Order 66), to the lead General of his "secret," in the winter built-up army.

On Cannapopa Wi or February 8th General Sheridan in turn telegraphed both Generals Crook and Terry, that the time had come for the Final Solution. And, he was using the command code of EO 66 (Executive Order 66), which ordered them both at once, to commence their winter campaigns against the Non-Treaty Signing hostiles. With that, the Great Sioux War of 1876 had officially begun, and there was no turning back now, as we all turned to face our destinies once again.

These were very unsettling times, because this 'EO 66' was strictly about extermination of the original inhabitants and their way of life. Now they want you to think that they were just trying to force roughly somewhere between 600 to maybe 2000 Teton Lakota and Cheyenne warriors and thousands of innocents to return to their Reservations, but really it was their version as they saw it of the Right of Conquest.

The Bluecoats, for the remainder of February started sending out a lot of scouts to survey the landscape, and more importantly, to also get an idea of where the campsites were located. The Bluecoats also attacked anything moving anywhere around them that appeared to them to be hostiles. And, their "shoot first and maybe talk later policy" was scary, because a lot of the First Ones were constantly in fear of their lives, on a daily basis. It was really a tense time because, for the First Ones, everyone had to keep their guard up at all times, and there was no letting it down--as in peace, for them.

The good thing was that when the Bluecoats were not grouped up in the main force, they always rode everywhere at all times, fast and furious, like they were scared or something. Then on top of that, they were always shooting all wild and blind, such that one had to be on guard for any sounds of gunfire. And everybody wanted to know what the Bluecoats were really up to; what were their real plans? Tatanka Iyotake and Tashunka Witco were both aware of their plans, because we all had already talked about what they would do or try to do.

So, they instructed all Chiefs that their villages must continue to keep moving, so that they could stay at least two steps ahead of the Bluecoats. They must also do this moving under the cover of the moonlit skies, because the Bluecoats would not be out at night, so this was the perfect advantage for the Nations. Now moving a village in the snow is tough, but at least everyone was alive and well, so no one complained, and it was just something that they had to do, if they were to remain free.

In about the middle of Istawicayazan Wi (Moon of Snow Blindness) or March 1876, Bluecoat soldiers located a village that contained about 65 lodges, and they wasted no time in attacking it. And, once they had seized control of it, they burned it down and took the medium sized pony herd, but they quickly retreated from the field of battle, as soon as they received return fire. For some unknown reason, the Bluecoats thought that they were attacking Crazy Horse's village, but really it was a Sahiyela village, that was led by Ishi'eyo Nissi (Two Moons), Pteblok Ska (White Bull), and Mato Waniyetu Ota (Old Bear).

The strike team was sent out, and when they arrived the following day, they recovered many of their horses that the Bluecoats had initially taken. The group of innocents from the destroyed village were then taken to Tatanka Iyotake's encampment and they were immediately absorbed into his village. The loss of life was small, but this action was the first actual engagement of the War, and it was a sign of things to come.

The actions of the Bluecoats seemed strange to some, because they were just trying to kill the innocents and burn down the dwellings. As if by burning them down, they would then have nowhere else to go but to the nearest reservation, which really was like a prison for interment. But we had already accurately deduced this move on their part, and we already knew then what their tactics would be.

So this then was one of their main tactics, so we would then use this to our advantage. We would move to either of the two previously scouted locations and send out the word that it was time to perform the Sun Dance. The area of the Greasy Grass River was selected because it provided a natural defense from the Bluecoats—with many trees on one side across the river, and then a maze of high bluffs and ravines that overlooked the river, on the other side.

And besides, it was extremely hard to ride into this area and not be seen by any watching eyes. This would be where we made our stand, and hopefully this call to gather would be heeded by everyone who was seeking to continue in the ways of the ancestors. The call to gather was sent out in early to mid Pejito Wi (Moon of Tender Grass) or April, and people started showing up around the end of Canwapeto Wi (Moon of Green Leaves) or May, and the beginning of Wipazuka waste Wi (Moon of the Ripening of June Berries) or June, in droves.

And it really was an amazing sight to behold. All seven of the seven bands of the Teton Lakota nation were present, as were other various nations. And, the Sahiyela and the Arapahoe's were the most prominent of the nations that were assembled. The encampment was arranged with the Hunkapapas Lodges pitched up highest on the River, under a bluff. The Yankton and Yanktonai Nakota, and the Dakota Santee Lodges were next. And, then came the

Oglala Lodges, and then the Sicangru (Brule) Lodges, followed by the Minne-conjou Lodges, the Itazipacola (Sans Arc) and the Siasapa (Blackfeet) Lodges. The Northern and Southern Sahiyela Lodges were then followed by the Arap-ahoe's, and then finally a very few of the Ree (Arikara) Lodges.

The Great Lodge was located in the center of the encampment which was the largest village ever assembled since the time of the Seven Council Fires. Never before had these three nations come together in such way, and to be honest I was impressed with the fact that so many people had even shown up. There was anywhere between 600 to 2000 warriors present, depending upon the day and time.

The Sun Dance, which was a 12 day ritual of self-sacrifice, was seen as a way to instill a sense of tribal unity. The Sun Dance was then set into motion, and all of the assembled warriors who wanted to freely partake in this cere-mony were encouraged to do so. And even the mighty Tatanka Iyotake himself submitted to the ritual. It was during the ritual when he said that on his dream quest that he had a vision, of Bluecoated grasshoppers falling up-side down from the sky. And because of this vision, he stated that there was going to be a great victory against the wacicu Bluecoated soldiers.

About this same time, the Bluecoats launched their main spring offensive. It was a three-pronged

, or three-headed monster, whose plan was to have all three columns converge simultaneously on the Lakota hunting grounds. And, it was intended to catch the hostiles between the approaching soldiers, in a pincer type of maneuver that would destroy them.

The Bluecoats had assembled a rather large fighting force that consisted of about 1500 men. It included about 250 or 260 Crow and Shoshone warrior scouts all of which were moving up into the Rosebud Valley area, looking for a nonexistent village and, they were within the closest striking distance. This column by the way in which it was moving, appeared to have come from the Fort that was called Fetterman, because it was headed due north without any course changes.

Tatanka Iyotake, Tashunka Witco and Pizi, all decided first to send an envoy to their encampment with a message which was really a warning for them not to advance any further. And if they did, then they would have a fight on their hands. Then, if the Bluecoats continued forward, we would then send Tashunka Witco, with the mighty Sahiyela war chief Kumokwiviokta (Wooden Leg) with a combined strike force, to assault the column somewhere along the Rosebud creek area, to see if they could check their advance.

On the very sunny morning of the 17th day of Wipazuka waste Wi (Moon of the Ripening of June Berries), or June, a combined force of 500 Lakota and Sahiyela warriors who rode all night just to get there, rained down upon the soldiers. And this battle that the Sahiyela call, 'the Battle Where the Girl Saved Her Brother,' had begun. This Battle lasted for about six or seven hours and had many twists and turns was fought over both even and uneven ground, and contained three separate skirmishes.

The Bluecoats would have most certainly lost, if not for the bravery of the Crow and Shoshone scouts and warriors, who had on two separate occasions , saved the Bluecoats from certain disaster. There were many acts of bravery on both sides, and never before had the Bluecoats seen the hostiles fight with such bravery and tenacity. It was said that they had fought with an uncommon ferocity, and never before had they shown such a willingness to accept casualties.

One act of uncommon bravery and valor that stood out in everyone's minds was by the female warrior named Sina Ogle Ptehicala Tatanka (Buffalo Calf Robe), who was the sister of the great Sahiyela chief, Wablesya Hi (Comes in Sight). During the battle, when the Bluecoats had suddenly counterattacked, a fast advancing party of about 50 Crow and Shoshone braves had shot Comes in Sight's horse out from under him, and they quickly closed in to finish him off. But then from out of nowhere, up rides his sister Sina Ogle Ptehicala Tatanka (Buffalo Calf Robe), weaving her way through the middle of the advancing warriors, to scoop up her brother in the nick of time, to save his life.

She had ridden into the battle that day at the side of her husband, Sunmanitu Sapa (Black Coyote). And, it was her highest act of bravery that led to the battle from the Sahiyela perspective to be so named, which was an eternal testimony to her true courage and warrior's spirit. Now I was not there, but it was said that Tashunka Witco had used a mirror to signal flash his warriors and to coordinate his attacks, which is something that the Bluecoats just could not seem to comprehend.

Because it was as if the hostiles had coordinated their attack patterns based upon the weak areas in their skirmish lines. The hostiles also seemed to be fighting with a sense of urgency, and an uncommon valor. They did not quit and run, and they assaulted the Bluecoats as if they already knew what their troop movements would be. They also seemed to be waiting for the Bluecoats to shift positions to cover their exposed flanks, and when they did, the hostiles seemed to then attack the empty space or hole in their line, that the vacating soldiers had created when they shifted.

This was something that only experienced soldiers knew how to do, so where did the hostiles get this ingenious tactic from, they had all wondered? Tashunka Witco had set the battle plan up on the ride in, and he wanted his warriors to act as one. He had once found, strictly by chance mind you, a piece of mirror that was partially covered in the dirt, while riding by an old destroyed and abandoned wacicu wagon train that was in the distance.

He said that as he rode, when he got to a certain angle, the mirror had flashed in his face and then directly into his eyes. And this flash had attracted his attention and had taken him off his course to see what it was that was shining into his face and eyes. And once he found out what it was, and that it was what the wacicu invaders called a mirror, he had always known that it was a part of his destiny and that one day, it would be used for something great or important.

Then a few years later on a visit with his Sahiyela family members on his first wife's side, down in the southern part of the Great Grass Sea, he had heard of a trick that the Southern Sahiyela Chief Wasicu Huste (Lame White Man) had once used, to confuse their enemies of their whereabouts. And, it was to signal one another from great distances by using a mirror to reflect the sunlight to get one another's attention. And this was done without any actual movement, smoke signals, or drumbeats from either party.

So, once he realized how to use this special gift of knowing the Bluecoats battle movements, and more importantly of knowing how to attack their weaknesses, he just needed a way to make his warriors follow his instructions, without using his voice or hand signals. He had his eagle bone war whistle, on him at all times, but that could not be heard over great distances, and therefore would not be effective for what he had in mind.

This made him think of the mirror that he had found years earlier and of the story that his Southern Sahiyela relatives had told him. And then in the next moment's notice, he had come up with a brilliant observation. He wanted them to follow his movements, so he instructed them to stay alert for the flash of the mirror, which meant for them to follow his every movement right then.

So, if he rode hard to the left, they would ride hard to the left, and if he turned and rode at a slowed down pace to the right, they would turn and ride at a slowed down pace to the right. If they were separated, and he flashed the mirror to them, then that meant for them to come to him right then, as fast as possible. They would also ride in herds or flocks or in packs like the Tatanka always do and this would allow them to create holes in the Bluecoats' lines as they crashed into them.

Once a hole or weak spot was created, everyone would then focus on this area until the Bluecoats shifted to fill the hole. Once they shifted, everyone would then focus on the area that the Bluecoats had shifted from, and all of this should create confusion, and give them the opportunity to kill as many of the Bluecoats as possible. This is how he fought and held an enemy of superior numbers to a stalemate.

They were outnumbered some say, by as many as two or three to one, yet they were able to on three separate occasions, smash into the flanks of their enemy and wreak havoc on the Bluecoat soldiers. Tashunka Witco's battle tactics were so successful, that they drove the Bluecoat soldiers back and completely off the field. But strangely, the Bluecoats soldiers say that they won the Battle of the Rosebud that day, even though the Crows and Shoshone warriors had to fight hard to save them, right before they all quickly left the field.

But the most important things that had happened were that the secret army that consisted of three enemy columns had now been reduced to two.

And the combined forces of Lakota and Sahiyela warriors had experienced a great battle that day that they had won, plain and simple. This increased the happy spirit at the gathering for the Sun Dance at Tatanka Iyotake's encampment, even though Tashunka Witco did not participate in the celebration because he knew in his heart that an even bigger battle was looming and it also caused many more warriors to join up with their just and noble cause— the cause of living totally free in the old ways of their ancestors.

This also had given us more valuable time to begin the hidden movement of the innocents to the lands of the great white northern winters, called Canada. In three days, our secretly hidden advance scouts saw the signs of enemy troop movement that were coming our way, and we surmised that it was one of the other two columns. This column seemed like it had come east from the Fort that was called Abraham Lincoln. And our scouts were sure that among the Bluecoat soldiers, that they had first seen Pizi's main rival, the hated lead scout Bloody Knife because of the star spangled handkerchief that he always wore about his forehead which was a gift, they say from Yellow or Long Hair himself. And then eventually they saw Yellow or Long Hair himself with all of his men of the vaunted mighty Seventh Cavalry.

The Great Lodge was quickly convened and all of the great Sahiyela and Oceti Sakowin warrior chiefs were present, Tatanka Iyotake, He Topa(Four Horns),Wicasayata Pi Kagi (Crow King), Pizi, Hanhepi Wi Sapa (Black Moon), Ite Magazu (Rain–in–the-Face), Sloha (Crawler), Hump, Sunkawakan Sa (Red Horse), Ohpaye Kage (Makes Room), Wakal Wayaka (Looks Up), Cetan Sa (Red Hawk), Tahea Huste (Lame Deer), Wambli Gleska (Spotted Eagle), Mato Sa (Red Bear), Sunka Iye (He Dog), Tashunca Uitco, Ishi'eyo Nissi (Two Moons),Wasicu Huste (Lame White Man), and many more.

And it was decided that we would defend ourselves against the Bluecoat soldiers, using the battle plan that I had created. The key was to hold our aggression, and to figure out where the soldiers were, before we charged headlong into battle. Someone would have to scout the enemy, and we all knew that the action would take place on the plains above the bluffs.

Pizi decided that he would handle this part of the plan, and that no matter what; he would get the information that we would need to complete our plan.

The main bulk of the innocents were asked to leave and start heading in a northwestern direction, but to leave the teepees intact, so that it would appear that the village was loaded with many innocents. Now some innocents refused to leave, because they wanted to remain close to their loved ones, and as fate would have it, Pizi's family was one of these who refused to leave.

Now the question was, would the Wacicu soldiers take the bait and attack the encampment full bore? The mood was happy but tense, and we used the in between time to drill into our warriors the methods and tactics of the soldiers, and what our battle plan would be. Finally, eight days later on the morning of the 25th day of Wipazuka waste Wi, the signal alarm was sounded, and the wacicu Bluecoat soldiers were moving up to attack us.

The warriors were sent out to their respective places, and everyone waited for the next alarm to sound. By midday the alarm signal went back out, and the Bluecoat soldiers were finally attacking us from the north just like we thought that they would. Now would Yellow or Long Hair take the bait and ensnare himself in a trap of his own making?

Ironically the very first death of this Battle of the Greasy Grass was a ten year old innocent, a boy named Deeds, who had been out early, away from the encampment. He'd been forging about when he had come across a box of food that some Bluecoat soldiers had dropped as they hurriedly had ridden by. He was examining the box and its contents when the soldiers came back by to retrieve the missing box.

And upon seeing him, they immediately opened fire and killed him right on the spot. But he did not die in vain, because the gunshots that took his young life were the warning shots that the attack had commenced. And really, it gave us time to organize and ready ourselves for the upcoming onslaught. The Bluecoats had assumed that the hostiles would be scattering and trying to escape once they saw the troopers.

So, they felt that they could not wait until the next morning and from their position at the Crow's Nest, they decided to commence their attack at noon. Long Hair, just as we had figured split his column into two. Anc, his goal was to attack from both ends of the encampment, the north anc the south ends. He would then split off and attack the middle of the encampment with his personal strike force.

They immediately started shooting into the village from the bluffs, then came down a ravine, crossed the Big Horn River, and attacked from the north end. They were driven back across the River, but sadly Pizi's wives Coka El Naji (Stand in Center), and Martina Makoce To (Blue Earth), along with three of his daughters were killed by Bluecoat scouts including Bloody Knife, in the initial Bluecoat attack from the bluffs. When the shooting started, Pizi rode out and crossed the River much further downstream, at a ravine that is now called Medicine Trail Coupee. And before he left, he asked the warriors to hold and to wait for him to return, and not ride out blindly to attack the Bluecoat soldiers who were at the south end of the encampment.

He rode to what is called today, Sharpshooters Ridge, where he found the enemy right where we thought that they would approximately be riding toward his position. And when he had gathered his intelligence, he rode back to the encampment, to set up the trap. As he came back from down the ravine, he alerted the sentries that the Bluecoats may try to enter the encampment from this location, The Medicine Trail Coupee, and that they should be ready to repel these invaders. This is when he was told of the death of his loved ones, and although he was extremely hurt and in a lot of personal pain and anguish; the anger that welled up inside of him fueled his rage towards the Bluecoats.

The warriors were sent to their respective places, and he gathered his warriors and off they rode to push back the Bluecoats and to close the box. Tashunca Witco was focused and somewhat tense, because of the information from our secret scouts and the hardest part of any battle is the wait before the conflict begins, so he wanted to clear his head. So he and the Sahiyela holy man Pasu Zi (Yellow Nose) went bathing in the Big Horn River, and that was where he was when the midday alarm was sounded of the initial at- tack. They both hurriedly went to the meeting at The Great Lodge, and after the meeting he went to find his horse and then gathered up his strike team. He was said to have coolly and calmly called out to his warriors, that all who want to fight, should follow him, and at once they had mounted up to follow him toward the river.

Once they had all had gathered up, he then told them to restrain their ardor and to obey all of his commands and listen for his whistle. And, that they should remember, what Tatanka Iyotake, had just said at the meeting in the Great Lodge, which was that the lives of our women and children were in danger, that they should do their best and "let's kill them all." Tashunca Witco and his warriors arrived at the initial battle, crashing into the exposed left flank of the Bluecoats that were seeking cover in the timber, at the River's edge, creating massive confusion and panic.

And, they forced them to retreat and back up a ravine to a long high ridge to the north. Then, right according to our plan, his men doubled back much further downstream along the River, in a sweeping arc, that caught Long Hair and his men in a classic pincher move. That was like slamming the door shut in the Bluecoats faces.

When Tashunca Witco had initially attacked them in the timber by the River, the Bluecoats' retreat was created, and hastened by the death of Bloody Knife, who was shot directly in the head. This severely and completely rattled the officer in charge of the attack. I guess seeing and having B.oody Knife's brains and blood blown all over his face had scared him to no end. Pizi and his warriors arrived just when Tashunca Witco and his warriors were leaving, and they crashed into the soldiers with even more savage fury. Pizi, himself killed many soldiers with an axe. They did their jobs by keeping the Bluecoats occupied, and unable to reconnect with Long Hair. They were effectively cut off from one another, and that part of our plan was working perfectly, just as we had originally envisioned it.

Pizi, then instructed the warriors to keep these Bluecoats pinned down. And then, after he was sure that they were completely cut off, he took a portion of his warriors maybe half, to join the main battle to kill our target, Long Hair. Meanwhile, Long Hair did exactly what we thought that he would do. He followed the tactics that he had used eight years earlier, at the Battle of Washita River.

He tried to cross the River by using the Medicine Trail Coupee ravine, and was driven back by the sentries who were put on notice by Pizi himself. Some say, it appears that perhaps he was shot off of his horse, named Victory, and into the Bighorn River by a young brave named Ptebloka Ska, (White Cow Bull). And that this is what caused the Bluecoats to go back up the ravine and try to regroup.

But who really knows if he was really shot or not? But what we do know is that when they rode back up the ravine to the bluffs, they were surprised to find themselves boxed in on all sides except one, which was west the only way they could go, as we steered them into our designated kill area, which was around a series of hills that faced a plain.

They were too busy shooting back at an advancing enemy of superior numbers from two sides, east and south, without any knowledge of the terrain, and they did not know where they were even going. Then, when they got to a certain point, suddenly Tashunca Witco, with his warriors appeared out of nowhere. And, from the west they were then boxed in on all sides in a trap of their own design.

Tashunca Witco, using his eagle whistle to command his warriors' movements, crashed into the already weakened and exposed flanks of Long Hair's command. And just like at the Battle of the Girl Who Saved Her Brother, they rode in packs like the Tatanka, right through Long Hair's troops, causing them to start running in a panicked state. Ite Magazu (Rain-in-Your-Face) had split off from Tashunca Witco, and following orders, he created a wall of warriors from the north that cut off any means of escape out of the back door, so to speak.

And, the trap was then closed and tightened down, until everyone was dead or dying or wounded. Now, the only one of the Bluecoats who seemed to realize what was going on was a Crow scout named Ashishishe (Curly), who sensing danger rode like the wind, on a windy day in the fall and was able get to a point beyond the closing-door tactic of Tashunca Witco's mighty warriors. This action on his part, saved his life and he was then able to tell the tale, even though the Bluecoats did not for some unknown reason, ever truly believe his story Perhaps it was because he rode hard and was not at the actual final battle that killed Long Hair, but for whatever reason, Ash-ishishe (Curly) lived to fight another day.

Pizi and his warriors then joined the battle, and although they were last, they still were able to participate in the final kill. Now once Long Hair and his men that were with him, which included his brothers, a brother-in-law, a nephew, a newspaper correspondent named Mark Kellogg; several Indian scouts, and one Isaiah Dorman among others were all slain. Everyone then turned their attention to mop up the remaining pockets of Bluecoat soldiers that were grouped in various other areas.

Some of the Bluecoats did fight valiantly, and were heroic in defeat, but for the most part they never saw this coming, and they did not seem to grasp that our battlefield strategy and tactics were just plain old more superior and more efficient than theirs. Now this Battle was not what history has made it out to be, with Long Hair and his men, surrounded in a circle by hostiles. It really was like a buffalo run, with soldiers running wildly in all directions. Once Tashunca Witco and his warriors had done their parts and they dropped like Tatanka's do after being run down by warriors on horses.

Some soldiers did stand and fight, but they were simply overwhelmed, and there was a lot of mass confusion, and the battle came from all sides all at once. Long Hair was not the last one standing, and he did not enjoy a hero's death that day. And he had two wounds, one below the heart on his left side, and another wound to the left side of his head both of which could have been fatal. So it is hard to say who inflicted the actual kill shot, and a lot of warriors took credit for the actual kill that day.

The victory was swift and decisive, and it was by all accounts easy, all of the warriors said. The soldiers' tactics worked against themselves, because they should have stayed mounted upon their horses and moving, but their tactic of creating what they called a "skirmish-line" once again, just like at the Battle of the Girl Who Saved Her Brother, had worked against them. For once dismounted, they only had one option, which was to kill their horses which was to provide them additional protection against an overwhelming onslaught of hostiles. The warriors then shot their arrows in an arc that came from all angles and from on all four sides and the arrows blotted out the sun and rained down upon the defenseless soldiers.

Their weapons also had worked against them that day because they used the Springfield 1873 single shot carbine rifles, instead of the repeating rifles. The Springfield 1873 was more accurate over longer distances than the repeating rifles but having to reload after every shot doomed them because they were facing superior numbers, who used repeating rifles as well as the bow and arrow against them.

The Springfield 1873 also had another fatal flaw in its design. It was that once the weapon got hot from continual firing, the weapon tended to jam, as the hot breech tended to expand and jam the bullets that then needed to be removed by some kind of means, like with a knife, and as in any battle, this was disastrous. The Battle to Kill Long Hair was over in less than an hour, and once the shots from the Bluecoats had finally stopped, the wounded and dead of the First Ones were removed from the battlefield. And then and only then, were the women and old ones allowed to strip and mutilate the bodies of the fallen Bluecoat soldiers.

Now everyone was told not to touch Long Hair, because we had a plan for his body so he could be stripped, but not mutilated in any manner whatsoever. So after he was identified, we put a sentry to guard his body, to ensure that our plan was not changed in any manner. I had given Pizi a letter, and this letter was to be placed upon Long Hair's lifeless body, and it was addressed to the Great Father himself.

I went to Hazel Rhonda, because she had the best handwriting in the entire clan, and in her very best penmanship, she drafted two identical letters, as a warning to the person who was in control of the fallen soldiers. Hazel Rhonda may have been a child, but she had always been exposed to proper schooling. She was the best of our best in this respect, and she had and still does to this day have excellent writing skills, which is why I guess that she fell in love with teaching in her adult life. Because she had been required to do something so important, which was to help our family's friends live and be free.

So I challenged her in a positive manner, to draft me two letters, which she did in about two weeks or so. We went over and over again on the wording and finally they had the sound and tone that I was looking for. The letters looked identical to one another, which is simply amazing to think about. They were drafted in perfect English, and they had a distinct style and look to them.

The letters said, "To the Great Father, hence known as the President of the United States of America, we are sending back to you, your greatest solider, dead but not mutilated, as a sign of respect because he possessed the true warrior spirit that lived inside of him, the soldier. We want you to know that we are a humble and simple people, but we shall not be bullied nor forced from our lands. We want you to leave us alone, and respect our sacred places, and hunting grounds, and we are tired of your double-dealing ways and your words that have never had any meaning. Once again, we just wish to be left alone, and to live in peace and prosperity. In closing, our warriors are not scared of your Bluecoat soldiers and will be ready for anything that may come our way. We are watching you and this vigilance is eternal. Signed, The Teton Lakota and Sahiyela Nations."

Pizi said that he placed the letter on the body, really under a rock that was under Long Hair's head, so that it would not blow away in the wind. But strangely, history has never ever spoken of, or even mentioned this letter and it was as if it never ever existed. But we all know that it did, because we still to this very day have the identical copy of it. And we could only imagine what the face of the person who found it on the Battlefield must have looked like. Stunned, I am sure! But whatever happened to this letter is the real question and more importantly why has there never ever been any mention of it?

The Bluecoats pulled back and were delayed in their troop movements, as they regrouped their forces, and devised a new strategy. This delay gave us the additional time that we needed to get the innocents safely tucked away and beyond the reach of the Great Father's armies, in the ancient land of the Sahiyela's Grandmothers, called Canada. The innocents did not simply vanish into thin air, away from sight, never ever to be seen or heard of, ever again like a lot of First Ones Tribes and Nations suddenly did, when their land was forcefully taken from them, in the eastern parts of the so called United States of America.

So the Battle of The Greasy Grass was a successful diversion and strategy, and because of it, the innocents from both Nations were not exterminated. And more importantly, these two Nations, as history has shown, did not die out and become extinct. The Oceti Sakowin were right in their actions, because they were dealing with a person, the Great Father, who had broken every treaty that he had signed in good faith, with not only the Lakota people but with all Native people or First Ones, that his position of power or office in this society had come into contact with, to date.

After the Battle of the Greasy Grass, everything changed, and the Bluecoats changed their strategy, by first increasing their troop strength at the Agencies, and then they seized all horses and weapons belonging to the First Ones at the Agencies for fear that they would be given to the resisting bands. Even though almost two thirds of the First Ones had already given up, and lived on a reservation, they still lumped everyone together as a whole. And, because of the resisters they played the blame game, and made everyone pay for the actions of a few, or really less than a third.

In Canwapekasna Wi (Moon of Falling Leaves), or October, when they felt that they were finally ready this time, they surrounded the villages of both Mahpiya Luta and Can Wape Sa (Red Leaf). First, arresting the pair of them in a very public way, conveniently in front of the various newspaper correspondents and then secondly holding them responsible for not turning over individuals who arrived into camp from the hostile bands. They made it very rough on everyone, and they even used starvation as a new and primary tactic on all Agency inhabitants.

They brought in most of the troops of the entire Federal Army, some say it was over 90 percent, and then in Wantiyetu Wi (Moon of Starting Winter) or November , as a test of their updated plan, they discovered and then defeated a village of our Northern Sahiyela brothers and sisters, in what is known as the Dull Knife Fight. In Wiotehika Wi (Moon of Hard Winter) or January of 1877, they battled Tashunca Uitco at the Battle of He Sumanitu Taka (Wolf Mountain), and then at Clear Creek, Spring Creek, and Ash Creek.

They were relentless in their pursuit, and they had more resources, of men and an endless supply of weapons most notably this time, the Winchester Model 1873 repeating rifle. They used a new weapon, called a Gatling gun and that, along with an improved cannon, which was developed during the so-called Civil War, which was called a Hotchkiss gun. They now did not even have to get close, to be effective. They could now kill at a greater distance, and the people of the horse culture on the Great Grass Sea did not have a chance to even get within striking distance.

They strangely then began sending certain men out on peace delegations, to talk the hostiles that were still trying to live in the old ways. And, to convince them to surrender to the Bluecoats because, the old ways were finished, and now gone. And, low and behold, the First One that was sent out was none other than Sinte Gleska, himself.

He now appeared to be in their pocket, more than ever, and he was a different person. It is said that the Great Father had also decided that they must break the hold and sway of the Great Chiefs, and that this was to be done by any means necessary, which really meant, to devise a way to kill them off.

All of the Great Chiefs were targets and were on some kind of secret list. And, there was even talk of bounties being given, for the death of a chief based upon a ranking system or hierarchy. So, once they had been fooled into surrendering to old friends and respected men of peace and honor, they could then figure out a way to kill them and to do it in such a way that it appeared, that the Bluecoats were not actually involved.

Even though we all knew that they were the phantom menace, who hung out in the shadows, and who was behind the curtain pulling all of the strings, like the puppet master does. The Bluecoats, seeing how successful their starvation tactic was working, started to use it as their main military tactic against our friends. And, no matter where you were in this crazy situation, called "Nation Building," or really stealing the land and you can call it what you want starvation was used as a major tool of their type of diplomacy.

They first starved the ones on the Reservations or the Agencies, to keep them weak and under their control, because in any jail, you want to control the prisoners and, to keep their energy levels, as low as possible so that one could control any breakouts. Because they would hopefully, be too physically tired to become obstinate and be much easier to control.

So all of the Indian Agency trading posts were the primary dispenser of this kind of care, the starving kind of care. The Congress of the United States, on February 28th of 1877, then voted to repeal the 1868 Fort Laramie Treaty, which took back the Black Hills, along with 40 million more acres of Oceti Sakowin lands, and more importantly permanently established the Indian Reservation.

This Congressional Act, which was also known as the February Act of 1877, replaced the Manypenny Agreement, which was a sleight of hand way to unilaterally claim the land, for white settlement. And, it modified the boundaries of reservations stated in the 1868 Fort Laramie Treaty, and only full- blooded Indians residing on the Reservation are allowed to the Agreements and to benefits from this Act as well as past treaties.

But the problem around this Act was that it states that the government purchased the land from the Reservation, even though there was no valid record of this transaction. At the same time the Indian Agencies forced the Reservation chiefs, by using this starvation tactic against the Innocents, to sign away the land, even though the chiefs did not know at the time what they were signing, and more importantly the ones who were actually forced to sign this fake bill of sale, did not represent all of the Teton Lakota Nation.

Then at the same time, the Bluecoat soldiers were killing off or burning up any and all food sources, in the field of battle that had any value that could be used by the hostiles, to aid them in their cause, for it is kind of hard to fight if you are hungry and cold. Food then becomes a weapon and a way to defeat your enemy. The Bluecoats chased our friends relentlessly in the early months of 1877 and trust me when I say that 'there was no rest for the weary.' and it was a series of running gun battles.

So, although they fought the 'game' fight, the Bluecoats were able to grind them down, and break their spirits for eternal war, or the prospect of it. They fought as hard as they could, for as long as they could. And finally, when they were certain that their families and friends were truly safe in

Canada, because of Pizi and Tatanka Iyotake's guidance, they rode over the border, and into freedom to the lands of our Sahiyela grandmothers, Wood Mountain Saskatchewan with the Bluecoats right there hot on their trial, ready to pounce and exterminate them.

The Canadian government provided them with security against persecution. And, the Great Father's Bluecoated soldiers could not finish them off right when they almost had them, all lined up and ready for the kill. The outlaw bands in the early spring of 1877 began to surrender en masse. And in Canwapeto Wi of 1877, Mahpiya Epata (Touch the Clouds) and Woqini (Roman Nose) surrendered with their bands at the Spotted Tail Agency. While Tashunca Uitco and his band, which included Sunka Iye (He Dog), Wicasa Tanka Sikala (Little Big Man), Kagi Maza(Iron Crow), and others surrendered at the Red Cloud Agency.

For the next four months, Tashunca Uitco stayed in or near his village, as rumors began to circulate that Tashunca Uitco was going to slip out of his village and return to the old ways. Things now appeared to be more complicated than before. Because before, there seemed that there had only been one choice fight or surrender, but now nothing seemed clear.

At the Agencies, the wacicu had all of the power, and the First Ones who wanted to do well, spent all of their time just getting the wacicu to like them. This created a new world, which was one of deceit, betrayal, backbiting and continual gossip and constant lying. Tashunca Uitco respected his Uncle Sinte Gleska, but he knew that the Bluecoats had created this new world, and that his Uncle was now deeply a part of it. Also, he knew that the Red Cloud and Spotted Tail agencies did not like one another, nor did they like him and his band.

He did not have that many people that he could really trust. And when he asked for his own agency that would be on the Beaver Creek, on the west side of the Black Hills, he could really feel the distrust and tension. The Great Father wanted him to come to his lodge in Washington, so that they could show him off as a war trophy. But Tashunca Uitco declined the invitation, no deal, or at least not until he got his own agency. They also asked him to be in a Wild West Show, but he said no, because he did not want to be put on display and to him, they only wanted to just further humiliate him.

The Bluecoats then wanted him to help them to fight against Chief Joseph and the Nez Perce who had escaped detention and were on the run for Canada. Which he ultimately would not do, and which caused a lot of tension with the Bluecoats. Then, a well-placed rumor that an Indian woman named La Kicun Wiya (Woman Dress) was to said to have started, began to circulate at all of the Agencies. Namely, that Tashunca Uitco intended to kill General Crook, at a meeting that was to take place between the two, at Camp Robinson.

Crook then decided that he was too dangerous to have around anymore. So he ordered that Tashunca Uitco be arrested and be sent away to be in exile at a prison called Fort Jefferson, which was on the far tip of the Florida Keys. He then also sent extra soldiers to ensure that this would happen. But when they got to his village encampment, he had slipped away to his Uncle, Sinte Gleska's agency be- cause his wife Aikita Sapa (Black Shaw) was ill, and he wanted to make sure that she was safe in the lodge of his parents.

On the way back, he met up with the Bluecoats, or really a large group of Indians who were wearing the Bluecoats of the wacicu soldiers, that were looking to arrest him. They took him to Fort Robinson, and once he arrived there, they led him to the guardhouse to be jailed. And once he realized that they were leading him to jail, and not to meet the officer in charge, he whirled around and tried to resist.

But Wicasa Tanka Sikala held his arms behind him, and in the struggle to break free, a private named William Gentles bayoneted him twice, as he then slumped to the ground. Tashunca Uitco's last words that he uttered to Wicasa Tanka Sikala, and the others who were present, were, 'Let me go my friends, for you have got me hurt enough.' They laid him on the floor, and when his father and mother arrived, he was said to have stated, 'Father, it is no good for the people to depend on me any longer, I am hurt bad.' He died a little before midnight, on Canwapegi Wi (Moon of Colored Leaves) or September 5th, 1877, and the next morning his body was turned over to his elderly parents.

About a month later, when Sinte Gleska's Agency was moved to the Missouri River which always seemed a bit underhanded, his parents moved his body to an undisclosed location somewhere near Wounded Knee, according to legend. In reality, Crook himself probably was the one who had ordered his murder, in the first place, to remove the Bluecoats greatest threat, and the Lakota's greatest warrior, and one of the true masterminds behind the death of Long Hair. So his killing was a revenge killing. And it was done in such a way as to make it appear that it was a separate incident, and not a part of some grand master plot or plan, by the phantom menaces.

Upon hearing of this, we were all determined to dispatch Wicasa Tanka Sikala and anyone that had anything to do with Tashunca Uiltco's murder. Because, the Bluecoats made sure that it looked like a soldier had killed him, but we all knew the truth. Because why would Wicasa Tanka Sikala, actually receive a medal, for his role in Tashunca Uitco's death? A medal. And, after Tashunca Uitco's death, he became a scout for the Bluecoat soldiers, because the Bluecoats would not let him escape to Canada for protection from our retaliation, so this treacherous person, was saved from us, by joining them.

He then joined the Agency police force, and he did all kinds of dirty and down low things to please his wacicu masters or overlords. We tried very hard to redrum (murder) him on many occasions, but the Bluecoats always watched him like a hawk, because they knew of his value to them. And, they wanted to keep these types of people in their service, because he was capable of anything and would do anything to further their cause.

In 1879, a group of Chiefs requested an audience with us. And at this meeting, they told us a strange story about how young children were disappearing without any trace. Some were saying that they were being stolen away, to some place far away back east. We checked with our sources, and what we found out was horrible and extremely hurtful.

A group of 84 children, in the first group, were sent back east to a place named Carlisle, in the state of Pennsylvania to the newly established United States Training and Industrial Boarding School. It had been founded by, the former Indian fighter, (Captain) Richard Henry Pratt. This school's mission was to remove young Indians from their native culture and refashion them into members of mainstream American society. This was extremely troubling, because I could only imagine what it must be like to be snatched from your loved ones, and placed into a place, that gave you an American name, made you cut your hair, forced the English language upon you, and denied you, your native customs and traditions.

And if you spoke your native tongue, you were punished until you complied with their demands. You then could not relate to your own people. When they came back, these children were in a strange place, like being in a strange limbo or grey area no longer accepted by the tribe, and certainly not accepted by the wacicu. Years later, and purely by chance, did we find out that this tactic of 'cultural swapping' was used in other places throughout the world like in a place called Australia. And, the victims there were known as the 'stolen generation,' were captured and culturally swapped, in what just seemed like to be an updated form of slavery. All of this was just very troubling, and it seemed like it was only just another attempt to further divide the First Ones on many more different levels.

Everyone on the Reservations seemed scared and extremely frightened. And over the next 24 years, more schools that were based on the Carlisle model, were established outside of the Reservations along with 81 boarding schools and almost 150 day schools, on the Reservations themselves. Education became a main point of emphasis, and something that my family focused on, because we were determined to make a difference in the lives of our friends.

This is because our friends had accepted us without hesitation, unlike other First One Nations or tribes. When we were escaping the reach of the long knives, they took us in, and had helped us to survive in the wilderness of the Great Grass Sea Plains, and eventually to grow as a family. So we became determined to aid our friends, the Oceti Sakowin, and to save as many of the children as possible and keep them free and safe within the tribe. So, education once again came back into focus for us, on a grand scale and it once again was something that had plenty of meaning for us, and our new family members, as a whole.

Then shockingly, two years later on Wasuton Wi (Moon of Ripening) or August 5th, 1881, Sinte Gleska, was killed by Suka Kagi (Crow Dog), some say because he sold some land that did not belong to him. While others say that he stole a crippled man's wife, but in the end, it was just another ex- ample of some of the strange and mysterious things that were happening to our friends. Some say that he was always too quick to flaunt his power, and to boast about who he knew within the wacicu federal government, and that the wacicu themselves had grown tired of his behavior and thus he had to go.

Well, whatever the real reason, the wacicu officials dismissed the killing as the culmination of a quarrel over a woman. But everyone knew that it was the result of, and part of the secret plot, to break the power of the Chiefs. This killing shocked everyone, because he was the wacicu's man in their pocket, and if the one chief who had gone over to the other side was killed, then any and everything was possible.

Who would be next, we all wondered? And, what was the real reason behind his murder? All of the remaining Chiefs must be protected and watched over no matter what. The shadow warriors were then placed in key locations, all over the Oceti Sakowin Nation to protect the remaining group of great Chiefs from anything or anyone that had sought to harm them.

PART SIX

SEMPERFIDELIS/FIDELDENFENS
OR
ALWAYS FAITHFULL
DEFENDER OF THE FAITH

QUOTE:I DO NOT AGREE WITH WHAT YOU HAVE TO SAY, BUT I WILL DEFEND TO THE DEATH, YOUR RIGHT TO SAY IT.

In between the murders of Tashunca Uitco and Sinte Gleska, in late 1880, we got word that Pizi was coming back with the innocents from exile, and that he wanted to see me as soon as he got back across the border. We eagerly rode out with food and blankets, and we reached them in about a two days ride. He was happy to see me, just as I was also, to see him. He told me everything of his time in Canada at Wood Mountain and how the conditions were tough and extremely harsh. Strangely, he did seem different though, like a changed person.

And, I have always attributed this to the loss of his beloved wives and family, at the battle of the Greasy Grass that had changed his outlook. He seemed sullen and somewhat withdrawn, and really like his spirit had been broken by all of this. The weather in Saskatchewan was extremely cold in the winters, actually much colder than what they had all experienced before and they were literally all freezing and starving to death.

A lot of folks, after the first year of exile, were talking about going back, but Tatanka Iyotake refused to even acknowledge this, as an option. Because, he stated, that the Bluecoats would be waiting for them to exact revenge for the killing of Long Hair. Pizi in the beginning agreed with him, but after a few months he openly stated that they were strangers in a strange land, and that they must eventually return to the lands and stars that they were accustomed to no matter what the consequences. And, if they were to die, then at least it would be in the lands that they were familiar with.

Tatanka Iyotake and Pizi went back and forth, for nearly two years or more, until finally Pizi one night, just stood up and calmly stated at the Tribal lodge meeting, that he was going back no matter what, and that anyone who wanted to join him was welcome. He was not trying to interfere with Tatanka Iyotake's leadership but living in such hard conditions just did not make any sense to him anymore. And, besides he had gotten word that other Bands had surrendered, and nothing had happened to them. So, maybe it was just time, to go back home, before anyone else died from the harsh conditions.

About a little less than half of the people assembled, decided to go back with him, while the others decided to stick it out and remain with Tatanka Iyotake and Wanbli Gi. On the morning that they left, he warmly bade both Tatanka Iyotake and Wanbli Gi goodbye, and they set out and eventually slipped unnoticed across the border. And after a few weeks, they were back in their native homelands.

He thanked me for all of my suggestions and guidance, and he felt that despite the hardships, everything had been worth it, because the innocents had survived and given. that, the Oceti Sakowin Nation would live on. He also stated that he had grown tired of war, and that they had to come up with a new strategy because the wacicu were not going anywhere. And, so they must all change or be destroyed. The old ways were finished, and they must come up with a way to survive in the land of the wacicu.

The right of conquest had overtaken them, and they just had to accept the fact that they were now not the keepers of the land any longer. And, just as they had used the right of conquest to acquire their lands, the wacicu had now used this very same idea to acquire their lands from them. He was going to surrender, and he hoped that I could help him. Much like I had helped Mahpiya Luta to understand more fully the ways of the wacicu, so that he could help to make a difference in the lives of his people.

Pizi finally surrendered on Wiotehika Wi (Moon of Hard Winter) or January 3rd, 1881, at Fort Yates. And, he was settled on the nearby Standing Rock reservation, where somehow in a twist of fate, he became friends with the Indian Agent James McLaughlin. Then in another twist, only six months later, Tatanka Iyotake, after leaving Chief Wanbli Gi in charge of the ones at Wood Mountain—one who did not wish to ever return to their homelands, Tatanka Iyotake surrendered with his band of nearly 200 innocents, on Canpasa Wi (Moon of Red Cherries) or July 19, 1881, at Fort Buford.

There, he stated that he now wished to regard the soldiers and the wacicu race as friends. Two weeks later, he was transferred to Fort Yates, which was the military post that was next to the Standing Rock Agency. Tatanka Iyotake, it seems had seen the errors of his ways, and also more importantly that what Pizi had been saying for years, was true. And, that only his pride was the thing that had kept them all, both freezing and starving at Wood Mountain.

After Pizi had departed, it was his young son, Si Kagi (Crow Foot) who had asked him, why he was so intent upon proving his point. And who had said that his stubbornness was making their quest pointless, because in the end, they were just dying as strangers, in a strange land. And, that his pride had held them all as hostages.

It was this very same son, (Si Kagi) that he had sent as his peace representative to surrender his rifle to the commanding officer at Fort Buford, and it appeared that he too was now a totally broken and beaten man. He was said to have stated that, "He had wished that it be remembered that he was the last man of his tribe to surrender his rifle." He had also asked for the right to cross back and forth into Canada whenever he had wished.

And, he also wanted his own reservation on the Little Missouri River, near the Black Hills, but they knew that they had him; so they shipped him away as their sign of how they truly felt about him. Everyone seemed down and disheartened, and most felt that all was now lost, and hopeless. But what they all seemed not to see, was that they were able to save the innocents, the survival plan had worked, and their Nation was not totally wiped off of the face of the mako (land), like so many of the other 16,000 original tribes of the First Ones, in the United Snakes.

Sadly those were exterminated without a trace, and therefore were wiped out from history or really 'his story.' Around September of 1881, we received word through our sources in Xenia of some very troubling news, that our mother had died on November 22, of the previous year 1880, and that she was buried in a nice church cemetery that lie on the outskirts of Bath which is a town in Beaufort County, North Carolina.

It appeared that someone, whom we suspected was Master Jack hac paid for an extremely nice burial plot, with an expensive headstone, and this head-stone had an equally expensive black wreath on it. My Madre was in good health, but she had contracted scarlet or yellow fever on a trip to the West Indies, and after a prolonged battle, she slipped away one night in her sleep and was gone. We were all stunned and saddened, by the news of her passing, and we decided that we would be making a trip to Bath, North Carolina to try to retrieve her body.

All of the Ackitas Chanzee were determined to make the trip, but I decided that we should keep the scouting party light and use a smaller number of warriors so that we could move quicker and faster. Mamie came to me, and asked me if I would consider letting L'Ouverture also accompany us on the trip, but I said no. Now I said no, like I had always said, because I did not want him to participate in the family business, and I wanted better things for him than I had experienced.

I also realized that I was gone a lot, which meant that my time was very limited, as it was for all of my family members, and because of that, I did not have a great relationship with him. I mean I did have a good relationship with him but we had never ever not even once, had ever taken a trip together with just him and me. So he seemed a bit proper towards me whenever we were in each other's company.

Mamie recognized this and she always wanted me to have a better rela-tionship with him, and at some point I would have to being his father make amends with him, and bridge this gap. He seemed to have a great relationship with everyone else but me and it bothered me, but I always held my ground because I wanted him to live and have a normal life. He was very smart, and he could have been any- thing that he wanted to be, and I did not ever want him to be a warrior for the House of Calais-Vega.

Everyone said that he was funny and smart as a whip, and that he was an extremely fast learner. But I forbade him to participate in any warrior ac- tivities, and to be honest that seemed to hurt Mamie the most because secretly, as his mother, naturally she seemed to have a desire for him to follow in my footsteps and one day to become the Prime and leader of the House.

As I now look back on it, she was proud of our only son, and because he was the baby of our bunch of children, and the only boy, she had a relationship with him that was different than with the girls. They had this closeness be- tween them, and they were always together, and they did more things with one another than with anyone else. He always held her hand whenever they were out in public walking around, as he had always done from when he was a little little boy from when he had first started to walk.

Mamie, I later found out, had even gone to Tatanka Sica in private behind my back, to ask her for a favor that I must never ever be told about. This was that she wanted Tatanka Sica to privately train L'Ouverture in the young warrior ways of the House. She felt that he had an certain something that she had first seen in his father, from when they were little kids, and when she got older and more mature, she realized that it was the sign or mark of the warrior, that I had learned from mi Abuelo. This same mark or sign was what the Council of the House had seen, when they picked the Three Commanders, and her request was to please trust her, when she said that she saw this in L'Ouverture too.

Initially, Tatanka Sica did not want to do it, because she would have not felt comfortable about disobeying my orders, and really for going behind my back. And, she was to always remember that I was the Prime. But Mamie used her charm and wily skillful logic to persuade her to at least try it, at least once, and then she could make up her own mind. Also she would not be ac- tually lying to me, she would just not be telling me of what she was doing in secret so if she saw it in this manner, then she could ease her conflicted mind about lying to the Prime and her Master.

Well Tatanka Sica finally relented, because Mamie can be very persuasive in her observations, and after the first session was over, she saw a certain something in L'Ouverture that could not be mistaken. He did have the mark of the warrior; it was undeniable and he was an extremely fast learner. And, he already had a battlefield skill set that was extremely impressive and quite unique for someone who was not supposed to have had any previous warrior training.

So she began to train him in secret and away from prying eyes, and he became her secret shadow apprentice. So after a year, and many months, the news of my mother's death came. And this is when Mamie sensing an opportunity, decided to approach me about letting him participate in this very important mission for the House of Calais-Vega. She simply would not take no for an answer. And she continually worked on me, to get the answer that she wanted to hear.

I was like "...no, he can't ride a horse," but she was like, "...no, his horse-riding skills are top notch and probably better than yours." I was like, " .. no he has no in-the-field experience," but she was like, "...well Balaam, how or when will he ever get it?" Then surprisingly Tatanka Sica approached me, one day when we were in the field, returning from an observation mission. And she flatly stated that she felt that L'Ouverture was ready, because he now displayed a highly above average and superior skill set, for in the field- of-battle activities, and he was already at step four of Abuelo's young warrior training model.

He was a "crack," and she really meant crack shot, with everything from a Derringer to a W. Model 1873. And he possibly could, even in her opnion because he was in the shadows, so she did not have a way to openly test it match or rival Aaron's proficiency. And before he became her apprentice, it appears she thinks that he was already flawless with either hand, when wielding a bushido.

She then told me of Mamie's favor, and how in her opinion he was now ready, but his only flaw was that at times he lacked discipline. But, because he was in the shadows, and a secret with no peers, she could not properly have him disciplined in front of everyone else, like we all had publicly been, which is how you grow and become mature. But in time, he would gain what we all had acquired through endless training.

She said she felt that his lack of discipline was mainly because he was always quick to improvise, or take a chance on a course of action, because he was a great situational thinker and he possessed a very high intelligence quota, as his schoolwork could attest to. And, this is what made him ap- pear to be reckless in his choices, because he had not yet learned to take his time, and see all of the angles, before he decided on a proper course of action required to get the desired result, which was an in-the-field strategy that you just had to learn through experience. She then said that if I let him accompany us, that she would watch him like a hawk, and that he was her secret appren- tice.

All of this caught me a bit off guard, because she was my apprentice, and it was not like she had lied to me, or anything, she just had not said or dis- closed anything, and on top of that, she was not the only one who had exhibited this type of behind my back behavior. And if the truth could re- ally be told, it really got me now as I think back about it, because I really had no idea that any of this was even going on and also more importantly because I pride myself on knowing everything, that involves my family, yet I had been hoodwinked so to speak. So after constant pressure, from all sides, I finally relented, and everyone seemed happy and empowered by my act of attrition, and all seemed all right and okay in the House of Calais Vega.

The trip would be a fast moving one, and I would take the Terrible Three and L'Ouverture, while the rest of the Akicitas Chanzee would be on guard duty. The two Hell Raisers, Stacey and Alphonso, would be in charge, and I would leave Our Friend named Destiny behind so that they would be in charge of it and it's usage, along with all of our assembled weapons which would make the two of them very, very happy, because they both just loved weap- ons and the situational use of them. But really El Diablo would be truly in charge, and Tatanka Sica and I would both hold his face and look deeply into his eyes, and tell him to watch and stay closed to the compound, and to bite anything that came close to the compound while we were both gone and, with him secretly in charge he would be serious and on-point about his assignment and everything would be fine and in our control.

The total trip across and down and then back up and over, should take about a month, and it will be a hard ride, each and every day and it would consist of many long days and extra short nights. The place that we were going to was located in coastal plains area of North Carolina. It is the oldest town in the entire state, being first incorporated in 1705 and it is said to be the first nominal capital of the state before New Bern was established. It is located on the Pamlico River, close to the point, where the river empties right into the Pamlico Sound

We would dress in civilian style clothes and play the role of Freedmen Citizens, seeking horses for our expanding homestead in the Dakota territories. We would take an extra horse just in case we could liberate her body, so that we could bring back her earthly remains to be buried with honor in freedom, in a beautiful place of our choosing. Because in keeping with our tradition, I was both duty and honor bound to see her resting place, and really so that I could bring some closure to our greatest mystery, for my brothers and my sister and myself.

The information seemed credible enough, because it had come from a usually exceptionally reliable source within the network of information that we had always used. But there was something about it that I just could not put my finger on. For some reason, that just seemed, not right. My instinct was telling me to be wary and on guard, because this whole thing just seemed too neat and honest, but I am not about to trust just anybody or anything that I hear.

There was also something about the town of Bath itself that I also could not put my finger on, but hopefully in time I would remember. I also made a deal with Mamie that I would write down my experiences each and every night, a love letter so to speak, from me to her, so that when we got back, she could gain a sense of what I learned about him, or what he had learned about me, so that she could read how her men came together like she had always wanted. She was proud of us both, and she wanted us to get closer to one another, so that we could enjoy one another and really bring our expanding family closer and more rock solid from the inside to the outside.

We were talking on one of our usual right-at-dusk walks and talks, and she had stopped as I was telling her about my gift for her. Upon hearing me, she just walked very rapidly up to me, and hugged me, and I could feel the warmth of her tears on my shoulder. We stood there for a long time as I just let my woman hug me up to her delight. Mamie was standing there as we left that day, just beaming with pride, as her two men rode off together on our first adventure with one other, and hopefully we would use this time to grow closer to one another.

The entire House had turned out to wave good bye to us, and as we thundered away, into the day, I looked back to see my beloved Mamie one more time before we got too far out of eyesight and she had this big old grin all over her face, which made me kind of laugh and smile all at once.

L'Ouverture sure could ride his horse, and he rode like he was a part of the horse—somehow slumped forward in his saddle—almost like he was learning forward on its neck, with the reins loosely in his hands, palms up, with little or no effort, like it was a trot in the park which meant that he was not expending any energy, so the ride was not tiring him out. I started writing the very first day, and she was going to get a kick out of her gift of my love letter to her. He could also shoot his rifles very straight from his horse, while on a dead run, and if we rode up on any game as we thundered through the landscape, the Terrible Three all had a hard time getting off any shots. This kind of became the joke between the five of us and his accuracy was pinpoint and true he never missed his mark, which really meant that we all ate really, really well the whole trip there.

We rode hard in the day, and each night when we had stopped to rest, all five of us, had a good time with one another, as we enjoyed each other's company and the meal together. Mamie was right, he was funny, a somewhat mischievous trickster who liked to laugh, and he simply was a happy child. And, I saw why his sisters all just loved him to no end. He was respectful, and pleasant, and open and honest and he always asked direct questions when he wanted to know something.

I got to see his real side for the first time, as he dropped the formal and proper role with me, and opened up to me, like he always did to everyone else. Then one night, I suddenly realized that he looked like both of us, my beloved Mamie and me which really made me smile. On another night when the ride was over, when it came to mealtime, he pulled out of his knap sack, a big ole rabbit that he had caught and dispatched in the morning before we had saddled up for that day's ride. He had set up his trap the night before when we first got there, and he never even let on, that he had gotten that night's meal for us all that day, nor at any time during the ride.

He was a cool customer and he flowed effortlessly. And, he had this good energy about him that seemed right. The five of us had a great trip going across and then down, and L'Ouverture and me really enjoyed one another's company.

Tatanka Sica also beamed with pride, and one night I took her aside in private and asked her if we were okay. She looked puzzled, and asked if she should not be asking me, that question? I was like, "No, you are my apprentice, and so your health, education, and welfare are always a concern of mine."

And, as Tatanka Sica, I trusted the decisions that her role required her to make, and to please always remember that Mamie came to her as Tatanka Sica, and not as my apprentice Kara Grace. I did not need her to be conflicted in her mind about anything, and my love for her was never ever in question in my mind. I also wanted to thank her, for giving me an opportunity to truly meet my son, for the very first time. And I added that it would not have even been possible, if she had not made a grown-up decision and followed her heart and mind.

She was right about him, and he did have the mark of the warrior, because it appeared that it was in his blood, the whole time. I just did not want to see it, because I thought that my way was right for him. Not understanding that he had to make his own way, no matter if my true goal had really been to somehow keep him safe, and away for the dangers associated with the job of providing protection for the House.

My words made tears come to her eyes, as she hugged me tightly, and held me for a long time. I guess she was thankful, because she had assumed that I would be mad at her, and she needed me to know that at no time had she ever lied to me. She respected me too much to ever do that, she tearful said, as she then pulled herself together and became her usual self.

In about two weeks of hard riding, we finally got to the outskirts of Bath, North Carolina a little before dusk, and we went right to church. The church had a steeple bell tower, and it had a graveyard directly adjacent to it, that had five neat rows of headstones. There was a gate that you had to ride through on the approach to the church, with a fence that had been somewhat started but not yet completed and there were heavy woods behind the church that boxed the church in.

We dismounted about a quarter of a mile away, and Tatanka Sica set up the battle plan. And, she decided to set up a triangle perimeter configuration around the church, and just take out time and observe the scene. We would use hand signals and she wanted L'Ouverture to stay with the horses and watch how we surveyed the scene for any signs of trouble. He was in a great position off the road, concealed behind some rocks and thick underbrush, and he also had a great view of the road in both directions.

L'Ouverture had a funny look of disappointment, but his role was vital, because not only was he watching the horses, but because he was also watching our backs. And, he would be our secret wildcard shooter if the situation turned serious. Also, he was to follow our hand signals to a tee, and if we said shoot, he was to pour it on just like it was basic target practice.

Tatanka Sica positioned herself at the point of the diamond or triangle, so that she could always have her eyes on him, and we took our time and set up properly. I took the proper precautions, as I always did, but this time I had a sense of something—but I could not make it out clearly, as I slowly rode Pegasus through the gate, without even looking in the cemetery's direction, like it meant nothing to me. There

were the headstones, and I could see the head stone that was on the 4th row, that had an expensive looking black wreath on it, that was in plain view for all to see.

I continued forward, riding ever so slowly past the church. And, as I got closer to the back of the church, my ears started to hear faint sounds, as my nose began to smell the familiar smell of horse dung, in the air even though there were no horses present or in sight. As I kept riding, I could see a dung trail that lead from the back of the church towards the woods.

I dismounted and relayed a signal to Gabriel who was positioned on that side of the church to be alert, that something was not right. And, that danger could be lurking nearby, by using the eyes up hand signal that we all use, which consists of using your index and middle finger in a V shape, right in front of your eyes. He then alerted Aaron and Tatanka Sica, and we all then were on alert for danger, because something was going on. I then slowly walked back towards the woods, and then I backed off, as I decided to circle around behind the back of the church using Pegasus as a shield between the woods and me. I walked at a moderate pace, and just as I got to the other side, I could see Aaron, who was giving me the hand signal to look up, and that something was moving about in the church steeple tower. I then looked back at Aaron who was directing my attention to Tatanka Sica, and I could see her giving to me the hand signal from her position as if she too, had sensed that something was not right, not only up in the bell tower, but also more deep into the woods directly behind the church.

I replied with the horizontal flat palm signal that meant for us to hold and wait for them to make the first sign of movement, and then I gave to her the neck slash signal, which meant for us to take the hostiles out and ask questions later. She then relayed the same signal to both Aaron and Gabriel and we braced for a confrontation. I then remember seeing Tatanka Sica waving all wildly to get my attention, and she was alerting me that L'Ouverture had disobeyed his orders, and had left his position, just about the very same time that he came riding up through the gate.

He smoothly guided his horse directly to the cemetery and then he saw the expensive looking black wreath that was positioned on the headstone. Then he went directly to the fourth row. He stopped his horse directly on the small path that lay behind this and every row, and he just smiled as he yelled out, " Over here, I have found it..." and then as he turned his head slightly to the left, in the general direction of the church itself, a rifle shot rang out from the bell tower, and a bullet struck him right above his left eye, killing him right on the spot, and in that instance, the L'Ouverture that we all loved and admired was forever gone. His lifeless body crumpled from the saddle and crashed onto the ground, as his blood just ran out, to form a medium sized dark wine colored pool in the dirt. I just remembered yelling "NO!" as I raced to his body, and scooped him up into my arms, as I tried to stop the bleeding with my hands pressing hard upon the bullet wound that was in his lifeless head. I do not remember much of anything else, and everything got blurry and it was as if time itself had stopped, but I could hear numerous rifle shoots and sounds whizzing about in the air, and I could sense a general madness or chaos all around me and L'Ouverture's body. I then just cradled his body in my arms, for a very long time, as tears started to stream down my face, and I was both dazed and all bloody, but everything else did not matter, not even my own safety. My tears were for the loss of my only son's life, because once you are gone you are gone, and there ain't no coming back. My tears were for my beloved Mamie, because I have always sought to protect her, and shelter her from any and all hurt or pain that this life brings to each and every person, but this was going to hurt her, in the worse way and it would be something that she may never ever get over for as long as she lived on the planet.

Her survival was going to now depend upon us, her beloved family, because it was, she, who persuaded me, against my wishes, to bring him. And, this then meant that she was going to eternally blame herself and we, her family, are going to have to keep her safe. And, she will need around the clock attention, as we nursed her back to health. Because her spirit and life force was going to take a severe hit because of this mess, and she may not even want to stay with us.

My tears were for myself, because I thought about the wonderful child, that I had just met, who was my beloved's and my child, a part of us both, and I almost because of my foolish and stubborn ways, missed out on knowing someone wonderful. Yes, my tears were for my daughters, who loved L'Ouverture like he was each and everyone's own child. The girls loved him, and they too would be heartbroken over his passing.

I had tears for many, many people, and all of this did not seem real or true, but sadly it was. Then after a while I could sense the Terrible Three, all standing around us, and when I looked up at them, they too all had tears streaming down their faces, as they too wept in the open, and without bashfulness. Tatanka Sica started crying so hard she fell down, and Aaron and Gabriel could not get her to stand up, for quite a long time. I finally started to move, because I could not be down, as well as my apprentice, so I forced myself to finally move.

I carefully wrapped up his body in a big blanket, and then hoisted it up onto the back of his horse, right behind the saddle. I surveyed myself, and I was a bloody mess, but I had to forget about this, and check on Tatanka Sica. I pulled her up, from the ground, and made her walk and snap out of it. Gabriel back-filled me in on the information that they had gathered, as Aaron took point to watch our exposed backs to the road.

This was a clever designed trap, that was created to kill one person, and that person was supposed to be me. The Terrible Three had tortured the two men in the steeple Tower, the spotter and the actual shooter or triggerman. There also was another man at a campsite that was where the horses and the campfire was located, and all three of them were easily and quickly captured and forced to tell what they knew, before they forfeited their lives.

A very rich man, had paid for their services, and they were to simply lie in wait, for anyone to appear at the gravesite, and if someone appeared no matter who it was, and went to the headstone that had the black wreath on it, that they were to kill this person on the very spot and then bring back the body to him for his inspection. He had paid double top dollar, and he said that, if they were able to accomplish this task for him, that he would further sweeten the deal on the backside.

He had even paid for an elaborate and expensive funeral that had a horse drawn carriage. The coffin was buried, and there was not one, but two grave diggers and it even had a pastor who read from the Good Book, and who blessed the dead person who had passed onwards to the next life. The headstone had the name ' Hermosa Perla' which means Lovely Pearl in English, beautifully engraved upon it, and the black wreath was placed upon the headstone by the head funeral director himself.

They were to wait for six months and he would advance them anything that they needed, but they were to stay on guard, and stay alert, because he needed this particular task completed. They did not know his name, but one in their group did, and he was some rich gentleman who used to originally be from Cumberland County. So no name on the sponsor, but they all had their suspicions and it was looking like it was our old Master Jack, who was the prime suspect in L'Ouverture's murder.

The next thing that we knew, it was Aaron drawing our attention by using hand signals, that a rider was approaching, from towards the town, as we took cover and waited to see what was what. He rode up into the gate, looking around like something was the matter, and Aaron just shot him right off his horse with an arrow, and they then took him to where the other prey were already stacked up. He was the person in charge, and he refused to talk, and give us the in- formation that we were seeking.

They rolled him up with rope, so that his arms were bound down at his side, and he could barely move. He played hard, until they tied his hands to a small table and then started cutting off his fingers two or three at a time. And it was then, after other of his body parts started being lopped off, like his ears and then his nose, it was just a matter of time before he told us everything that we needed to know. Their patron was a Mister Edward Teach Esquire, who was a very powerful and influential citizen of the state and he was paying for the whole thing, which was some kind of secret deal, which was to be done out of the public eye, and off the books.

He had a house in Bath, on the eastern side of Bath Creek at Plum point. His house, which has always been in his family, was near the home of an Ex-Governor of North Carolina named Charles Eden. The four of them had been selected because of their unique skill sets that they had learned and then developed, as members of the Grand Confederate Army in the Great Civil War amongst the states. They did not know why he wanted someone killed, nor did they know why he had paid for such an elaborate funeral service, and they all had actually wondered to themselves, just who was the person in the coffin.

Bath was chosen because once the deed was done, they would be whisked aboard a waiting ship, through Beaufort Inlet, which would take them into the Atlantic Ocean, and then down to New Orleans, Louisiana for a restful vacation. He was only following orders, he said, and that he had told us everything that he knew, and we had already disfigured and maimed his person, so could we please let him go? As soon as he said that he had honestly told us everything he knew, I stepped behind him, placed the black wreath upon his head and then using my bushido, cut his throat from ear to ear.

We dragged his body to the back of the church and stacked it up, like we have always done to our prey or victims, and everything was in a line, the four dead men, and their five dead horses. We dug up mi Madre's grave and to our surprise the coffin was empty! Empty! He had done all of this to kill me, and he had spared no expense to entice, entrap and then dispatch me.

I then decided to send this Edward Teach, a personal message from me to him, as I then burned down the entire church as well as set the surrounding brush on fire also. All of which was probably a very eerie scene, for the eyes to behold—smoke, fire, death, destruction, and four dead killers. We rode for a long time, as tears just continued to stream down Tatanka Sica's face, but we pressed onward to create some distance between us, and the trap.

That first night of his death, no one said anything to one another, as if we were all strangers in the night to one another. We did not even eat, and we all were quite worried about Tatanka Sica, because she had lost all of her rock solid composure, which was one of her greatest strengths and attributes. After two days, I decided that the Terrible Three needed to see me pull it together, because we still had many miles to go before we made it back home and to the family.

The next night, after the day's hard ride, I pulled Kara Grace to the side, just her and me, and put my arm around her, and made her lean onto me. I did not hate her, nor was I even mad at her, and his death was certainly not her fault.

His lack of discipline caused his death, and no one should blame them-selves, because his actions although noble, were reckless and showed a lack of observation skills on his part, because you should never let your passion cloud your judgment.

This was going to be hard on all of us, because his death was a painful reminder that what we're going through, as a family in our quest for true Freedom was serious and nothing to be dismissed nor joked about. Kara Grace was concerned about Mamie, because she felt that Mamie would somehow blame her, and that this would affect their wonderful relationship with one another. But Mamie would not blame her I said, she would blame herself, and so Kara Grace should not try to blame herself. And, it was okay for Kara Grace to grieve, but we needed Tatanka Sica to return because danger was lurking everywhere around us, and we needed her insights and wisdom.

And, if to get herself together, she wanted to relinquish her position of Tatanka Sica, until she could again focus her mind it was okay. So Gabriel was appointed Tatanka Sica, the House of Calais-Vega's Shirt Wearer and Pipe Holder, and although he did not want it, because he felt that he had not earned it, he accepted the position and stepped up to the challenge.

We rode hard and in less than two weeks we were back at our compound. As we rode in, around noon, El Diablo was first to meet us. His low shrieking howl sounded out in a manner that seemed as if he could sense that some-thing very bad had happened. And then everyone started to ap- pear and gather around us, to say welcome back.

There was this eerie silence, as the Two Hell Raisers were the first two to sense that L'Ouverture was missing as they used eye contact with Aaron to get their answer, and then as Mamie appeared sort of half running, all excited because we were back, all happy and smiling, and then the look of horror appeared on her face as she realized that L'Ouverture was not with us and missing. Then she started to violently shake and scream as she real-ized that a body was over the back of his favorite horse, as a collective gasp, and then screams and yells along with crying were heard all throughout the crowd.

Mamie then looked at me, shaking her head no, no, as her eyes rolled back into her head, as she passed out and crashed hard upon the ground. We gathered her up to take her inside, as Gabriel delivered the bad news to all that had assembled. We took L'Ouverture's horse, and body into the barn area, and removed his body from the back of the horse, to prepare it for his going home ceremony.

His body was bathed, and then anointed with oils and wrapped in a beautiful set of sheets, and then placed upon a funeral pyre with all of his favorite things, after which all was then set a fire, as we stood solemnly at attention until it burned down to nothing but ashes. Kara Grace stood at attention wearing her robe with the hood pulled down over her head, and at some point, she removed it, to reveal a totally bald head to everyone's shock and amazement. All of her long and beautiful hair was gone, and she was almost totally bald to her skin. She did this as a sign of herself inflicted sorrow about the loss of her apprentice, and she was still greatly affected by all of what was going on, as if she was hurt to her deepest core. Some people openly cried, while others seemed numb and in shock or denial, and everyone was visibly shaken by all of this, because he was much loved. At the end, we scooped up all of the ashes, and placed then into a nice urn, so that we could properly scatter his ashes at one of his favorite places when the time was right.

All of our five daughters were crushed by the loss of their much beloved baby brother, and they too were in various forms of either denial, or shock or hurt or extreme sadness, but Mamie was worse, as I knew that she naturally would be. And she was unconscious for days and days. She did not even go to the ceremony, and she seemed like she had lost her mind, or really the ability to focus it. When she finally opened up her eyes, she would not eat, or drink and her mind seemed like it was a very far off and away place.

I thought that we were going to lose her, and everyone was scared and anxious, and she appeared to not want to remain with us any longer, as if her will to life force or energy had been snapped or sapped by the death of our only son. Finally after about three weeks of this behavior, I could not take it any longer so I took a couple of horses, and took some hard tack, and scooped her up in my arms, and rode out far into the Sea of Grass, beyond the Bad

Lands. I made a small fire, and just held her in my arms, talking to her until she came back to me and us.

It took about 4 days for her to join us again, but I guess, after my constant talking to her, telling that we all loved her, and that it was not her fault, nor did I blame her, and then finally if she was going to die, then I was prepared to die also, because she was the sun in the sky of my world. I was awakened by her moving around, to get a blanket for me, as she weakly smiled back at me, and said thanks. We stayed out just her and me for about three weeks, and we stayed until she was about back to her old self.

We talked about everything, and we played with one another in the grass, as if we were teenagers again, and when her laugh came back, I knew that she or we would be able to make it. One day she looked me right in my eye, and asked my why did people have to be so evil with one another?

Why could we not all just live in peace and respect one another? All that I could say was that to me, it appeared to be something very familiar about this whole thing, and that I had my suspicions.

This whole thing appeared to have been a way to either trap or really kill me, and only one Blanco knows what my weakness is, and how to use it against me. Our son was in the wrong place at the wrong time, and no matter whom it was who showed up at that headstone, that person was to be killed, and that is a fact. L'Ouverture was with us only a short time, but we were truly blessed to be in his presence, and we were all better because of the experience of knowing him.

Time does heal all wounds, they say, but for me, time would never heal the hole in my heart and mind because of his loss. But I was not alone in my feeling of loss, and we all had been fundamentally changed by his death, but in the end, the part of her healing was needed, and Mamie enjoyed this healing time with just her and me. Everybody was happy to see us, when we finally got back to the compound, and we were met by Kara Grace, who rushed to Mamie, as they hugged one another and went off, by themselves to walk and cry and talk. El Diablo, who was wagging his tail in affection, trailed closely right behind them.

When they finally came back with El Diablo happily in tow, a couple of hours later, they both were back to being themselves, but Kara told me that she did not know when she wanted to resume her role as Tatanka Sica Gabriel also informed me that the Akicitas Chanzee had all voted, and that L'Ouverture had been given young warrior status, and therefore in the family records, it will show that he died while on his first mission in the field, while in service for the House.

That would really help both Mamie and Kara Grace, I thought, and it was like a blessing because he being a determined young warrior, was what they both had seen in him, and what they both were so determined for me to see and understand.

I then took Mamie off to the side and gave to her the letter that I wrote to her, while we were on our trip down south. She looked a bit startled, but she took the letter and went inside and sat down in a chair and began to read, as tears formed in her eyes, and she laughed and smiled, and when she was finished, she took my hands in her hands and she just beamed at me, as she stared into my eyes for a long time. She finally said that she loved me, and that she really appreciated my gift to her because she got her wish fulfilled, and her men had truly come together and bridged the gap that had been between them.

She then hugged me tightly and she just held me for what seemed like hours. The whole time, that I was dealing with Mamie's and the rest of the family's mental health concerns one day at a time, something was nagging at both my mind and soul, and I just had to know the truth. For the whole thing seemed like it was very familiar, and it was like I was forgetting something, about this Edward Teach that I needed to or was supposed to remember.

So, I started to consult my resources and after a secret trip that Gabriel and his apprentices, the Two Hell Raisers, took to a library in St. Louis, to find a rare copy of a certain book, 'A General History of the Robberies and Murders of the Most Notorious Pyrates,' we had the answer. Edward Teach was known in history by the name of Black Beard, who was the notorious English pirate who operated in both the West Indies and the east coast of the American colonies. Once I heard the name Blackbeard, and that he died on November 22, 1718, things really began to come together in my mind.

Blackbeard had been given a pardon in June of 1718, by Governor Eden, along with some property, that was adjacent to his, in the sleepy town of Bath, which was located in Beaufort County. But some feared that he could not be trusted, and once his money ran out that he would eventually return to his old ways. So, the Governor of Virginia, Alexander Spotswood, arranged for him to be killed in a cleverly designed trap that he completely financed, using the Crown as his muscle.

Blackbeard was killed in a tense battle on November 22, which was why it was chosen as her burial date, to coincide with Black Beard's death. And, this Edward Teach fellow just had the fake lavish funeral for his hero Black Beard, who never had gotten to even have one. So it was Master Jack after all, who had set this whole trap up to kill me, and I see that his obsession with pirates had taken on an entirely new level.

There could be no one else but him, because there were just too many things that coincided with one another for it to be anybody else. For this person has bought Black Beard's old house and property, claiming that it was his family's land, and heir property, and he was even using this fictitious surname of a real pirate, like pirates often did while engaged in the business of piracy, so not to tarnish the family names. Black Beard's property even had a secret sailing slip, and I see that Master Jack had further diversified his wealth, because this Edward Teach was a highly respected arms maker, and dealer for the Confederate States during the so-called Civil War.

He had a couple of ships that he renamed Queen Anne's Revenge and Adventure, which were the names of Blackbeard's actual ships, and he used these very fast sloops, especially, the Queen Anne's Revenge to outrun the Northern Blockade for the Confederacy during the Civil War. During this time, Ocracoke Inlet was his favorite anchorage, because it had the perfect vantage point from which one could see any approaching ships traveling between the various settlements of the northeast Carolina coast. So the Yankee's never had a chance of ever catching him, because from far off, he could see their sails in the air, and he would simply slip around or through their nets and out run them into the Ocean.

He also was a serious rum and cigar maker, and he had a home, and rum making property located in Jamaica. He also had a small cottage that lay by the sea on New Providence Island, and this was his vacation home away from home, he would often boast, it was said. So Master Jack's alias was Ecward Teach or Thatch, and this Edward Teach seemed to just come to life. only just a few years before the beginning of the great civil war. So becoming Edward Teach allowed him to do all of his dirty business right out in plain sight, while the great southern gentleman Jackson Bernard Strickland Esquire could just sit back and reap the benefits and rewards of this secret lifestyle.

So all that this really meant was that this Edward Teach or whoever he really was, was now public enemy number one for the House of Calais-Vega and we were determined to kill him or die trying. Because the Ackitas Chanzee, were determined to avenge the murder of L'Ouverture and an eye for an eye is what we all saw as the only resolution for his murder. We started using all of our resources, to track down Master Jack who now seemed to be reliving the life of Edward Teach, and we would take our time and do this right, no matter how long it took, because after all we were dealing with a very rich, powerful and resourceful individual who did not wish to be tracked.

All of this did not sit well with me, because I had often wondered just what happened to all of the various plantation owners' factors of production, which are land, labor and capital, after the so called great Civil War. It appeared that these owners went from plantation owners, to the leaders of corporations. And it has always been interesting to see, how all throughout the south, that these vast and mighty corporations seemingly sprung to life, just around the same time that the plantations ceased to exist and had vanished into thin air.

News then came that Tatanka Iyotake on Canwapeto Wi or May 10, 1883, had been allowed to rejoin his tribe at the Standing Rock reservation. He had been held since 1881 at Fort Randall, as a prisoner of war, because it was feared that his mere presence might incite riot and or rebellion, at Standing Rock, when he had first surrendered. So when he had first gotten back in

1883, the Indian Agent in charge of the Reservation, James McLaughlin, who was now Pizi's friend, and so called mentor, was determined to treat him as he would any other Indian man, with no special privileges, and he even had the nerve to force him to work in the fields with farming tools and do what our friends consider as woman's work.

But Tatanka Iyotake knew his own authority, and he used his gift of gab, to enhance his place with McLaughlin's superiors along with a visiting delegation of U.S. Senators. Then surprisingly in 1885, we all heard that he had been allowed to leave the Reservation, and join Buffalo Bill Cody's Wild West Show, the same show that Tashunca Uitco had refused to join before his death some 8 years earlier in 1877. It was said that he earned $50.00 dollars a week, for riding once around the arena, and he was a very popular attraction.

It was said that he always cursed his audiences in Lakota, and he even charged for his autograph and picture. He even on one occasion, met the Great Father (Grover Cleveland) and even shook hands with him, although he claims that he did not even know who he was at the time, and only did know, after he had left and went to the hotel that evening to rest for the night. He quit after only four months out on tour, because he grew tired of the wacicu and their simply confounding ways of mockery and hero worship.

When he came back, to the Standing Rock Reservation, he lived in a cabin on the Grand River, near where he had been born. He refused to give up the old ways, as the Reservation rules required everyone to do, still having and living openly with his two wives, and rejecting the religion of the wacicu, although he did send his children to the nearby Reservation Christian school at the Fort (Fort Yates), because he believed that the next generation of Lakota would need to be able to both read and write in the wacicu's language.

He was still a powerful chief, and everyone knew it and more importantly you could also feel it, like you do wind in the air, on a windy and cool day. In 1887, the Dawes Act, which was also known as the General Allotment Act or the Dawes Severalty Act, was adopted by the Congress, on February 8th. It was authorized by the Great Father (Grover Cleveland), to survey Indian tribal land and then divide it into allotments for individual Indians.

The real hope was to achieve at least six goals, which were the breaking up of the tribes as a social unit, the encouragement of individual initiatives, to further the progress of native farmers, reducing the cost of native administration, the securing of parts of the reservations as Indian land, and the most important goal was, the opening of the remaining land to white settlers for profit.

This Act would force the native tribes to adopt the values of the new dominant society and hopefully, make them see that the land was real estate, which was to be bought and developed. It was not something to be valued and cared for because it represented something that produced and sustained all life, and something that embodied their existence, their identity and an environment of belonging.

The social unit was viewed as a highly cohesive group that was led by a chosen chief, who used aging traditions to exercise power and influence among its members. These strong knit societies were led by powerhouse men, who were opposed to any changes in their lifestyles, and ways of being. And more importantly, they objected to the Euro- American lifestyle of property ownership.

That, then was the real reason why the Bluecoats had first sought to break the power of the Great Chiefs, because without them providing leadership to the tribes, they were rendered ineffective, which would open the way for the opening of the remaining land to white settlers for a profit. So the Dawes Act paved the way for the final act in their plan of stealing the land. And, it was the last piece of the proverbial puzzle, or the final nails in the coffin so to speak. The Dawes Act would then finally lead to their new end game, which was the abolishment of the tribal governments by abolishing tribal jurisdiction of Indian lands. This would make everyone unable to have their rights heard and understood by their own kind, and thus creating an even bigger division amongst each tribe member. As each one when it came to the law, would then have to fend for themselves.

As I, and the others, all saw it, the 1887 Dawes Act was just another insult and slap to our faces was ratified by the Federal Government.

In late 1888 and early 1889 the original 1887 Dawes Act was ratified by the Federal Government, in order to legally sell more Lakota lands. And of course, it was opposed to by both, Tatanka Iyotake, and Mahpiya Luta, but somehow the amendment was mysteriously signed. And we found out much later, that the government agents used subterfuge to obtain the necessary signatures, by using children's sig- natures, possibly the stolen 84, to make it seem that the Lakota could care less and were willing to part with more of their lands.

Also more importantly, in 1889, a Northern Paiute of those who were known as the Tovusidokado, from Mason Valley, which is now in the area of Nevada, began a movement that would spell further doom for the Oceti Sa- kowin. His native name was Wovoka, but he changed it to the wacicu American name, Jack Wilson. And he was seen as some- what of a prophet, because of a vision that he claimed to have experienced from the Christian God, during a solar eclipse on Wiotehika Wi (January) 1 of that year (1889). He stated that he stood before God in Heaven, and he had seen many won- derful things, along with many of his ancestors.

God also showed him a vision of a land filled with wild game and instructed him to return home and tell his people that they must love each other, not fight and live in peace with the whites. The people must also work, and not steal or lie, and they must not engage in any of their old practices of war. If they abided by these rules, then they would be united with their friends and families in the other world, and there would be no sickness, disease, or old age.

God then gave to him the Spirit Dance, which was a five- day event, and commanded him to bring it to the people and if it was done properly, the performers would secure their happiness and hasten their reunion of the liv- ing and the dead. In Jack Wilson's mind, if every Indian in the West danced the new dance to hasten the event, all evil in their worlds would be swept away, leaving a renewed Earth, which would be filled with love, faith, and food. Many Western Indians quickly accepted this new religion and, it was termed 'Dance in a Circle,' which was a variation of the 'Round Dance' that many First Ones routinely practiced.

It was a circular community dance that is held around an individual, who from the middle leads the ceremony, and it often included prophesying, exhortations, and intermissions of trances. Wovoka also had another vision that followed his first one, and in this vision, the Christian Messiah, Jesus Christ had returned to Earth, in the form of a Native American. The Messiah would raise all the Native American believers above the earth, and during this time the waccicu would disappear from all Native lands, and the tatanka herds along with all of the other animals would return in abundance.

The word Spirit, which translated into Oceti Sakowin, means 'Ghost of their ancestors would then return to earth,' which is where the Ghost came from in the term, Ghost Dance. All of this created a craze all throughout the West, as many tribes who had grown tired of the wacicu and their double-dealing and lying ways of nation building, sought a way to rid themselves of their new masters. In Cannapopa Wi (February) of 1890, the Federal Government once again broke a treaty with the Lakota, by adjusting the Great Sioux Reservation of South Dakota, into five smaller reservations, which was done, once again to accommodate wacicu homesteaders.

Representatives from many tribes all over the West, starting in Cannapopa Wi and Pejito Wi (Moon of Tender Grass) or April of 1890, were sent to visit Wovoka, and learn the dance and then go back to their tribes and teach their own people, the essential elements of it. The Oceti Sakowin representatives were Mato Nahtaka (Kicking Bear) and Tatanka Ptecela (Short Bull), and when they returned, in Canwapeto Wi of 1890, they bought this new religion back to their people, with another variation or twist.

This was that the Oceti Sakowin while performing this Ghost Dance would wear special shirts that Hehaka Sapa (Black Elk) had seen in a vision of his, and these shirts had the power to repel bullets. This variation surprised and bothered the wacicu, because in Jack Wilson's original version, it was supposed to be a non-violent dance, and revolve around peace and harmony. But now, the Oceti Sakowin had added its own elements to this, and had fundamentally changed this dance into something else that was far more sinister than its original design.

It was like that this dance was now a way to begin again the old ways, and to teach and preach insurrection and civil disobedience to the masses. This dance had to be carefully watched at all times, along with anyone who was associated with this new movement. And they would not take any chances, because they were not going back, only forward.

And their nation building strategy or plan would not be stopped or delayed by anyone or anything, and especially not because of a dance.

The Ghost Dance had been quickly accepted at both the Pine Ridge and Rosebud reservations, and so Mato Nahtaka (Kicking Bear) went to Standing Rock to visit Tatanka Iyotake and try to get him to join the Ghost Dance movement in a leadership capacity. But, although Tatanka Iyotake, was intrigued by its message and meaning he politely declined the offer, for many reasons for he realized that a lot of people would be affected by his decisions going forward, and he needed to stay away from anything that could further bring harm to his people.

So he would listen to things, but he would no longer become involved at a high level. His family was growing, and he just wanted to enjoy them, and watch his children grow up. But the spies who were watching Tatanka Iyotake reported back to James McLaughlin, that he had been visited by Mato Nahtaka, and that this could indicate that an alliance could be brewing.

Then a carefully concocted rumor was spread about the reservation, that Tatanka Iyotake was the real leader of the movement and that he was about to flee the Reservation with the Ghost Dancers. So, McLaughlin ordered Tatankapah (Bull Head) to take a group of men to his cabin, and arrest him before dawn, so that his followers could not react and aid in his rescue. Around five something in the morning, on Wanicokanwi (Moon of Middle Winter) or December 15th, (1890) in a freezing drizzle, 43 men, which consisted of 39 police officers and 4 volunteers, surrounded his cabin, as Tatankapah (Bull Head) and Chankpidutah (Red Tomahawk) went inside and placed him under arrest, and then they took him outside, as they quickly tried to leave.

Tatanka Iyotake's camp was quickly awakened by all of the commotion and noises, and a fairly large crowd had quickly gathered and surrounded the cabin and the police officers. To the assembled crowd, there was a lot of confusion, as to why he was even being arrested in the first place. And then the police officer's story suddenly changed, to one which said that the Indian Affairs Agent (McLaughlin) had just wanted to see him about a pressing matter, and that he would be coming back when their meeting was over.

Tatanka Iyotake sensed that something was not right, so he refused, and then resisted. This caused a massive struggle, and during the commotion, it was claimed that Mato Yukape (Catch the Bear), in defense of Tatanka Iyotake, fired his rifle and the shot struck Tatankapah, who then reacted by discharging his revolver right into Tatanka Iyotake's chest, just as Chankpidutah simultaneously as if he had been secretly instructed to do so, fired his revolver directly into the back of his head.

Tatanka Iyotake crumpled to the ground in a heap, and they say that he was dead before he even hit the ground. In that very fleeting instant of time, the Oceti Sakowin sadly had lost an inspirational leader, fearless warrior, loving father, gifted singer, a truly friendly one towards all others type of individuals, who was deeply religious, prophetic healer and holy man, and someone who simply could not be replaced on any level. Needless to say, all hell broke out, and within minutes it was all over, as six police officers lay dead, with two more mortally wounded, and Tatanka Iyotake and seven of his followers, along with two horses all lay dead upon the ground, with numerous more people on both sides injured or wounded.

Federal Bluecoat troops had to be called in from Fort Yates, to quel the panic and restore order, because to many people including myself, it was just a case of plain old murder. And more importantly, it strongly appeared or seemed that killing him, and not merely arresting him, was what the po- lice had come to Tatanka Iyotake's cabin for, in the very first place. The news spread quickly and people came from both far and wide, and the news of his passing really hit us in the House of Calais Vega very hard, because within the space of 13 years, three of the greatest chiefs of the Oceti Sakowin had been murdered, for no real and tangible reasons.

All had lived their lives to the fullest, and they all, in their own ways had sought to protect their people, and their deaths seemed so senseless and without reason. The mysterious puppet master, who was the phantom menace, who resided behind the curtain and in the shadows, and who was pulling all of the strings had struck again. And, the real men of valor and honor were now, forever gone, to be seen no more in this life.

Then exactly 14 days later, after Tatanka Iyotake's murder, on Wanicokan Wi (December) 29th, near Chankpe Opi Wakpala (Wounded Knee Creek), which is on the Pine Ridge reservation, another twist of fate occurred, which eternally scared us all once again. Two weeks earlier, over 200 members of Tatanka Iyotake's band who were fearful of any reprisals, because of the death of the 8 police officers fled the Standing Rock Reservation, and joined Sinte Gleska and his band at the Sahiyela River reservation with Si Tanka (Big Foot) as it's the leader, because he was a half-brother to Tatanka Iyotake, and who was also on the Federal Army's list of troublemakers.

His band all left to go and convene with the remaining chiefs, so that they could try and make some sense out of what was happening, and more importantly, why was this happening right now, at this exact moment in time and really, to ask for more rations and aid because for some reason, they were being starved to death, to keep them in line. But with 200 more mouths to feed, Si Tanka (Big Foot) had no choice, so he left his Reservation, with about 350 people all in total, to seek out help and aid for the new additions.

On the way to Pine Ridge to see Mahpiya Luta, on midday of the 28th of Wanicokanwi, 1890, they were intercepted by a 100-trooper scout detachment of the 7th Cavalry, southwest of the badlands, near Porcupine Butte. The troopers escorted them about five or six more miles, until they got to the Chankpe Opi Wakpala (Wounded Knee Creek), where they told Si Tanka to make camp for the night. Later that night, the rest of the 7th Cavalry under the command of a Col. Forsyth showed up. And, he instructed the soldiers to surround the encampment and to position the four Hotchkiss cannons up on the surrounding hill, pointed down and towards the tipis. The soldiers now had 500 troopers, and they seemed restless and out for blood, because they still seemed upset over what had happened at the Battle of the Greasy Grass, which had occurred 14 years earlier. That next morning, the troopers sought to disarm the Lakota, and during this confusion a medicine man named Zitkala Zi (Yellow Bird), began to supposedly perform the Ghost Dance, and state that the ghost shirts were bullet proof.

A struggle between two soldiers and one man over the one man's weapon broke out, just as Zitkala Zi (Yellow Bird) threw some kind of strange powder or dust into the air, and the soldiers thinking that this was some kind of signal, then began to open fire as commanded by their commanding officer. Now who shot first, was really not important, but what was important was that the soldiers were so enraged and out of control, that they chased down and killed the fleeing individuals. Many were shot in the back, and to everyone's horror and shock, many were defenseless women and children.

Some of these escaping people were killed over two miles away from the Creek itself. And then, to add more insult, the remaining children who had survived the initial canon and rifle fire, were coaxed out of their hiding places, within the surrounding ravines and crevices in the rocks and then rounded up and killed or really butchered and mutilated just like the 7th had been done after the Battle of the Greasy Grass, by the women and old folks.

Si Tanka was shot, and he fell in a way that appeared that he was trying to sit up, or get up and warn his people but sadly, he bled out and died, and then froze in that position. The troopers were reported by eyewitnesses to have said, "Remember Custer," or "Remember the members of the 7th who had been killed at the Big Horn," or "Remember the Battle of the Big Horn." Then, on Wanicokanwi 30th, the very next day after the massacre during a blizzard, the Drexel Mission Fight, which was the very last ever, military conflict between the Lakota and the Bluecoats, occurred on the White Clay Creek—also located on Pine Ridge Reservation.

The soldiers of the 7th, were sent to round up Lakotas who had fled the Rosebud Reservation, because of the massacre. And, in the ensuing fight, the mighty 7th Cavalry was pinned down in a valley by a combined force of Lakota warriors. Amazingly, to their rescue came the 9th Cavalry, which was an all Negro regiment that was nicknamed the Buffalo Soldiers, and who had distinguished itself by battling the Apaches on the southern plains.

This action struck a nerve in me, and the warriors of The House, because in our minds, "Why would Negroes want to fight for the same people who owned them just 25 years earlier?" Well, when the 9th showed up, and displayed their brand of ferociousness and heroism in a driving snowstorm no less the Lakota just gave up and surrendered en masse to them. But in reality, they had surrendered only to them, out of the respect that they had always shown, for their dark-skinned and buffalo-like haired brothers.

Then on Wiotehika Wi 2nd, 1891, after a three day blizzard had subsided, the military and eastern media showed up along with the military hired civilians to bury the frozen dead, as the media had a field day snapping pictures of the gruesome so-called battle site. The dead were all rounded up and then buried all together in a mass grave up the hill, where the Hotchkiss canons had fired down upon the innocents.

The military reviewed the situation. And despite numerous attempts by the commanding officer General Miles, to get Forsyth permanently relieved of his command—because Miles felt that Forsyth had deliberately disobeyed his orders and had commanded a deliberate massacre—the Secretary of War, Redfield Proctor, reinstated Forsyth and promoted him to the rank of Major General. Then, even stranger, 22 troopers who had participated in this massacre were awarded the Medal of Honor, which is the highest award that any Bluecoat soldier can achieve in the service of their country, for valor and heroic actions.

We decided right then, that because of all of the craziness and death that was all around us involving our friends which had crushed our hearts and minds, that it was time for a family vote, to see what we were doing next. And, if our journey had to keep moving, then we would do so. The Akicitas Chanzee, under Gabriel's visionary leadership had gone on a westward scouting mission. And they had been over the mountains to the Columbia Plateau, which was a region that then included parts of what is now, western Montana, Idaho, Oregon and Washington states. In Idaho there was a magnificent lake, Skeetsure (Coeur d'Alene), and beyond that in Cascadia there were extremely fertile lands, in this place called the Yakima Valley region, and there seemed to be a certain peace that resided in the lands. Everyone seemed intent upon staying unto themselves, and people with color are viewed as human beings and not someone's former chattel or property. The vote came back, and five of our family members wanted to stay, because it is customary for the wives to stay with their husbands' clan. But the rest of the family wanted to stay together, and to continue westward, and to be like Lot in the Good Book, and not look back. I remember when we went to visit our friends, to tell them that we were leaving and moving onward and that we were thankful for all of their love and support. It was hard, because my family had become intertwined within the Oceti Sakowin, and there was a certain amount of sadness, as we bid everyone good-bye because things would never ever be the same and everyone knew it. But in the end, we were all family with one another, so we truly were not saying good-bye for good it just was for now, and of course we would be back to visit. Mahpiya Luta and Pizi both seemed a bit sad, as their eyes twinkled and shined like they do when one is about to cry. We left in early spring of 1892, with snow still covering parts of the ground, and within weeks, we had reached the beautiful Skeetshue (Coeur d'Alene) Lake in Idaho that became our newest settlement and forward base camp.

We quickly became friends with the Skeetshure/Skitsuish or the Pointed Hearts, who were called by the first French traders into the area, the Coeur d'Alene (Hearts of Awls), as well as the Spokans who lived due west, and the surrounding area was well-stocked with game and good hunting. We also scouted Cascadia, and the rumors of the peace and tranquility that was all over the lands were true and reassuring. The lands also had this wonderful green and alive look to it, and I guess because it rained a lot, the water re-newed everything it touched, and it made everything beau- tiful and soft looking for the eyes and to the touch.

We had heard of a place, Siahl, that was named for a great Siab (high status man or chief) of the Duwamish tribe, and that it was close to a great gateway or passage to the ocean. Siab Siahl also known as Sealth, See-ahth, Seathle, or Seathl, was the son of Shweabe who was a Siab (chief) of the Dkh Suq Absh (Suquamish). And as a boy, in 1792, while at the summer village at Restoration point, he and his father were the very first ones to see the British Captain George Vancouver's ships, the HMS Discovery and the HMS Chantam, passing through the Khulch (Puget Sound-Strait of Georgia Basin), on the search for new and unclaimed lands for the Crown and Kingdom of England.

Once the ships saw the summer village and people on shore, they anchored offshore and very close to Restoration Point. And, his father was the first to greet the strange new visitors, to their lands. This began Siab Siahl's lifelong journey of self-discovery and self-awareness for him and his people.

He was a renowned man of peace and in his lifetime, he did a lot to foster amicable relations with all of the European- American newcomers to the area. His leadership and guidance allowed them to not only survive but also thrive and prosper in the region. And, he and his descendants have places of high esteem in the area's history and tradition.

So, we once again voted, and we left in search of this place. And in about three weeks' time, we reached our destination, which fascinated everyone because it was so emerald green and pretty with hills and unique looking flowers and plant life. The Duwamish themselves, are members of the Lushootseed people, which are made up of primarily, two distinct sets of people, the doo-AHBSH (People of the In- side) and the hah-coo-AHBSH (People of the Large Lake), along with the People of Lake Sammamish and the People of the Snoqualmie River Valley.

They lived in cedar plank longhouses that were low slung and close to the ground, which always faced some form of water, and had wonderful carvings upon the exterior. They were a generous and peaceful people, who reached out to us, and who treated us as equals. And, we decided to move again, and this time set down some real roots, because we had come all of the way across the country and we could not go any further, because the land had run out.

The area was comprised of many hills and fresh water lakes, and the gateway to the saltwater ocean, which was called the Kh-ulch (Puget Sound-Strait of Georgia Basin), which was like a great water road that they traveled on, and it was right there beckoning our call. The Duwamish showed us all of their secrets. For instance, how to split the long boards from the straight grained cedar wood, to make or build many things that would be useful to our basic survival in our new land, like our own longhouses, and our own totem poles, which displayed our family's own unique story. And also, how to construct canoes, how to fish in the ocean, as well as in the many lakes, and on the Duwamish, Black, White and Cedar Rivers.

They showed us how to farm and cultivate the land, and grow wapato, which is a potato. And they also showed us how to forage in the summer and fall for acorns, fern roots, and bulbs. And also of all of the numerous berries— like the huckleberries, the strawberries, blackberries, raspberries, salmon berries, serviceberries, thimbleberries, and salal— which were either eaten fresh or dried and formed into cakes to preserve them for the winter.

They taught us how to fish for crayfish, salmon, clams, freshwater mussels, and other seafood, which were abundant in the area all of which sustained us, and helped our family to continue to grow and prosper. We also were shown how the tribes did things in a yearly cycle, like dispersing in the spring, coming together in the summer for the salmon runs, and hunkering down in the longhouses during the winters.

Time flew and two years passed quickly, and we were all saddened when we heard the news that on Wanicokanwi 5th, 1894, Pizi had died at his home on Oak Creek in South Dakota. He had settled down and become a farmer and a Judge of the Court of Indian Affairs on Standing Rock.

And, he was extremely friendly with all wacicu settlers, because of his relationship with McLaughlin. His passing was hard for me, because before he had left for Canada, we had become extremely close, and we were kind of like brothers, but after he had come back from Canada, he was simply a different person.

As I look back on it, the loss of his family at the Battle of the Greasy Grass, had broken his once proud spirit, and he seemed bitter and conflicted in his mind. Then in 1898, the Curtis Act was passed, and this Act dissolved tribal courts and governments. And, it was the culmination of the Federal Government's attempts to destroy all Indian tribes and their governing bodies, and to open Indian lands to settlements by non-Indians and the railroads.

It was ironic that the Curtis Act closely followed on the heels of the Dawes Act. In itself, it had a negative effect on all Indians, as it ended their communal holding of property, by ensuring that everyone in the tribe had a place in the tribe, and a home and land to live upon. Time flew again, and two years passed quickly and before you knew it, it was the year 1900, which was the official beginning of the 20th Century, for the so-called civilized man or human being.

Then, a mere six years later in 1906, came the next insult, which was officially called The Burke Act, which was also known as the Forced Pending Act. This was passed to ensure that the Secretary of the Interior had the power in his discretion, to issue a land patent to an allottee. And to really decide, whether or not to sell or to keep the land, and to decide if the land be liquidated and sold to whites.

So, if the Secretary of the Interior decided that the allottee was unfit or incompetent after which he could act in his official capacity, and legally authorize the sale of the land right out from under the allottee, with or without his or her approval or consent. This was because, he Department of the Interior, controlled the land patent and therefore, also its use. The Department of the Interior had already decided beforehand, in some kind of underhanded way, that over 90 percent of fee patented lands would eventually be sold to whites.

More time flew by, and then before you knew it, we got word first two years later that the mighty Wasicun Thasunke (He-Has-A-White-Man's-Horse), had died on Wanicokanwi (December) 16, 1908. And then one year later, in late Wanicokan Wi (December) of 1909, that Mahpiya Luta, had died on the 10th day of that very same month and that they had buried him near his home on the Pine Ridge Reservation. He lived 90 years, while married to the same woman Hiha Waste (Pretty Owl), for over 50 plus years.

And he was remembered as a quiet and simple man, who was direct in his speech, and extremely courageous in his actions. He loved his Nation and he was the only First One to have beaten the Bluecoats in a war. He also held a position of being totally uncompromising against wacicu forced submission.

He was a great and legendary speaker, and he was a visionary and the supreme leader of his people, during his entire time on the planet. He always showed poise and confidence, and he was simply awe inspiring to even behold, or to be around. He never lost his dignity, and he always kept his head, wits, and his senses about himself, and he was a man's man, and a true warrior.

He was to me, simply one of a kind, and he outlived all of the other great warrior chiefs of the Indian Wars, and he was also my friend. So, it was with much sadness when we all (the Akicitas Chanzee and myself) went back to the lands of the Teton Lakota to pay our respects at his gravesite.

And we were quite the sight, all dressed up in our Sunday fineness, with top hats and suits or dresses, as we humbly paid homage to his life and legacy and memory. Mahpiya Luta was a hero of mine, and I have never ever been either ashamed or afraid to say it either, because in this thing called life, the truth will always set you free.

Then in January of 1910, word had spread around that Bass Reaves had died, in Oklahoma and he was the first Negro to be commissioned as a Deputy U.S. Marshall in 1875. He had worked for 32 years as a Federal Peace officer, west of the Mississippi river, in the so-called Indian Territories, for Isaac Parker who was a federally appointed federal judge for the Indian Territories. He served with much distinction and honor and he was even friendly with the Terrible Three and he was a good man and an even greater person. It was a sad day for the entire House of Calais-Vega when we all heard the bad news. He will always be missed!

A few years later, my Grandson Scarlet Cloud, came to Mamie and me, to ask our permission to go away to college in the wacicu world back East, in the Federal District of Washington. My second oldest child Christine Lydia, who we all called Chris or Tine was the first of my children, to get married to a fine Oceti Sakowin young man named Whitehorse (Sukawaka Ska), who was related to the great and highly admired Teton Olagala Lakota Chief Wasicun Thasunke (He-Has-A-White-Man's-Horse) and then to have children.

They had identical twin boys, who were named after the Great Scarlet Cloud (Mahpiya Luta) and the Great Crazy Horse (Tashunca Uitco). And, the boys were always inseparable with one another; just like their aunts H and P were all of their young lives. They had even adopted a passed down tradition from their aunts, which is to call one another Cekpapi (Twins), and whenever one or both said it, we all knew who they were talking about at all times.

Christine or Tine, as life had it, became an educator, and she became quite the teacher, principal and then administrator, and then for the all of the Reservation schools of the Oceti Sakowin. She had worked closely with Wasicun Thasunke to ensure that the children were taught and stayed on the Reservation, and not shipped away back East to the Carlisle Indian Industrial School, like Wasicun Thasunke's own son Samuel had been made to be. So, because of her strong educational background, and her constant traveling back and forth back East with Wasicun Thasunke's delegations, to lobby or campaign for Governmental support for improved rations and humane treatment, and the educational rights of the Oceti Sakowin and then for all of the First Ones, she became privy to a lot of information regarding scholarships to colleges and universities.

So one year, before the boys were to graduate from high school, she made it her business to make them apply for Federal scholarships and grants and see what would happen. Both of the boys were extremely smart and quick studies, and Tine and her husband Sukawaka Ska (Whitehorse) were both excited with their studies and the possibilities that lie ahead for them. Scarlet Cloud was the more reserved of the twins, and Crazy Horse was the more dark- sided of the boys, and he had this edge that seemed a bit sinister and hardened, like mi Abuelo.

Scarlet Cloud enjoyed reading and he was always reading and studying, and he had this zest to learn. Early on, he wanted to be a teacher like his mother, while Crazy Horse was the straight-up warrior, and he knew and said what he wanted to be at an early age, which was to be a gun toting, multi-sword wielding, star throwing Akicitas Chanzee for The House of Calais-Vega through and through. Nothing else in his life ever seemed to matter.

He lived for battle and he would always listen intently to all of the mission debriefings as if he was soaking up any and all knowledge of battlefield situations and experiences. It seemed as if he was just patiently waiting for his turn, and that he already knew what his destiny was and would be.

They would play and battle one with one another starting from wher they began to walk, and everyone would laugh at all family gatherings because it would only be a matter of time before they were going at it, as if they seemingly could not help themselves when it came to engaging in their playful contests.

They would always want to see who was better, or who could do this or do that, and both of them had an extremely strong will and desire to be the best. And, this always reminded me of the game that Pizi had spoken about that he had played in his youth with Woqini, who grew up to become the mighty and respected Sahiyela Chief for his peoples. They grew up outside, so the Great Grass Sea, as well as the Badlands were their initial playgrounds. They began early on as little boys, hanging out with El Diablo's pack, and they loved to rough house and play with the wolves, who became so comfortable with the boys that they would even allow only them and at first no one else, to join the pack and to practice howling and growling at the light of the moon. They did everything quicker than everyone else, and they were extremely competent horse riders at the age of 8 years old. And, by age 10, they were going out on their own and hunting and fishing and learning their way through life.

They made their own tomahawks without anyone's assistance, and their tomahawks were made better than most adult warriors were which really seemed to please their father and, they really became efficient in using and throwing them. They had even secretly traveled to the Bad Lands to get their wood for the handles, and both of their tomahawks were of course identical to one another. As long as their schooling was done, their parents had no problem letting them roam and learn the old ways of the Oceti Sakowin warriors.

Their father Whitehorse (Sukawaka Ska), loved to take his sons out with him, to hunt and fish and he wanted them to be more than reservation First Ones, and he had this pride whenever he saw them or spoke about them. Both of the boys were hurt by L'Ouverture's passing but Crazy Horse was extremely affected by his uncle's death, and he it seemed never got over this, or his hatred for the person named Edward Teach. And, all of this fueled his dark sided nature even more so.

They both began their young warrior training and they both excelled and rapidly went through the initial stages of learning in an easy and breezy manner which made everyone in the family marvel at their abilities, and there was even talk of them mirroring L'Ouverture's rapid progress. Before long, they were the apprentices of the Hell Raisers, and they really started to make their marks, and there was no turning back. And, they both had this 'certain something' that was undeniable, and it was the mark of the warrior.

Tine was extremely happy and satisfied on a personal level when the scholarship papers began to arrive, and she was over the rainbow, when Howard University in the Federal District of Columbia, which is a tuition based institution of higher learning, offered Scarlet Cloud a full academic scholarship. Crazy Horse, as we found out later had only halfheartedly applied, for the various scholarship offers, be- cause deep down inside, he had no wish to attend any waicuc schools, and he only wanted to continue his young warrior training and one day, become the Tatanka Sica Ohitike for the House of Calais Vega.

Howard University was originally a project of some members of the First Congressional Society of Washington, to create a theological seminary and establish a university for the education of Negro clergymen and once established, it was named after the civil war general, Commissioner of the Freedmen's Bureau and later Indian fighter Oliver Otis Howard, who was also one of the Ohio Howard's who as a family, had been involved in the cause of the freedmen since their days of service for the underground railroad.

Howard University's motto is Veritas et Utilitas (Truth and Service) and its funding comes from an endowment, private benefaction and tuition. And, Tine felt that this would be a great fit for Scarlet Cloud, because his passion for learning could be enhanced if he truly wanted to grow and follow his dreams. We, my beloved Mamie and myself of course said yes, with a sense of pride, and we liked the fact that he had come to ask us first, which seemed kind of neat because, what child comes to his or her grandparents and asks whether he may have our permission to go away to college?

Scarlet Cloud wanted to follow his path of schooling and be a teacher and a lawyer one day, so he applied himself educationally, and turned away from his warrior training and accepted the offer to attend Howard University, in the Federal District of Washington. He knew that warrior training was necessary, but there always had to be a better way, and besides he could still do his warrior training, just on a reduced basis as he concentrated upon school. We were all a bit sad as we bade him farewell at that train station, but we knew that in life nothing is for certain except getting a quality education.

And of course, Crazy Horse was the very last one to say goodbye to him as they hugged one another and whispered something into each other's ears. Once Scarlet Cloud enrolled in Howard University he was always either first or second in his classes or studies, and he seemed to thrive on the educational challenges. All of the family, especially his parents were extremely proud of his accomplishments, and devotion to his studies.

He stated openly that he now wanted to study law, and to one day become a judge, so that he could attack the ignorance and prejudice that resides all throughout the legal system regarding freedmen and women of color and the First Americans. "The needs of the many outweigh those of the few," he would always say in his letters, as he dove headlong into his studies with the same determination that he had exhibited at a young age in his warrior training. He was always sending us, his family, his used schoolbooks.

And, he created an extensive reading list for my personal consumption, like the combined works of Alexandre Dumas, which were, The Count of Monte Cristo, The Three Musketeers, Captain Paul, and George. He also sent to me a lot of works that were written by great Negro writers and people who were committed to changing the everyday lot of the Negro, like the impressive David Walker's Appeal 'To the Coloured Citizens of the World, but expressly to those of The United States Of America' which was first published in September of 1829. One day a package came for me, and when I opened it, it contained a letter and a book called The Souls of Black Folks, which was written by a W. E. B. Dubois in 1904.

This book Pop-Pop—he said in his letter, had changed his whole perspective about colored people, and it was all the rage at school, because it changed the way that people of color looked at one another. Dr. Dubois was the first Negro to receive a Ph.D. from Harvard University in 1895, after first attending Fisk University from 1885 thru 1888, and then Harvard and the University of Berlin. He taught several language classes at Wilberforce University from 1895 through 1897, and then from 1897 through 1910, he taught history and economics at Atlanta University.

While at Atlanta University, Dr. Dubois edited 14 publications and was the editor and founder for both a magazine and a newspaper. In 1910, Dr. Dubois became a co-founder and member of the board of directors of the NAACP, which stood for the National Association for the Advancement of Colored People, and the editor of the NAACP publication, which was called (The) Crisis. Scarlet Cloud seemed taken with this W.E.B. Dubois individual, and he then also sent to me the other works of Dr. Dubois, The Suppression of the African Slave Trade to the United States of America" (1898), The Philadelphia Negro: A Social Study, (1899), and an article, that was in a monthly periodical called The Atlantic Monthly (1897).

Scarlet Cloud stated that once he even had the distinct honor of meeting Dr. Dubois, even if it was ever so briefly, and in passing. One afternoon in the hallowed halls of Congress, he did get a chance to look into his eyes, which are the windows of one's soul, and see the determination and pride that Dr. Dubois displayed at all times. It was as if he could see the measure of the man, and, that he was speaking and living the truth.

And the only other person that he, Scarlet Cloud, had seen with the same measure was me, Pop-Pop, his much beloved Grandfather. Dr. Dubois when given the chance had excelled just as I had when Master Jack had given me "mines." And to him, Dr. Dubois was possibly one of the greatest colored men alive, right then as we all lived our lives on this planet.

Dr. Dubois had inspired him to be a better person, and to see that education is the key for our mistreated and ex-slave people. The House of Calais - Vega had always had a policy of strict isolation and we had always sought to stay far away from the long knives and their crazy and befuddling ways of nation building. But where were we going to go now, we have almost reached the shores of the Pacific Ocean, and we cannot run any further, unless we all get in a boat and sail away to some distant shores or republic and so, we must partake in the ways of this country.

We cannot just sit back and let injustice and ignorance rule the day, and as Dr. Dubois skillfully stated, "Men must not only know, they must act." Now Dr. Dubois has some very strong opinions about Booker T. Washington and his method's for uplifting the Negro race, but Dr. Dubois understands that in this world there are many ways to 'skin the cat' as they all say, and no one way is the best or most sure, so he does not have the time or passion to judge Mr. Washington's methods, as long as they did not collide or hinder those of his own. Dr. Dubois has also made me really think, Pop-Pop, about what I want and also what is both my role and place in this whole thing, called the United States of America, as the century turns over.

My goal was to come to Howard University, graduate and then come back home and become a teacher for The House. But now things are different Pop-Pop, and I feel alive and growing, and I want to make a difference on a real level and in a real way. I now want to go to New York City, right after I graduate and not come home and to get a job. And to, pursue a graduate degree, while I figure out how to somehow get into law school.

Dr. Dubois has sparked something in me, Pop-Pop, which makes me want to be a better person in so many better ways. Please also know that I will not turn my back on my warrior training, Pop-Pop. And I work out constantly, and because of The House, I have a certain discipline, that pro- vides both comfort and satisfaction on a lot of levels. Yours truly, Scarlet Cloud your grandson.

I then started to really dive into the work of Dr. Dubois, and I began to see why my grandson was really so taken with him. This W.E.B. Dubois was really a very impressive figure, and he was most certainly "a man amongst men," and he had this confidence that came through in his works, which could not be mistaken or ignored. I remember writing Scarlet Cloud and thanking him for exposing me to this Dr. Dubois, because his words really made me think, and contemplate everything.

Scarlet Cloud graduated in four years, ranked third in his class, with hon- ors, and a double degree in History and Economics. And, my daughter and son-in-law, they (the ones in the family, like Crazy Horse, who had accompanied them on this important trip) all said, were extremely proud and handshaking parents at his graduation, when they called his name, "Scarlet Cloud Calais Vega Whitehorse (Mahipya Luta Calais Vega Sukawaka Ska)," out loud, as the next graduate, for all to hear who had assembled at the place on Howard University's campus that is called the Yard amongst the many and loud cheers and hand claps, by his classmates. After the ceremony, he introduced everyone to a fellow graduate, a fine-looking young lady named Beatrice Josephine Thomas as his girlfriend.

She, who was with her equally proud and beaming parents and grandparents, was from Harlem USA, she proudly proclaimed with distinction and with a certain flair for the dramatic, as everyone laughed in approval. The two families really enjoyed one another's company that day at dinner and in the days that followed. Crazy Horse even took the two graduates out for a drink, at The Willard Hotel, and Scarlet Cloud and Ms. Beatrice were both shocked and pleasantly pleased when he ordered three glasses and a bottle of the establishment's finest champagne.

The two graduates even took two graduation pictures, which they said was for both sets of grandparents. And, I always remember the look on Mamie's face when Tine and Whitehorse, came to Siahl or really King County and personally gave our picture to us, as tears of a grandmother's pride and admiration streaked down her lovely face. Scarlet Cloud moved to New York City and got a room in a boarding house that was located at 267 West 136th Street in Harlem. And when he finally came home, that next summer to bring his fiancée home to meet his entire family, he would say his address over and over again, 267 West 136th Street in Harlem, as if it meant something not only to him and her, but also and more importantly to the ones who knew what he was talking about in the first place. But none of us did, so it did not matter anyway. He was home with a visitor so everyone was on their best behavior, even Crazy Horse who had been warned by not only his grandmother, and mother, and aunties and girl cousins, to not horse around today and give this real city girl the wrong impression about us vagabonds and prairie dwellers.

Scarlet Cloud's girlfriend was talking with the rest of the girls, who had taken her off to the side, to kind of like feel her out. And, Ms. Beatrice Josephine told them right to their faces in a low sounding voice, so that what she was saying was just between them. That she first wanted to be clear, that she loved that man, with a conviction that exceeded her own expectations, as all of the girls faces broke out in either big smiles or big grins, which meant that she was saying the right thing whatever it was.

Because, she had never ever met a real man before she met him, and she is from Harlem so she had been around the block before when it came to all men, which meant that she always had had men and boys up in her face all her life, and so "she ain't no body's fool." But this thing between her and him was different, and it made her, have to take a step back and observe this whole thing, from the outside of her body. He is kind, always generous to the poor or downtrodden, sweet, humble to a fault, hella handsome, rational, bright, an athlete, a great orator, has a sense of humor and likes to laugh because it is good for the soul he always says, has a great heart, is courteous, a gentleman, a student and scholar, and he has this unwavering discipline to his daily workouts, that seems almost fanatical in its design.

His parents should be proud, for just because they are not seeing him every day, they should take some solace in the knowledge that he was giving his Family name and its people a good showing because, the Howard University and the Washington Federal District of Columbia crowds, are tough crowds. And, for him to have come in and held his own with his books and earned the respect of his classmates and instructors, from day one by being a student with an enormous amount of mental and physical discipline, was and still is, extremely intriguing. He then sailed through his studies, and he simply was on the roll throughout his time in the Federal District. And, he graduated with a certain amount of ease that made everyone be in awe and jealous to a certain extent.

When he moved to New York City, he asked me if I know of where a good church was that he could regularly attend, because he knew that to my parents, having a good church to go to is always important, when trying to raise a family or a village. So the next thing that I know, only a few days later, he told me he had met a man, at a neighborhood soup kitchen where he (Scarlet Cloud) had volunteered his labor, who had invited him after they had had a wonderful discussion about the way of the world, to his church and low and behold, it was none other than the Abyssinian Baptist Church.

Abyssinian Baptist Church, traces its origin to the year 1808, when a visiting free Ethiopian seaman and some Negro parishioners left the First Baptist Church of New York City, in protest over being restricted to racially segregated seating that was either in the very back of the church or way up in the balcony section. Imagine that! They renamed their new congregation the Abyssinian Baptist Church after the historic name of Ethiopia, and the man that he had met was Adam Clayton Powell Sr. Adam Clayton Powell Sr.! Adam Clayton Powell Sr. had been the pastor of the church since 1908, and he is truly one of the most respected Negroes in Harlem and the entire city for that matter.

Scarlet Cloud just has this way about himself that draws you to him and his energy and way of being feels real, and true. Everyone just wants to do right for him, and then throw in that he lives in a building that has a lot of interesting and creative people always in and out of it with always something very profound and uplifting going on within its walls. He found the building somehow, in less than two weeks of being in Harlem, and somehow, he moved in with no job and limited money. And now, has secured a room and the trust of the owners, because he always pays his rent before time, and not on time like respectable people with good intentions, always do without question. He quickly got a job, and is thrifty and conservative in his spending habits, and he is extremely resourceful, like his grandmother Mamie he always says which then makes him always smile that smile of his, when he thinks about the very mention of her name. And after meeting her, Ms. Mamie Elizabeth and his grandfather Mr. Balaam, I see why you all are happy and enjoy one another. Because of their love for one another, you all have survived together as a group and flourished in this sometimes-crazy land. You were not day-to-day, exposed to the evils of America and this world that it, America is in, and you all love one another in a real and tender way. Then throw in that he is fine, and yes, I know that I did say that before, and extremely well-groomed in a natural and fresh sort of way, and he always smells good, like lilies or honey-suckles, she laughs. I am just hooked like the fish that is being pulled into shore or into the boat. I love that man!

Then when you come here, to you all's home, and everyone, and I mean everyone is just so nice and pleasant and the natural surroundings are just beautiful and breathtaking. I now know what he meant when he tried to de-scribe how where he was from looked like, and what his life was like for him when he was there. I will never, ever forget and forever remember when he said that his life and all of its surrounding natural beauty, was like something that he had remembered that his grandfather had once said and still says about his grandmother, which was that whenever he sees her, " life itself is not measured by the breaths we take, rather by the moments that take our breath away."

All the girls sighed and awed as Mamie and Christine Lydia both smiled at one another, and then each one from the littlest to the oldest, began one at a time to give a real and meaningful hug to our newest family member, and to really tell her that she finally was home. Meanwhile, as Scarlet Cloud and Crazy Horse began their usual playful rough housing antics, like they were doing their own version of the Che-hoo-hoo, with one another, everyone laughed and said that they wondered how long it was going to take for them to start up. "Not long," one of the little ones yelled out loud, as everyone really started to laugh. And, it was good to see my grandson Scarlet Cloud, because he brought happiness and smiles and laughter with him on his visit to the House of Calais-Vega. Even his usually serious and stoic Cekpapi (twin), Crazy Horse was laughing, smiling and extremely happy, as if a piece of him, had been reconnected to his soul and being. We had not all laughed like this as a group, since before L'Ouverture had died. And, that was many, many, moons ago!

In a little less than a full year, about eleven and a half months, we received word that Beatrice Josephine and Scarlet Cloud had eloped to somewhere in Europe, (which we found out later was the Greek Isles) and gotten married, and that Scarlet Cloud was returning home with a surprise. Before they ar-rived, Crazy Horses started acting all funny, as if he knew something, and he told me and his grandmother, that he saw in a dream that we had new blood in the family, and it was girl blood at that, and to please keep his dream a secret, which we naturally did. When Beatrice and Scarlet Cloud showed up at the train station, they had a baby girl with them who was less than 3 months old, and whose name was Zana Thomas Calais-Vega Whitehorse.

Zana means Lily Rose in both Hebrew and Greek, and in the Slavic countries it means beauty, or the one who has all of the beauty and is the one that gives it away. They had gone to the Greek Isles for their honeymoon, and so they sought to pick a name that would always remind them of their first trip anywhere, and in this case abroad as husband and wife. And they had sure picked the right name for this child, because this little girl was an amazingly beautiful and happy child and everyone was taken aback while in her presence.

My daughter Tine immediately started crying the moment that she saw her first grandchild, as did all of her four sisters and of course even their beautiful mother Mamie, had tears of joy in her eyes. For Zana has the softest looking curly reddish colored hair, with eyes like my mother and skin like Mamie, that shined and glistened in the sun, and you could tell at three months old on the mako that she was her daddy and her uncle's girl, because of the way in which she admiringly looked at the both of them whom she probably assumed was the same person. For she was the most happy when they held her, and she could be crying because she was wet or hungry, but once they held her, all seemed right in her young world.

Scarlet Cloud was extremely happy and quite the proud parent, but it seemed as if his mind was somewhere else. And when we finally got a chance to talk, just him and me, he disclosed that looking at Baby Zana was rough for him, because he had serious concerns about her future and the world that she lived in. He stated that the whole world seemed on guard and on edge, and especially in Europe, the major powers had gone through great lengths to maintain a balance of power, which resulted in a complex and confusing system of military and political alliances throughout the entire European continent.

It seemed as if Germany was in the middle of it all, as no European nation wanted to do anything to set the German Empire off. Because Germany always seemed poised and primed to wage war due to their vast industrial and military base. Germany and England were in a serious arms race or arms buildup, with one another, as each nation had sought to one-up the other, and they both are devoting their industrial bases to the production of the equipment and weapons necessary for a prolonged European conflict.

So with all of this happening, it seemed inevitable that a spark would occur that creates a conflict which escalates to an all-out total world war, which would not only envelope the whole of Europe but eventually also the entire world. I asked "why did it bother him so much, because in the history of the European world, the history has been about war, plain and simple. So why should he become enmeshed in this craziness"?

Well Pop-Pop, he said, because if the Great War comes, and the world chooses sides and becomes involved, then my daughter will be affected by this mess. Her generation will be affected by all of this, and she did not ask to come here, so I feel somewhat responsible, and protective. I therefore must stay alert and abreast of the situation, and it is not easy being a parent, and I can only imagine what you have had to go through with all of the children in our family that you and Grandmother have always been responsible for since the days of the great battle for our freedom. I told him that I have always tried to worry about just the things that I can control and nothing else. That may seem like a simplistic observation on my part, but it has helped me to gain a peace of mind and has eased my worries. This life has never ever been easy for us as a family, but we have never taken on the worries of the Blancos and made them our own. Also because he is now a city person, and lives in one of the greatest cities in the entire world, he has become affected by the news and the times.

He has enjoyed living in the city, and he loves his place and space in the flow of time, and he loves being alive at the turn of the century, because of the promise that technology offers and affords the so-called civilized man and woman.

So, because he now has converted to the city ways, he feels connected to things that do not involve him and his family on any real level. Yes, it is an exciting time for mankind, because something new is being invented just about each and every day and, he should not be fooled, because times may change, but man and his nature do not.

Man is who he always has been, which in most cases is brutally selfish and prone to war, and the lust of power that comes with it. Do you understand? I asked him, which was just about that time, that Crazy Horse burst into the room, all happy and smiling with baby Zana, who was asleep, cradled ever so lightly up in his arms.

He first looked at me and said, 'Howdy Pop-Pop.''Cekpapi' (Twin) he said, as he smiled, all lovingly at his brother, as they hugged one another and smiled brightly at one another. He then said all happy like' I am so glad that you and your wife are both here once again, and my Tuzaya (niece) is beautiful and such a blessing.

Let's go take her for her first horse ride, and introduce her to her new world, and will you accompany us Pop-Pop?' Please? I could not help but to say yes, and everyone was shocked, in a funny but happy way, because before they knew it, the three of us had snuck off for a ride and to everyone's chagrin, we had also taken the Family's newest blood, our beautiful and precious baby with us. After about almost a hour, of riding and laughing with one another, El Diablo comes running up at full speed, growling something as he had like this smile draped all over his face.

The twins looked a bit perplexed by his behavior, as I just laughed and laughed. Your Grandmother has told him to tell us that it is time for us to come back home, and that oh yes, we are in trouble, for sneaking off. We all laughed and turned back for home, as El Diablo stayed close to Crazy Horse who was still holding baby Zana, wrapped close to his chest as El Diablo kept looking up and howling in a low voice of approval, as if he was talking directly to her, as Zana still somewhat asleep, ever so slowly lightly opened up her eyes, then yawned, and then quickly drifted contently back to sleep.

When we finally got back, we were met by a posse of females, which included all of my daughters along with Kara Grace, who quickly took the baby from us, as a female led snicker went up about the crowd. And, for the rest of their visit with us, no male hands even touched the child. And, she passed from female hands to female hands, as everyone took their turns holding our beautiful girl child, as Beatrice and Scarlet Cloud just beamed with parental pride.

In less than a year from Scarlet Cloud's confession to me, on June 28th, 1914, Archduke Franz Ferdinand of Austria was assassinated in Sarajevo by a young Bosnian-Serb student named Gavrilo Princip. And one month later, the world was at the brink of war, and Scarlet Cloud had been right and very prophetic in his observation of what was going to happen. The various combatants chose up sides, because of this alliance or that accord or secret treaty, and the amount of casualties and killed grew to numbers that were unprecedented and unheard of up until that time in human history.

The years of 1914 to 1917 were some of the bloodiest and grueling that the entire world had ever seen before, because technology was being used to kill by more advanced methods. These weapons of mass destruction were unlike any other weapons that had been used up until that point in time, and the loss of life on both sides of the combatants was staggering. The United States had initially pursued a policy of neutrality and isolation, trying to avoid any conflict trying to be the ones that brokered a peace settlement.

The Great Father Woodrow Wilson seemed to be playing both sides over the middle as he desired to push the League of Nations as the primary peace-maker, and yet he wanted a role as the one who demanded and got a peaceful solution. But there were too many factors happening on the edges, and out of sight, that appeared to draw the Great Father personally into the conflict. He was being pressured on all sides, as he sought re-election, and even members of his own Cabinet appeared to be outwardly and publicly betraying him at every turn.

Then came a mysterious sabotage in both Black Tom and Kings Island, New Jersey that reeked of the smell of Imperial Germany. Then, in 1917 came the news that the British had intercepted and decoded the Zimmermann Telegram, which supposedly suggested that Mexico should join the war as Germany's ally. And, if the United States were to enter the war, then Mexico should declare war against the United States. And in return, the Germans would promise Mexico military support in reclaiming the old Mexican territories of Texas, Arizona and New Mexico.

This telegram, along with a massive covert domestic propaganda campaign by both the American Protective League, and the Committee on Public Information, was to feed the general public's pro-war sentiments by using newsreels, newspaper advertisements, magazine stories, newspaper articles, photos, and large print posters. This occurred along with the continued sinking of US merchant ships, all of which worked in tandem, to publicly force, by the will of the people, the Congress to declare war on Imperial Germany on April 6th, 1917. Because even though the Great Father President Woodrow Wilson had won re-election on his pledge to continue to keep the United States strictly neutral and out of the conflict, he was behind the scenes totally supporting Britain in many ways.

Namely, by having U.S. merchant ships sending munitions and food to Britain along with his overlooking of Britain's illegal mining of international waters in support of the blockade of German ports. He also started preventing shipments of food to Imperial Germany, and he acted as if he was just trying to figure out a way to get the general public on its own, to want the United States to enter the war. And then, he would publicly act using the total might of the U.S. Military.

His plan seemed to have worked on all angles, because despite having a relatively small standing army, it drafted around 4 million men as young men flocked from far and wide, and even as far away as from the Island of Puerto Rico to the war effort. And it seemed like in all of the newspapers that all of the talk was of war, and the need to stop Imperialism at all costs.

The next thing that happened was that a new Tatanka Sica Ohitike for the House of Calais Vega needed to be appointed in the traditional manner. For there had not been an Tatanka Sica Ohitike who had gone through the tests since Kara Grace, and it was time to get back to our ways that are described by The Codes which are our governing principles. Gabriel had been handed the title of Tatanka Sica Ohitike when Kara Grace stepped aside, because of her self-inflicted mental wound regarding the death of her secret apprentice, L'Ouverture.

Gabriel did a great job, in the role, he was fair and honest, and a great battlefield tactician. Until he got hurt while out on a mission, when he had his horse shot out from under him, severely breaking both of his legs. So his days in the field were finished, as he struggled to regain the use of his legs and to just be able to walk properly, and without any assistance or a cane.

Aaron did not want the responsibility, because he wanted to have some softness in his life (having a wife) and to have a family, but he knew the importance of the role, so he became the next Tatanka Sica Ohitike, but, 'only for a few years,' he openly stated. So eventually after he stepped down, there had not been one ever since, and the upcoming tests would determine the new leader of the warriors of The House of Calais-Vega. Crazy Horse seemed like he was the obvious choice and the hands down favorite by most of the warriors of The House because his two Masters, Alphonso and Kara Grace both had personally groomed him and added their own touches to his fighting style.

Alphonso was his original Master, and he had learned much from him, but Crazy Horse felt that he needed more, and that the one person who would make him the complete warrior was none other than the legendary Kara Grace herself. Because even though she did not wish to be Tatanka Sica Ohitike any longer, as her self-punishment for the death of her much beloved secret apprentice L'Ouverture, she still was very much involved in the training of all warriors, and she still participated on some missions that were deemed of strategic importance to the House. She was still dazzling and an amazing master of the bushido, and no one wielded their bushido's like she did, so learning the ways of the bushido from her was both an honor and an education.

She at first did not want to, and she politely declined his request. But after his constant persistence, and finally because he had told her of his troubling dream, in which he was fighting himself in an epic battle, and he needed her expertise to help him to beat himself, she finally accepted his request. And he excelled under her tutelage, as everyone knew that he would.

The date and time of the tests was announced, and low and behold, there came a letter from Scarlet Cloud that was addressed to me. He stated that we would be seeing him very soon because he wanted to partake in the tests and become Tatanka Sica Ohitike. His letter sent waves of questions through the House, because why would he want to be the leader of all warriors, when he lived such a long ways away?

What was he up to? Was he moving back home? What was his angle? Did I really know what he was up to? There were nothing but questions, questions, questions that only he, Scarlet Cloud knew the answers to. He showed up by himself, without his lovely wife and beautiful child, about two weeks after the letter had arrived, and Stacey his Master met him at the train, and they immediately set into a strict and grueling training routine to get him into even better shape.

They showed up in about a week at the compound, and Scarlet Cloud had this hungry look of determination, and he seemed somewhat standoffish and withdrawn. He did not smile or even talk much, and he was like a completely different person. The day of the tests loomed large and when it finally arrived, it came down to a test between three people, Scarlet Cloud, Crazy Horse and the very young in age, but polished Temujin.

Everyone took their seats and watched in amazement as all three warriors passed each and every part of the tests almost perfectly, but after the sixth and final test, there was a tie, and dead heat between Scarlet Cloud and of course as fate would have it, his Cekpapi (twin) Crazy Horse. Temujin of course was thrilled to have even gotten that far, though he was far beyond his own personal expectations, and everyone was downright pleased that he had gotten that far, which was a testimony to his skill set and passion.

So, in case of a tie, it had been so written, that a mock battle with wooden bushido's and padded suits with helmets would take place on a circle, and the rules were simple.

Whoever was made to yield or whoever was either pushed out of the circle or knocked off their feet, was the loser, and the winner was the new Tatanka Sica Ohitike. So, without much fanfare or talking, the final test or battle began, and it was furious and rough.

Initially it looked like Crazy Horse was about to lose, because every movement he tried, Scarlet Cloud was right there with a stronger counter movement, which was a strong suit of his Master Stacey's fighting style. But just when Crazy Horse looked like he was down and out and was about to get tossed outside of the circle, he abruptly changed his style, to that of Kara Grace, which was a touch of mi Abuelo and myself, all thrown in together, that employed a complicated but simplistic style of defense to offense pattern of bushido wielding.

The action was wonderful from a warrior's perspective, and it contained ups and downs, back and forth, and a lot of the crowd seemed at times distressed, as the two of them went at each other like they were mortal enemies, and not twin brothers. A lot of the women folks could not even watch, and even Mamie winched and squirmed about as she at times hid her face, so that she could not see the two of her grandsons savagely going at it, against one another. Scarlet Cloud got Crazy Horse down to one knee at one of the sides of the circle, but somehow Crazy Horse remained calm and gathered himself in his mind and began to knock Scarlet Cloud back with a series of head and upper chest, and head blows and the final one took him off of his balance.

He then used a powerful reverse roundhouse kick without even looking, that was simply stunning and a thing of beauty to behold, that pushed Scarlet Cloud up into the air, until he came crashing back down to mako (earth) flat upon his back. And, with that it was over, and both seemed like the loser, as Crazy Horse ran to his brother and helped him up and then hugged onto him for what seemed like an eternity. Scarlet Cloud told him in his ear, in a way that only Crazy Horses could hear him that he loved his cekpapi (twin) and he was happy that he had always continued his training which was what had enabled him to move further along his path.

This was the key to his great victory, and he had finally come out of their shadow, and he now stood in his own light. The family all gathered around the two contestants, and everyone seemed relieved and happy because the great battle had taken everyone's energy and it had us all sweating and panting for breath. Scarlet Cloud spoke to everyone and then he disappeared into the longhouse dwelling with tears in his eyes.

Later on, when the night came, and the ceremony was to begin, to officially pass the title to Crazy Horse, we got some bad news. Scarlet Cloud was gone, and he had taken Our Friend Named Destiny with him! The Akicitas Chanzee set off in hot pursuit of Scarlet Cloud, who had about a five to six hour head-start on everyone. Why would he steal our family's most prized heirloom and procession, we all wondered and what was his endgame or reason for such a dastardly deed?

Stacey, his Master was heartbroken, because he felt that his apprentice had deceived him and everyone else, and his main goal was to kidnap Our Friend Named Destiny. That is why he had entered into the tests, because by our laws, if he had won the right to be called Tatanka Sica Ohitike, he could have taken Our Friend Named Destiny, for whatever reason and to God knows where, and it would have been perfectly alright and okay. So he rode all night and the next full day to arrive at the train station ahead of the Akicitas Chanzee, and his train had already been gone by about an hour when they arrived.

Crazy Horse immediately bought four train tickets for himself and Aaron and the two Hell Raisers, and then sent the others back to report their findings. And the four of them went straight from there to New York City, to 267 West 136th Street in Harlem in search of Scarlet Cloud who had a two days head start on them. They found out that they had moved, about 7 months ago into a bigger place that was, about 8 blocks away, and they were given the address.

Beatrice, who looked very pregnant, (seven and half months) looked a bit stunned when she saw Crazy Horse, Aaron, Stacey and Alphonso all standing in the hallway, all suited down with nice ties on, with fancy English styled top hats, and long coats. And Zana, who was hiding behind her mother, squealed and ran from around her legs and jumped up into her beloved Uncle Crazy Horse's arms, as she repeatedly said his name, "Uncle Crazy, Uncle Crazy..." over and over again with her childish glee, as she cheerfully played with and patted his below-his-shoulders length hair with her hands, as everyone laughed and smiled. Beatrice let everyone in, and as they helped to ease her down into a chair, she stated that he had come there, to check on her, and Zana and to make sure that he had everything in order and after a fine meal out as a family on the Avenue, he had gotten some of his things and was now gone.

He had enlisted into the Department of the Navy, specifically the Marine Corps, and he had left yesterday to proceed to the Federal District of Columbia to report for active duty. Crazy Horse sent Aaron and the two Hell Raisers immediately down on the next train to the Federal District of Columbia, to trace his trail. And when they got there it went cold, at the gate of the Navy Yard, because, although they tried hard on numerous occasions, they could not gain access to the military base or facility.

But as we found out later, he was not even there, and he had already been sent straight down to Parris Island, South Carolina, to the Marine recruit depot and instruction for his 8 weeks of basic training. Crazy Horse stayed in Harlem, to attend to his sister-in law's needs, and to experience his niece, and more importantly, to try to gain an idea of what his cekpapi was truly up to or thinking. She stated that Scarlet Cloud was determined to fight against Imperialism, and he had a few friends who were members of the Negro Army combat regiment that was known as the Harlem Hell- fighters, and they all had pledged to make a difference.

But Scarlet Cloud did not see the Harlem Hellfighters as an elite Army organization, and he was looking to see some real action, and not any so-called mop up duties. So, after some studying and speaking to various people, he decided that he would enlist with the Marine Corps, because of its legendary and historical significance beginning with the founding of the Continental Marines on November 10, 1775, by the Second Continental Congress in Philadelphia. The Marine Corp's Latin motto Semper Fidelis, (Always Faithful) also had attracted him and in the end, he viewed the Marines as a better fit for him personally.

He had also done some banking, after he had enlisted, and he had them to open up a new bank account, and he also had his identification slightly modified to be in line with his new papers, all of which did not make sense and seemed both shady and shaky. But she asked us to trust him and re-member that he had never ever done wrong to her or their child, so I naturally was compelled to trust him no matter what I thought or was thinking. Be-cause after all, he was the complete love of her life and their love for one another was total and based upon the truth.

He then said that he had to go visit the homeland of his ancestors, on a business matter, but he would return to say goodbye to the both of them before he had to report for active duty. But why then did he take 'Our Friend named Destiny' with him Crazy Horse wondered over and over in his mind? Crazy Horse paid all of the bills for the next two years and left Beatrice and Zana enough money to live on for at least 12 to 16 months, and also some additional money to buy themselves train tickets so that they could always come out and visit the Family, at any moment's notice.

We would not want her having to get around and do things for herself with new blood in the family on the way. And once he had gotten back, he would send two female warriors back to blend in and live amongst the city dwellers, to assist her with her needs, as it got closer to her time.

About three weeks after they had all gotten back, letters from Scarlet Cloud, that were addressed to Mamie and me, and Beatrice, and also ones addressed to his parents and to his cekpapi, started to arrive, from Beatrice because he was mailing everything to one central point, which naturally was his beloved wife.

And, he tried his best to get us, his readers to understand his position and his logic. He stated that although it appeared that he had thrown away his pride and dignity and committed a great crime against the House, his justifi-cation was righteous and true. Because Our Friend named Destiny, was truly a great and powerful weapon that could make the difference in the Great War. He had not stolen it, but in fact he had only borrowed it, and he would be bringing it back.

He also stated that he had gone to his superiors and told them that no matter what happened to him, that it was his request that his family's heir-loom be returned back to his family. For he had illegally taken it, which was not right, but he had done so because it was extremely sharp and it may come in handy on the mission that they had been as-signed to carry out by executive orders of the President. So, if at all possible, it needed to be re-turned, and he had sworn and written papers that testified to his intentions.

He also humbly, both wanted and needed our forgiveness, and when he returned, he would immediately come home and turn himself in, to be pun-ished by the Akicitas Chanzee. He then began sending letters that were addressed strictly to the Akicitas Chanzee, which described in great detail how the Marines Corps was organized and operated.

He was in the 4th Brigade, 2ndArmy Division and in the 5th Regiment of regulars, and he would be going to France as part of the American Expedi-tionary Force.

He was in the Second Battalion, in the 43rd or F Company and in the 4th platoon. He chose the Marine Corps, because of its storied and legendary past, and he wanted to participate in the action on the fronts, and with the Corps he knew that he would get his wish. He stated that a platoon was the basic independent unit of organization, and it was the principal training unit, and usually it consisted of up to a dozen people.

So, four platoons together make up a company, and four companies formed together creates a battalion and battalions that are grouped to-gether, form a regiment. A regiment consists of about 4,000 to 5,000 soldiers, and then if you put together 2 or 3 regiments, you get what is called a division. In the Marine Corps, brigades are only formed for certain missions, or special expeditionary duty, and thus a Marine Corp brigade keeps the reg-imental structures intact.

And therefore, the 4th brigade consists or is a part of the Army's 2nd Division, which consists of the 5th and the 6th regiments, along with the 6th machine gun battalion. After their basic instruction at the depot, they would be going to Quantico Virginia for additional training, and then at some point be shipped over to France for duty. The training was tough on some but for him, it was not even as hard as The House's Young Warrior 1st step training level is, and it was like this is what he had trained all of his life for.

He loved learning how to shoot rifles and machine guns, and how to properly use explosive devices, and learn offensive and defensive procedures and tactics. He had a great time with the hand-to-hand fighting, and he loved the marching and running and the constant drilling. He loved being a razor or implement of war, and all that he lived for was to train and eat and breathe war.

He seemed, his superiors had observed, to be the one in the regiment who was good at any and everything, and he had quickly mastered a lot of skill sets. He was given an expert marksman ranking and award, and he was initially assigned to the snipers' group because of his expert shooting skills. He also was first or second in all of his training classes, and although initially he had been promised by his recruiter, the rank of Second Lieutenant, because of his educational background, but he would only get it after he agreed to have the initial rank of Private, and then had successfully completed his training examinations and then review by the examining board but for some reason he was given the rank of a corporal.

A Corporal, he knew was better than a Private, in both rank and pay grade, but when he had first heard Second Lieutenant, come from out of the mouth and off the lips of the recruiter, the pay grade in truth had affected his decision.

For the money that a Second Lieutenant makes would help his growing family and would help to ease his worries about not being there for the birth of his second child. He would use this snub as motivation, because he was also there to prove a point, in the words of Dr. DuBois which were that, "the modern day turn of the century Negro was just as competent as any other race, to be in command, and lead the fight against the new evil in all lands of the world that is called Imperialism."

He would show them all, because after all he is a warrior of The House of Calais-Vega. The next letter from Scarlet Cloud was telling us that the 5th regiment had been organized at the Philadelphia Pennsylvania Navy yard on June 7, 1917, with Col. Charles Doyen in command with Major Harry Lay as adjutant. They sailed on June 14th 1917, aboard the auxiliary cruiser De Kalb which was part of a naval convoy that was commanded by the serious and stern looking Rear Admiral A. Gleaves, whose flag ship was the U.S.S. Seattle, and on June 26th, 1917 they arrived at St. Nazaire France.

They, however, did not arrive without incident. Because eight days out of port on June 22, at 10:15 pm, they were attacked by enemy submarines, which are underwater craft. And, two torpedoes were fired, one of which passed ahead of our ship, while the other one passed astern of our ship, the De Kalb.

The situation was tense and grim, and from where my platoon was standing on the deck of the ship, we could hear the guns of the ships firing at will, at something that at first we could not see, and then all at once, an alert was sounded that pointed us towards a location. And, then we could see the torpedo as it whizzed towards us just near or at the crest of the surface of the ocean and then as it got closer, we could hear the hardworking sound of its engine as the torpedo luckily passed us astern. This incident brought back the seriousness of our task that lay at hand, and for the next four days until we made port, everyone was concerned and apprehensive about the remaining portion of our trip.

Then two days later, on June 28th, 1917, his Battalion, the 2nd, disembarked from the ship, along with the Third Battalion. And, as they put boots on the ground, Scarlet Cloud had been surprised to see a rather large amount of Negro stevedores, someone said 500, who had been brought over by the U.S. Army, to help discharge the massive amounts of ships and equipment of both the Army and the Navy. The whole situation at the beachhead was one of total chaos and confusion.

And for whatever reason, the Negros were catching the blame, for this chaos even though the Army and the Navy have always been at odds with one another for one reason or another. No one listened to one another and the situation, as a matter of fact was really like an all-out free for all and do it in your own way kind of affair. Way over here across the ocean, and so very far from our homeland, and they were still being treated as the servants, cooks and cleaners, and the butt of jokes, like buffoons and coons.

Just where is the honor in that? He said that he reflected, and he just shook his head, about the whole mess. Because it truly was a mess, and for some reason it bothered him in his mind, as they marched away and from out of sight of the landing area and went to a camp site which was a short distance out of St. Nazaire. We began the training exercises, and we were given duties that were along the Allied Line of Communications.

The 5th and 6th Marines of the 4th Brigade were not allowed to wear their standard khakis, and they were forced to wear the standard uniform of the Army, as so ordered by none other than, General Black Jack Pershing himself. His logic was that he did not want to differentiate any US soldiers from one another, and because he was an Army man and in control as the Supreme U.S. American Expeditionary Force Commander, he would naturally want everyone to reflect the look of the Army, plain and simple. And, the Marines were after all detached to the Army's 2nd Division.

The Marines had only the eagle, globe and anchor on their soft covers to distinguish them from their Army counterparts. So, after a lot of turmoil and way too much discussion, it was decided that a patch would be created so that you could tell right away, just who Marines Corps was and who was Army Infantry. A black shield with one five pointed star and an Indian head with a full war bonnet was selected, and the origin of patch had two different stories, one was that the black was for mourning, and respect for their casualties, the shield was for defense, and the star was for the Second division Commander Brigadier General John A. Lejeune, as was the Indian, because Lejeune's nickname was 'Old Indian.'

The other story said that the patch was derived for a U.S. Coin, the Buffalo and Indian Head Nickel or Five cent piece which was first minted for use nationally in 1913, and still was in circulation at the time. But the patch became something that the Marines rallied around, and each regiment came up with their own variation. In his next letters he spoke about what his days consisted of, and he would always cut right to the chase and not beat around the brush, in his observations.

We did a lot of inspections and had a lot of regimental reviews by a lot of higher ups, but all in all, they were all wondering just when they would be given the honor of representing the Department of the Navy, and it's Marine Corps Brigade of Regulars on the field of battle. We were relocated to the Bourmont training area, and once there we marched and drilled even harder and we practiced advancing against machine gun nest, in packs, and we conducted drills against simulated attacking foes, and how to create a field of concentrated fire that was designed to mow and wear down any advancing enemy. We also used different tactics, because Pershing saw what a waste of lives trench warfare was, and that American lives would not be a part of any murderous frontal assault.

As the British and French, who combined were losing almost 7,000 soldiers a day in the trenches in their stalemate with the Germans, so he decided to change his tactics. He would now go on the offensive, using speed and the element of surprise along with the rifle and the bayonet, to break through the trenches and into the open. Americans were better in the open, which could take advantage of their superior fighting and shooting skills.

It was like our superior officers were waiting for something, and they were taking their time to do whatever was right. His next letter, spoke of a feeling that everyone was having, and that they would be moving towards a jump off in the upcoming weeks, because Imperial Germany had just signed in early 1918, the Treaty of Brest-Litovsk with Russia. And, its new leader, had capitulated and given up and really quit the Russian part of the war on the Eastern front, as the Bolshevik revolution ravaged all throughout Imperial Russia.

So the two front war was now over, as the Eastern Front closed down, and the Germans would be launching a massive offensive on the Western Front, to capture Paris which would theoretically end the war before the full strength of the United States military could be added to the conflict.

So, they would throw their best divisions that were stuck on the Eastern Front, at the Western Front, and everyone knew that the mighty and famed 347th Division of the Imperial Army Group Crown Prince would be somehow right in the center of the assault. Because the 347 Division was the elite of the elite, the crack shock storm troopers of much distinction and bravado, who were both feared and admired by all of the contestants of the Great World War.

The next letter spoke about a German Spring offensive that began on or around March 21st, as the Germans attacked the British 3rd, and 5th Armies. But the Army's 2nd Division was still being held in reserve, and in a holding pattern. And as the action picked up, we were being moved closer and closer to the front. So in his in next letter, dated May 29th, 1918, he spoke of how just two days earlier on May 27th, Imperial German Storm troopers from the 347th Division, had broken through the French lines in Aisne, by striking into an area that lacked substantial defenses or reserves.

And this tactic had forced the entire French 6th Army, into a full retreat. The Germans moved quickly and in no time, they had advanced all of the way to the Marne River, and they were now, in some areas only 40 miles from the City of Paris. They would finally be seeing action, even if it was to only block their advance towards Paris, and everyone was excited and ready to get it on, and that he would be writing back when he could. They were supposed to be moving to an area called Mont Didier, which was northwest of Paris, to be held in reserve until the moment was right.

He did not want us to worry and he would be fine, and everything would play out like it was supposed to, because as per his Young Warrior Training for the House of Calais-Vega, every day was a great day to die. We did not get another letter from him, for a while, but Crazy Horse seemed to know or feel that he was okay, and that was all that mattered to us. The next letter that came was dated July 6th, and his Brigade had been relieved after 31 straight days of fighting and they were now resting and refitting (R&R), at a place that was known as the line of defense or the army line. They had participated in a great battle that was called the Aisne Defensive, which became an offensive action against desperate and determined Imperial German soldiers. And, war is like the ultimate contest of wills and desire, he recounted.

The 4th Brigade had been asked to block the German advance, and they sent us in motor trucks, and other transports down to the vicinity of a place called Meraux. And, we then deployed across the Chateau-Thierry Paris Road near Montreuil-aux –Lions, in a gap that was in the French line. And we rushed down the road as far as we could go because the fleeing refugees and the retreating French army had the road all clogged up.

When we got to about a little north of the village Lucy-le-Bocage, we were about to dig in, when a French Colonel suggested that we were going the wrong way, and that the Germans could not be stopped and perhaps we should retreat. Before anyone could respond, Captain L. Williams re- plied, "Retreat, Hell! We just got here!" as everyone kind of like nodded in approval.

We checked their advance, and pushed them back, in tough hand-to-hand fighting, and at a place called Les Marces farm, I got the first of my many, many kills from long range. I wasted no ammunition, and at one point I had 22 one shot kills in a row, before I severely wounded but did not kill my next victim. Then on June 6th, we of the 4th Brigade were asked to re-take the Belleau Wood area, which elements of the German 237 Division had taken, and turned into one big death trap only 3 days earlier.

The place was a heavily wooded and forested area that the Germans had fortified with machine gun nests, and gun emplacements, bunkers, snipers' nests, and land mines. We battled them back and forth for three weeks, and it was during this mighty battle, that I first used Our Friend named Destiny. I have figured out a way to keep the bushido (blade) awake, and it allowed me to slice through any and all things. It is amazing how powerful you feel when it is in your hand, and nothing can withstand its mighty onslaught. It feels so amazingly light in your hand, and it is as if you are just waving a wand or something and it enabled me to be very effective in slicing through the enemy.

Because I wanted to get this over with as quickly as possible because, on one day alone, June 6th, which was the first day of the Offensive, 1,087 men were either killed or wounded.

And, Our Friend named Destiny allowed me, and us to make quick work of our enemies. We took the woods inch by inch, to the surprise of everyone, which was mind boggling. We received a citation from the French Army and citizens, but it did not feel like a victory, because the cost of victory was extremely high for a lot of good men were killed or wounded.

Like, our commanding officer, Colonel Albertus W Catlin, who was se- verely wounded on the first assault, and seeing him in such a bad way inspired us to try even harder. We are now getting ready for the Aisne-Marne Offen- sive, which should be jumping off sometime within the next two weeks. I will write when I can, Scarlet Cloud Whitehorse.

The next letter was dated July 21, 1918, and he was at a place called Taille Fontaine, and he had been there since the 19th. The Aisne-Marne or Soissons

Offensive, had taken only two days to complete, and they had simply crushed the enemy and had taken their will to fight from them. The offensive was over quickly, so quickly that they had been removed from the front-line duty, and, they really had not even had a chance to inflict much damage on the enemy.

He would write again soon. The next letter was dated August 2nd, 1918, and they had not seen any action in weeks. After they had left Taille Fontaine on July 22nd, they had been billeted from July 24 and 25th in an area around Nanteuil-Le-Haudouin, and they stayed there until July 29th. They had been moved on July 31st, by train to an area around Nancy, and they would be there until at least the next week. The Brigade had gotten some great news, because on the 25th of July, Brigadier General John Lejune had been named commander of the 4th Brigade, and then on July 29th, he was named commanding general of the entire 2nd Division. "General Lejune was a hell of an officer, and his presence would immediately uplift us all. He is a soldier's general, and a man's man, and all of us would do anything for him, because he commands so much respect. He also understands us, and his demands never exceed his expectations," he wrote. He would write back very soon.

His next letter was dated September 1st, and he was in an area about 20 kilometers southeast of Toul. They had been moved on August 5th, to the Marbache subsector, near Pont-A-Moussou, which is located on the Moselle River. They were doing intensive training for the impending St. Mihiel offensive, which would be in a few weeks. His next letter was dated Sept 22, 1918, and they were still in the Toul area doing a rest and refit (R&R) after completing the St. Mihiel offensive.

The offensive was from Sept 12th thru the 16th, and we really took it to the Germans, and they seemingly just wilted under our advance. He was getting very comfortable using Our Friend named Destiny, and he had used it to dispatch many Germans. And, he could not believe just how sharp it was, and how it could and would cut through anything. He had been promoted to first Sergeant, and then after the offensive, it was some talk that he would be promoted to Master Gunnery sergeant. His deeds he said had become the talk of the entire Division and Brigade, and he was always the one who took the lead and pushed the advance.

The same letter had another date, Sept 28th, 1918, and Scarlet Cloud said that he was back, and on Sept 25th, they had taken a train ride to an area south of Chalons-Sur-Marne, with their headquarters at Sarry. Then on Sept 27th, the 2nd Division was placed at the disposal of the 4th French Army.

They had been selected by the Commander in Chief of the Allied Armies, as his special reserve, and were being held in readiness to strike a swift and powerful blow at the vital point of the enemy's lines.

They had been moved around a lot, but they had not seen any action in over two weeks, and some of the guys were getting restless and seeking action, but he used the down time to train and rest and write to us. He said that he often wondered what the country of France was like in peace times, because the people seemed friendly and that they did not appear to see the color of one's skin as any prerequisite for judging the character of one's soul. If everything worked out, he would love to bring his family back, so that they too, could experience the beauty of the people, and of the countryside.

His next letter was dated Oct 11th, 1918, and they had participated in the Champagne Battle of Blanc Mont Ridge, which include the capture of St. Etienne that took place from Oct 2nd thru the 10th. On the 10th they had been relieved, and they went to the Sommes Suippes-Nantivet area. The Battle of Blanc Mont Ridge was intense, but they had made quick work of the enemy and as a reward, the people of the area had given to them the town's secretly hidden supply of champagne, Moet et Chandon which was established in 1743 by Epernay wine trader Claude Moet. The original name was Moët et Cie (Moët and Company), and it had quite the international following and prestige. It was the favorite of Napoleon, the Tsar's of Russia, the Duke of Wellington, the Queen and King of England, and most of the nobility of Europe. The commanding officers let them drink as much as they wanted to, and it was funny as they ate their military issued meals, and instead of drinking water they drank champagne like it was water, and like they were nobles and royalty of the Americas. He had also by the way been pro- moted to the rank of Lieutenant. His next letter was dated Oct 16th, 1918, and on Oct 14th, they had marched to the Vadenay-Bouy-La-Veuve-Dampierre area north of Chalons-Sur-Marne. They had been provisionally placed at the disposal of the 9th French Army, to hold a sector in the region of Attigny-Vonlq-Aisen River.

The same letter had another date Oct 31st, and they had been moving around a lot. On Oct 20th, they had been temporary detached from the 2nd Division, and had marched to the Suppies-Nantivet–Somme area.

And then on Oct 21st, they had marched or hiked to Leffincourt, and then on the 23rd, they had marched to Mont Pelier. They rested for a day, and then on the 25th to Les Islettes, and then on the next day, the 26th to Ex-ermont. They had stayed there until the 31st, when they moved south of Landres-et-St.George, and the word was that they would be joining the Meuse-Argonne Offensive, which was to begin on around Nov 1st, 1918. He would write back when he could, and that he loved everyone, and that he missed his family.

There were rumors that the Imperial German Army had had enough, and that they were really close to collapsing and if everything worked out, the next Offensive would break their backs, and their will and possibly end the war. He was ready to get back to his family, and to meet his newest child, little Ms. Devi Dominique Thomas Challis Whitehorse. Devi was of Hindi origin and its meaning is goddess. And his wife had said that everyone expressed that she is even more beautiful that her older sister Zana, as if that was even possible, because Zana's beauty was the kind of long told tales and legends. So, the name Devi really fit her, and the name Dominique was of French origin, so he could only imagine what it would be like to see her, and her older sister grow up and become women of the 21st century. He really appreciated his family, and he really appreciated his grandmother and me, for being the source of strength for our entire family.

'Our Friend named Destiny' was fine, and we should not worry about it, because he will ensure that it gets back home to where it properly belongs. Because with great power, comes an even greater responsibility, and he now realized that although his intent was noble and just, that he had no business taking it, even though it has helped to turn the tide of this ill-fated war. He would write back when he could and that he was proud to be our grandson.

The next thing that happened was on Nov 10th, when Christine Lydia and Whitehorse (Sukawaka Ska), with Crazy Horse's wife Ruth Anne Harriet, who was carrying their baby daughter Ericka Terri, all came to Mamie and me, looking worried and very troubled. Ruth Ann stated that ever since his twin had gone to participate in the Great War, Crazy Horse had begun having dreams that seem to be real and lifelike. He was not himself, and he would be sweating badly and moving about. And he was not dead still like he most times always is when he was asleep. And, when she had asked him what his dreams were about, he seemed defensive and at times confused. He had finally told her that he was going into war with his twin, during each battle, and he was on edge. Then last night Crazy Horse woke up yelling and crying and in a bad way, and he was extremely despondent and heartbroken. He was so loud he even woke up and scared baby Ericka Terri, and even she could sense that something was up with her daddy. He would not leave his room, and he was crying and unable to speak or even walk.

Something had happened to her loving husband, and she needed our help to figure out what had happened to him, before his mind seemingly unraveled from the grief that he was enduring. She was scared! Because he was and is, the mythical rock of ages for the House of Calais-Vega and if he is spooked, then something terrible must be up. We all immediately went to him, and when he saw Christine and Mamie he fell into their arms, with tears streaming down his face.

After what seemed like a long while, Mamie had finally gotten him to calm down, as she held him in her arms, while Christine held the both of them in hers. And after a long time, he seemingly gathered himself and then with a lot of courage, he looked into our faces and said that his cekpapi (twin) was dead. Christine Lydia and Whitehorse were absolutely both stunned and shocked by his revelation, and there was this eerie and absolute silence that they both exhibited.

Whitehorse wanted to know how his son knew that his brother was dead, and how he could be so sure. Crazy Horse had seen his death in his dream quest that he had had every night that Scarlet Cloud had gone into battle, in the European wacicu's great world war. He actually had a bird's eye view of all of Scarlet Cloud's actions in every battle that he had fought in, and he was right there with him. He was somehow connected to his brother on like an astral plane or level, and it was as if he was right there, seeing and experiencing everything like his guardian angel or watcher.

Crazy Horse had always had dreams or visions that had always manifested and were always true ever since he was a little boy. He had come to me in his teens, naturally with his twin in tow, and asked why he was chosen to see such things, and this thing bothered him, and was like a curse or bad omen. He hated it, and it was a very draining experience, because it was as if he was watching things unfold, that always came true. Why was his dream quest, such a horrible thing, and why was he the one to witness such things? Well Crazy Horse, I explained to him, you are special and one of the true chosen ones, and this gift was something that he had to learn to accept and live with.

So, that is what he did and as he got older, he tried to be calm, and just learned to accept his gift. So, when he said that he knew things, I always accepted it, because he was always right. But this was a tough one, because he had seen the death of his beloved twin, and if he was crying and hurt then it must be true. We all wept and held one another, and we just would have to sadly wait for the official word.

The next day, on Nov 11th, 1918 news came over the telegraph wire, that the Armistice had occurred, and that the Great War was finally over. Scarlet Cloud had died in one of the very last battles of the Great War, so very far from home.

In four weeks, Beatrice with both of the girls arrived at the train station, and when she saw Crazy Horse and Ruth Anne standing there, she started crying, and as they rushed to comfort her, she reached into her purse, and pulled something out. And, in her hand was a letter from the U.S. Department of the Navy, stating that First Lt. S.C. White had died with honor on the field of battle on November 10th, 1918, while on duty and participating in the Meuse–Argonne Offensive.

Two Marines all decked out in their dress blues, had knocked at their door, in Harlem U.S.A., to deliver the bad news letter, and she had blacked out and had cut her head in the fall. When she had gotten herself together, she came personally to deliver the news to us, because she did not want to send a telegraph or write a letter with such hurtful news. She needed to be with us, and to be able to rest her mind, because she was in a bad way herself, because she had lost her lifelong mate. And more importantly, she did not know how she was going to continue on without him.

So, we sent for her parents, and then we officially let everyone in the family know, even though they already knew it seemed. We took her into our hearts, and we helped her heal, and really made her realize that we were, and will always be her people and that she was home. Her blood had been joined with ours, and she was now a part of our unique collective of human beings. In a few weeks Crazy Horse and Kara Grace walked up seek- ing an audience with me and asked if we could we all take a walk, in the beautiful countryside of King County. Crazy Horse was ready to talk about what he had seen in his dream quest, and he needed to do so, to finally clear his mind.

Scarlet Cloud had led his men through heavy artillery and withering ma- chine gunfire, as they were the first to cross the river once the two footbridges had been laid across it. They crossed the east bank and once they drove the enemy back, they established themselves in the heights that cov- ered the bridgehead, and they held the high ground to protect the troops that were able to cross the river. Scarlet Cloud sensing a counterattack, ordered his men to hold their positions at all costs as he sent one man back to head- quarters to report that they were massing their numbers for a possible counterattack on the newly established bridgehead. And, that they should dig in and repeal the attackers at a point right above the bridgehead, and not get too forward and spread out too thin away from the bridgehead as he took as much ammunition that he could carry, and he went off by himself in the dead of night, to the point and most forward position.

From this position and using his tomahawk and Our Friend named Destiny, that sounded like a magical humming or singing wand, he killed many, many Germans. It looked like hundreds, as he cut into and through them like a saw does to wood, and he was amazing and quite the true warrior and he had even stacked up the dead bodies in such a way that they were protecting him like a shield from their rifles and pistol fire.

He would then one by one take their positions and then use them and their own weapons against them, so that he could save his precious ammunition that only worked in his weapons. Every soldier that he killed, he would take their weapons and then stack up their bodies, and he then used all of the dead soldiers' weapons against the next approaching and unsuspecting groups of soldiers. It was like a slaughter and a blood bath, and they never had a chance, because they had no idea of what they were truly up against, because it was as if he was hunting them down as if they were his ultimate prey.

He also had used a trick that he had devised at a previous battle in a heavily wooded area, of wearing a German helmet with the dead man bones faceplate—that all warriors of the House wear whenever they are in the field of battle—to really confuse and suck in his prey. Because, when they saw the distinctive design of the Stahlhelm helmet, and not the Brodie helmet design, they assumed because of the darkness that he was one of them. And, once he got close to them, he was vicious and an absolute razor and tool of war.

He diced and sliced off many body parts and through all types of metal and weapons all with an uncommon ease. It was a macabre and grisly looking scene, and if you were weak of the heart it may have spooked you. He caused mad confusion, and he terrorized his prey to create both havoc and fear. And, he had used the mushroom chews to move at a pace that seemed almost inhuman to behold. He was breathtaking and red rum (murder) was his business, and he was like a killing machine that had no peer or mercy for his enemies in the field.

It was as if hell had opened up, and out he sprang like a terrible beast, like he was one of the devil dogs that stands guard at the gates of Hades itself. He had even lowly but clearly howled and growled, sounding every much like El Diablo when he was about to attack his prey, and the sound alone was simply frightening and downright scary for the weak and ignorant.

He had held them off all by himself, for over ten hours until daylight arrived, and until he was mortally wounded by a German trick. They killed their own men to get a shot at him, and he took a round in his hip, right on his hip joint. But he still gallantly fought on, and when he realized that he was slowly bleeding out because he could not stop his wound from bleeding, he was determined that he would not allow them to get their hands upon Our Friend named Destiny, because he realized just how truly a powerful and awesome weapon that it truly was.

So, he impaled it into the biggest and widest tree that he could find, and he had held onto his position until it had cooled back down and had gone back to sleep. And, if the Germans had not sacrificed their own men, to kill him, he probably would have lived to fight another day. But to his credit he had fought all of the way to his end, and even in his diminished state he still took a whole lot more with him.

Scarlet Cloud's last words were as if he could see an outline of Crazy Horse standing there, and as if they were directed right at and to him—his twin. He said that, "You my Cekpapi, Crazy Horse are going to ultimately be okay, and you have to have the strength to let me go." He continued, saying that they had never ever been alone, from one another, and that Crazy Horse would just have to learn to mentally let him go and keep on moving forward. For the young warriors of the House needed him and his expert leadership abilities.

He would always be in his heart and mind, and he was proud to have been his brother and cekpapi (twin), and friend. He hoped that Crazy Horse had forgiven him, for stealing their family's most prized heirloom, and that he would always love him for being the better warrior. Tell Grandfather and Father how he had died in good way, and that he had died a very honorable and noble death.

Tell them that he was not scared, because every day was truly a good day to die, and that he cherished everything that The House had taught him about being a true warrior. He then slumped back, against the tree, and quietly died with his eyes glazed wide open. And, about at that same time Crazy Horse had seen his life force leave his body and dissipate into the early morning air.

I remember suddenly just hugging Crazy Horse as Kara Grace hugged us as well. All mourned the loss of a great and mighty warrior for The House of

Calais-Vega. In early May, on Cinco de Mayo 1919 (5th of May) a transport appeared on the service road that goes to the compound. It stopped in front of the compound's main house as everyone walked towards it to see what was going on, and why was it there.

The door opened and well-dressed soldiers slowly came out and got in two columns or rows, as a distinguished looking officer finally appeared, walked down the center of the rows, holding something that was wrapped up in a very nice-looking red rug or blanket as the men snapped to attention and saluted as he walked by them. He was met immediately met by the young warriors, who were on duty, and he requested to speak to the leader or the person in charge.

He handed the blanket to another officer, whom he identified as a Captain Carlton, who immediately snapped to and stood very rigid at attention, while never breaking his attention or gaze forward. In a southern drawl he introduced himself to me as Major Jonathan Ray or J.R., for short, Harris. He was tasked by his boss, back in Washington, Col. Albertus W. Catlin to personally come there today and pay his and the Corps respects to the family of such a proud and noble warrior.

As Crazy Horse and Ruth Anne slowly approached everyone, The Marines seemed a bit taken back, at the sight of him, because he was the spitting image of his twin brother, and it was as if they were looking at a ghost with just much longer hair. Major J.R. Harris nodded at Captain Carlton, who then handed the beautiful red-colored blanket to Crazy Horse. And, as Crazy Horse unwrapped its contents it revealed Our Friend named Destiny and Scarlet Cloud's blood drenched tomahawk and Crazy Horse upon seeing them, just closed his eyes and clutched them both closely to his chest with both arms as tears slowly streamed down his face. Ruth Anne wrapped her arms around Crazy Horse, and she slowly rocked and comforted her husband as everyone stepped forward and then crowded around to touch and to say hello to Our Friend named Destiny, and to welcome it back home.

Major J.R. Harris also had Scarlet Cloud's things which were in a trunk with a funny looking locking mechanism that Scarlet Cloud had requested in writing, to be taken back to his family, in the case of his death. Major J.R.

Harris wanted to speak personally to me alone, but I requested that the leading warriors of The House also be present to hear what he had to say. Mamie asked some of the other soldiers if they were hungry and if they would join us for the meal, because it would be an honor for our family, if they would be our guests.

They all looked at Major J.R. Harris who nodded in approval, and they all said yes Ma'am to Mamie, as she just smiled that pretty smile of hers, as if she was going to give them any other choice. As they all got in a line for food, I took the Major to the workout area, and every Tatanka Sica Ohitike of The House along with their past and present apprentices were waiting for us.' Mister Calais, and assembled leadership, Major J.R. Harris began, we at the United States Marine Corps want you to know of the exploits of your grandson First Lieutenant. S. C. White'.

He was a man amongst men, and he was quite any amazing officer and true warrior, when it came to his fighting ability. He wanted always to be the one who had first contact with the enemy, and no matter the situation, he made it his business to get there first and show everyone who was in command of the field. He had like an extra gear when he ran, and he had this burst of speed that he would use, that propelled him forward, as if he was really riding on a horse, and this helped him to cover long distances in no time at all.

He had this fierce determination when he was in battlefield mode, and although he was quiet and serious, the only reason that he ever gave for his rugged and rough behavior, was that he could feel that his Cekpapi was watching, and he needed to show him that he had the mark of the warrior. .At the Battle of Meuse River Crossing and Heights, he had somehow got his men and himself across the river and was out in the front, as was h s usual and customary position, since the Aisne Offensive.

They had made it through barbed wire, machine gun nests, and up over to a position that was established by Lieutenant White, in the heights or hills above the beachhead on the Meuse River. Lieutenant White had determined that they must hold their position, because if the enemy could retake the heights position, they could rain down superior fire-power down upon the beachhead and effectively trap our men on the wrong side of the river. Because the river crossing presented a lot of problems, due to the enemy's clear sight of fire.

And, once you made it to the other side, going back was just not a good option. His scouts, that he had sent out to spy upon the enemy, could see that the enemy had stopped running, and were organizing and amassing their forces for a clear counterattack, which would be directed down the hill, and towards the beachhead. So their positions where the chokepoint was at and must be held at all costs and everyone must be prepared to die, for the sake of the 2nd Division, 4th Brigade of Regulars.

He would create an additional chokepoint out beyond their most forward point location, which he would man himself. Do not worry for he was going to red rum every single one of them all, and he would be alright because, his cekpapi was always with him. And then, he sent one man back to the beachhead headquarters to give them an idea of what the enemy was trying to do. They must dig in above the actual beachhead and be prepared to spring forward at a moment's notice, as one single unit, and more importantly they must not, at no time ever split their forces.

He then took two rifles and extra ammunition, his usual weapons, and then took off running into the darkness of the tree line. We then do not know what actually transpired or really happened from that point forward, but from what we have been able to piece together he killed every step of the way, as he moved up further and further into the darkness. When he ran out of ammunition, he started to stockpile the bodies of his victims in such a way as to use them as shields against the bullets.

He then took their weapons and used them in his killing spree, against the advancing enemy soldiers, and it was ingenious and showed both guile and great cunning. He created a lot of spread-out killing nests, which were designed by him to use as mini kill zones as he guarded a fairly large area and, in these nests, he stockpiled the weapons that he was gradually accumulating. When he ran out of US Military issued ammunition, he started using his tomahawk, and his hand made dagger, but especially the family heirloom sword, and it is at that point that the number of his actual kills starts to increase in frequency.

He just literally chopped them up, and it was in a very ghoulish and savage manner, I might add. The field was littered with wrists, arms, hands still holding their weapons, heads still in their helmets perfectly sliced in half with a single slash or cut, ears, guts, legs, bodies cut totally in half, blood and brain parts, and everything else. Some bodies were impaled with star looking metal stripes, and others had gashes and or savage looking, ripe looking wounds.

He also had sliced through numerous metal things like guns, rifles, motor emplacements, machine guns, 3 long range field cannon barrows, and really anything that he came into contact with, and of course many, many of the enemy soldiers. From our information gathering, it appears that one single so.dier had stood up to almost a whole battalion and almost won, as he effectively battled them to a stalemate.

He was the messenger of death, and if not for enemy snipers he may have won. The German Field Command Officers that we were able to interrogate, seemed both impressed and literally afraid of Lieutenant White, and if one single man was able to accomplish all of this, then what must a whole Division of them be like, some had openly wondered. He was amazing some had said, and more like a machine other had said, and he was armed with an incredible glowing sword, that hummed or created a sound when he swung it, others had openly confessed.

He had a very unique fighting style, and it was unlike anything that the German soldiers had ever seen before, and his feet were just as deadly as his hands, forearms, knees, elbows, and teeth. He moved at an incredible almost inhuman speed; they had testified. And he was extremely elusive and really cunning and sneaky. He used one of their own Stahlhelm designed helmets, which were invented in 1916, along with a officer's long field jacket, to confuse and confound them, and lure them into his cleverly designed traps. And it was as if he was hunting them down, like they were his prey!

They also said that he could speak fluent Deutsch (German), which he also used in his illusion to draw them into him. Because it seemed as if he were one of them, and as soon as he had gotten you into a certain range, or distance from him he had you. If not for a lucky shot they had said, that wounded him on his hip, and started for him to bleed, and the bleeding is what eventually slowed him back down, and back to normal speed. They were finally able to kill him from long range by sacrificing one of their best young officers along with his best platoon.

And it took five shots to finally stop this weapon, and even though he was mortally wounded, he still did an incredible amount of damage and death upon them, as if he knew that he was dying and did not have a lot of time. When they finally were able to determine in the early light of the next morning, a lot of soldiers, had gathered around to see what they were finally able to kill, and as a sign of respect, they were told by their Generals to not touch his body, and "do not touch his weaponry", which consisted of two American Military Officer side pistols, a handmade dagger, a tomahawk, a sword, stacks of German rifles and ammunition and a flamethrower that he used for some reason unknown.

They wanted to study everything about this soldier, and especially his incredible sword. For somehow his fabulous sword was impaled deeply, with only the white jade handle showing, into a wide trunked tree, and it was stuck hard and was unmovable, which was baffling in itself. Every German officer had asked the very same question, which was "what was the metal that the sword had been made of" and how was it so exceptionally sharp and such a deadly weapon?

How did this soldier make it glow like, that they had all asked? Where did that humming-like sound come from? Also, what kind of super soldiers did the U.S. Marines create and were there any more like him? He was by all of their accounts, the most deadly and accomplished killer that the modern-day 20th century warfare had ever seen or witnessed before. And, one man was responsible for such an enormous amount of death, destruction, and misery that total surrender, seemed like the best and only option to all of the Germans in their quadrant or part of the field of battle.

Although there was no way to confirm his kill totals, some German Officers had openly stated that it was thought that he had killed anywhere between 500 and 900, or really possibly even many, many more men! That's

500 to 900 or even many, many more men, in the darkness of a moonless night by one man and a sword and a tomahawk and a handmade dagger, all done with minimal effort, but with maximum efficiency! For some of the German prisoners had said, that he did not look like he was even trying hard, as if he was just simply waving his hand. He killed with either hand and it was as if he were an assassin whose goal was to slay them all. They also said that he had a way of throwing his tomahawk that made it seem as if it were child's play for him, and his accuracy was astonishing and quite remarkable. His delaying actions enabled us to prepare for their counterattack, which never came, as we now know why, which ultimately saved us thousands of countless American lives.

When we approached them early that next morning, they immediately surrendered and gave up to us. And when we found his final resting place, we were stunned with what we had seen. He gave them one hell of a fight, and to his credit, he was not the retreat kind of person, and he always went forward, which is where his focus always seemed to be up on.

As word filtered back of his demise, everyone was hurt by his death, but honored to have served with such an outstanding Marine. As we gently placed his lifeless body onto a medical stretcher, and took his body back down the hill, to the beachhead, everyone stood to attention and held a fixed salute until the body had passed, in his honor.

Even the German prisoners saluted because they were finally safe, now that he was dead, which for some unknown reason appeared to suit them just fine. Once we had gotten his body back to the beachhead, a lot of soldiers just came up to touch his body in some kind of way, as a way of signifying the mourning of his passing, and how he had affected us all, on some level. The solidarity amongst the men for his passing was extremely touching, and it showed just how much, that they truly respected their fallen brother in arms.

He was eventually buried with full military honors, as per his written wishes under a great tree, and on that day, everyone in the entire brigade had turned out for his going home ceremony. The German field command was just about to liberate the sword from the tree, when we had initially arrived at the battle scene. And, to be totally honest they seemed more intent with gaining control of the sword, than with us even being there, as if we did not exist which kind of alerted us to the importance of studying it ourselves.

What we know is that, it is not made of any metal found anywhere here on the known earth, our experts have told us. This metal is not found anywhere on the known periodic table, and this fact only adds to the mystery of its presence here on earth. And it appears to be, according to many historical experts, well over 5,000 years old or maybe even far older than that. The green jade hilt and white jade handle with gold inlay seems to have been specially designed for the blade, and all together it is an extremely im- pressive piece of work to behold.

The skull carvings on the handle also add to its mystique, and the sword has this glean to it that kind of like mesmerizes you. It is very light in weight, but yet it's exceptionally sharp, and it can cut through almost anything, and Lieutenant White seems to have known or somehow discovered the secret that unlocks its immense power. This whole episode had been a series of baffling and hard to believe stories.

And truthfully, everyone had a Lieutenant White story, about how he did this or that. But what we do know for sure was that he was by all accounts a quiet, but intensely focused soldier, who was a gentleman and a scholar off the field. But, when he was on the field, he was one of the most coldblooded killers that the world had ever known.

One soldier a Lance Corporal Juan Olmo who was from San Juan, Puerto Rico who had been a good friend of his ever since basic training, spoke of how he had a way of throwing his tomahawk that was both vicious and with uncanny accuracy. And, it was like it was a part of his hand, and he was simply a tomahawk master.

He was always training even in his downtime, like going on daily training runs of two to five miles, and it has been said that he even trained on his days off. He was at first a crack shot and so we started him as a sniper, but at the Aisne Defensive he displayed such bravery and skill, that he was able to save a group of wounded soldiers as he had abandoned his sniper position and then passed through an intense field of machinegun fire to aid his fellow

5th regiment soldiers, who were pinned down and about to be overrun by a rapidly advancing column of enemy soldiers. Lieutenant White reinforced their position, defended and then held the foxhole, all by himself until the fighting had stopped.

He had also taken command of the field, when all of his officers had been killed or wounded, and the soldiers had all rallied around him, and his battle-field experience and tactics. He then next made a name for himself with his daring deeds of heroism and killing ability, at the Battle of Belleau Wood, and he rose quickly through the ranks. No one has risen as fast as he had, and I mean no one. He started out as a Corporal which was a clerical oversight and mistake, because based upon his educational record he should have been made a Lieutenant right out of the gate when he had first signed up.

But, he displayed the kind of valor and bravery and leadership on the field, that making him a Lieutenant was a no brainer, and also simply because his men requested it. Hell, and if the truth could really be told, at the rate he was going, if the war had lasted any longer, and he had lived, he would have made General within the year. It was said, that in the Great War, that initially it had begun as a war between good and evil, but over time it became something different, because although it had begun as one thing, it had changed into something totally else, which was evil and sinister in its design.

Because, it became more and more about the ways to use modern technology to kill, and less and less about the reasons that created or caused this massive loss of human life. So to fight true evil you must fight it with a different kind of evil, and to some, Lieutenant White in the flesh personified that different kind of new image of what evil actual looks like. It is as if he had tricked everyone and had held back on his true abilities on purpose. It was as if he somehow did not want to show his true potential, and only did so when he was locked into combat on the field of battle.

He cheated us Mr. Calais, because if we had known we could have studied him, to learn of his immense tactical and ruthless fighting abilities. We could have learned from him, in a real way, and become even more efficient in our brand of fighting ability and style. We now have so many questions, like was he one of a kind, and where in the world did he learn or acquire such a superior fighting ability and style?

What did we think he meant when he said that his cekpapi was watching? What did we think that he meant when he said that he would redrum every single one of them all?

Where did the strange skull type markings that seemed to be burned or seared into the palms of his hands come from, and where did the strangely painted battle faceplate, he wore under his helmet come from? He had let on to only a few of his friends in the regiment that he had learned all of this from his family, and if so, we in the Marine Corp want to thank you for giving us such a home-grown killer. The Germans for some unknown reason had begun calling us Teufel Hunden, which in English means "Devil Dogs," after The Battle of Belleau Wood, and it has been thought that they did so because they respected our fighting ability and classified us as a version of an elite storm trooper. And for the official record, it is at Belleau Wood, that then Lance Corporal White first had displayed his uncanny fighting abilities that, everyone has their own personal story about. And, have testified under oath that they had personally witnessed, 'so help them God.'

Even more amazing and baffling is, that when the German's willingly surrendered to our advance scouts in large masses that morning of Nov 11, 1918, at the battle of the Meuse River Crossing and Heights, the one word that they all said over and over as they thrust their hands into the air in surrender was "Teufel Hunden, Teufel Hunden." So what did they know that we did not, and how was Lieutenant White able to inflict such mental terror into the minds of the enemy?

It seems like his tactic was to either kill them or scare them, or really a little bit of both.

And a lot of the prisoners had this wild-eyed look of absolute fear or fright, when we came to make them surrender. We came looking and expecting an uphill fight, because they held the high ground, but what we got was a lot of frightened and scared men, who had been exposed to some- thing frightening that completely scared the bejesus out of them in a real and horrifying manner.

This, in retrospect was the very last battle of the Great War, for us in the Corps, because later in that same day on Nov 11, 1918, we had learned that Imperial Germany had agreed to sign the armistice that effectively, right then and there ended the war. And, to think that he did all of this with a sword and two side arm pistols, a tomahawk, a flamethrower, and a handmade dagger is even more astounding and for some in the Corps, hard to grasp. He was simply mind boggling and Sir, your grandson was a unique and amazing warrior," he concluded.

He looked at all of us, trying to judge our reactions, as everyone smiled and come up to personally shake his hand, and to say thanks for the detailed debriefing. I also noticed that both the Major and Captain had made it a point to take out the time to each privately speak to Crazy Horse, and I saw the Major give him a card, that I assumed had his name or his superiors name and title printed or embossed upon it. As I sat there thinking about what he had said, about Scarlet Cloud's heroic deeds, I thought about his identical twin brother, Crazy Horse, who is by far the better and more accomplished warrior between the twins.

For he is the one who stayed home and learned his craft, and profession, and all that he ever wanted to be was a warrior for the House of Calais Vega. He is the current Tatanka Sica Ohitike, and he is a far more accomplished master of death than his brother ever was. Scarlet Cloud was not even a full-time warrior of The House, and everything that he had truly learned was before he had gone away to college.

And if Scarlet Cloud, who it appears was seduced by the dark side of the blade and the effects of total and true war, as evident by his 'redrum (murder spelled backwards) them all,' comment, was able to accomplish everything that he had done, all by himself, what must Crazy Horse, who has always been the far darker and sinister of the twins be capable of, with Our Friend named Destiny, in his hands I wondered to myself? I shudder to think of what his dark sided influences could drive him to do, if God forbid, he was ever placed in a similar situation. Heaven help them, whoever they are, for he is truly the perfect storm!

Therefore, with the time that I have left on the planet, I need to monitor him as well as all of the warriors of The House, because they will all now have this even harder and somewhat sinister edge about how they conduct or carry out business while in service for The House. Because after L'Ouverture had passed, they all seemed to have a newfound and darker edge. But now, I can only imagine what they will all truly be like, and therefore capable of.

Because they seem to always, only get harder when one of their own passes, for whatever reason, out in the field.

Kind of like always kill first, and then talk about it later, or really kill first and then do not talk about it at all. We all left to join the daily meal, and, the Marines, at every dinner table, were telling stories of Scarlet Cloud in the field of battle.

He was the talk that was on everyone's lips, and the stories about him really helped our family to heal and get past this big and crushing blow because, he was one of the bright lights, of the next generation, of the Warrior Class of The House. And he would now influence all of the generations by his deeds and exploits on the field of battle. He was the embodiment and essence of what all of the Warriors of The House now wanted to be like and strive towards. A highly educated intellectual killer with no peers or equals, and one who was willing to die for what he believed in, because to him, "every day was a great day to die."

As the soldiers settled in, and enjoyed the food and the family, and the happy laughter, talk and playful banter of the family, I asked Crazy Horse to ask all of The Tatanka Sica's to join us for a quick private moment. I asked Aaron to pull the trunk to family's room of honor. And, when everyone, including Mamie was present, we pressed the lock on the trunk, and opened it up to see what Scarlet Cloud had wanted us to have.

Inside of the trunk were six unopened and dirty bottles of Moët champagne, his picture of Beatrice and him smiling and posing on their honeymoon in France and Greece, two medium-sized canisters, a letter that was addressed to The House, two different kinds of German Army helmets, a German Lugar pistol with ammunition, a bundle of French cheese that was encased in a waxy covering, his Howard University Graduation Ring and his

Wedding ring that were both wrapped up in a fancy scarf, a Hamilton watch, his suit, white pin stripped shirt and fancy tie that he wore on the day that he reported for duty, a nice pair of soft brown leather shoes with socks in each shoe, some books one which was how to learn French and the other how to learn German a couple of writing tablets, an inkwell and an old fashioned feather writing quill, maps of Philadelphia, Paris France, the whole of France, along with one of South Carolina and North Carolina, a medium length Imperial German Army sword which had a fancy handle, his personal identification, his wallet, some letters from us his family, and from his wife, a fancy dagger with a jewel incrusted handle, and letters that were addressed to Beatrice, Zana, and Devi.

In the letter that was addressed to The House, he stated that he had discovered a way to rapidly awaken "Our Friend named Destiny," and it involved using the mixture of fluids that are combined to create the fiery and extremely hot flame that a flamethrower emits. He had first seen a flamethrower used in the Aisne Defensive, and he had been impressed with how hot the flame had actually gotten.

He then realized that, if the stories from his childhood and beyond into his adult life, about 'Our Friend named Destiny,' were true of how it had fallen from the sky from well beyond the atmosphere of our world from what is called Outer Space. And, of how the rock that it was created from itself, was also created by an extremely hot heat source, and thus the metal must get stronger when exposed to any heat.

The hotter the heat, the stronger the metal so why not use the fluid from a flamethrower to generate the desired response? So he took the fluid from a discarded flamethrower, and put it in these two metal canisters, and if they could study how a flamethrower operates, and what are the principles behind its use, they may have found a way to unleash and awaken the ultimate weapon. He had used a flamethrower to heat up "Our Friend named Destiny," at the Battle of Belleau Wood and he was easily able to effectively vanquish all of his foes that stood before him as he swept through the woods like a street sweeper, and cut through everything in his path or field of vision.

But the funny thing, to him is that it seemed like he was just waving his hand the whole time, and nothing else. It was not hard or difficult, and really his Acitkas Chanzee training was harder, intense, and was the real test of one's will. The liquid solution also kind of like bonded with the bushido, making it appear to smolder and linger on the bushido. This gives it this really neat looking on fire and flaming kind of look that stays super-hot for a long while, and unless you submerge it totally under water for a few minutes, it takes a really long time just to cool down, and then totally go back to sleep.

Water is the equalizer. So always remember that once it has been awakened by any reasonable hot heat source, Destiny has no peers and no equals, and it could be arguably, the most dangerous and destructive weapon, on the entire planet, because of its cutting ability. I also see why for centuries upon centuries men have been willing to die to become its master, because the sword has an ability to first seduce and then turn its master towards the darker side of the human mind. I know, because I have been in its grip, and I have personally felt the satisfaction that is felt when one is able to kill so effortlessly, without reason or a sense of purpose, and really just because one can. Respectfully yours, signed, Scarlet Cloud.

We all were silent and very somber, until Crazy Horse who was holding one of the champagne bottles in his left hand, stated that we should all have a drink in the honor of Lieutenant Scarlet Cloud Whitehorse...one of the finest intellectual warriors that has ever been created, or really produced, by The House of Calais-Vega, as everyone rose or stood at attention and, then slowly smiled in appreciation and began to clap in unison. Just about then, as if right on cue, Zana with her little sister Devi Dominique in tow, suddenly burst into the room, both of them affectionately looking for their much beloved Uncle Crazy, as we all laughed with delight. "Uncle Crazy, Uncle Crazy, we've been looking for you!" Zana proudly proclaimed, as Crazy Horse just kind of slightly shrugged his shoulders a bit and started smiling.

And the newest little one, Devi, to everyone's surprise, and without saying a word and with a big ole smile on her little pretty face, made a beeline straight into the arms of Kara Grace for an 'uppy.' Kara Grace just smiled away as she picked up Devi and held her tightly as Devi's little arms wrapped around her neck, and she just hung on for dear life it appeared. "This child seems like an old soul because she already appears to know the order of things," Aaron proclaimed, as we all then really burst out and laughed.

Yeah, I thought, I need to make sure and watch them all, even these two who happen to be some of the youngest ones in the family right now. I need to watch them all, because the dark side was lurking closely by. I could feel its presence all around us in the room, in a real way. It felt strong in a real way, and this feeling appeared to dominate the room.

PART SEVEN

FORTE SET LIBER/
DUM SPIRAMUS TUEBIMUR

STRONG AND FREE WHILE WE BREATHE
WE SHALL DEFEND

QUOTE: FAITH CONSISTS IN
BELIEVING WHEN IT IS BEYOND THE
POWER OF REASON TO BELIEVE.

Time seemed to really slow down for me when Scarlet Cloud had died so far away from home, fighting for a country that never ever cared about our kind of people. For his death made me think and truly appreciate his short but very fulfilling life. And, we had always had this way with one another of stimulating one another's minds in a positive manner.

My grandson always made me think and want to grow and strive to always be a better person. He left home, and came back as a man and a father, and a husband, and a thinking human being. I will always miss him, and it is like a part of our lives, or a piece of who we all are, has been taken from all of us, never to ever be seen again on the face of this place called earth.

Then throw in the fact that we could not even get up and go and see his grave without going half the way across the known world, to a place called France and it all seemed to me, to be such a waste of a bright light, and even greater person. His so-called intellectual principles had gotten him killed, and if the wacicu had never had any honor, then why should he have had any for them?

Fighting for freedom in another country, halfway around the known world, when you were not really totally free in your own country seems absurd, and a waste of energy, time and effort, and very much pointless. The codes that mi Abuelo had created were created or established for a reason, and this reason was real and honest. We need to revive the codes and forbid our young ones to have any kind of contact with them.

But that means that we must keep moving and continue on our path, and not let our choices define who we are or what we want to be. Because in the end, as I look back on it, it has been the choices that were made that have affected our lives in a real way. I now think about the choices that different people in my life have made, and how these choices affected their eventual outcomes. From Master Vega, to Old Master Strickland, to Mamie, to Osbourne Anderson, to Pizi , to L'Ouverture, to Scarlet Cloud, etcetera.

And, all of them made choices that in one way or another affected their lives, in some kind of way, be that good or be that bad. That is what we all do as human beings, and this then is the human equation that binds or ties us all to one another. The choices that we make as we live our lives are this connection to one another, and that is why it is important to learn from our choices and continue to grow de- spite the setbacks or rewards.

This is not an exact science or anything, and through wisdom and age we hope that we have learned enough to make the right and proper ones. I look at my own life and think of the choices that I have made, some of which the consequences are far reaching. I realize that my choices have de- fined not just me but my whole family and subsequent generations, because my choice of actions have turned my whole family, especially the children of my brothers and sisters, along with my own, into a bunch of cold blooded and highly educated killers. My choices have led to redrum (murder) and the deaths of my loved ones, all in the very name of freedom itself, when we mentally have never ever been truly free. We thought that we were **free,** but freedom in this country, has been only just a word or a lofty ideal, and not a true state of mental and physical being. So I have killed to get free, and I have killed to remain free, and in the end, I had to learn that nothing in this life is free, for there is a cost associated with everything in these so-called United States.

But to me, the real question is was I right or was I wrong, to pursue this line of reasoning and logic? Could I have tried another way, and did any of this truly matter in the end anyway? And, more importantly instead of going through any mental exercises, was it just what it was and nothing more? For who am I to even try to judge myself, when I have only done what I thought was right, to save my family and friends?

I did what needed to happen at that particular point in time, and if I had to do it all over again, I probably would have done the exact same thing, just in another way. My choices have created the person that I now am, and my family is here, alive and prospering despite the obstacles that were in our path as we sought a new beginning. Some things on my path or journey have been extremely tough to comprehend, and grasp, and through everything, I have continued to grow, as a thinking and breathing person.

But all in all, my wife and family are still around me and have continued to love me despite all of my shortcomings. I am what I am, which is a Warrior for the House of Calais-Vega, and I can think of nothing better to be than that. For being a warrior has sustained and nourished me and kept us all alive in this strange and wonderful place called the United States of America.

We have been told of place that lies to the north of our location that is called Alaska, and it has a very tall mountain there, that is called Mount McKinley, and it supposedly is the 7th tallest mountain on the planet. Alaska also has some peculiar natural occurrences, like for some days in the summer there is virtually 23 hours of sunlight or in the wintertime 23 hours of darkness. Everything supposedly grows big and huge up there, and it is such a big and mighty place, that there are many places that the wacicu have never seen, set foot in, or laid eyes upon before.

And Mamie wants us to see this place and try and experience some of the much talked about wonders before our natural time is up, and we go to meet our one and true maker. The House is in excellent hands and the Leadership Council has some fine minds on it, which will always do the right thing when it comes to the survival of The House and its members. But we are going to have to always be aware, and stay on guard, because they now know about 'Our Friend named Destiny,' and just as important, who we are.

Destiny is the ultimate prize and weapon, and it needs to be watched at all times. Scarlet Cloud, when he came out from the darkness and into the daylight to become a National Hero, exposed us for all to see, and they now have an interest in The House of Calais-Vega, and how we do what we do. So, vigilance must be eternal and everything and everyone needs to be watched, at all times, and nothing must be left to chance. For, these are, as they have always been, very dangerous times...

EPILOGUE

Balaam hears the sound of someone approaching, and he turns to see Tecumseh, Hannibal and Shaka walk into the room and walk straight over to see what Saladin had created. They all stand behind him, and view the image, as Saladin wipes his hands on a rag and then stand's up, and then turns to hug Shaka, Tecumseh and Hannibal, and he then eases back a few feet to view the image then asked them, well what do you'll think"? They all started smiling and said that they all thought that it was a nice picture and that he had captured Pop Pop's image to a tee. It was lifelike and it showed that he was a very creative painter, with an interesting and unique style. They all then walked over and hugged Balaam, and Tecumseh said, 'Pop Pop it was time for dinner, and that he had been requested to please come now, before it gets any colder'. Okay please tell her that I am on my way, and that he appreciates her at all times. The three of them start smiling and they playfully hop and jumped kind of like back out of sight.

Saladin tells his grandfather to please stay seated, and to please close his eyes, as he turns the picture around so that his grandfather can see what he has been creating all of this time. He then respectfully asks his grandfather to please open up his eyes, and to Balaam's surprise, the image did look like him, and it was done in a very nice way. This should really help the people at the University to see that the boy has got some real talent, and that he would be a good addition to their art program. Saladin leans the picture back upon the easel and walks over and proceeds to give his beloved Pop Pop a hug. Balaam hugs him back, and asks him, what is this for? Saladin says what is what for? Are you talking about the hug? Yes, says Balaam. It is just because I love you, and because you were a good model and did not complain and whine.

THE END

Sitting Bull

www.ingramcontent.com/pod-product-compliance
Lightning Source LLC
Chambersburg PA
CBHW052046240626
47153CB00006B/2242